To Debbie

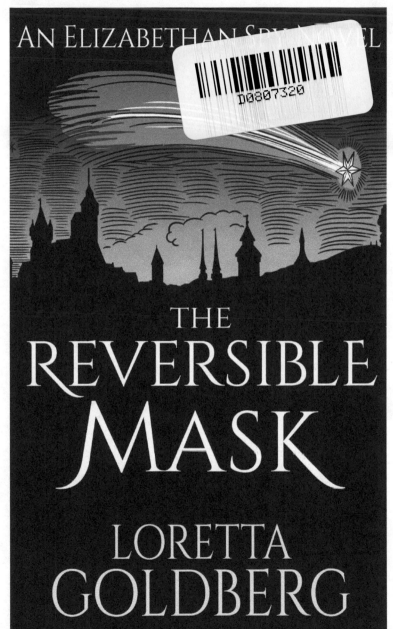

AN ELIZABETHAN SPY NOVEL

THE
REVERSIBLE
MASK

LORETTA
GOLDBERG

Best wishes
Loretta G Goldberg

The Reversible Mask

M

MadeGlobal Publishing

For more information on
MadeGlobal Publishing, visit
our website
www.madeglobal.com

For Jane, my better seven eighths,
whose support is beyond thanks.

PART ONE: SEEKING

CHAPTER 1
AT THE PATH'S FORK;
Palamon and Arcite

Oxford, August 1566

S ir Edward Latham stood in his stirrups to glimpse the distant ceremony. He did not care that he was disrupting the look of a procession in which he had an honourable place. *From this far back it is almost comic,* he thought, with a smile that flashed intense amusement before disappearing into his dark mood. Rows of scarlet robes billowed, undulated and bent in unison as Oxford's deans, scholars, masters and students greeted the jewel-encrusted apparition that was their queen, Elizabeth. Latham couldn't tell which black or blue hoods were lined with silk or rabbit fur, according to sumptuary rules; or which masters who'd once tortured him with mathematics were coiled in a longing to rise. But they wouldn't be invited to stand until after long orations in Latin.

It was late afternoon when, finally, the royal procession inched into Oxford. Cheers of "Vivat Regina!" were thunderous, although many in the crowd looked exhausted, having waited for hours. Latham felt a jab through his russet doublet. He turned. David Hicks, with whom he had been sharing accommodations during the progress had reached over with his whip end. "Ned, hold," Hicks said, as if to a pet dog. "We're painted scenery, bushes not flagpoles. Don't risk the Master of Revels' disfavour."

Latham nodded and sat. He ran a gloved finger around the inside of his ruff, feeling a heat rash on his neck. "I wanted to see gouty Johnson on his knees; he was contemptuous of my algebra. I marvel you don't."

Hicks grinned. "Too much tavern learning. I missed those equations." Having saved his colleague from a reprimand, he eased his horse back and left Latham to his thoughts.

Latham's feelings about this royal progress were complex. He resented the discomfort and expense, the accumulation of small miseries for all but the sovereign. But he didn't reject court ceremonies. At a distance, he could *almost* smirk at them, but *almost* was the keyword. Up close, when *he* was the bowing one, he thrilled at being a courtier and knight. At heart, he was a traditionalist, and protocols affirmed feudal hierarchy's vital role in warding off anarchy. He had sound reasons for his ambivalence and was acutely aware of his inconsistency. For the moment he resumed his pageant role, offering the crowd a gracious wave and smile.

He occupied a tricky position in the retinue: behind him, the convoy spread out for half a mile, embraced by continuous cheers, while in front of him the noise diminished as speeches began. He was close enough to recognise the language of the eulogies–Greek, Latin and English–and Elizabeth's replies in the respective languages. But he couldn't hear the words, the irritating fate of a courtier midway down the line.

A sudden stillness, eyes lowered to conceal smirks, signalled the delivery of a royal joke. *At the expense of some scholar or cleric who once criticised her*, Latham thought. The rapier of royal wit thrust into a stationary object. Who was pierced today? It could be politically important, but he'd missed the repartee. His reputation would grow if he could repeat the quip, suffer if he couldn't. Who to ask without embarrassment? *I watch my sovereign feted through the passing of ancient staves, masque performances, speeches I can't hear, tediously alike in length. But jokes break predictability, signifying policy or someone's fall from favour.*

He was running through his contacts among councillors' clerks or ladies' maids when the procession stopped at Christ Church. The entire convoy was now in Oxford proper. Supplications were rebutted with laughter that rolled down the line, as students thrust manuscripts at courtiers, ladies-in-waiting, falconers.

"Enough," Latham heard in response, in many regional accents.

"Move along now."

"Let go of my bridle."

"I can't promise Her Majesty will read it."

In addition to these unsolicited offerings, poems in Greek, Latin, and even Hebrew, written on parchments oranged by the setting sun, had been pasted on walls, doors and eaves. Suddenly he was nostalgic for his student days. The city had been spruced up—building exteriors painted, roads fresh-gravelled, roving animals and beggars expelled—but Oxford's rambunctiousness still came through. A speech, Elizabeth's response, titters again. Damn. He'd missed a second joke.

At twenty-two, Edward Latham was handsome, energetic and cultured. He had chiselled features, flaxen hair, and polished teeth that gleamed through a ready smile. Unusually tall but not reed-thin, his athletic physique was admired by both men and women, whether he was at the archery butts or dancing the galliard. He had the required three languages for an Elizabethan courtier and could bring listeners almost to tears with his lute playing. Elizabeth had knighted him at the beginning of her reign, to reward his prominent father for swearing the Oath of Allegiance to her. Latham's future seemed assured.

But his eyes told a subtler story. They were not the candid blue one expected in a blond. They were hazel, tinting green, brown or pewter, according to the colour closest to his face. Chameleon eyes. Today, his russet doublet with beige satin-slashed sleeves enhanced their brown.

Latham looked around. He was hemmed in by prime reds, blues, yellows. David Hicks was wearing blue with alabaster-white satin slashed sleeves that accented his silver earring hoop. *I used to see life in prime colours*, he reflected. *But now I see everything mixed: clay-burnt ivory ground black darkening my blues; chalk-stone white smearing India-resin reds.* His sigh had the heaviness of an older man.

A scent of early yellow gorse made him cough, and the heavy silver cross under his shirt leapt with his chest spasm. This cross was a lodestone to his restless mind; it was the need to conceal it that was his problem. As a doctrinally conservative Catholic serving a Protestant queen, Latham had almost concluded that he could not reconcile his religious faith with fidelity to the State. To Catholics, Elizabeth wasn't only a heretic, but a bastard with no right to rule. She was the daughter of Henry VIII by his second wife, Anne Boleyn, but the Pope never annulled Henry's first marriage. Catholics believed the Tudor-Boleyn union was invalid; its issue, Elizabeth, illegitimate. Legally, a bastard could not rule England. Henry's will and last Parliament named Elizabeth an heir but didn't declare her legitimate. So although Elizabeth was crowned without challenge, Catholics could reasonably assert that her title was faulty. A few months into her reign, it became clear she was a heretic, too.

Latham had sworn allegiance to her when he had knelt for the giddy shoulder-tap of knighthood. His elevation had occurred before she had shed her earlier ambiguity and changed England's religion, banning public Catholic mass and requiring her subjects to attend Protestant services. But she winked at private observances. Pragmatic Catholics said: "Life is tolerable. God will dispose." Latham wasn't that pragmatic; daily he felt the tension between Protestant governance and his faith. What if he was dying and couldn't find a priest in good order with Rome for last rites?

This concern was not mere fancy. Latham's mother had died of the sweating sickness when he was three. His father, much older brothers and sisters, even the servants, had always been tight-lipped about what rites she had received at the end. It had been the last year of Henry VIII's reign. The king had broken with Rome years before, but some Catholic institutions still functioned. By the time Latham was old enough to ask questions, the boy-king, Edward VI, was ruling as a Protestant. Within a few years he died of tuberculosis, and Queen Mary, Elizabeth's older half-sister, was ruling as a Catholic. Latham's father kept his youngest son shielded from religious schism, no talk of it allowed in the house. The family bent to the laws of the day while privately remaining steadfast Catholics. Latham was vaguely aware that something awful had happened to his older brother Nicolas's household during Queen Mary's reign; awful enough for Nicholas to abandon England and settle in Ireland. He still didn't know what it was. All this protective circumspection made him yearn for clarity. Other peoples' secrets annoyed him.

He couldn't remember his mother's face at all. The flat portrait in the hall, the stone effigy on her tomb, its chiselled features mimicking the portrait, had nothing to do with the presence he vaguely remembered: a calm immanence floating toward him in a miasma of lilac-moss perfume, followed by a long embrace.

What *was* etched in him was visiting her grave with his father. On the way there and back, they passed a priory closed by Henry VIII during his Dissolution of the Monasteries and awarded to a favoured courtier. It was a dismal place: iron gates ripped from their hinges; holes gaping where stained-glass windows once told the redemptive tales of saints; the broken roof yawing to nature's spite. The courtier had been in such a hurry to turn once-sacred property to his own purposes that he'd bombarded buildings with cannon. For young Latham, the fresh-looking gashes in the walls were an extension of his mother's death. His sadness only lifted when he got home and climbed trees or skimmed stones across their pond's surface.

This experience made him sensitive to the conflict between personal faith and state allegiance, which filtered into unlikely levels of society. Just last week, near Elizabeth's palace at Woodstock, he'd almost come to blows with his travelling companion for this progress, David Hicks. It was over a girl of about four, who was clearly touched in the head. The poor wee thing, she'd scurried into the tavern, swinging her hips at the gorgeous strangers crowding the dining room. Her ruff, embroidered kirtle and bonnet showed she was from a family with means. Excited by her grand audience, she piped in a high chant:

> *The little bastard's come to town.*
> *Will she burn or will she drown?*

She sang it a second time, then squatted on the floor, brushed spindly rushes apart to get bare wood and twirled a top. Agitated, David Hicks pushed through the crowd to grab her, ready to call her a knowing traitor, or possessed, and summon the constables. A partisan for the Elizabethan government, Hicks was unfailingly kind except when afraid of Papists. The tavern owner ran in front of him, arms spiralling and yelling that she was mad, harmless. Silent local customers found something important to stare at on the walls.

Latham swept her into his arms and edged to the tavern door. The girl laughed delightedly at his flaxen hair and pulled it. She had the deepest roundest blue eyes he had ever seen.

"Stop, David!" he shouted. "She has no more ken than a cat in heat. She'll end in Bedlam if her family isn't rich."

She began her rhyme again, from the safety of Latham's arms. Obviously, her parents were fervent Papists. A skinny servant woman bustled in, white-faced with fear. She grabbed the girl from Latham, saying, "She has the cunning to get away from me, but no idea what she says. Please believe me, sirs." Latham picked up the top, bowing as he handed it to the woman. "No harm," he said, staring at Hicks. No one mentioned the incident later, but seeing dissent so close to a royal palace was a shock.

Being Catholic under Protestant governance created problems, but Latham also took his knighthood seriously. His options felt narrow: hell or self-exile. Prime colours; red, blue. To stay endangered his soul; to leave was a betrayal. To stay and dissent was a betrayal. His father and sister had compromised, and he loved them. His thoughts went round and round, causing him sleepless nights.

"You must go on this progress, Edward." his father had insisted. Appointed Justice of the Peace when he had sworn allegiance to Elizabeth, Latham's father had put his Catholicism again into a private realm. A decent man, he had reverence for his responsibilities. He was grateful for work that filled his waking hours, for he'd never re-married after the death of Latham's mother. "It's an honour, especially this year," he impressed upon his son. "All of Europe will be watching the queen and her court. Her Majesty is hosting the Spanish ambassador; rumour says she might marry the Spanish king's nephew, Catholic Archduke Charles. Then there is the issue of English policy on Protestant rebels in the Spanish Netherlands…"

Latham's father was right about the importance of this year's progress. Tension between Spain and England had flared when Dutch Protestants, tired of religious persecution by their Catholic Spanish King, Philip II, had begun destroying churches, beating priests and refusing to pay taxes. Elizabeth the Queen despised rebellion, while Elizabeth the Protestant abhorred the burning alive and torture of her co-religionists. Her Protestant subjects pushed her to aid the rebels; her Catholic subjects hoped a Spanish army across the channel would frighten her into allowing public Catholic mass. All watched for signs.

So far, Elizabeth was playing the good host to the Spanish ambassador, displaying her popularity among the crowds and relishing lavish entertainments in her honour. Erudite disputations at Oxford were to be the climax. "See our reformist scholars," she intended to imply. "Our Protestants aren't smashing and plundering bandits." She wanted friendly relations with Spain despite religious differences, and it seemed that Spain saw its interests the same way. In this bubbling cauldron of faith and power, no one knew what the leverage points were.

"As a loyal Catholic courtier," Latham's father had concluded, "many will notice you. Her Majesty will notice you."

At this, both had laughed. Edward had told him that when envoys from Catholic countries visited, Elizabeth often brought one of her Catholic courtiers close. She would incline her head toward him and whisper loudly to the envoy, "See how moderate I am to loyal papists. If only your prince emulated me, there could be peace." When the audience ended, back the token Papist went to midway in the line.

Latham had obeyed his father, so here he was on the arduous haul from Middlesex to Surrey. He had emptied his purse to buy silks, velvets, peahen cap feathers, soft leather dress boots with floppy tassels and hard, gleaming riding boots. Out of ready coin, he depended on the pittance Elizabeth gave her junior courtiers.

Cautiously, he fingered a missive in his pocket. He touched the vellum, then drew his fingers back, as if it were scalding. He sat up and waved at milling spectators. But then his hand, of its own accord, crept back and his thumb rubbed the broken seal.

This letter, with its elegant calligraphy, offered him a way out. It was from his childhood friend, Henry Stuart, Lord Darnley. A Catholic cousin of Elizabeth, Darnley had married Catholic Mary, Queen of Scots, who was also Elizabeth's cousin. Both Elizabeth and Mary descended from Henry VII, Elizabeth being his granddaughter and Mary his great-granddaughter. But no one questioned Mary's legitimacy, and for this reason, some thought her claim to the English throne the valid one. It was a claim Mary refused to relinquish, despite her dynastic line having been omitted in Henry VIII's will. Darnley's letter invited Latham to leave England and serve him at the Scottish court, in the coveted position of Master of the Horse.

As Latham imagined life in Scotland, his heart soared. He could go openly to mass, worship with Mary herself! End his daily struggle over faith versus loyalty to his sovereign. He glanced at the head of the procession, where Elizabeth was being escorted by her Master of the Horse, her swarthy favourite, Robert Dudley, Earl of Leicester. Darnley was offering a parallel position, at the head of the line.

But. There was a but. To leave legally, Latham needed travelling papers approved by Elizabeth. She would be incensed when he told her that he wished to serve Mary–born-in-legitimate-wedlock Mary–instead of her. There was no active conflict between the queens, but implicit rivalry could spark religious unrest at any time. That mad girl in the tavern showed how fragile stability was.

Beneath Darnley's seductive vellum there was another letter, on thinner parchment. Latham had crumpled it after tut-tutting at its plea. However, his treatment of the paper did not diminish its importance to him; he replayed it as the procession inched forward.

My beloved little brother, his sister Katherine had written, *I beseech, demand, disprove your premise if you were amenable to reason, DO NOT LEAVE ENGLAND.* There it was: faith, kin, country, colliding. Katherine had been named after Katherine of Aragon, Henry VIII's first and only lawful wife. Stubborn Spanish Katherine had refused to let Henry go, which precipitated the king's break with Rome. Yet here was her namesake urging Latham to adapt.

Stay, Edward, she wrote. *Papa practises outward conformity. You are "Sir" through his fealty. Even Father Williams renders to "Caesar Caesar's," though he visits us privately every day. Why will you not settle for the same? Cool your impatience. We heard from Crofts of the Council that Parliament will tie the Queen's tax subsidy to her marriage or the naming of an heir. Before Easter, we might have King Consort, Catholic Charles, with mass being allowed soon. Why would the Spanish envoy come on this tour if King Philip of Spain hadn't blessed the match with his nephew? Consider, if Her Majesty dawdles, which she has been wont to do, there's the chance of an early shroud; she was a sickly girl. Throw not all away, Edward. You're full of black bile despite the cheer you paint on the face you turn to the world. It drowns your judgment. Dear brother, take the purge I sent you, then ask the physician to let blood, two quarts. See if a royal affiancing is not trumpeted before you are cleansed. But whatever your course, know I will always love you.*

Generous Katherine, Latham thought. He was grateful for her unconditional love. But if black bile sludged his judgment, airy blood filled her with self-pleasing vapours, endangering her soul. Elizabeth would not marry right now. A king consort brought a fixed alliance, and Latham could not imagine this sovereign accepting certainty. Nor did he believe in an early death for her. Elizabeth's girlhood illnesses had not come from a sickly constitution, he believed, but the absence of power. Once the crown had been placed on her red hair, she had shown great resilience, surviving smallpox without a mark. Who but a witch did that? No, Catholic hegemony was unlikely. Still, the Spanish envoy, a suave noble named Gusman de Silva, was on good terms with her. He might be able to ease restrictions on English Catholics. Latham had not decided what to do.

A blue-gowned student carrying a slate caught Latham's attention. He was looking for a discreet place to relieve himself. Latham leaned over and grabbed a fistful of coarse linen. The jokes he had missed; perhaps the student could help. "Hold, sir. Did you hear Her Majesty's jokes?" he asked.

"Ha, ha, ha!" A sun-reddened face, a fuzz of auburn beard, earnest grey eyes smiled up at him. He waved his writing tablet. "I wrote them, yes. They won't appear in any history of Magdalen College. No, sir. You know Dr. Humphrey, Magdalen's president?"

Latham nodded. Lawrence Humphrey was a radical Protestant who'd chastised Elizabeth publicly for ordering her clerics to keep wearing the white and gold surplices of Catholic services, and for her own gorgeous clothes. Humphrey railed that such vanities corrupted the new religion. For Elizabeth, familiar garments bridged old and new. Too much plain black was a social leveller, threatening the glittering hierarchy over which she presided. Similarly, she'd written a law protecting the polyphonic choirs that were anathema to radicals like Humphrey. Her conservatism raised Catholics' hopes that she might go further, but nothing else had changed.

"What about Humphrey?" Latham asked eagerly.

"Can you believe that after calling our queen vain, he primped in his plushest regalia!" the student answered, highly amused. "Her Majesty said loudly, the Spaniard grinning at her side..." he glanced at his tablet: "'This gown and habit become you very well, and I *marvel* that you are so straight-laced in this point.' Humphrey went red. She added, 'But *I* come not to chide.' A complete rebuke!"

"And the joke at Christ Church?" Latham handed him tuppence.

The youth thrust the coins into his pocket. "Oh, that. Thomas Kingsmill didn't hear her put Humphrey down. He praised her in Latin for her great wisdom in appointing Humphrey. She replied in Latin that his speech would have done well had his matter been good! Kingsmill had no idea why he came up short, but everyone else did. I will publish it someday. Now, sir, let me go!" Laughing, he spun away to piss.

Publicly exposing her clergy's hypocrisy was a departure from predictability. Latham's heart leapt. Perhaps his sister had a point. Mentally, he ran through the scheduled events, the many agendas accompanying any royal visit to a university, wondering which ones would be significant. Individual scholars would seek patronage (much was expected this year for the queen's debate champion, Edmund Campion); the university wanted endowments; the sovereign would monitor her future governing class. On this occasion, Elizabeth would want to establish her intellectual credentials with scholars and diplomats.

On a subtler level, through entertainments, Oxford intended to express opinions to Elizabeth indirectly that would be unacceptable in plain statements. It was a game the university played with the support of her principal councillors. To urge her to settle the succession by marrying or naming an heir, a spectacular play in English was on the schedule, extolling marriage. *Palamon and Arcite*, by Richard Edwards, was based on Chaucer's *A Knight's Tale*, featuring a beautiful blonde princess who had sworn chastity, but was compelled to marry one of two competing knights to preserve the realm. The programme also included a debate in Latin on whether the sovereign alone determined the succession, or whether a parliament, in the absence of a named heir, could. This was the hottest controversy of the day, and Oxford was hinting that Elizabeth's next parliament would press her on the issue. In this way, obliquely, subjects and sovereign conversed.

Check, not checkmate. Latham had laughed when he had read the programme. Elizabeth would find a way to get her tax subsidy and retain her freedom, especially with this warning. As he considered the events, he decided the Latin debate on natural philosophy was the most likely to offer clues to future royal policy. The erudite and popular Edmund

Campion would stand as the queen's champion. Campion's parents were Catholic, and he was rumoured to have Catholic sympathies, but he was due to be ordained as a Protestant deacon. One of the new pragmatic men, Elizabeth would want to show him off.

The procession broke up, and courtiers sought their lodgings. Feeling his entire life was on hold, Latham joined Hicks in their small tavern room.

In the great hall at Christ Church three evenings later, court and queen were watching *Palamon and Arcite*, the spectacle scheduled to take two nights.

PALAMON: I saw Emilia first! She is mine!

ARCITE: Nay, I did. As the sun marks the dial, yes, your eyes fell on her first. But you cannot say if she is a goddess or maid. A mortal cannot claim a Divine. Your love must stay chaste. But when I espied her walking hither and thither relishing the May sun, I knew her for a ready woman. Therefore, I saw Emilia first.

Palamon and Arcite were young knights who had been bound since childhood by kinship and sworn oaths. Both prisoners of war of the Duke of Athens, their bond had shattered in their lethal quarrel over Emilia, the duke's sister. Emilia had sworn her own oath: lifelong chastity. But as the tale unfolded, she'd be compelled to marry one of the knights. The playwright, Richard Edwardes, was hammering home the point that England's semi-divine sovereign maid must do the same. To make sure no one could possibly misunderstand, since the performance was open to the public, Chaucer's blonde Emilia had red hair.

The hall had been transformed into a theatre. The ceiling

had been gilded, and a multitude of candles on walls and in chandeliers cast dazzling light. A temporary stage had been built with retiring rooms for actors; their doors painted to resemble palaces. By tradition, the monarch was part of the performance, so Elizabeth sat on a cushioned throne under a gold cloth canopy on a dais, partly facing the audience. To accommodate a huge crowd, scaffolds had been erected along the hall's sides. There were boxes on top for aristocrats; standing room below for lower classes. From his box, Latham had a clear view of the stage, queen, ambassador and the audience. Elizabeth's lips curled in contemptuous amusement. She knew what Edwardes and his councillor sponsors were up to.

PALAMON: You betrayed our lifelong tryst.

ARCITE: Nay, 'tis you that is false. Forsooth, now each man will be for himself!

Which of Latham's senses first trumpeted the disaster? Was it the lurch beneath his feet, when he realised he was looking up at the box that had been level with his a moment before? Was it the squeal of unseasoned timbers releasing their bolts? Was it the sight of spectators' mouths gaping like beached fish, or their shrieks?

Time moved with exquisite slowness as the scaffolding on his side of the hall cracked. He had time to note Elizabeth's steely calm as she leaned forward to assess the damage before guards hurried her to safety; time to see Palamon and Arcite, who first tried to shout over the disturbance, scrambling in unknightly haste off the stage, dragging a squawking Emilia.

Time sped up. The scaffolding collapsed with a roar as Latham's box fell, crushing those below. A piece of wood hit Latham on the temple, and he lost consciousness.

He woke up later; how much later he didn't know. He was lying on a table, beside other benches and tables. When he turned his pounding head, he could see bodies laid out all around him. Shadowy figures hovered, bending, bandaging, dosing, murmuring, giving purses of coins.

Voices swam in and out of his woolly brain. "Her Majesty is heartily sorry for your mischance." Again and again.

A piercing female wail hurt his ears; some new-made widow.

A male voice said deferentially, "Three dead, my Lord: a brewer, a cook, a scholar, all of the standing audience. The five injured are being tended by Her Majesty's physician. They will recover, God willing."

Latham gathered that Leicester was here, deciding what to do next.

Leicester's deep voice seeped through Latham's muddle. "...and bury the bodies. They swell so quick in summer. We can't wait for the scholar's kin to come. The coroner will rule it misadventure, anyway."

Latham's head throbbed beneath his bandage. He sat up and bent to retch into a bucket solicitously held out for him.

"You have a bump and a scratch, nothing broken," Leicester told him, using the mellifluous tone with which he soothed jumpy horses and dogs. "Go back now."

The bang of nails on wood, the rustle of debris dragging on floors, told Latham that they were still in the hall. Not much time had passed at all. To his amazement, they meant to go on with the play.

The audience returned, standing warily beside the remaining scaffolds. Palamon, Arcite and Emilia came onstage to work out their destiny, in which one knight would die, and Emilia would marry the survivor.

The tragic accident seemed forgotten as the audience submitted to ingenious effects that lasted until midnight, culminating in a hunting scene. Painted sets of groves along with tree-lined paths intersecting the stage created the illusion of a forest. Packs of real hounds in the courtyard bayed; an actor outside a window mimicked the bark of a mighty stag; horns blared backstage. Students shouted that there was a hunt on. Filled with excitement, some ran to the windows.

Elizabeth loved their confusion. Laughing and clapping, she said, "Those boys are ready to leap out the windows to the hounds!" Her eyes crinkled, her radiant smile embracing all around her. This smile had no shadow.

Afterwards, Latham walked back to his room, somewhat dazed. Three deaths simply erased. Three unshriven souls. But for God's grace, it could have been him. What *were* his mother's last rites?

He pondered his sovereign's coolness as the scaffolding broke, princely remedies dispatched, the completeness with which she put tragedy behind her, responding to the spectacle of the later scenes. She was formidable, in a way he found hard to like.

"Damned papists. You'd think that witch-girl came here and multiplied," David Hicks said moodily, as they fought a chess game to a draw in the early hours of the morning. "They're whispering evil omen." He hadn't gone to the play, meeting friends at a cockfight instead. But everyone knew about the accident.

Latham studied Hicks's vivid green eyes, slightly dulled by drinking. Freckles on his forehead and a snub nose gave him the appearance of lightness. He was a congenial companion at court, but behind the guileless look was a tough shrewdness. Roistering, which Hicks called "tavern learning," was how he made an abacus of human contacts. He was both ambitious and a partisan for his government. It was generally known at court that Latham's family was quietly devoted to the old faith, but Latham was careful not to reveal his doctrinal beliefs to Hicks. In the close quarters of a shared room, he used a dividing screen to conceal his cross.

"The play resuming directly," Hicks continued. "I think Her Majesty right not to deprive the actors of their chance at fame. We may never come again."

"You weren't there," Latham retorted. "A son, a brother, a family provider lost; no waiting for kin to bury them. Such mischances should be given all the proper observances."

Into the frosty silence, Hicks shouted, "Dried thistle-cunny!"

"Dung tongue!" Latham answered.

"Beetle-brain!"

"Mouldy plum with no pip!"

Soon they were laughing, for they competed to collect insults they heard during the endless saddling up, packing and unpacking. Latham asked, "What do you make of Edwardes' play? I know you read it at the Master of Revels' office."

"Why, it shows that Her Majesty, like Princess Emilia, must marry and provide an heir for the realm. Oxford meant to send the message, and Sir Thomas had no wish to censor it."

"I saw something darker," Latham mused. "What bond could be stronger than sworn oaths between cousin knights, a bond cemented by being wounded in the same battle and prisoners of the same captor? Yet this bond shatters instantly over an Emilia they glimpse from their prison window. Only one of them lives."

"Shattered bonds, eh?" Hicks looked at Latham, suddenly attentive. "Maybe you see what you seek. Edward, be careful. You are prey to melancholy. Take a purge."

"That's what my sister Katherine writes."

"She's wiser than you, friend. That play is a prettied-up version of the old tale extolling royal marriage. Nothing more." Hicks's eyes softened. "I mean it about the purge. We've helped each other on this trip, found common things to laugh at, which is no small thing. But even if we were in a perfect garden, you would still trip over a half-eaten rabbit and dirty your hose. Do you have a particular worry?"

It was a frank offer of friendship, but Latham wasn't inclined to be part of Hicks's abacus. He busied himself putting chess pieces away, ignoring the puzzled hurt in his companion's eyes. Hicks was soon snoring, a heavy rumble that soon settled into a low purr. Eventually, Latham drifted into a dream: silk filaments binding kin, church, country, sovereign, fraying at one moment, knitting at another; a bombarded priory repairing itself, getting hit again. When he woke, he was still uncertain about his future. To his relief, Hicks seemed to have forgotten their last conversation.

The last of several Latin debates conducted over three days, along with banter between Elizabeth and the Spanish ambassador—jokes signifying policy—finally clarified Latham's future.

Elizabeth loved Latin disputes, listening happily for hours while her courtiers desperately wanted sleep. But it was advisable to pay attention because a slack mouth could inspire her to ask the mouth's owner his opinion on the point before the last. It wasn't just mischief on her part; it was a way of getting to know her future civil servants. Latham drank a tonic of balsam, gold flecks and saffron to stay alert.

Debates on the efficacy of various medicine; on whether debt valuation changed if a coinage was debased after contract signing but before settlement; and on whether Parliament could act in the Succession, had all gone well. The climactic contest on natural philosophy was to consider whether the lower bodies on earth regulated the motions of the heavenly bodies, or the other way around; and whether the moon, through magnetic force, influenced the tides.

Oxford's celebrated scholar, a sweet-faced proctor, named Edmund Campion, due to be ordained as a Protestant deacon, argued for the Crown. Stepping on stage at St. Mary's Hall, Campion put new science, classical astronomy and mythology together, couching his proposition in the language of tribute.

"The tides are caused by the moon's motions. Further, the lower bodies of the universe are regulated by the higher, the highest of which, in the sublunary sphere, is the moon. At the peak of the sublunary sphere is the moon goddess, who therefore regulates the moon and all below." Since Elizabeth was often called Cynthia, the moon goddess, Campion implied that his sovereign was a prime mover in the cosmos. The flattery was custard-thick, its logic fanciful, but it turned out to be impossible to dismantle.

The first opponent argued that the lower bodies regulated the higher. He cited an ancient theory that the heavens were formed by distilling corrupt earth and water into the purer air and fire, which in turn improved the earth. "Meteors are expulsions of earth's gross matter," he stated.

Meteors, terrifying slashes of the sky, Latham thought. While the Latin rolled around him, he recalled one when he was a child. His nurse told him to avoid looking directly at it because that would displease God and he would never have a quiet soul. Latham had peeked through his fourth and fifth finger; a sliver of a look, surely too quick for God to notice. But he sometimes wondered if his dark moods were punishment for that childhood effrontery.

Bringing his attention back to the argument, he tried to visualise corrupt matter soaring from earth, shedding grossness. Where did the ancients think the expulsions began? Volcanoes spewed smoky vomit, but lava plunged back to earth. At what height did gross matter purify? The top of a cathedral spire? Or the ether, where angels whirled? It was easier to believe in invisible magnetic fields than up-plunging boulders.

The next contestant proposed that as the higher and lower bodies never touched, it was not provable that they acted on each other. The final contestant argued that all the others were wrong. Citing the Renaissance scholar Paracelsus, he said that the four humours governed mind, matter, and the firmament, not the moon.

Latham found the contest futile, its pointlessness masked by being in Latin. But Elizabeth's eyes gleamed as she followed each point. The moderator declared that no one had disproved Campion's first proposition, that the tides were caused by the moon's motions; therefore the second proposition and his conclusion also stood. Campion won.

Latham was the token papist at supper, close enough to hear Elizabeth and the Spanish ambassador talk. In French, she asked de Silva what he thought of her champion, soon to be a deacon in her church.

"I own to disappointment, Your Majesty," de Silva replied with a mischievous grin. He enjoyed teasing Elizabeth, knowing she wanted to impress Spain, but he never crossed a line that could damage diplomacy. "Let me explain. His name has two possible derivations. First is Campo, warrior champions used by ancient kings to fight for the crown in non-judicial trials. Your Campo certainly showed chivalry, linking you, Madame, with Cynthia and the regulation of the sublunary sphere and what lies below."

Elizabeth blushed.

De Silva continued smoothly. "But to me, your Campion is more like his other namesake, the moss campion. Your Majesty may not know this alpine bloom. Its pink or white petals are perfect, like your Campion's practised fusion of science, Ptolemaic astronomy and myth. The plant is delicate, making the most of the shallow, stony soil in which God decreed it must exist."

Latham looked down to conceal his grin. He knew where de Silva was going. By reducing the Queen's champion to a fragile flower, he was challenging Oxford's stature.

Elizabeth riposted. "Shallow soil? Come to your matter now, my Lord, or your moss campion will be stillborn under the frost of Our disapproval."

"Pithy, Your Majesty. You surpass princes and scholars in wit." De Silva laughed and bowed his head. "Allow me to knot my argument. The moss campion adapts to a dry climate, but England is loamy and wet. No one knows this better than I, who wheezes in your dank mornings. I expected more invention from an English campo, where bushes, grasses and trees thrust up in happy abundance. A campo worthy of Your Majesty would fight spontaneously, without preparation. Where is your campo's native wit?"

"Ah," Elizabeth laughed, "You want to test my scholars with an extempore debate. No practice, no looking anything up. Granted! But you buried your meaning under such verbal clods of soil that only someone of considerable parts could extract sound seed beneath."

Pleased with herself, she called for a Latin extempore debate the next day.

Campion stood for the Crown again. This time the subject was fire. He didn't find a way to imply his sovereign was the goddess of the element, but linked the legend of Prometheus, the effects on the brain of lightning, and the culinary results of slow versus fast cooking. Tactfully, he refrained from mentioning the Spanish Inquisition's burning of heretics.

"So," Elizabeth demanded of de Silva at dinner, an event in which Latham was again the token papist. "Campo or moss campion?"

"Campo," De Silva conceded. "Permit me to praise the learning of your scholars."

"Well, I am glad that's settled," Elizabeth replied. "Tell my good brother, King Philip, that your moss campions must stay only where they grow naturally. Our climate will rot them." She frowned, leaving no ambiguity about her authority.

It went by so fast that Latham had to pinch himself to grasp the meaning: no loosening of restrictions for English Catholics. He glanced at the other guests, wondering what they made of it. Bemusement showed on Leicester's face; metaphors were not his strong point. Two Oxford deans were in conversation with each other, while three young nobles concentrated on their wine. Only Sir William Cecil, Elizabeth's Principal Secretary, was listening, eyes ferally alert in his warty face.

Latham leaned forward, straining for the Spanish ambassador's response.

De Silva inclined his head. "I take your meaning but beseech you to think on your own King Canute, who presumed to alter God's design by trying to stay the tide. An ignoble failure."

Lives were being disposed of here, in quip and counter quip. Elizabeth was saying Catholicism wouldn't thrive in England. De Silva accepted, but she wasn't to overplay her hand like Canute in meddling beyond her land, no matter how much her subjects sympathised with Dutch Protestants. Spain wanted open sea lanes to defeat its rebels.

Elizabeth retorted, "We do not contest with God's design, no matter we're called the moon goddess Cynthia. That bog-brained king was pagan Dane, not pure English like me."

The deal: each would leave the other alone. For now. Neither mentioned marrying Catholic Archduke Charles. Secretary Cecil kept his expression bland, his thoughts unknowable.

When the festivities ended, Latham waved off Hicks's invitation to join him at a card game and lay on his bed, arms behind his head, staring at the ceiling. Policy was made today, he brooded. And it was done with wordplay, nothing written. Everything would stay the same. *Semper Eadem*, 'always the same', was the motto Elizabeth chose when she was crowned. Today it had a smidgeon of truth.

Latham's hope for a better balance between his faith and allegiance to the State died. Elizabeth's rebuke of Humphrey and Kingsmill *was* a sign: that she meant to control her own radicals. Darnley had written that Mary was an active monarch: she had marched her armies twice already in her four-year reign, to counter an insult and consolidate her authority as a Catholic monarch. "There's clarity here," he promised. Latham was young. He yearned to *do* something.

The royal visit climaxed at twilight with Elizabeth's Latin speech.

"Those who do bad things hate the light, and therefore, because I am aware that I myself am about to manage badly, I think that a time of shadows will be fittest for me." She spoke fast, in a high, light voice. Her disclaimer enchanted the scholars. Inclining her head becomingly as the sky darkened from blue to black, she praised the students for their excellent disputations and blamed herself for the limits of her own learning. "Therefore I will make an end to this speech full of barbarisms, if I may first add two prayers: that while I live you may be most prosperous, and when I die you may be blessed." To the cheers that greeted her speech, Elizabeth responded with tears of gratitude. They meandered down her cheeks, upon which the cheers grew louder, more ecstatic, bringing forth more tears. Light seeped away, stars began to wink, a multitude of torches flared.

Is it real, or theatre? It hardly matters, Latham mused, for the exchange between rapturous subjects and gracious monarch fed on itself. Edmund Campion would soon be a Protestant deacon. If Elizabeth attracted scholars like him, there would be little room for men like Latham. As a community, English Catholics would wither.

Latham looked down the path of his future and saw stifled words, stillborn thoughts. This was not his destiny. A tombstone floated in front of his eyes. He did not recognise its location, but the light was hard and brilliant, the cemetery ancient. He knew, though he couldn't say how, that it was his gravestone. Of white marble, it bore an Italian inscription in gold paint: Edward Latham, valiant knight. His birth year, and a blank. It wasn't a morbid vision, but cheerful. He would be known, but not for actions in England. So. To Scotland, without travelling papers.

The next morning, he sought out the Master of the Revels for permission to return home. He found him at Christ Church Hall supervising the dismantling of the stage. Sir Thomas Benger had a sad, basset-hound face, a mismatch for an organiser of entertainments. It was well known that Elizabeth wasn't thrilled with her Master of the Revels, because she hadn't granted him the privilege of passing the office to his son. Too many plays extolling marriage, perhaps. Sir Thomas often gave out that he was overworked and underpaid. He was so preoccupied with what he didn't have, that he could be inattentive to what was happening in front of him. He didn't interrogate the young courtier who had been seated near Gusman de Silva and now bowed so respectfully to him.

"A beloved elderly retainer is mortally ill," Latham told him, painting grief on his face.

"Sir Edward Latham, isn't it?" Benger shouted over the noise and dust. "Noted. Go. Loyalty to servants is a noble virtue. I wish certain great others showed like care."

An hour later, Latham gave the stable boy a note to deliver to Hicks, then rode out of Oxford. Gulling Sir Thomas was shabby, he thought with a touch of shame. When Elizabeth learned her Master of Revels had released Latham without inquiry, his remaining hope of preferment would end. Still, Latham wasn't Benger's keeper. That guilt he could bear.

His estate, a three-storey fifteenth-century mansion with a brewhouse, stables, orchard and woods, was near Reigate in Surrey. Soon after leaving the main road, he had to jump the ditch and wait when a farmer with carts of vegetables passed. Then a flock of sheep. Away from the royal progress route, where everything Elizabeth saw was paved or re-gravelled, Latham saw flouting of regulations. Ditches and drains that were supposed to be cleared annually hadn't been, shrinking the road. In addition, trees soared above the prescribed height, blocking the sun from drying the road, so even a hot, dry day could be a slog through mud. Usually, indifference to laws made for the public good infuriated Latham. But this time it suited him: he was confident he could reach Scotland without papers.

He checked the steward's accounts and wrote a letter to Katherine. Confirming his decision to leave, he asked her to supervise his estate in return for its profits. Then he consulted his astrologer. Dr Pell's office in Reigate was permeated with the dust of threadbare old age and fading magic. A second-floor room with low ceiling beams, it was bursting with books, piles of parchments, and jars of strange-smelling substances. Three tallow candles gave a flickering taupe glow to a chart spread on a low table.

The room was drab, but the man himself had a radiant serenity. Pell's kindly eyes gazed at him. Latham felt a jolt of astonishment; a sense that he could see right through the blue irises to Dr Pell's fluttering gentle soul, one burdened by too much prescience.

"Scorpio's your birth sign, of course. But Jupiter in Leo," Pell began, hunching thinly over the chart. "You have huge ambition, but not of the usual sort. Presumption is your lifeblood and flaw. It helps you snatch truths from what is hidden. But you strive to influence your patrons, and this temerity robs you of your deserved rewards. Taurus rising, with vibrations of Venus, Mercury, Jupiter: peripatetic travels to far lands, separation from ancestors."

He uncurled and grasped Latham's wrist.

"Dear boy, I cast your chart at birth. Much then was just possibilities. Now I see shifts. Several shifts. Many live, many die from your dealings. You have triumphs, failures, an unquiet soul. Love, yes, but fleeting; folly in wisdom; courage among shadows. A long passage. God be with you, Edward. The 30th September is propitious."

Latham jumped up. "Dr Pell! That date cannot be right."

"The 30th September 1566. The chart is clear. This is goodbye, dear boy."

Latham was horrified. It was now the 23rd. He had just seven days to go three times as far as from Oxford to Reigate, some of it on the horrible roads he'd been laughing at. But crossing a foreign border without travelling papers must be done on the propitious day. He embraced Dr Pell and clattered down the stairs.

He had to reach Berwick-upon-Tweed, England's northernmost fortress, by the 29th. During an uncle's garrison duty he'd visited Berwick, hawking in the marches and taking wherries to the various bastions. He had a friend there who could find a boatman to take him to Dunbar, Scotland, as long as he was ahead of any hue and cry.

By dint of riding sixteen hours a day, changing horses frequently, and hiring guards as needed in lawless areas, he arrived at an inn two miles south of Berwick on 29th September. Dusty, bleary-eyed, his thighs calcified into the shape of the saddle, he slid to the ground bent like a goblin. But exultant. He drew into his nostrils the heady tang of kelp fertiliser, thinking it more bracing than the musky dung of southern fields.

Scotland and England had been at war for centuries. As he neared the border, he heard in the voices of farmers from whom he bought ale and bread a commingling of Scots and Northumbrian dialects, forced long ago. There were burned-out churches and rubble piles that had once been homes. Many dwellings now were primitive: clay and wood, under whose roof livestock and livestock eaters co-habited. Easy to knock down or fire, easy to rebuild. Eagerness to fit all he saw into his concept of a simpler life, he told himself that clay and wood were less entrapping of a man than the immovable brick of his Surrey house.

Cross-border cattle rustling still went on, but the peace treaty signed three years into Elizabeth's reign was holding, made by Protestant parties in both countries. Latham thought it ironic that the labours of heretics would enable him to reach Catholic Queen Mary. He smiled as he massaged his back and eased himself upright. Peace had benefited this area. The inn had a settled feel: mature vegetable gardens, placid barley fields and grazing meadows. In his second-floor private room, the sun was setting when he opened the window. He gazed at its traditional back garden, with a hen house, spindly lawn and stables.

It was bucolic. But not for long. A party of workmen and officials rode into the stableyard and dismounted. They shouted, the inn's dogs barked, their own answered with growls. Aghast, Latham recognised the men's badges: the bear and staff of Elizabeth's Master of the Horse, her favourite, Robert Dudley, Earl of Leicester. Were they after him already?

The Northumbrian innkeeper went out to greet them: peremptory exchanges and pointing fingers signified demands, initial refusal, resentful acquiescence. Minutes later, he knocked on Latham's door. "An unexpected visit, sir, Leicester's men. Engineers, a builder and clerks. They come to replace rotted pilings under the bridge and draw plans to fortify the walls."

It is nothing, Latham thought, his limbs unclenching. "One must say yes to the Earl of Leicester," he said, wanting to be agreeable. "Do you need the room?"

"No, sir. I have lodgings for them. But they say a courier and magistrate from London, Cecil's men, are riding posthaste after a courtier fugitive. They could arrive around midnight. Or tomorrow. Or not at all. Lawless brutes out there." He grinned. "But when they come, I must ask you to move."

Now that *was* to do with him. When the innkeeper left, he stood paralysed, gripped by profound lassitude. "It will end on the 30th September, not begin," he whispered bitterly. "Curse false astrologers." His mind began the stuff of resignation. The punishment might not be unbearable: interrogation, public reprimand, banishment from court, his father incensed but Katherine standing by him, partial rehabilitation after long shame.

But offering himself up for chastisement? "No! I'll make this night's witching hour my friend," he muttered. How had anyone learned his plan? Not from Hicks or Benger, who thought he was home. Or Dr Pell, who would never discuss a client's chart. Katherine was the only one he had told. Cecil kept must have an informer in her household; he watched covert Catholics. Well, he wasn't going to win this one.

Anger replaced melancholy. His thoughts raced. He couldn't rely on his Berwick friend to find a boatman to Dunbar. He'd have to get to the river tonight. Then what? Even getting to the road silently was a problem, with the inn dogs. Achieving the river didn't guarantee success, either. Rivers usually marked borders, but this section of the Tweed led to the fortress of Berwick, which was England for two more miles. The bridge would be guarded; he couldn't walk or ride across. "And even if I cross undetected, I'll still be in enemy territory." What? *Enemy*? He was amazed at that rattling word. "No, this is my country. I'm English."

He hadn't thought it through. He'd rushed here with no contingency plan. He prayed for inspiration, forgiveness, mercy, and to wake at the right time. Then he pinched out the candle. Hours later he jerked awake, in deep darkness. When he looked out of the window, he realised that dark was a relative condition. The near-full moon behind striated clouds cast a diffuse brightness of blue, white and black, patterning the ground. Mysterious and frightening, but navigable. A gift.

He moved fast, dressing in comfortable travelling clothes and thick hose. He thrust money, jewels, and Darnley's invitation into his waist pouch, made a bag of wood ash from the room's fireplace to blacken his hair, slipped his dagger into a sheath at his belt and strapped on his short sword. He left his court finery behind. Only a fool would abandon such wealth; hopefully, any pursuers would assume he was nearby.

Holding his hard boots in one hand, their laces tied, he felt his way downstairs, stopping at every groan of the wood underfoot. On the landing, snores from Leicester's men were muffled by a door. At the cellar door, he stepped over the drunken heap of stinking wool cloak that was the night soil collector and cellar guard. *Marvellous omen*, his thoughts rattled. Another gift: the cellar wasn't locked. Picking up the guard's lantern, he went into the cellar and took a rope, smoked meat to give the dogs, and an apple, in case he needed to steal a horse. He pulled on his boots and girded himself for the terrors of the night.

Outside of the front door, he stood, getting his bearings. In the courtyard, the two large dogs–fortunately leashed–growled softly, clearly considering a full-throated fuss. Latham threw one hunk of meat at them, waited for them to compete over it, then strode forward and threw the second piece. When the growls turned to chewing, he opened the gate to the road.

The night painted the roadside trees as tall as cathedral spires, the woods behind great naves and cloisters. He imagined skeletal fingers scratching at him from the underworld, or winged demons springing from behind trees to tear his throat out. Even so, the charismatic night beckoned him on. Men didn't call this the witching hour for no reason. At every owl hoot or leaf rustle, at the constantly changing shadows, he stopped to calm his dread.

He sat beside a ditch to think. What would he do when he reached the bridge? Could he cross under it? He had done it as a child, swinging by his hands from plank end to plank end, like a jungle chimpanzee he had seen in the bear-baiting arena. Jack-an-apes, the agile beasts were called. He assumed that the bridge's plank ends still jutted beyond the barrier railings. There were pilings with diagonal braces every fifteen feet or so–the supports Leicester's men had come to repair–and he could rest against them. He was taller and heavier now, but had an archer's strength. If he reached the other side, he would then have to hike around the outer walls. Dawn might catch him short. Hopefully, the spirit that woke him at the right time would inspire him with the solution.

He got up and walked on. Soon water slapped rocks, and the pungent odour of rotting fish filled the air. He was there. Above him, a torch bobbed as a guard patrolled, spat over the side, turned heavily and walked back. Latham blacked his hair and face with the wood ash, looped the rope around a plank end and pulled. He was relieved when it held. Then he felt intense regret; he was committed. He levered himself up and felt for the next plank.

Now he understood the challenge. The blue-black light, adequate for walking, robbed him of depth perception. He had to do everything by feel. Dangling, with knees bent to hold his boots above the roiling waters, it was agonisingly slow, creeping one hand to the next plank, keeping balance while he found the firm place to grip, then swinging his heavy body over. His worst moment came when he realised that the spaces between the planks weren't even. In one case there was no space at all, so he had to spread-eagle over two planks to find his next hold. The rope was useless; he let it go. When he collapsed against the first piling, he was exhausted and sweating. It was going to take much longer than he expected; the pain in his shoulders was excruciating. He wondered if being racked was worse. The current and wind sent waves slapping against the seaweed-slimy support.

He pulled himself to the second piling, then the third. He clung, gasping, to the diagonal bracing. One further pull, and he sat on the beam joint. His palms were bleeding. With his teeth, he worked at splinters he could feel. Above him, the guard's tread approached. Latham yearned to end this mad adventure, to return to what he knew, with all its constrictions. To call out to the guard: "I surrender for a hand up and a pot of ale." He imbued the owner of the tread with the angelic goodwill to spare Latham the consequences of his choices. Again, his future hung in the balance. The 30th September, Dr Pell's propitious day; how would it end?

He eased himself down to try for the fourth piling. Pushed by a wave, something hard and horizontal bashed his calf. It was excruciating. He clenched his lip and felt around it with his other foot. He forgot the pain in delirious joy: it was a raft, put there for repairs, but tied too loosely to the piling. Gingerly he lowered himself onto it and found the paddle. He listened for the guard to pass, then cut the rope. The tide swept him along the river's westward curve. There were shouts as the bridge receded, the swish of a net falling short, a flash of light followed by the whistle of shot overhead—the guard no angel after all–but Latham was beyond reach.

"Thank you, spirit." He started to laugh. It was four miles in the river to West Ord, where the river *was* the border, but the tide would do his work for at least half the distance. As he drifted, he let his hands trail underwater, enjoying the healing coolness. The diffuse radiance from the moon was amplified by occasional points of lantern light from farmhouses.

When the river stopped being tidal, he paddled around an island to the northern bank. His raft banged a gravelly mud bank, a *Scottish* gravelly mud bank. He cut off a piece of his shirt and bandaged his palms, lit his lantern, clambered up a grassy hillock and collapsed. Staring at the sky, he lost track of time, though he was profoundly awake. The guard would tell Cecil's men. There might be a formal protest, but he had Darnley's invitation. He had done it.

After a while, he walked again and was soon in pasture land with fenced fields. Nervous sheep baa-ed as he passed, and he smelled the acrid residue of a doused hut fire. A little further on, a horse whickered nearby. He approached the noise and held out his apple. A moment later, a wet nose pushed his wrist down, teeth nipping at the treat.

He climbed over the gate and studied the animal. A sturdy mare, she seemed placid, though plump. He wrapped a jewel in a handkerchief as payment, tied it to the fencepost, and mounted. Her flanks forced his legs apart wider than he'd expected. He chuckled when he discovered the reason: she was pregnant, which was why she had the freedom of the field. As the sky greyed to dawn and mysterious shapes took on names –maple, ram, cow, hut–he trotted the horse, getting to know her peculiarities.

Before entering the nearby woods, he looked back. He could no longer see the river. But he felt Katherine's embrace; heard his father's stoic disappointment; and rebukes from his older brothers, Edward and Nicholas; saw a puzzled David

Hicks; heard Leicester's animal-soothing voice. A cold wind of loss whipped about him. He would miss them all. A tear crept down his cheek. He licked it, tasting salt. Exile, but his choice.

Dawn seeped pink, a rabbit bolted, and a distant wheel screeched. There was a road beyond the woods. A fierce autumn sun leapt into the sky, enclosing him in a world of whispering red, gold and yellow leaves that looked as if they had been scraped from their prime element. He had been tested. Had he triumphed? He patted the pocket holding Darnley's invitation. The court was at Jedburgh, not far from the border, so that was his destination. Laughing, he urged the mare through the brilliant leaves.

CHAPTER 2
A TALENT
MANIFESTS

October 1566

Latham had to wait two weeks before meeting Mary. Incapacitated by stomach pains and convulsions, she languished near death for hours before a French physician revived her with tight bandaging of her feet and legs. When Latham asked a councillor if it was the dreaded childbed fever–she'd given birth in June to a healthy son, James, now in the care of the Catholic Earl of Mar at Stirling Castle–the councillor pulled on his beard and muttered, "No. It is some other malady. The queen's husband has the blame for it."

Calling Darnley "the Queen's husband," instead of "King Henry," and accusing him of making Mary ill, told Latham that he might not find the clarity Darnley had promised. In fact, Darnley wasn't even in Jedburgh; he was in Edinburgh. Latham had delayed leaving England for a year; he sensed now that, beneath the surface courtesies of Scots courtiers, lay volatile power struggles.

Still, while he waited for his audience with Mary, he bought fresh clothes and luxuriated in attending mass. Despite the hint of future trouble, these were happy days: celebrating mass openly, and wearing a cross over his doublet instead of under his shirt.

He realised how robbed he had been by the Elizabethan liturgy. To him, the Protestant assertion that bread and wine in the Eucharist symbolised the body and blood of Christ, rather than embodying Christ's presence, repudiated Christ's own words:

> *I am the living bread which comes down from heaven...*
> *Unless you eat the flesh of the son of man and drink of his*
> *blood, you shall not have life in you.*

To make the flesh and blood purely symbolic took away the mysticism in the mass, making faith, on which redemption rested, unnecessary. It was heretical pragmatism, a vile secular hedge.

The heresy itself was blatant. What made it insidious was that Elizabeth kept the music and vestments of the Catholic mass. She washed the feet of the poor on Maundy Thursday, healed by touch the swelling of the lymph nodes called scrofula, even crawled to the cross on her first few Good Fridays, as if she were Catholic. English subjects were confused about why doctrinaire Catholics made a fuss. Unaware, they were slipping into heresy. It was hard for Latham to find words for how relieved he was to immerse himself in the traditional liturgy.

Nevertheless, when he finally bowed to a recovered Mary, he tried: offering her heartfelt thanks, then amusing her by demonstrating how he had concealed the heavy cross under his shirt on the Oxford progress, even while undressing in a shared tavern room.

"Well, Sir Edward, we'll find you a filigree silver cross of quality someday," Mary said, motioning him to rise. He saw little sign of the effusive confidence her admirers had always extolled, but her beauty was compelling. She managed her unusual six-foot height with grace. Today, her milky skin was highlighted by a cream smock with a pleated v-collar under a black velvet dress, exposing a soft neck that hinted at allure. Her sweet, spicy perfume of rose water mixed with burnt orange peel and marjoram wafted over him. Strain showed in crows' feet framing eyes that were ready to brighten with anger or brim with tears at any moment, arousing a protective instinct in her supporters.

She treated Latham with courteous wariness–he was her husband's servant, after all–but she enjoyed his account of crossing under Berwick Bridge, hand over hand, from plank to plank; laughing at how he had used the river current to waft his stolen raft to the Scottish bank. As the court was conducting legal assises at border towns, hearing criminal cases, she dismissed him.

Latham left for Edinburgh, finding Darnley in the falconry house of Holyrood Palace. Pleased to see him, Darnley's lips curved into a warm smile. The universal first reaction to "the Queen's husband" was simply to gasp at his long-limbed, androgynous beauty. His cornflower eyes were puffy today, Latham noticed, but he was still handsome. Under cropped auburn curls, he had high cheekbones and a long symmetrical pale face. His eyebrows were thin and arched, while his wrists, forearms, and thighs had the sinewy power of a tiltyard jouster and athlete. The lips welcoming Latham were soft and full, intimating sensuality and petulance.

"Ah, Edward," Darnley said, offering a gloved hand to kiss. "You see me king, of some poor sort. Mama wrote from England, telling me to hire you. She expects you to report to her, but of course, you won't. Let us get horses and ride. Things are at a standstill in this accursed court."

He led them to an empty hillside house, surrounded by neglected but lovely gardens. It was near a collegiate church, abutting the town wall. "One of my retainers owns it. It is peaceful, with sweet air. Kirk o'Field, the former Provost House.

As soon as they had brushed leaves and bird droppings off a bench, and were sitting with their long legs extended, he burst out: "How much humiliation must a man take?" He hadn't asked how Latham was, or how he had crossed the border without papers. "I want to live abroad. You could be my Master of the Horse there, too. But the nobles and my wife are making a tremendous fuss. My mother is a Tudor, descended from Henry VII; my father's a principal noble here. I have noble blood and have sired the royal heir. I should be crowned king. But the queen will not grant me the Crown Matrimonial. Without the Crown Matrimonial, I have no legal status. I'm proclaimed joint monarch, until I'm not. Do you know what will happen to my son if poor Mary dies? She's been sick; I went to see her. I will not be his regent unless I am crowned king. She is thinking of placing James into Elizabeth's care–she's his godmother—the Protestant Elizabeth you just left!"

He brushed a tear from his eye, looking hurt and bewildered; Latham couldn't tell if he was more distressed by Mary's suffering or the blow to his pride.

"I expected more, Edward. Mama never criticised me. Why does my wife?" he ran on. "Eve was carved from Adam's rib. After courting rituals, which I did to perfection for months–lute playing, dancing, singing, love poems–the man rules the woman. It is in the Bible. Look..."

He took two silver ryals from his waist pouch and handed one to Latham. Its inscription read 'Henricus & Maria,' with Darnley's head dominating Mary's. "As is natural," Darnley scowled. "When Mary denied me her bed, she recalled all these coins, minting this one instead." The replacement ryal's inscription read 'Maria & Henricus,' with the Scottish coat of arms and thistles. "What a public slap!"

With cautious sympathy, Latham returned the coins.

Darnley glanced slyly at him. "You came for freedom of worship. I've done a lot for Catholicism. Scotland is legally Protestant, but due to me, high mass can be heard in Edinburgh for all who wish. The Kings of Spain and France have praised me. Well, there is more to say, but I will seal your appointment, and we will celebrate tonight."

He's at the apex of power, Latham thought, *but a soul with ripped stitches, crying out for some more-robust being to salve him*. Darnley's incompleteness exerted a charismatic tug.

Wine, more wine, the scorching native brew called whisky, and whoring. The "celebration" of Latham's appointment went on for days. As Darnley's servant, when summoned to accompany him to a brothel, Latham had to go.

Now, he was no virgin. As a teenager, he had responded to the wife of a Reigate merchant deficient in conjugal duties. Nicholas, Latham's older brother by ten years, had told him that court gallants stuck to married women, so that an accidental belly swelling would not be career-ending. Latham luxuriated in ample breasts, and the intoxicating, exotic scents and textures of a brushy Venus mound, and its beyond. Periodically, he worried about sin and stayed away. But then he told himself: "I do not covet her estate; she covets me." The affair lasted two seasons with no pregnancy, and they parted as dear friends when he went to Oxford.

There, he was drawn to the principal bell ringer, a talented musician who introduced him to another world of sensual and intellectual pleasure. This sin he confessed. It went hard at the confessional, the priest lambasting him on how deeply the Church abhorred the practice.

"Let him who is without sin cast the first stone," the bell ringer had protested, when Latham met him the next day, to end the affair. "That hypocrite cannot throw a single pebble," the bell ringer added, pacing his bedchamber in high passion. "He is being investigated for… sundry acts." He did not elaborate, but Latham got the hint. In the end, he viewed this affair as *Greek*: Plato; Alexander; not definitive.

So Latham was ready for Eros in Scotland, but not for Darnley's frantic hedonism. The third night, while Latham was relaxing post-coitus with a pretty red-haired girl, he asked, "Have you known the king long?"

"Oh, yes, sir. Regular, from when he came to the city. Girls say he sometimes drinks himself to sleep and forgets to do anything. Now, go or pay again. You're nice, but I've got another customer."

This vaunted royal marriage was trapped in circularity, Latham realised. Mary had drawn away because of her husband's obvious defects. Darnley sensed only the rebuke, with exquisite sensitivity, and consoled himself with rousting, and worse. Latham gleaned from palace gossip that Darnley had plotted with faction leaders the previous year to get the Crown Matrimonial, clipping Mary's power in favour of his and theirs, murdering Mary's private secretary in the process. In reconciling with Mary, Darnley informed on his co-conspirators and publicly acknowledged error, enraging those whom Mary exiled. She was now negotiating the return of a conspirator; things felt unstable, the factions potentially vicious.

One night, Latham found himself in difficulty with the plump brunette Darnley had bought for him. Her vagina appeared both accommodating and stifling at the same time. As he softened, he saw scorn creep into her tired young eyes. He summoned a vision of firm thighs, a flat chest, and sinewy wrists. He hardened, blocking out distractions–the goblet falling to the floor, moans from the next room–and performed. The brunette was not impressed.

Later, Darnley came to his rooms. "Ah, Edward, what a cabal of cows. I'm sorry. Naught pleases a man like one of his own." His lips implored over white teeth.

Undressing was a comic marathon of unbuttoning and untying, kicking off shoes and rolling down hose; lust kept aflame by lingering kisses, rough stroking, and laughter. After lovemaking, Darnley got up and gazed at himself in Latham's mirror, sighing contentedly when Latham murmured, "God made you blessedly comely, Sire."

"You're quite good, too," Darnley responded, returning to bed and giving Latham a playful dig in the ribs. "Let me tell you what humiliated me most…"

Back to his favourite topic: wounded pride.

"When I announced I wanted to live abroad, Mary assembled the court, giving precedence to certain nobles she prefers to me. In front of foreign diplomats, she asked, 'What are your grievances, my husband? State them for all to witness. How have I hurt you?' What could I say? 'My wife implies I fail in bed? She removed me from first place on Scottish coins?' I mumbled that insufficient honour is given me, which made me look even more the fool."

Latham pointed to the wine flagon and risked unsolicited advice. "If you drink less and avoid factions, she'll unbend, in time. From what I've seen, Scots nobles are mature and highly-seasoned in malice. You're just twenty. They'll outmatch you." He felt older than the two years separating their ages.

"Nonsense, I'm king," Darnley scoffed. "Don't *you* join the rebukers."

They enjoyed several more encounters, but then came the wages of excess. In December, when Darnley took off his shirt, his chest was covered in white, foul-smelling pustules. Shockingly, he didn't seem to think this an impediment to coupling. Latham gaped in horror. This wasn't an early sign of syphilis, pox, *Grandgore*, as the Scots called it. All men knew it began with one red sore. Darnley's case was advanced.

"No, Your Majesty. Please." Latham knelt in terrified deference.

Suffused by desire, Darnley glowered. But he retained a vestige of decency. "Ah, Edward," he conceded after an eternity, "you're right." He bowed and left.

The next day, he summoned Latham. "I'm taking the mercury treatment in Glasgow, my family stronghold. We've got plenty of armed retainers; I'll be safe." He looked frail and frightened; perhaps Latham's warning had sunk in. "You serve my wife, the queen; keep an eye on things."

An hour later, he was gone. Latham reduced his alcohol to a minimum, washed often, and went to mass regularly. He was in terror of contagion, too embarrassed to consult the French physician who had saved Mary. The one he found in Edinburgh was a dour Presbyterian. "A night with Venus, a lifetime with Mercury," the doctor hooted, his face gleeful with spite. "The pox isn't in you, but it will be a long time before you're certain. Sores can erupt three, nay, five years after whoring, so patients relate. I have no personal knowledge, praise God."

Treatment consisted of being fumigated with mercury vapour; drinking mercury brews; painting the sores with mercury. Teeth loosened, gums rotted, but it often worked.

Latham watched for a red sore. Daily he inspected himself in the mirror, ran his hands over his body. He seemed clean, but resolved to be chaste for "three, nay five years."

At first, it was easy because he was frenetically busy. He escorted plate to the Mint for Mary to melt down to pay her soldiers; carried messages to her far-flung supporters; checked on the royal son. With long days in the saddle alert for bandits, directing court entertainments to project the image of a functioning monarchy, Eros had no chance. Latham served Mary well.

In January, she went to Glasgow and brought Darnley back with the promise of renewed relations when he was fully purged. He chose to complete his cure in his retainer's house at Kirk o'Field. Mary furnished it, and he moved in with his servants. She visited daily, sleeping in the spare bedroom on Wednesdays and Fridays.

Latham visited on 9th February, the day before Darnley was due to return permanently to Holyrood Palace. The bedroom smelled of sulphur from the daily baths that constituted the final treatments. But Darnley was radiant. "I'm cured, Edward, skin clear. I told the queen, my good wife and love, of any plots I heard about, for which she thanked me, and inquired. Our hearts were leaden so long, horribly afflicted; but God lightens them, thanks to his divine mercy. We'll be joyful. Mary has been a loving, natural wife. Life stretches before us."

Was this a hint of redemption, or was everyone playing for time?

At 2.00 a.m. on 10th February, a crack, sounding like multitudes of cannon firing at once, shattered sleep. In Holyrood Palace, everyone ran for weapons. It seemed to have come from about a mile away. Latham attended Mary when she got up, white-faced, and sent her long-time supporter, James Hepburn, Earl of Bothwell, to investigate. When a messenger returned with the explanation for the explosion, she was paralysed with shock, then collapsed, weeping.

There was no invasion. The house at Kirk o'Field had been blown up; everything around destroyed for hundreds of yards. The entire building was rubble, and Darnley and two servants were dead, presumably from the blast.

At dawn, the news got much worse: The king and one servant had escaped by climbing through a window, using a rope and chair. They hadn't been injured in the blast, but thugs waiting outside had strangled them. A local woman reported hearing Darnley pleading for mercy.

This made the crime pre-meditated regicide. Kirk o'Field belonged to allies of Darnley. Since it had good physical security, treachery was incontrovertible. Next day, placards in town accused Mary and her supporter, Bothwell, of regicide. Her reign faced an existential threat. Latham had been in Scotland for less than five months; he'd had a fast, rude education in the vulnerability of monarchy to factionalism when badly managed. Numb with horror at Darnley's death, Latham took to whisky to dull his pain.

On 14th February, Mary summoned him. Still pale, she said, "I need an envoy in Paris who was with me on the night my husband was murdered. I was no part of this crime. You, above all others, can recount that when we heard the terrible explosion and knew not what it could be, you witnessed my shocked innocency. You are to raise funds from my brother-in-law, King Charles IX, and my cousin, Henry, Duke of Guise."

Latham was still on his knees when she thrust a sealed packet at him. "This letter puts you under the care of the Duke of Guise. You must swear to deliver it before going to the French court."

When Latham rose and swore, she smiled. "We'll formalise your appointment tomorrow, in the great hall.

There, she did something Latham had never expected. To raise his rank high enough to represent her, she bent over him and tapped his shoulder with her ceremonial sword. He was being knighted a second time.

It was frigid in Holyrood Palace. The witnesses—nobles, diplomats, guards—hunched deep in their furs, while even heroic embroidered Hercules shrank on the wall tapestry.

She did more. "I'll earl you in England," she whispered. "Someday," the syllables floating almost inaudibly on her condensing breath. Latham alone heard her. She was wearing the deep black of mourning, but her hazel eyes held Latham's in a conspiratorial glint. He felt a thrill of secrets shared, the conviction that, at this moment, no man in the world mattered more to Mary, Queen of Scots, than Edward Latham, newly made "Sir".

In his bedchamber was her parting gift, an exquisite filigree silver cross.

From Paris, he sadly watched the disintegration of her authority. Everyone was too shocked by Darnley's murder to respond to his advocacy. In May, when she married Bothwell, widely suspected as the leader of the regicide, the French court turned against her.

A mere few weeks later, pre-dawn hammering on his apartment door woke him. Rubbing his eyes, he shuffled to it, knife drawn.

"Open, in the name of Henry, Duke of Guise," the visitor rasped. The Duke's liveried messenger told Latham the awful news: Protestant Scots rebel lords had overthrown Mary, imprisoned her, and forced her at knifepoint to abdicate in favour of her infant son, James. "She's done, your queen, as of the 15ᵗʰ June. News is spreading fast. You have no status, no valid papers from the new regent or salary. The duke will hire you, temporarily. Come, dress and pack before town criers are about."

"I'll earl you in England," Mary, Queen of Scots whispered, knighting Latham with her ceremonial sword. His eyes lingered on milky skin that hinted at allure, while he allowed her sweet, spicy perfume of rose water mixed with burnt orange and marjoram to bathe him in pleasing vapour.

No! Sweating, he jerked awake; his recurring dream. It wasn't February 1567, but July 1569. He was still in the Hôtel de Guise, the Paris headquarters of the Duke of Guise. He had bumped his head on the frame of a bed made for a boy in a servant's room. Mary had miraculously escaped her captors in 1568 and fled to England, where she was now confined in a castle. The second queen who had knighted him was imprisoned by the first queen who had knighted him. He was a third clerk for Henry, Duke of Guise.

Latham rubbed his head, got up and went to his desk. He lit a candle and took out his diary. Any new patron would demand a written account of his service in Scotland. People always asked, "What is Mary *like*?" She fascinated everyone: her rise from infant Queen of Scotland under the regency of her mother, Mary of Guise (her father, Stuart King James V was killed battling the English); to Queen Consort of France; then, after the death from illness of French King, Francis II, Queen of Scotland. The greatest Christian lady in the world was the expectation. Then her dizzying fall. What's she *like*?

Latham paged through to his description. He had worked at it, but had to admit it read like a master of the horse justifying a purchase: weight, height, features, health, complexion. On a separate page, he wrote about her seductive aura of tragic mystery, the truth in his dream. He stopped. An ink drop hit the desk surface. She had protected him, beyond what a subject might expect from a sovereign terrified for her own safety. He noted how she had preemptively put him in Guise's care. Then he sanded the paper dry and snuffed out the candle. He no longer had a master of the horse's salary of 200 pounds a year, with mounts and clothes. With twenty pounds and board, he could not waste candles.

His dream wasn't fantasy. She had promised to make him an earl in England, although she had flicked the words so casually that he wondered if he had invented them.

A year after her abdication, he was still shocked. He grieved the vestige of potential decency in young Darnley choked out, and the collapse of Mary's authority in her foolhardy quest to balance violent factions against each other.

"I loathe rebellions," he muttered, putting his rewritten text away. But as he pulled off his nightshirt and dressed as plain clerk Edward, his youthful energy returned. "Come, fool," he grinned, slipping on his shoes. "See the irony: Master of Horse to third clerk. It is a mordant joke on your pride."

He needed to tackle the day's minutiae: bills to pay; oats deliveries recorded; salaries dispensed. The courier had brought in two packets, one which looked diplomatic. Latham's temporary job was to copy and forward all letters to the duke, who was away fighting a Huguenot (French Protestant) rebel army, and had taken his regular secretaries with him.

Though Latham didn't love being a clerk, he was enjoying the reprieve from military drills Guise ran when he was in town. The duke required retainers to be ready to fight. In addition to cavalry charges, there was the loading, aiming, firing and cleaning of arquebus and muskets. And exercises in night ambushes. Like most courtiers, Latham was good with horses and sword; he was pleased to learn guns. But he hated night ambushes, which seemed simply murderous: slithering under tent flaps; or laying a ladder quietly against a wall and bursting through bedroom windows, waving swords. He didn't believe his destiny was to be an assassin. However, Dr Pell had muddled his chart. He lived here dangling, the air breathable but a little foul.

He paused before going to the servants' hall to break his fast, but realised he wasn't hungry. He decided to finish scribing and eat later. He lit the candle and untied the first packet. To his surprise, it was for him from David Hicks, with an enclosure. His heart leapt; he longed for news of home. But his enthusiasm quickly dissipated. What could Hicks, now serving Elizabeth's Principal Secretary, Sir William Cecil, say that he wanted to hear? He put it aside.

The second packet bore the Hapsburg seal. From the Spanish Embassy, it was addressed to Henry, Duke of Guise. Spain still hadn't crushed Dutch Protestant rebels in the Netherlands, while in France, Catholic and Huguenot armies battled. There was a natural affinity between Catholic Spain and the most fervent Catholic family in France, the Guises. The letter would be about that.

Latham broke the seal and bent to copy the letter. It was a jumble of Roman numerals. He whistled; it was the first encrypted text he had seen. He copied carefully, checking horizontally and vertically. In doing so, he noticed recurring numbers. His toes tingled, a pleasant sensation as it travelled up his spine to his scalp. The tingle contained a thrilling thought. What sport to break the code! He made two copies; one for the duke's files and one for himself, sending the original off with the duke's courier.

He stared at the numerals. First, he tried systems he had heard about: A as I; E as I. A as IV, or X. Gibberish emerged, and a dull irritability settled on him. Perhaps he had no gift for this.

He leaned back, stretching his arms. *Try logic*, he thought.

Frances de Alava was the Spanish ambassador, so his name should be at the end. Diplomatic letters usually began with the word *Trusty*. Any letter from a Spanish ambassador to the Duke of Guise would mention faith, for the Guises were France's most fervent persecutors of heretics. Spain wanted Guise to stop French Huguenots helping Dutch Protestant rebels. With these principles in mind, he tried again.

Just before the date at the bottom of the letter were the numerals II XIII V XXIII VIII. The date itself was in modern script. It was an inaccurate date, ahead of the calendar by three days. That had to be a clue. And in its falsity, 23 July 1569, the 23 was penned with a flourish. Were 2 and 3 the key?

Latham attacked the last six numerals. With mounting excitement he tried A as II, L as XIII. 2 was one key. He was stumped at the V, but then he remembered hearing that using the same number for recurring vowels was too easy to break. Codes advanced the number by a second key. Perhaps 3 in the date signified the number by which repeated vowels advanced. It worked, and he converted the numbers to modern script: 2 13 5 23 8. Alava.

Laboriously, the text emerged.

Trusty and esteemed Duke, True Defender of the Faith,

Foul as it is to allege meddling in our affairs by your citizens, this matter compels it. Thousands of beef-fed German and other mercenaries came into our Netherlands provinces. If not for these reinforcements, our foot would break the rebel neck. Now the rebels survive a season at ruinous expense to us. Where did their leader, William of Orange, get money? Thirty thousand pounds must have been paid. Our spies report no transports of treasure to the territories, and our bankers in Florence, Genoa, Antwerp and Augsburg report no notes of exchange. We believe your Huguenot nobles managed it. We know your King wants peace within France and would wink at a Huguenot subject helping our rebels if peace resulted. But you Guises have always been strong for the faith.

Can you find the meddler? The secrecy suggests one great hand only, not the joint industry of many. King Philip's appreciation will be bountiful if you succeed.

> *Your trusty brother in faith,*
> *Frances de Alava,*
> *23 July 1569.*

Excited, Latham put down his quill and ran his fingers through his hair. What a tantalising mystery! Thirty thousand pounds could buy eight to ten thousand mercenaries. The previous year, the Dutch had mounted four invasions, and Spain had eventually defeated all of them. The Dutch rebel leader, William of Orange, was out of money. But money had come; he had raised more troops and created a small navy much tougher to annihilate. As Alava wrote, the secrecy suggested few were involved. Having decoded the question, Latham felt he owned it. No, it owned *him*. He longed to find the answer, but it was Guise's affair, and he'd never be told who'd finagled the money. It was the curse of being third clerk.

He picked up Hicks's packet. David's letter was two sentences. The first begged Latham to do him the honour of meeting him that afternoon at The Yellow Cock's Spur, a tavern across the River Seine near the College of Navarre, whose claret David had enjoyed as a student and longed to try again. Latham smiled at his friend's tact; it was cheap enough not to embarrass Latham. The second sentence suggested a fallback meeting. The enclosure from his sister Katherine was also succinct. *My dearest little brother, we stand surety for your good behaviour. Please meet Master Hicks for the terms and other great news. You can trust him, Your ever loving sister, Katherine.*

After stabling a borrowed nag, Latham picked his way along a mud alley to the tavern's entrance. A faded sign depicting a yellow-breasted cock with a red comb and silver spur swayed in the breeze. The tavern's whitewashed walls were stained, its oak door gouged in spots. The place had known better times.

"Rodomontade!"(braggart) Hicks shouted at Latham, beginning their old game of insults.

"Hircine avec lientery embouche!" (smelly goat with diarrhoea of mouth) Latham retorted. "You can't match that."

"I yield," Hicks said, "if only to get out of the sun. It is good to see you, Edward. Three years, eh? You look well, if low in funds."

Hicks had cropped his auburn hair in the current fashion and was clean-shaven. A broken front tooth was new. Latham wondered if he did dangerous courier work, or whether he'd just brawled. He wore a workmanlike sword at his waist, and the leather strap around his neck suggested a sheathed knife between his shoulder blades.

After a quick embrace, Hicks opened the door. Inside, wall lanterns cast a wan yellow light. The air was cooler but heavy with sweat, yeast, and the cloying sweetness of cheap wine. They found seats at a long table.

"When I was a student, I came here after cockfights," David began.

"So you wrote," Latham remarked. "Cardinals now condemn the sport as cruel. Provosts throw cockers into the stocks. There aren't many fights."

"A betting man can always find a pit," Hicks laughed. "Word spreads from here. Cockers use a derelict building, bribe watchmen, throw a pit together and disassemble it when done. This is something of a free-thinking area. Friends of the Dutch rebels come here to learn what they're up to." He watched Latham absorbed this information.

Latham was interested. The Yellow Cock's Spur might have been past its glory days, but was more than it seemed.

Rasping nearby made Hicks chuckle. "See? I told you." He twisted and pointed at a small square table against the wall.

Latham heard "...tough-breasted." Cockers were planning a fight.

"About cocking," Hicks went on defensively, "I know you now for a thorough papist, but surely you agree it is rank hypocrisy for the red hats to have a quarrel with bird fights when they happily burn some poor peasant who thinks bread in the mass is bread and the little wine he scarfs just wine. Poof! Up in smoke goes poor peasant Guillaume!"

Latham frowned, his expression cold. He loathed the Inquisition, but he wasn't going to get into arguments with a representative of the English government.

"Sorry," Hicks backtracked. "I'm not here to debate."

Relaxing, they looked around. At the end of their bench, one gaunt student played three simultaneous chess games while watchers bet. A scholarship boy playing for food, Latham concluded. At another long table, card games were in progress. Along the walls were more private tables. At one, four gowned proctors argued with hands as well as voices.

Money, the getting and spending of it, occupied his thoughts. Chess winnings feeding a student; cockers paying off a watchman; thirty thousand pounds buying mercenaries for the Dutch rebels. Who sent that money? Thrusting the mystery away, he got up and went to the serving hatch, where he ordered whatever dinner for two his five *billons* would buy.

A waitress brought a flagon of rough claret, an oregano-infused stew with stringy lumps of an unidentifiable beast, turnip and cabbage pieces, and two hunks of bread.

"As I remember it," David laughed. "Oregano disguises near-rotten meat. Listen, I speak with two tongues today. One's official, the other personal. I'm soon-to-be-kin to you. I'm going to marry your second cousin, Isobel."

Latham reached over the table, clasping Hicks's hand. "I give you joy of your marriage, David." He hadn't seen Isabel for years. She'd been a pretty child and was well-dowered. Her branch of the family was Protestant, in good standing with the government. Hicks had worked his abacus of contacts well.

Then Latham sat back, staring into the stew, remembering his father's plan to marry him to the daughter of a nearby baron. Joining the two estates would have enhanced both. Negotiations had begun before Latham left on the royal progress to Oxford, in 1566. Without knowing why, he'd felt a trap closing. The prospect of that arranged union had infused his decision over whether to leave England with urgency. The baron's daughter had married the following year, taking her lovely land into a rival family.

Eager to forget how he'd let his father down, Latham met Hicks's eyes. "It is a good match, David. If you're to be kin, you must have met Katherine."

"She heard I was coming to Paris and visited me in London, with messages for you. Oh, how she turned my rooms around!"

Hicks started to laugh, and Latham laughed with him. They both saw indomitable Katherine, blue eyes bubbling with determination to improve the condition of the wretch in front of her.

"She dusted every book," Hicks continued, "rebuked the landlady for over-salted mutton, threw out mouldy carrots. She poured the foulest purge I've ever taken down my throat, which kept me in for two days. Against my wishes, she hired a man to scour each week. She has a great heart, Edward, but can be a touch shrewish."

"She presses," Latham agreed, "but was always my forgiving friend. When my mother died we had servants, but Katherine decided she must tell me what to do, but be on my side. I was three, she was nine. How does she look?"

"Sanguine in health, comely, a few grey hairs dulling the blond, but no wig. One of her messages is that Williams went to Rome, but she found a substitute."

Latham frowned. Williams? Then he remembered. Father John Williams, Katherine's priest. So she still heard mass privately. Good.

Hicks grinned. "We know all about John Williams, and the substitute John Smith. Ha, ha, ha! Priests. Such plain aliases! Why not Eustacius Tollander? Don't worry. Sir Nicholas Bacon says, *Her Majesty makes no windows into men's souls.* She's more moderate than her father, and brother and sister monarchs. That holds as long as the realm stays quiet. We've had ten good years of prosperity and peace."

Latham was irritated by Hicks's proselytising. "Katherine's other messages? She wrote that my kin stands surety for my good behaviour."

"Reluctantly. They deplore your leaving. I say this officially and personally. You muddled east and west, the rising for the setting sun, when you left Elizabeth to serve Scottish Mary, whose imprudence… "

"Stop!" Latham interrupted. "I didn't choose one queen over another. I sought a liturgy not chopped about by heretics. I won't contest with my former sovereign; I left to save my soul."

Hicks sighed. "Your act has a certain virtue, but you put amazing weight on a few words in the mass. It doesn't matter now. Her Majesty believes you left for reasons of religion, not opposition. She has accepted your father's proffer, which Katherine nagged him into making. Your kin stands surety with their lands and yours for your undertaking to do nothing directly against Her Majesty."

"Oh, I can swear to that. I'm against rebellions. Change should be lawful, done without violence."

"I never doubted it." Hicks showed Latham a formal letter. "Here is a note of exchange on our embassy banker in Paris. You'll receive twenty-five pounds annually. One of Cecil's men is running your property, relieving Katherine of it."

Latham reached for the banker's note.

Hicks pulled it back, grinning. "Not yet."

"That's only half the net revenue from my estate."

"Yes, I saw the accounts. Her Majesty levies a little tax. It is still more than Guise pays you. Her Majesty dislikes the Guises; they claim Mary should rule England. She hopes you can find a patron less hostile to her interests."

"Is that a condition?"

"No. She recognises the difficulty your lack of travelling papers makes. The condition is that you always tell us your whereabouts. The money changer will be proximate to you."

"Clever."

"Cecil *is* clever. That completes my messages." Hicks drank the rest of his wine.

They turned to the contests again. The scholarship boy was gorging bread and cheese; he must have won. But one of the card players was begging for money. Clambering onto the crowded table, he sang,

> *I see your scorn rejects my pleas,*
> *For one testoon to win my ease*
> *From chafing wrists debts' chains devise,*
> *How bitter I myself despise.*

He got some coins, but judging by his pout, not enough. A student who refused him sang:

> *Kinship and friendship are death.*
> *The more I give, the deeper the debts.*

Money rules my day, Latham thought. *I'm bought by my kin or Guise. And where did the Dutch get thirty thousand pounds?*

"Let me tell you about money," Hicks said, leaning close. His sudden intensity told Latham they'd come to the real purpose of the meeting.

"I was so amazed," Hicks continued, lowering his voice. "You know Elizabeth loves gifts: jewels, silk hose, rare books, maps, new devices like the music box. Well, one morning in May, a foreign delegation carrying a heavy chest came to the Presence Chamber. Some councillors and maids attended Her Majesty. I was with Cecil. These strangers pulled out diamond-encrusted belts and ribbons, cascades of pearl strings, bags of unset rubies and emeralds, every imaginable set pin and brooch, gold vases, other valuables. It looked like royal treasure."

"Were they genuine?" Latham wondered where this was going.

"Vouched for."

"Who vouched?"

"Richard Clough, Thomas Gresham's factor. He knows gems better than anyone."

"I remember." Gresham, a great English merchant, acted for the English Crown in the Netherlands. Clough moved between Antwerp and England; both men had excellent reputations.

"What value did he give them?" Latham asked, intrigued.

"Sixty thousand pounds."

Latham tried to control mounting excitement. Sixty thousand was twice thirty thousand. It couldn't be coincidence! Loans were often secured by collateral assets of twice the loan. Was he on the track of the Dutch rebels' thirty thousand pounds? He wanted to leap on the table, wave his arms, stamp his feet, dance. He clutched the bench white-knuckled, grinding his heels into the floor. Why had Hicks come to Paris to tell him this?

Affecting indifference, he drawled, "So? Queens get many gifts."

"But this gift was rejected! Let me paint the scene: Her Majesty takes off her gloves and runs her hands through the rubies and emeralds, tries the pearl strings against her sleeve, fits a diamond ribbon to her hair. She picks up a gold agate vase and strokes its every detail. I have never seen such longing in a woman. Certainly more desire than when I proposed to Isabel!"

"Come, David, Isabel will be eager on the day."

"I'm not so confident," Hicks sighed. "No desire could compare with this. Her Majesty's hands trembled like a child whose body shakes when he sees a honey-cake he can't have. Tears snaked down her cheeks. Then she collected herself. She said she must reject every one of the gorgeous baubles. She couldn't take one as gift or purchase. And, with trumpeting emphasis, she said she couldn't use any as collateral for any purpose whatsoever. They must be returned forthwith, even though offered by her esteemed sister, whom she fervently hoped she wouldn't offend."

"Elizabeth has no sister," Latham interjected.

"Figure of speech."

Latham nodded. Monarchs referred to each other as "good brother, good sister" even when unrelated. "What livery did the foreigners wear?" He held his breath.

"Gold-thread chains on a red shield, a cheerful angel on each side."

Latham exhaled slowly. He wanted Hicks to identify it, not him.

After a pause, Hicks did. "The Navarre coat of arms."

So Elizabeth's "esteemed sister" was the Huguenot Queen of Navarre, Jeanne d'Albret. Her son, Henry, was fighting with a Huguenot army against Latham's employer, the Duke of Guise. Elizabeth had always admired the Navarre family.

"What happened then?" Latham asked.

"Leicester pleaded for the jewels to be used to help the Dutch rebels. Her Majesty jumped up in high temper, swearing she'd never sanction rebellion against a lawful prince like her good brother, Philip II. She wouldn't sully her name by association with rebels little better than low-born vandals and pirates. One would have thought her a papist she was so adamant! Instead, she offered to mediate."

"Where's the treasure now?"

"Her Majesty ordered it returned. You should have seen the foreigners shrink with grief. The point is, riches can be rebuffed even by one who yearns for it. The use has to be right. The whole thing moved me profoundly."

Latham knew this wasn't the full story. But did Hicks think it was? His green eyes were moist with admiration of his queen's self-denial. So the Queen of Navarre sent the treasure to London, hoping Elizabeth would use it to help the Protestant cause. Elizabeth rejected it publicly, to assure French and Spanish eyes she wasn't intermeddling in their lands. Knowing Latham worked for Guise, Cecil sent Hicks to tell him, expecting Guise, in turn, to tell the Spanish ambassador in Paris, to reinforce whatever account the Spanish ambassador in London, who was an implacable mischief maker, sent. Thus the *apparent* story. What was the right question to get further understanding?

He tried: "You came here before the jewels were taken back to Navarre. Where did Clough go? Straight to Antwerp?"

"I offered to arrange passage, but he declined," Hicks said. "I think he mentioned approval for going via Hull, but the room was noisy, and he might have said something else."

He twisted to look at the card players, his expression wistful.

Latham drew a sharp breath. Hicks knew only what he'd seen with his own eyes. He didn't know about the thirty thousand pounds buying German mercenaries for the Dutch, so the significance of Clough going via Hull escaped him.

Latham assembled a scenario. Hull was the closest port to Hamburg, where Lutheran banker friends of the English merchant, Thomas Gresham, did business beyond the reach of Spain's spies. Elizabeth didn't have the jewels; too many eyes could betray her. But Gresham, with fortified houses in

England and the Netherlands, could store them for the Queen of Navarre. If Gresham held the jewels, Clough's valuation could raise thirty thousand pounds. Elizabeth hadn't stopped Clough going via Hull. She'd winked at the transaction while making a public display of avoiding involvement.

Latham had the answer to the thirty thousand pounds. The Queen of Navarre was Alava's meddler. Teasing a plot from odd facts was intoxicating. He'd have to decide what to do with his knowledge; it could make him powerful, or dead.

He'd found his talent. Material riches and status wouldn't come his way after abandoning his patrimony. He'd been Master of Horse in Scotland, but the vicissitudes of court politics weren't for him. The triumphs Dr Pell had prophesied would come from knowing. With knowing, his lowly foot could direct his ruler's head.

Would he use his talent for good or ill? *Many live, many die from your dealings*, Dr Pell had predicted ominously. Now Latham felt such a rush of power he had to force himself to breathe, his excitement intensified by having to conceal it from Hicks.

He got up. "I must get back to work. May I have the note of exchange?"

Hicks laughed. "Not yet. You must account for your time in Scotland. What is Mary *like*?" This was for Cecil. Latham was amazed at how those who scorned Mary could never get enough tales about her.

"She has a great heart," he began thoughtfully, as he sat. "When she sent me to Paris, she insisted I put myself in the care of her powerful kin, the Guises, before going to court. As if she knew she'd be deposed. What monarch would be so protective of a servant with her own safety at risk? As to what she's like, she makes a man believe he's the tallest, strongest, smartest creature in the world."

Hicks responded tartly. "Well, Queen Elizabeth reminds a man that *she's* the tallest, smartest creature in the world. Puffing up a man is un-kingly, and sows confusion. Mary is imprudent at best, a husband-killer at worst."

This was Mary's problem: the undying suspicion that she had ordered Darnley's murder.

"Don't accuse an anointed sovereign of murder without proof," Latham said.

"We've seen letters." Hicks sounded tentative.

"They must be forgeries," Latham snapped. "I was with Mary the night Darnley was killed. If you'd seen her reaction, you couldn't accuse her. I admit she was imprudent, and couldn't understand Scots factions. But murdering Darnley? No." Pained, Latham pinched the bridge of his nose. "It is possible they'd found a rapprochement. He certainly thought so, the day before he died."

Hicks shifted tack. "Alright. You haven't seen the letters. What did you do when Darnley got sick?"

Latham described his work for Mary.

Hicks nodded, then circled back to English concerns. "Some call Mary nefarious, although I don't, yet. She didn't divorce Darnley or apply for a papal annulment. Then she married the accused murderer, Bothwell. How can you explain such acts?"

Latham thought back. "Try good intentions, bad judgment. She was only twenty-four. Annulment or divorce might have damaged her son's claim to the Scottish and English thrones. She couldn't assume she'd have more healthy babes. And marrying Bothwell seemed like good policy. He was a long-time supporter; the factions tolerated him, until then. He was Protestant, so she thought that would appease Protestants, while the Catholic Earl of Mar was bringing up her son: something for everybody. But everyone hated Bothwell as king. Consult your natural kindness before accusing Mary of worse than folly. Quiet won't last; the factions will compete to control James. Have I given you what Cecil wants?"

"A final question. Why didn't Mary come to France, to her powerful kin, the Guises? Why come to England, where she maintains a claim to the crown? Elizabeth had no choice but to imprison her. We fear our own quiet now, indeed we do. She may have protected you, but wherever she goes, there is chaos and bloodshed. If she's imprudent, her folly bites with an adder's venom. I say this to you as kin, beyond my commission: we can never free her. There is no hope you'll serve her again in Scotland, despite public noises about compromise."

Latham nodded, reflecting. *I'll earl you in England.* What had Mary meant? Did she offer Latham what she thought he wanted to grab a day's service from him? Or did she expect to rule England soon, and be able to bestow English titles? He wouldn't tell Hicks about the earldom, and he had no idea why she'd fled to England instead of France. A terrified woman would choose England because it was closer, forgetting her unresolved claim to its crown. A manipulator would have commitments from English Catholics to make her Queen.

He didn't want to know the answer. "I can't say, David. I revere her for protecting me in her own crisis. Thank you for the warning. It is our secret."

Hicks gave him the banker's note, and they said goodbye. Latham went to the stables to retrieve his nag, but Hicks stayed. Latham grinned. Would he join the card games, or meet some friend of the Dutch rebels?

Back at the turreted Hôtel de Guise, Latham entered through the servants' door. Restless and excited, he had to decide what to do with his knowledge. Hearing faint music in the hall, he realised he needed to play awhile to find his direction. In his room, he picked up a folio by Francesco Canova da Milano, a lute composer whose pieces had intricate contrapuntal lines. The music suited his mood. Bass, tenor, treble lines commented on each other, came to a moment of glorious resolution of dissonance, then trotted off again. The last chords sounded like an exhalation, a pause. Nothing concluded with him, even though there were no more notes on the page.

Latham played, one part of his mind accepting the challenge of the composer's technical demands, the other resolving what to do with his discoveries. His first service was to his faith; he had a duty to not act against Elizabeth. Could he advance two imperative lines without them getting tangled?

After a last chord that left his emotions still churning, he decided on his next step. He wrote to the Duke of Guise using Alava's cypher. It was a calculated risk that the adventurer in him relished.

Your Grace, this letter is proof of the snooping cur I am, meriting prison or worse. However, I have learned the source of thirty thousand pounds. I remain your devoted servant, eternally grateful for your generosity in finding a use for my poor abilities. Edward Latham, Knight, by the grace of Mary, Queen of Scots.

He received no answer, but, when fighting between the Catholic and Huguenot armies reached stalemate the next month, Guise returned to Paris and summoned Latham to the library. As a page led him down a long corridor, Latham looked again at the portraits of Guise ancestors. The family claimed descent from Charlemagne. Being a dubious claim, they trumpeted it. Guise Lords Spiritual stared out sternly, famous for the enthusiastic burning of heretics; Guise Lords Temporal were implacable warriors; Guise women, plump skin palpable, were fertile breeders of the next militant generation. Latham touched the filigree silver cross on his doublet. He was relieved to wear it openly, but even he found the Guise dynasty's zeal extreme.

In the panelled library, a tapestry of Charlemagne's victory over the Moors dominated one wall. The table was full of books and maps. The duke stood at the head of the table, legs spread and arms crossed, radiating feral capability. At nineteen, he was the same age as Darnley was when he was murdered. But there was no incompleteness in Guise. His pink-blond hair was cropped, and a forthright nose sprang from his face. He had a thin moustache but no beard, while his mouth could open in an irresistible smile one moment, clench with rage the next. Huguenots had killed his father and several uncles, and he was now the family's head. The burden of Charlemagne's lineage sat on his shoulders, and he embraced it.

He wasn't the only person in the room. In a deep-set window ledge, a second man sat, reading. When Latham bowed to Henry, he stood. A black, pointed beard framed his clever, narrow face, and he wore the sober blacks and whites expected by Spain's ascetic king.

"Well, Latham, knight by the grace of my poor cousin, Mary," Guise began with a sneer. "You decoded without permission. It was a simple enough code, concocted by my esteemed friend here, the ambassador of Spain." The duke nodded to the other man.

Frances de Alava, Latham realised.

"No doubt you think I'm a simpleton, to make a code a third clerk can unravel," The duke said testily.

"No, Your Grace. I think of you as *busy*." Alava bowed.

"Good," Guise replied, "because one day the world will find that I'm as subtle as the next rogue." He laughed briefly; then merriment gave way to anger. "Any other day, Latham, I'd kill you for such a breach, but some find your presumption useful. So you'll favour us with the important fact you wouldn't tell my trusted courier."

Latham had thought about how to reveal the Queen of Navarre's aid to the Dutch without implicating Elizabeth. He repeated Hicks's account of a treasure brought in by foreigners wearing gold and red livery, and Elizabeth's orders that it all be returned.

"Gold on red. Navarre," The duke said to Alava. "There *was* a transport of treasure, but your spies had their pointy noses sniffing in the wrong directions. They missed it coming back."

Alava sat and studied his manicured fingernails with a smile. Latham wondered if he suspected the jewels hadn't come back. Inwardly, he prayed Alava wouldn't probe.

He was relieved by Alava's response. "I'm not surprised Navarre's our meddler. Your Grace, is it possible to admire your man's enterprise?"

"I don't see how knowing this helps. Navarre is beyond my reach," Guise said. "I hope King Philip still appreciates our work for him."

Latham suppressed a smile; the duke was now taking credit for his discovery.

"His Majesty will reward you, as promised. May I address your clerk?"

Guise nodded.

"Now, sir," Alava said, "you repeated a practised account by the witness Hicks. With the current irritants between Spain and England, Elizabeth would be mad to hold the treasure. Still, despite this affecting tale of renunciation, the rebels got money. You're a thinking man. Who was the lender?"

"Your Excellency, these jewels are notorious," Latham replied. "I suspect an envoy of Navarre's received Clough's written valuation and took it to Hamburg or Bremen, eluding your spies. The lender could be any banker there."

"Logical," Alava agreed. "Tell me, Latham. You left the court of Elizabeth after several years, then served the unfortunate Mary, and now His Grace."

"Not for long," The duke said. "I loathe skulkers."

"Yes, Your Grace," Alava said. "I propose to relieve you of him." He turned to Latham. "What moves you?" His black eyes bored into Latham.

Latham tried to explain his philosophy. "Your Excellency, Your Grace, I look first to my soul. I worship according to Rome. But the Almighty also decreed temporal hierarchies, so I oppose disrupting social order. How would it be if the moon got petulant about the impurities of the sublunary sphere and leapt to embrace the sun? What would happen to tides? Harvests? Without proper order, all is calamity. I abhor rebellions. Huguenots fighting the French king; the Scots who deposed Mary; the Dutch rebels fighting Spain; are Protestants fighting Catholic overlords. But I also would oppose Catholic rebellions against my former Protestant sovereign. I won't do anything directly against Elizabeth's government. I left, and that's enough. The Almighty gives us free will to choose good or evil. My countrymen, in legal proceedings, chose heresy. Their destiny is their affair."

The duke had jiggled his foot while Latham spoke. "Anyone can spice up Ptolemy with a dash of Paul," he sneered. "Doesn't make him reliable."

"I think he's sincere," Alava said. "Let me hire him. He's lived among heretics, knows their ambitions, liturgy, jokes. And he's not known in France. I'll send him to monitor Huguenot strongholds, and share his work with you. He's more useful doing this than causing you grief. You know Latin, Latham?"

Latham nodded, bemused, as the duke happily released him.

While packing, he began to laugh. *Last week, I was dangling. Now I know my talent. I have twenty-five pounds a year of my own, and an employer who'll pay me to support the faith in Europe. From one decoding!*

Alava's first remark when they met in the courtyard was, "Latham, I mentioned Latin because King Philip knows only Latin and Spanish. Latin is the only tongue for avoiding misunderstandings, so use it for text and code. Now, what is the Queen of Scots *like?*"

CHAPTER 3
FIRST URGENT
INTELLIGENCE

O ver the next eighteen months, Alava used Latham gently, sending him to Huguenot strongholds. Latham used aliases he chose himself: Ignatius Andrade, commodities merchant, in Navarre; Piso Prosperino, commodities merchant, in La Rochelle. His job was to report troop musters and arms imports, and chart prices of iron, steel, rope, and grain. Sharp increases in these goods suggested a mobilisation that wasn't yet visible. Playing traders amused Latham, reminding him of masques he'd acted in as a child.

He also had a paper filled with the names of "dear friends" who'd graced his bed during his travels. He'd been chaste for three years, after the dour Edinburgh physician who examined him after Darnley got syphilis, proclaimed, "Sores can erupt three, nay, five years after whoring." Three years to the day Latham was clean, and he followed Eros's promptings. He avoided brothels, but a care-worn widowed inn owner in one town, lively artisans' wives in two others, an irresistible groom with a gappy grin he'd met at a market, tip-toed to his bedchamber, charmed by his manners. Some even volunteered information helpful to Spain.

He hadn't uncovered plots or performed decoding feats, but Alava was satisfied. A genial employer, Alava enjoyed drinks with Latham in taverns, always eager for stories about Mary. Spying for Spain had so far had left Latham's face wind-chapped, and his stomach sour from bad food, but his conscience untroubled. He hadn't had to suborn anyone into political betrayal.

Now, in September 1571, Alava slid a gold goblet of rich burgundy across the table, motioning Latham to enjoy it while he finished what he was writing. They were alone in the library of the Spanish embassy, not a tavern, which was a first. Puzzled, Latham wondered if Alava was celebrating some triumph; but from what he could see of the page margin Alava was notating, that didn't seem likely. He was adding to Latham's last three reports, as if for someone else's eyes. Sudden anxiety spoiled the taste of an exceptional vintage wine.

Alava finished, sanded the pages, adding them to a small pile. He looked up and smiled. "Truc peace in France or another truce? We don't know yet. A long cease-fire here changes everything. I have a new assignment and alias for you."

Latham nodded uneasily; Alava was withholding something. "The simplicity of war," the Spanish ambassador continued. "Hordes assembling now, or soon, or not. You say not."

"The peace of St. Germain holds, Your Excellency. About a year now," Latham affirmed.

Alava sighed. "As Christians, we're supposed to rejoice at saved lives. 'Thou shalt not kill,' and all that. However, Madrid's miserable and worried. Any French Huguenot not being savaged here is free to help Dutch Protestants rebels against us. The location of mischief just changes. It moves, dear Latham, to royal palaces. This truce stipulates that Huguenot leader, Admiral Gaspard de Coligny, join the king's privy council. Our enemies will now be at court, gaining influence. There are negotiations to marry the king's sister, Marguerite de Valois, to the Huguenot commander, Prince Henry of Navarre. All this is against our interests…"

A knock on the door interrupted him. Two workmen came in with sheets. Behind them, a man trundled in a cart with a flat crate on it. To Latham's astonishment, they took down Alava's portrait, wrapped it and carted it away. An ominous blank dominated the wall, the hook awaiting some other face.

Latham gasped.

Alava coloured. "I was going to tell you. I'm sorry those fellows came so soon. Yes, I'm recalled. His Majesty appointed a replacement he thinks fitter for the task ahead, which is hearing conspiratorial whispers rather than belching artillery. I advised Madrid that you have a talent for this, but another ambassador will get credit for your triumphs."

"Should I return my alias papers?" Latham asked.

"No. I'm adding, not substituting, an alias. Monsieur Hercules Felipe Gidon is a soap seller who supplies the Louvre Palace. The mongrelly name will account for your accent. We've set up a producer with the best Spanish soaps. You'll use your sales to report who visits whom at court. With new influences there, troublemakers will get busy."

The workmen came back and hung a new portrait. When they left, Alava said, "Your new employer, Don Juan de Zuniga y Requesnes."

Latham read disdain on Alava's face.

Painted Zuniga sat on a white Arabian horse, armour-gloved hands cupping the pommel. His salient features were frowning eyebrows and brilliantly oiled black hair.

"You're tall, Latham, and Zuniga is meagre, particularly his hands," Alava explained. "This painter put him on the smallest Arabian, so the ratio of man to mount wouldn't insult him. He also used armoured gloves to make something substantial of his fists. Zuniga will dislike you. He sees plots in every cellar and attic, and will demand details about alliances that might not exist. He'll know about bedfellows" –this with a cautionary wink—"Well, I've done what I can for you, Edward. May God keep you in health. My secretary will finish your instructions."

He stood abruptly as if he was weary of this moment in his life. Draining his goblet, he walked out without looking back.

Latham waited half an hour under Zuniga's brooding face, reconciling himself to another period of libido-restraint. Then Alava's secretary came in, carrying a wool cloak with a modest fur collar. "This will suit for Monsieur Gidon. We've made friends with some palace grooms and stable boys, so you'll be able to buy information from them. Here are the names. But we never succeeded with the woman who sees most but says little." He tittered, then covered his mouth.

"Who is she?"

"Mademoiselle Hélène Michaud, mistress of the royal laundry. She holds her position because she's kin to your former master, Henry, Duke of Guise. We assume she informs for him, but none of our agents has won her confidence." Another titter. "Well, I must get ready to leave. Sell soap, Gidon/Latham. May God smile on you."

Latham enjoyed becoming an aggressively charming, obsequious soap seller. He was fond of his creation: pushy, desperate Hercules F. Gidon; he liked him far more than Zuniga's disdainful clerk, to whom he brought his reports. Gidon didn't detect any imminent plots, because the respite from hostilities served all parties, and Zuniga was displeased. He refused to meet Latham, hinting through his clerk that he suspected Latham was lazy, timid, even false, and he knew what to do with such rogues.

Latham stayed unfazed because he was making progress

on his long-term strategy: cultivating the mistress of the royal laundry, Helen Michaud. He gave, determined to ask nothing until she clearly wanted to talk.

The moment he uncovered his barrels of soap for her grumpy inspection, he understood Alava's clerk's titter, and the difficulty in winning her confidence Homely and middle-aged, her demeanour suggested that if she'd ever invited kisses or fondling, that openness was long gone. Consequently, she was much neglected by men primed to be ever fruitful and multiply, men for whom any breedable female, regardless of station, provoked momentary notice. That kind of man didn't see women like Hélène; he looked through them. The mistress of the royal laundry knew it.

Edward Latham wasn't like those men. From their first meeting, he felt intense empathy for her. She dazzled him with her similarity to his sister Katherine's governess. "Beauty and the Beast" the family had called them, with perfect unkindness. Slender Katherine, with her long blond tresses and unblemished white skin, floated about trailed by this governess, oddly enough also named Catherine. Governess Catherine was short and dumpy, her oily, wide-pored complexion prone to blackheads. But if you closed your eyes and opened your ears, her mind was astonishingly sharp. Her quick wit put her noble charges to shame, yet the family treated her as nearly invisible. Catherine yearned to be noticed, appreciated for her care of her charges, which expressed itself through a stern imparting of facts, equations, and grammar. Young Edward had seen through her unprepossessing shell to the warm heart inside. He gave her all the dependence a trusting child could, earning her unstinted devotion.

So when Latham as Gidon bowed to Hélène, he saw governess Catherine. He knew at once, with a thrill of power, that he could manage her. He understood that rank had given her what his governess lacked–a fiefdom to rule–for the laundry was a semi-autonomous state.

He treated her with the courtly manners due to a duchess. Their acquaintance extended beyond the price of soap. During card games, he elicited her views on everything but politics: degrees of quality in silk and linen; the virtues of various slickstones and stew-presses; how she taught employees their skills. Occasionally he asked her about gossip he'd heard around the stables. He charmed her because he liked her, and was genuinely intrigued by the enterprise she ran.

She ruled her empire with ferocity, generosity and piratical avarice, and soon let him glimpse its inner workings. It was a wholly female world, yet nothing like a convent. Judging by the piping calls of "Mère," "Tante," "Grandmère," it was populated by generations of a few families, some of the lowest social class. There were separate rooms for different fabrics, a room for repair, where smocked girls aged eight to ten laboured on shirts, overskirts, petticoats, sleeves, breeches and doublets, supervised by Hélène's deputy. Bare-legged waifs carried baskets of soap or bottles of soapwort juice for velvets, or piles of soiled garments. Older women twirled fabrics in cauldrons stinking of uric cleanser, while others mangled and ironed. The oldest hauled water buckets to the cauldrons and logs to the fires.

Eventually, Hélène explained the laundry's finances to Latham. When she did, he understood how to bribe her. It took two stages. One morning, she beat down his price for soap mercilessly, saying that she received a fee set by the Treasury for running the laundry, out of which she paid expenses. But expenses had gone up with the debasement of French coinage. Only her shrewdness enabled her to survive, she assured him. Opening her official book, she showed receipts and treatments of every garment, audited and certified by a royal bookkeeper. Based on this accounting book, things were indeed tight.

Knowing there was more to it, Latham grinned as he handed her back the book. He kissed her hand and agreed to her price. Next week, he sold her a year's consignment of luxury orange-scented soap for half its cost. Ecstatic, Hélène opened a triple-locked cupboard and showed him two more books. She was ready to talk, anticipating an infinite stream of bargains.

Her first unofficial book consisted of typical palace skimming. Only slightly corrupt, it documented tips for the quality of soap applied or precedence in service; the sale of fabric ends, spoiled gold and silver thread, a precious gem snipped from the doublet of a courtier fallen from favour, candle ends, and a fraction of each soap and wood consignment. As they sipped the cognac Latham had brought her, Hélène told him that she shared her earnings with her staff, who had to sign for their portion. Kinship ties and signatures or thumb marks would keep her safe, she believed. When Latham asked Hélène how she spent her profits, she said she invested in provincial inns that her relatives managed. She hoped he'd patronise them on his travels.

Her second unofficial book went beyond normal skimming, and there were no employee signatures or thumb marks. This was Hélène's alone. It accounted for intangible transactions: information told and secrets kept for a price. It was in a crude code, but Latham made out Henry, Duke of Guise, next to information told. Hélène was willing to be suborned. And they seemed to favour the same political side. But for months, despite her willingness and his enthusiasm, she couldn't point him to any plots against Spain.

Finally, in early July 1572, she named a Dutch courier, Albert Braak, who served a French captain. The captain had left Paris, leaving his courier behind. Why, she didn't know.

When she described Braak and his master, Latham immediately grasped their significance. His instincts screamed that a plot was underway. The captain was gone, but teasing information from Braak could revive Latham's flagging career as a spy,

"Albert Braak is a courier for a Huguenot visitor, Jean Haguet de Genlis, who struts like a general," she said, pocketing Latham's five testoons. "He tried to keep his identity secret, but his groom boasted to my cousin, the falconer here. Genlis came to meet that Huguenot leader now on the privy council, Admiral Coligny. Then he left in a hurry, puffed and happy. Left Braak behind. What do you think of that?"

"First," Latham asked, "is this something you also sold your kinsman, Henry, Duke of Guise?"

She blushed. "Couriers don't interest him."

Latham was relieved. If Hélène didn't know who Jean Haguet de Genlis was, she understood less than she'd heard. "It is not worth what I paid you, dear Duchess. Please do better."

"Ah, I must satisfy my favourite customer. Braak is a gambler, mostly loses. He'd be minnow to a fisher of men like you. Ha, ha!"

Latham went still with excitement. He knew three facts. First, in 1567, Jean Haguet de Genlis had fought with Huguenot Admiral Coligny against French royal Catholic forces; they were fellow soldiers. Second, Genlis had joined Dutch rebels holding the city of Mons, which the Spanish were besieging. Third, Genlis had escaped, met Coligny and left Paris happy. Now came Latham's conjecture, his instinct: while it was natural that Genlis would seek safety with a powerful friend and comrade in arms, it was more likely he was raising a French Huguenot army to invade the Spanish Netherlands and relieve the Spanish siege of Mons. This was exactly the mischief Alava had feared when he had bidden farewell to Latham. This would be urgent actionable intelligence for Spain.

"What do you know about Genlis, Duchess?" he asked Hélène.

"Nothing, and I couldn't care less." Hélène sniffed contemptuously. "He came with Dutch servants, acted Dutch himself, obsessively washing every day. He may have noble rank, but he gave me nothing "unofficial," even though he used a month's cedar soaps in two weeks and two rose-scented soaps for his whore. Only Braak and a manservant remain. They wash and wash too, and they're as tight-fisted as their master. There is something *small* about Huguenots!"

Latham burst out laughing. "Small-minded indeed, Duchess. Contempt for the mystery of the mass, and no concept of paying properly for soap. A pox on them."

He took his leave, thrilled with her information.

He had to prove that Genlis was raising troops to help the Dutch rebels at Mons. If he were right and could thwart Genlis, he'd be shaping events, not just finding facts. No one thought the Dutch rebellion would last six years, but it had. In this context, Genlis with a few thousand troops was a real threat.

The next day, rays of a late afternoon sun dissected the street's stone buildings, painting them golden and brown. Braak, Latham's tousle-haired, bow-legged quarry, glanced behind him as he turned into a side street, prompting Latham to slip into the shadows. They weren't far from The Yellow Cock Spur tavern, where Latham had once met David Hicks.

The tavern wasn't Braak's destination. He turned a corner, and another, stopping outside a stone building with a wooden addition on one side. It looked like an old school that had been hastily expanded during Paris's population surge in the 1520s. The addition leaned against its host, each decrepit construction propping the other up. The roof sported a sad-faced stone lion with half a mane. The windows were dark, but fresh horse dung in the street indicated life inside.

Braak peered at the side of a window frame, opened the door and went in. Latham walked to the same window. A freshly scratched spur was visible on the flaky shutter; easy to sand off. He grinned. A clandestine cockfight, as David Hicks had said. More men approached as Latham left.

He needed a drink before suborning Braak. Back at the Yellow Cocks's Spur, every post had a horse tied to it, and inside, a crowd of men in livery drank companionably, there to collect their employers after the fight.

Latham squeezed onto the end of a bench and called for ale, thinking about his task. He had to confirm that Genlis had left Paris because he'd raised the troops he needed; that this force was going to Mons; and what Genlis expected to gain by leaving Braak behind.

He stared at the thick white froth in his tankard, trying to imagine the next hour. Hélène had said Braak was a loser. Latham intended to cover his losses with coin, jewels and fur trim, and had dressed opulently. In addition, he'd sewn onto his doublet sleeve a little red rose with white inner petals nestling on green leaves. It was the Tudor emblem, meant to mislead Braak about his allegiance. Latham expected that if Braak faced debtor's prison when his urgent duty was to rush messages to Genlis, his gratitude would overcome caution, and he'd betray Genlis. But what if Braak won? What if Hélène was wrong about his haplessness? Latham had no alternative plan. He pushed this worry aside; he trusted Hélène's assessments of men gone bad. On these subjects she was wise.

Getting what he needed from Braak would require better playacting than he'd done before. Up to now, in the guise of a trader, he'd mostly assembled facts about commodity price movements. *Today is different*, he mused, *I must dig out of Braak a secret he'd never otherwise reveal, which means stripping him of agency.* He conjured up a world of deception. *Must I become a theologian of deception, like the old scholastics? Is there a hierarchy of deceptions, a netherworld where lies whirl in serried ranks? How many lies can dance on the head of a pin?*

"A turn and a half of the glass, friends. One more flagon," a servant near Latham sang. An hour and a half left of the fight. Latham had to go. He was nervous, that's all.

He returned to the schoolhouse, crossed the empty lobby, and pushed aside heavy curtains screening an anteroom.

Vendors were hawking food and drink; a few customers were relaxing.

Opening the hall door, he was greeted by heat and noise. Resin wall torches and candles set on traverse ceiling beams lit the room. The crowd was yelling. Clambering up on an elevated plank that formed the back row, Latham saw that a black-breasted red with a red comb had been fighting a streaky red with a yellow comb. Yellow comb was down, its owner dripping water on a gash in its throat, cajoling it through the umpire's counts.

"One. Two."

"Black! Black! Black!"

In the front row, Braak shouted as he increased his bet on the black-breasted red. On the count of three, yellow comb fluttered its wings, took an experimental hop, then sprang at the black's flank. The crowd roared louder as the black began to sink to the mat. As the umpire counted again, the crowd quieted.

"One, two, three…"

Silence. What might have been a death rattle came from one of the birds, but which? Then harsh whispers.

"Black rattles."

"No, no, it is the yellow."

"Four."

The black-breasted red stirred. There was one gasp from the audience, then two, then cheers. Yellow comb summoned the will to rake the black one more time. The black died instantly; the yellow a few seconds later.

"No! No!" Braak was hitting his forehead with the palm of one hand. To Latham's left, there was a heaving of communal movement, a cry, a thump. In the hot miasma, a man had fainted. People bent over the body while one wiped his face with a vinegared cloth. When his eyelids fluttered, he was pulled into the anteroom. The umpires called an intermission.

Latham used the pause to walk around, for the moment keeping away from Braak. It was a promiscuous crowd, from threadbare students to jewelled aristocrats whose servants swivelled as they watched for pickpockets. Not unlike the cockfights Latham had attended in England. The air was thick with mingled perfumes and sour sweat. Looking up, he laughed softly. In a far corner was the customary man-sized basket suspended by chains from a ceiling beam, used to string up a gambler who couldn't cover his losses.

The hall accommodated about three hundred people. The front row was empty, for standing. There was one row of flat boxes, then his row of planks on barrels, with divisions by three aisles. The pit was improvised too. Not oval, not round, its shape was determined by the length of planks making its base. Matting was nailed to the planks to prevent birds slipping. The barrier consisted of latticed wooden frames tied together. Seating and pit could be quickly disassembled if there was warning of a raid, as Hicks had told him.

Braak was standing by a cage, talking to another man. The man shook his head and backed away. Braak clutched his shirt, then the man handed Braak a purse. *Ha*, thought Latham, *he's wagering another man's money, having lost his own.*

Braak won his wagers on the next two fights. The change in his demeanour was astonishing, his blue eyes brilliant with hope. "Dame Fortune's come in on my side!" he cried, inducing his companion to stake more bets.

Latham wanted fresh air. It was quiet outside; the sky painted with the deep grey-blues of twilight. A street lantern had been lit at each end of the street, and pinpricks of candlelight appeared at several houses. A guard stood outside the building; two others manned the street corners. No sign of the regular watch, presumably bought off.

He returned to another intermission. This time he walked up to Braak and his companion. They were assessing the remaining birds.

"What do you think of this beast?" Braak was saying. They were at a hamper containing a big bird, all muscle, with white plumes streaked with black. Its breast gleamed with grooming.

It hopped from foot to foot, its head inclined as if hearing applause from past wins. An apprentice began to push balls of milk-soaked bread into its beak. Milk dribbled onto its powerful claws, which the apprentice tenderly mopped off.

"Ungainly," Braak's companion remarked.

"I think you do not go to many fights," Braak retorted, full of confidence.

"Parisians must be careful. My father will disinherit me if he finds me in the stocks."

"Pfff to that! This is a Fleming breed called Nord. No beauty, I agree, but a vicious pecker and its endurance legendary. I'll bet on it if it's paired properly. I have to make up travel money I lost. I go tomorrow." They moved away.

Latham squatted and appraised the bird. The apprentice was still mopping its legs. When his cloth brushed the bird's breast by mistake, Latham saw a tiny patch of white feathers through the black. The apprentice quickly interposed his back between Latham and the bird, but Latham had seen enough. White down had been concealed by charcoal, a sign of improperly healed wounds. The bird shouldn't fight at all. Anyone who bet on it would lose.

He moved to the last hamper, where bettors were staring at a straw-coloured cock with a curved yellow beak, yellow legs and a stiff red comb. Its powerful thighs stood well forward. Its cocker was gently massaging its under-wings with oil. The bird writhed with pleasure at the sensuality of the kneading while it strained against the hamper, provoked by the scent of nearby foes.

"It has a sound build and lots of spirit," one man offered.

"Holder and scraper," another agreed.

"You can't tell with a bird of this colouring," Braak offered. "Straw cocks are sometimes bred with common hens. The offspring look alike but show their underwings. I'm sticking with my Fleming Nord. I'd be a knave to bet against a beast from my own country."

He looked homesick. *A patriot as well as a fool*, Latham realised, with a pang of sympathy.

Many bettors deferred to Braak, since he'd won his last few bets. The crowd cheered as the umpires announced that the Nord would fight the straw. Latham joined the crowd around the bet-takers shouting for the glossy Nord. The odds against the straw were seven to two. Latham placed two silver shillings on the straw.

When the birds' spurs were fitted, the umpires gave the signal to begin. The two cockers thrust their birds together, brought them back to the pit sides, and released them.

The fight lasted less than two minutes. The birds swooped at each other. As the crowd roared, the straw managed to rake the Nord's unhealed wound. It tottered, one eye blinded, blood dripping from its breast. It stood its ground, seemingly impervious and baleful. Then it sagged and died. The straw understood its victory, preening, while its owner rushed into the pit and scooped it into his arms, laughing wildly.

The crowd was howling with frustration, some shouting that the foreigner had deliberately misled them.

"Now, gentlemen," shouted a bet-taker. "The straw won fair. Losers pay up, winners collect."

Latham collected his winnings.

"I am ruined!" Braak cried, as enforcers shoved him toward the debtors' basket. He was kicking and yelling, "Give me until tomorrow! One day."

"Thief! You're leaving tomorrow," his bet-taker shouted.

"I can't help you, Albert," his companion moaned. "You lost my money too."

One of the enforcers silenced Braak with a punch in the mouth, to guffaws from the crowd. The men swung him into the basket, tied his arms and legs to the rims, then gagged him with a linen strip. They searched his pockets for money, found none, took two rings from his fingers and then pulled on the ropes. The swinging basket ascended. When it was eight feet in the air, they secured the rope to hooks in the oak beams. Apple cores, eggs, wooden cups spewing drops of ale and wine rose in an arc and clattered against his calves and face.

Laughter roared around the hall, increasing until everyone was holding their sides or punching their neighbour's shoulder. When their noise stopped, Braak's protesting mews could be heard through his gag.

Latham stared at the basket. Braak had played his role perfectly; it was time for Hercules F. Gidon to play his.

Into the silence, the bet-taker shouted, "Pay up, Fleming. Your farm and your wife." He caused the epidemic of laughter to start again. It took a few minutes to abate.

When it did, Latham called, "Release him. I'll make good the bet." He took out two of the coins he had won on the straw and gave it to Braak's companion, who thanked him effusively and pushed out of the hall as fast as his legs would pump.

When Latham got to Braak's bet-taker, he gasped at the tally. The Fleming must have been losing for days. What a fool Genlis was to trust a compulsive gambler, Latham thought. He counted out his gold and silver coins, keeping back a few billons for a meal.

"It's not enough," the bet-taker said, calculating the shortfall.

The crowd's attention shifted to Latham. They chanted, "Strip him, strip him clean!"

Protected by enforcers, the bet-taker took Latham's kid gloves and three rings from his fingers. Methodically he cut the pearl buttons from his doublet, the silver buckles from his boots and the mink fur collar from his cloak. Latham willed his hand not to draw his knife. He'd prepared for rough usage, but the reality of being indifferently plucked filled him with rage. A vein in his temple throbbed. Gidon, soap seller and friend to Braak's cause, could endure this, he reminded himself.

Finally, the bet-taker stepped away, nodding sourly. "Enough. You don't need foes with this friend, you poor fool." The enforcers lowered the basket and set Braak free. He stood, massaging his wrists. Rubbish-spattered but unhurt, he began to grin. He seemed to be used to this kind of scrape. "I'm grateful to you," he said, offering Latham a dirty hand. "You look familiar. Haven't I seen you at the palace?"

"Monsieur Hercules Felipe Gidon, soap supplier."

Braak stepped back. "A trader saves me? How strange." His tone became frosty. "Why?" He stared at the embroidered rose on Latham's sleeve. "Ah, a special trader. No flower pleases more than the noble, er, the *royal*, rose. That explains your pearls and fur. Well, thank you."

"Come on, I need a meal," Latham muttered.

Braak nodded cheerfully and followed him.

"David Hicks, who serves Sir William Cecil, told me about these fights," Latham said as they picked their way down the outside steps, weaving through the jumble of people looking for their servants. Bells were tolling curfew in an hour and a half.

"We know you must travel tomorrow," Latham rattled on. "A hindrance like debtors' prison cannot stand, so we help you on your way." He allowed Braak to absorb this as they walked to The Yellow Cock's Spur tavern. Most patrons had left, and they got a private table. Latham ordered a Burgundy wine, along with bread and cheese, exhausting his funds. He expected a long walk home.

"Burgundy!" he said, raising his goblet. With his doublet and shirt shorn of buttons, and his cloak jagged where the collar had been cut, he looked like an escapee from the lunatics' hospital.

Braak looked stricken. "Gidon, I don't know what devil possesses me. Every day I wake up and say, 'No wagering, you're better than that.' I pray, I cast out evil, I'm pure. But within an hour, the devil whispers that only in the vortex of a wager does a man know ecstasy. Only then is he fully alive. The devil has me. I'll make it up to you, I swear. Tell me your address."

Latham snorted. "I'm sure you swear similarly pretty oaths to more people than you can remember. You make it up by completing your commission. Now Braak, let's drink to

Burgundy, your ancestral home, I suspect. The French ruled the provinces before Spain inherited them, so I know you welcome French help. They'll be glad to plant their flag again."

"Burgundy," Braak agreed. But before he drank, he called for warm water and soap.

"Braak, I don't have the funds for it."

Braak fished under his codpiece and pulled out a knotted handkerchief. "They missed this in the basket. Enough for washing water and hired nags to get us home before curfew."

Hélène's right about the Dutch obsession with washing, Latham thought, watching Braak scour his face and hands. He gave his own hands a cursory wipe.

"Yes," Braak said again, satisfied his hands were clean. "Burgundy is a joy to drink, and a better place to live when at peace. We gladly accept French Huguenot support. But no French flags. It is our time for independence. You know the French Huguenot leader, Admiral Gaspard de Coligny, has a deep affection for Prince William of Orange. There was talk of uniting the families last year, Coligny's sister marrying William, but she married another Huguenot leader. Still, kin at heart if not body." His bright blue eyes held Latham's.

Latham showed surprise; he hadn't heard this.

Suddenly suspicious, Braak asked, "How many tennis courts are in Whitehall Palace?"

Latham laughed. "Questions! About time. Four. I lost matches in each one." That was lie number one: he'd played the vain Earl of Oxford once, and after losing to the lower-ranked Latham, the earl refused to play him again. But there was no way Braak could know that.

"Who are you?" Braak pressed. "Not Hercules Felipe Gidon, soap seller, that's clear."

"For your purposes I am Gidon," Latham retorted, pointing to the Tudor rose on his sleeve. The pin of deception wobbled.

After a few more questions Braak relaxed and smiled. "We have to watch for spies, so our questions change from time to time. Perhaps it's better you don't name yourself."

Sensing success, Latham remained quiet, an expression of inquiry on his face. He still had everything to learn.

Braak couldn't tolerate silence. "Listen." His voice was higher, shrill. "We've been frustrated by English neutrality, so I was surprised by your help tonight."

"Queen Elizabeth is cautious," Latham offered, "but she watches Genlis with great interest. How have you met the difficulty of raising an army from the dispersed Huguenot lands? I know them well. Then there's the awkwardness of discreetly moving armed hordes."

There, he'd thrown his dice.

Braak smirked. "Captain Genlis is marching with thousands of infantry and cavalry. They set off from Chatillon. One thousand pike will follow in a month. As to moving, absolute secrecy isn't possible, of course. But it has turned out not to be necessary. I stayed in Paris to secure a right of way through the French king's lands. It came today, with royal signature and seal. The king wishes to appease Coligny. See, all hindrances removed." He leaned back, folding his arms. "What do you think of that?"

"What do *I* think? I say you jest. Right of way from the Catholic King Charles for a Huguenot army to invade the Spanish Netherlands through the king's own lands? No plausible deniability? I can't believe in it without seeing the permit."

"Would seeing it change English neutrality?"

"It will take time. But if I report seeing proof of your claim, it will make a strong impression."

"I carry a copy." Braak reached inside his doublet and thrust a paper at Latham.

Latham stared at it. "You astonish me. We saw Genlis as a shallow boaster, but what you say is true. Please accept our apologies."

He knew now that there was a French Huguenot army, and it was marching into Spain's territories with the French king's approval.

But he needed the destination.

After a pause, he added, "Genlis will join Prince William of Orange's German mercenaries waiting at Roermond. Combining armies makes sense."

Braak winked as he put his paper away. "That's what Orange wants. He wrote to Genlis insisting on it. But Captain Genlis grieves for the suffering citizens in a place he just left. More I cannot say."

Latham let out a sigh. His conjecture was right. Genlis intended to attack the Spanish army besieging Mons, and William of Orange was nowhere near Mons. Latham had effectively stripped Braak of agency and had all the information he needed. Around them, benches were scraping as remaining patrons made drunken farewells. He and Braak hired nags and joined the crowd on their journey over the Petit Pont to the city proper.

By the time they had said goodbye, curfew bells were tolling continuously, and men stood by the giant chains, ready to roll them out and block the streets. As Braak spurred his nag toward the palace, Latham shouted after him. Words tumbled out unbidden. "Braak, that Nord cock had old breast wounds hidden by charcoal! It fought once too often. Take care your Genlis doesn't do the same!"

"Ha!" Braak shouted back. He waved and resumed his trot.

Had he understood? Amidst the din of chains scraping, it was impossible to tell. Latham shook his head, wondering what strange goblin capering around his mind moved him to warn Braak. A desire to give Braak some agency and even the odds between him and Braak, a fairness denied to the black Fleming cock so impervious to pain?

He made his way to the Spanish Embassy, where he was shown into the library. He reported to Antonio Gomez, secretary to Ambassador Zuniga. Gomez was even shorter than his master, rotund, and with mousy thinning hair. He listened gravely, told Latham to wait, and went upstairs.

He returned after half an hour, saying, "His Excellency

is pleased, but unavailable. Our couriers are engaged. You'll have to take this information to Mons and deliver it to Field Marshal Chiappino Vitelli yourself. What weapons and escort do you have?"

"I have two swords and a knife. No regular manservant."

"Then we'll give you a pistol and escort part way. Can you shoot?"

"Yes, the Duke of Guise taught me." Latham turned the wheellock pistol around in his hand. It was beautiful, with a walnut handle inlaid with ivory, a damascene barrel, and a wheel of hardened steel. A servant brought a shoulder strap with attached powder flasks and a bag of shot.

"Don't I need a permit for this?" Latham asked. Pistols, especially the new models that used flint to spark the powder, were considered too easy to conceal, a perfect assassination tool. Only approved persons could carry them.

"There's no time. You say this army has already left Chatillon. Here's an official ring that will identify you when you reach Spanish lines. And a letter."

Latham put the ring on his index finger. It was heavy, old, and of fine white gold. There were a few scratches where Philip's face was set. Puzzled, he ran a finger over the flaws.

"The scratches prove its authenticity," Gomez said. "When Emperor Charles abdicated in 1556, in favour of his son, a few rings were re-set. Vitelli will accord it great honour; he served the father as well as the son. The camp password is "Don Carlos," though it might change by the time you arrive. I'll provide an escort for two days, then hire locally. You won't need to show the pistol at all if you hire shrewdly. You've done well; urgent, timely intelligence."

Latham read the letter, perturbed that Gomez, not Zuniga, had signed it. "I thought you said the ambassador was pleased," he protested. "This is your signature, not his."

"His Excellency *is* pleased, but not completely confident in you. Don't worry. You won't have any trouble. God give you a safe, fast journey."

CHAPTER 4
DANGER AT
MONS

Twelve days later, Latham walked his horse out of some woods and onto a dirt road. The moon had set, but blinking constellations shed enough light, and he doused his lantern. Gazing at the pale orange dot that was Mars, he mused: *A little god of war for the little army I've outrun.* Still, Genlis had around seven thousand. If Braak was right, a thousand pikemen were marching to reinforce them. A thousand men wielding fifteen- or eighteen-foot staffs, with their wickedly sharp metal ends, would make this force formidable.

He had barely slept since hurtling out of Paris. Nor had he washed properly; just splashing his face and hands in ponds or streams. Each day the water got more brackish since the weather was unusually dry. To make himself presentable at the Spanish camp he dabbed cedar oil on his skin. He was wearing a cream linen shirt with a blackwork collar under a grey doublet, breeches and light-wool cloak. Plain, but good fabrics. Confident that bandits wouldn't attack so close to two armies, he'd paid off his guards the night before, wanting to arrive unremarked and alone.

The pistol was in his saddlebag, and he had a knife and sword at his waist. Exhausted, and with a heavy cold, he begged God to keep him awake. However, in case the Deity was busy with other things, he roped his ankles to the stirrups.

"Just a few more hours," he murmured to his tired horse. Daylight revealed brown grasses and dead flowers, confirming a drought. Latham was amazed he didn't see fire's blackness. Soon the sun beat rider and horse into a torpor. Latham slumped over the horse's neck and dozed. Grateful for his inattention, the mare slowed to a plod.

Clanging picks on stone; clumping boots; a cacophony of shouts in Catalan, German, Italian, and Gaelic, over which soared orders in Spanish. These were the sounds of Spain's Army of Flanders, as its soldiers and masons raced to complete two thick stone walls that would seal off Mons from the outside world.

A mile from the camp, a *bisono*, a raw recruit, stepped out of a sentry hut and peered at a distant object. In the haze, it was a four-legged apparition floating on balls of dust, ballooning grotesquely on one side. Young William Boels crossed himself. Was it the Horseman of the Apocalypse, about to gallop? *Stop this superstition*, he chided himself. *I'm a soldier; there's another explanation.*

He tried to make sense of the shape, but noise distracted him. A week out of computing figures in his godfather's warehouse, he'd been unprepared for the din of army life. He put clerkly hands over his ears. Now he could concentrate. It wasn't the world's end; it was a large man slumped lopsided over a plodding horse. "Dead man down the road!" he shouted to the other sentry,

"I saw," snapped Lieutenant Juan Alvarado, coming from the side of the hut.

Boels realised that his superior officer had seen his fear. He blushed.

Alvarado, a leathery-skinned veteran, squinted into the distance. His acute eyes picked up a minute jerk of the reins. "Not dead, but near. Load the guns."

Boels frowned, looking puzzled.

Wearily, Alvarado explained, "Could be a plague-poxed saboteur. Rebels sent sick refugees to our camp last month. Bastards."

Boels crossed himself again, then opened the powder flasks and shot pouches. He loaded gunpowder and a ball into each barrel, then tapped powder into the pans. Alvarado's gun was an old matchlock musket, while William's was a gleaming new invention, a *snaphaunce* gun, fired by a flint. It was a gift from his godfather.

Both men were sweating in the heat. For days, clouds hinted at rain, but as twilight closed to night and night bleached to dawn, the rain found somewhere better to go. Violent internal tensions lay just below the surface of army discipline. The Army of Flanders sorely needed a success.

"Blow off the loose powder, or you'll kill us," Alvarado muttered. He resented having to train well-connected Dutch youths who used the army to advance family influence.

Unabashed, Boels stood and pointed his gun at the distant horse.

"Steady, there's time. Don't cramp," Alvarado warned.

He turned and stared at Mons' battlements, at rebel flags flapping in the wind. There were two: ten bronze coins on a red background, the symbol of the Sea Beggars' rebellion against Spain's tenth penny taxes; and gold lions holding silver arrows in their paws on a blue and yellow background, the flag of Count Louis of Nassau, brother of the rebel leader, Prince William of Orange.

The rebels had taken Mons without firing a shot. They

had promised citizens freedom from King Philip's taxes and his religious inquisition, whereupon the traitors chased Spain's administrators out and invited the rebel men in. Now the city would have to be starved into submission. But the siege couldn't begin until gaps in the siege walls were closed. The longer the siege lasted, the more Spaniards would get sick. Rebel lookouts jerked about the battlements like painted puppets, taunting the impotent swarm below. Alvarado spat at the flags, his daily protest at the army's misery. It was futile, the spit often blowing back in his face. Still, it gave him a second's triumph.

Alvarado turned back to the road. The supine rider was wearing a grey cloak. There was a lot of him: long legs and arms, and he had blond hair. A poxed rebel German, he guessed. Concerned, he glanced at the field to his left. Brightly coloured tents housing officers were only a half-mile off, along with stables and water troughs. Since there was no enemy near, the tents had been left outside the siege works for the sweeter air. Alvarado knew his company's new commander, a sergeant-major, was in the nearest tent. He'd arrived the previous night, and hadn't yet met his troops.

"Boels, that horse will go for the water trough as soon as it smells it. I must be able to cut it off. Don't fire until I signal. Remember how to send the ball straight."

Excited, Boels nodded.

Alvarado walked onto the field, carrying a musket and gun fork.

When the mare smelled sweet fresh water, it turned into the field. Closing his eyes, Boels pulled the trigger. Crack! Bright light pierced black smoke. The ball slammed into a tree in front of the horse. A branch fell to the ground and flared dry leaves.

Panicked, the horse started to gallop. Latham woke, tried to haul himself upright. Too late. Sprawled over the horse's back, he clutched the girth, coughing as his stomach bounced against the saddle. With one hand he drew his knife and slashed the rope tying his right foot to the stirrup.

"Halt, in the name of King Philip!" was screamed in Spanish.

"Don't..." he gasped between collisions with the saddle. "D-don't shoot." Pause. Thud

"King's... business."

Latham glimpsed a gun fork, burning match above the pan, musket pointing at him, the pointer wearing the red sash of a Spanish soldier. Frantic, he tried to work his other foot free. His words had been lost in the noise; the soldier didn't understand, or didn't want to.

Five hundred yards, four hundred, three hundred. Crack! The animal shuddered as the ball slammed its flank. Latham flung himself into the air as the horse's front legs buckled and it sank to the ground. Latham landed on his side, winded, too stunned to feel the pain of cracked ribs.

The Spaniard flung down his gun, drew his sword and ran up to him. "Traitor! Poxed rebel scum!" he yelled

"No traitor. King's business. Help me up," Latham was struggling to breathe. He rolled onto his back. The soldier pointed his sword, threatening. His embroidered corselet signified officer rank. A red diagonal cross over green and white horizontal stripes sewn on the corselet's sleeve identified his company. Latham raised one hand in a gesture of surrender and wriggled over to the dying horse. Caressing the rough hair of its mane, he rasped, "I'm so sorry."

On the road, several men were dousing the fire caused by the sentry's errant gunshot, while that young man was running across the field with two other soldiers. All wore the same colours as the leathery-skinned officer menacing Latham.

"Fool. Don't ever fire before I order," the officer snapped at the hapless sentry. "If it weren't for my speed, this horse would have got to the troughs, and you made me kill it. Now, examine our intruder for lumps."

He pointed at one of the soldiers, "Cover the road. There could be another." And to the other soldier, "Fetch the butcher."

Latham's mind raced: *intruder*, the term for an enemy. He was actually in danger.

He stared at his captor with mounting dread. Squat broken nose, scarred eyebrows; a street fighter who had pummelled his way up the ranks would determine his fate. He turned to the youth, white-skinned with clever eyes and the pout of a well-connected whelp, wondering if he could exploit the tension between the two soldiers. He caught the youth's eyes and tried to get up.

"Down," the officer ordered.

As Latham sat, he sneezed and coughed. Both men jumped back.

What's scaring them? Latham wondered. *Oh, plague.* "A cold, not plague," he wheezed.

"I've come on King Philip's business, with urgent intelligence for Field Marshal Vitelli."

"King's business," the officer scoffed. "I am Lieutenant Juan Alvarado, acting sergeant-major of the Eleventh Company. I decide what your business is."

A butcher was trundling a cart to the horse carcass.

"Clothes off," Alvarado told Latham. "Don't get up."

Latham undid the neckties of his cloak, fumbling with fingers bloody from the horse's wound. Then he untied the loops that fastened the onyx buttons of his doublet. Every move hurt, and he needed help to pull the shirt off over his head. While Alvarado tapped his foot impatiently, he undid his codpiece buttons, untied his breeches and the grey ribbons securing his hose. He rolled his breeches and hose below his knees.

Alvarado noted a pale chest pinking from the fall. Its well-tended skin contrasted with a face weathered by sun and wind. He assessed the intruder as not a courtier today; he lived too hard. But the filigreed silver cross around his neck, the gold ring on his finger, and the coddled torso suggested rank. His accent was foreign, but what kind was beyond Alvarado.

He glared at Latham, his ferocity masking an uneasy sense that he was out of his depth. If

King Philip stuck to Spanish soldiers, a man would know where things stood. But foreigners fought for, and against, Spain. Because the company's new commander wouldn't take over until tomorrow, the decision was Alvarado's to make. "Boels, check him for disease," he ordered the young Fleming.

Boels squatted beside Latham, trembling. Arms extended to their maximum reach, he poked at Latham's armpits and groin, and ran an index finger around the back of his ears. No lumps or sores.

"Clean, sir," he squeaked in a high voice. Heaving a tumultuous sigh of relief, he wiped his hands on his breeches then shook them violently, as if intending to launch them into the air.

Latham bit back a snigger.

"He could be in the early stages," Alvarado demurred, staring at snot coagulating in Latham's moustache. "Nothing showing, but sickness lodged."

"It's just a cold," Latham insisted.

"Do up your breeches and no more talk." Alvarado chewed his lower lip as he sorted through the options: a quick execution and the man's possessions forfeited to him and his men (the cross and ring were worth something); ransom for a greater payoff, though deferred; or deference to the man's claimed status. But if he were a plagued saboteur, Alvarado would be exposing his superiors to danger and himself to a charge of negligence. Could he risk it?

The search of Latham's saddlebag revealed travelling papers in the name of Hercules F. Gidon, a bottle of brown hair dye, a rolled parchment and the pistol. Alvarado turned the gun in his hands, put it on the grass then studied the travelling papers. An expression of malice crossed his pummelled face as he shook the bottle of dye. "A disguise? A king's messenger would have servants. Where are yours?"

"My journey was urgent and unexpected," Latham said. "The Spanish ambassador in Paris ordered me here. I paid off hired guards near Saint-Ghislain."

"Password?"

"It was Don Carlos," Latham said.

The youth started, but lowered his eyes at Alvarado's frown.

"Expired. Where's your letter of commission?"

"None for this journey, sir. My intelligence is for Chiappino Vitelli or one who serves him. Read the letter from the ambassador's secretary, Antonio Gomez."

Alvarado read slowly, his index finger tracing each letter. "We don't know Gomez.

Secretarial scribbles are all alike, could be forged. Do you have other proof of the king's favour?"

Latham handed him the ring Gomez had given him, with the current king, Phillip II's face, replacing that of his father, Emperor Charles V. *Gomez promised me Field Marshal Vitelli would know the ring, but will he see it?* Latham wondered bleakly.

"Hmmm," Alvarado said. "Our king's face looks newer than its setting. Suspicious.

Turn on your stomach."

As Latham turned over, he went clammy with fear. His mind raced for some words that would delay the impaling sword he was certain would come. No inspiration came. The officer's hot breath was on the back of his neck, reeking of infected gums. He prayed for forgiveness of his sins, prayed and waited. Impalement didn't happen. *The axe then? Reeking-breath won't waste a bullet.*

When nothing happened, Latham realised the street fighter wasn't sure of his ground.

The notion found its way to his tongue. With manic hope and ill-judged presumption, he said, "What if I am as I say? You'll be ill-served killing a loyal servant to your king and a greater man than you."

"Turn back," was the terse response. "Your breeches

rustled. Hidden pocket. Boels, find it."

Boels slit open Latham's breeches and found papers for two aliases.

Now Alvarado whistled. "Mr No One or Lord Too Many."

Wit from reeking-breath was so unexpected Latham couldn't help, through the pain of his chest, coughing out laughter. He could see how criminal he looked from the lieutenant's point of view. Wheellock pistol; blond hair, brown hair, at will; multiple identities meant no identity. It had been stupid to take all three sets of travelling papers. But he was afraid to leave them in Paris, where they could have been stolen. Aliases, he'd thought, were his asset. All that stood now between him and death was a scratched ring.

He marvelled that the men who would soon kill him were the ones he was trying to save.

Through an excruciating hacking guffaw, he thought: *What a satirist Dame Fortune is.*

"Ah, you laugh," Alvarado said, his mouth curving up. "You can see why your future looks short. I'll give you one more chance."

There was a hint of sympathy in his eyes.

"Boels," Alvarado said, "take the ring to the jeweller that the Ninth Company captured last week. You speak Dutch."

When Boels left, Alvarado allowed Latham to sit up. "What's your urgent intelligence?"

"It's for Field Marshal Vitelli," Latham snapped. "You'll regret it if you kill me."

"Is it about a relief army?"

Latham didn't reply, but blinked.

Alvarado laughed. "Another point against you. Scouts returned last night. The only relief forces near here are widows wailing over ghosts of dead rebels."

Boels returned. "Sir, he can't tell. He heard a few like this were made after the Emperor's abdication but never saw one."

"He felt it?"

"Yes, sir. Still couldn't say."

Alright. I've followed procedures for dealing with suspicious intruders,"

Alvarado pronounced. "The case goes against you. Expired password; no commission; excess identities; dubious ring, letter and intelligence; illegal pistol; foul malady. You're their man," he yelled with fury, pointing at the Mons battlements, "Thank the Almighty your malady earns you a quick death, because if you were healthy, I'd turn you over to the Ninth Company. But we can't risk the interrogator's health. Boels, that branch you shot. Strip its leaves. They can see it from the battlements. Time for the noose."

Don Cristobal Covarrulejo d'Avila, newly appointed sergeant-major of the Eleventh Company, jerked awake. Had he dreamed gunshots or heard them? His head pounded with a hangover from last night's wine. He leapt out of bed and ran to the close stool, just ahead of heaving up fatty duck and jets of pinkish liquid. *That's right*, he remembered. *I'm the new commander of the Eleventh Company, a group tainted by the corruption of its prior sergeant-major.*

"The usual sordid stupidity," his colonel had said as he signed Don Cristobal's commission. "Gutierrez invoiced for a full complement when a third of his men were dead. He spent the company's money while his men scrounged for scraps, even sold their physic to pay whores. It all came to light when he was ordered to Mons where he might have to fight. The rogue bleated for reinforcements! Probably he acted alone; his men certainly suffered. But a taint clings to them. The Eleventh Company needs a hard straight commander with warrior lineage. You can keep Gutierrez' page and halberdiers until yours arrive."

Don Cristobal wiped his mouth with the sleeve of his nightshirt. *Well*, he thought, *he'd meet his men today, assume command tomorrow.* Feeling better, he washed his face and sat on the bed. There was banging at the siege works. A bell rang, and the noise sputtered then stopped. Midday break. In the stark silence, he heard voices in the field, quite close. He picked out the word *noose*.

Jumping up, he opened the tent's flap. The vast field was almost deserted, other officers being at the siege works. Only a few washerwomen and stable boys were around. They were staring at something. Don Cristobal stepped outside. Three men with drawn swords were pushing, prodding and dragging another man across the field. A priest was striding with them, robe flapping and talking at the prisoner's ear. The prisoner was being hustled towards a tree across the road with one bare branch. A man was stringing a rope around the branch.

A hanging! Who were these men? Don Cristobal opened a box and took out three tin tubes, each one of a different thickness. He hadn't tried this device yet, having confiscated it from a Dutch apothecary just two days ago. The Dutchman was executed for refusing to pay the tenth penny tax. The tubes, which had double reflecting glass pieces, were supposed to bring distant images closer when fitted together. Don Cristobal felt vaguely ashamed as he remembered the apothecary's children clutching a soldier's breeches as they dragged the father away.

The apothecary had tried to barter the device, which he called a *looker*, for his life. But Don Cristobal had no authority to negotiate. *Enough daintiness*, he thought, thrusting guilt aside. *He was a hard straight man, as the colonel said; the apothecary was a rebel, tax cheat and heretic.* Still, he regretted the children's loss.

He fitted two tubes together and looked through the glass circle at the end. All blurred. His stomach heaved. He took a deep breath, substituted tubes and tried again. Suddenly a scratch in the leather of one man's jerkin nearly smacked his eyeball. He jumped back amazed, then looked again. God Almighty, the thing worked! He could make out horizontal green threads, horizontal white threads and red diagonal ones. Red diagonal cross on green and white stripes: the man was an Eleventh Company soldier. He put the device down. Knowing what to look for, he made out with his naked eyes the same colours on all of them.

His men. Then who was their prisoner? He looked through the tubes again, and a section of dusty grey cloak swam into view. The weave was first class. He shifted the tube to the man's shirt. Its blackwork collar was equally fine, if soiled.

This device was cumbersome, but it had shown him what he needed to see. His company, tainted by corruption, was about to hang a man of consequence. Maybe they were right, but he had to make sure. He thrust the tubes under his sheets, dragged on shirt, hose, boots, and shrugged into his corselet with its new red cross on green and white stripes. Grabbing his letter of appointment, he ran. "Stop! Eleventh Company, stop!" he thundered.

A soldier continued adjusting the rope around the prisoner's neck.

"Stop this hanging!"

An officer turned to stare at him. The prisoner was on a box, torn breeches flopping, so bowlegged from riding that he was already dragging on the rope. His eyes were bulging, but his expression was serene as if he'd already embarked for the next world. His connection to earthly life was tenuous.

"I am Don Cristobal Covarrulejo d'Avila, your new commander. Delay this hanging." He thrust his appointment letter at the officer who'd turned to look at him.

Alvarado read the letter and bowed.

"First," Don Cristobal said, "loose the rope. Let the prisoner sit. I don't want him dancing the gallows jig before time."

A moment later Latham was sitting on the grass, roped by the waist to the tree.

"Let us become acquainted." Don Cristobal now addressed the soldiers.

Head bowed, Latham only half listened as the commander's thundering yell moderated to a pleasant baritone. He was in the vortex of colliding emotions: his absolved soul strained towards the afterlife. He'd tasted an intoxicating freedom, glimpsed the long-dead mother he'd hardly known dancing a stately pavane. Cocooned in soft white-pink light, she beckoned him forward. The benign vision was brutally dispelled by his still-living flesh propelling air into his lungs. *Must I go back?* His soul protested. Re-entering his earthly skin with a miserable jolt, Latham felt the searing rope burn on his neck, the pain of cracked ribs, groans of stretched thighs. He lived, but for how long?

Struggling to conceal violent shaking, he willed himself to focus on his temporary saviour. The soldiers, suddenly anxious, were also gazing at Don Cristobal. He was stocky, with broad shoulders and muscled legs. Dark curly close-cropped hair framed an angular face. His ears stuck out, as if constantly attuned to danger. He had coal-black eyes, suggesting Moorish co-mingling in his ancestry. Now, these eyes burned through the men and their prisoner, sizing them up. *Pure-bred animal Spain breeds to win its empire,* Latham thought. But there was an anomaly: his clean-shaven mouth allowed shadows from his chin dimple to play on his lips, hinting at a playfulness belied by his razor-sharp features.

Alvarado introduced himself. "Sir, acting sergeant-major, musketeer of Seville, fourteen years' service." He named the others: pikemen with the blunt-tipped hands of former farmers; a lithe, swarthy cavalry officer, and the soft-handed recruit.

Don Cristobal stared at Boels, who'd reclaimed his gun. "Snaphaunce gun. Are you the marksman who woke me this morning?"

"Sir," Boels replied, blushing. "Lieutenant Alvarado will tell you I shot too soon, spooking the prisoner's horse and starting a fire. But I can hold a pike, and I have the algebra to calculate the ratios of guns and pike in mixed squares of any number of men."

"Well, that learning will serve you in ten years," Don Cristobal snorted. "This company has lost a third of its small complement. It has different problems from deploying hordes. Evidently, you're one of them."

Alvarado smirked. The recruit's face seemed half-sculpted in soft clay, awaiting maturity's moulding. Latham began to relax. There were things to observe, and he tried not to think about how long or short his reprieve would be.

"Now, let me inspect the prisoner," Don Cristobal said. He walked over to Latham and pinched his cloak and shirt. The fabrics were as good as what he'd seen through his *looker*. An aristocrat bred for court life, he concluded, who chose a harder path. He noticed the prisoner didn't have the blue eyes that usually accompanied blond hair. Instead, they were hazel, taking on the hue of his surrounds. Against tired pine needles they looked green; touched by the sun, they looked tawny. Chameleon eyes.

"These loyal soldiers say you're their man," he said, gesturing at the Mons battlements. "Are you?"

"I serve King Philip, and have urgent intelligence for Field Marshal Vitelli," Latham coughed. "The Lieutenant says I'm a poxed saboteur, but I only have a cold."

Don Cristobal noted the accented Spanish. "Who do you think he is?" he asked Alvarado.

"Mr No One or Lord Too-many," said Alvarado, "a saboteur. He has travelling papers in three names and hair dye." He handed over Latham's possessions. "He may be plague-poxed, like refugees the rebels sent us last month. He had no servants, no commission, his letter by an Embassy secretary we don't know. Also, a Dutch jeweller the Ninth Company captured couldn't authenticate the ring. If the ring is fake, the pistol's illegal."

Don Cristobal nodded. Small, concealable pistols using flints were banned in much of Europe. He looked at the ring, with its antique, scratched gold band and newer portrait of Philip II. He remembered his father saying rings of this kind were made when Emperor Charles V abdicated.

"Had the jeweller been questioned hard?" he asked Alvarado.

"He doesn't see well anymore," an infantryman conceded.

"Then his caution isn't surprising," Don Cristobal was angry; he didn't believe in torture's utility.

"The prisoner gave an expired password." Alvarado continued.

"How long?" Don Cristobal asked.

"Five weeks, sir."

"If the man came a great distance, and he's bow-legged from riding, is that long?"

"Our rules say two weeks are the limit, soon be shortened to two days. He says he has urgent intelligence, but would tell only Vitelli or one who serves him. He doesn't look like he merits an audience with the field marshal. I couldn't risk letting him into the camp. His intelligence concerns a relief force, but our patrols have seen nothing. He's a saboteur, sir."

Don Cristobal looked at the first travelling paper in the name of Hercules Felipe Gidon. Looking at Latham, he asked "Comment allez-vous, maintenant?"

Latham replied in accented French. "More comfortable than on an inquisitor's rack; less than in a whore's bed."

Don Cristobal tried halting Italian, Dutch, German. The prisoner replied in each tongue. Exasperated, Don Cristobal reverted to Spanish. "You have the advantage of me, for I'm out of tongues, except for Latin, which won't advance our mutual understanding. So, who do you say you are?"

In French, Latham said, "Sir Edward Latham. I'm English, a Catholic as you can see by my silver cross. I was a courtier at Queen Elizabeth's court, but left England for the sake of religion. I care nothing if you hang me, for I was shriven. But many of you will meet their Maker tomorrow if you ignore my intelligence."

His certainty gave Don Cristobal pause. "English expatriates do work for us, but why papers in such silly names? Hercules Felipe Gidon, strong man; Piso Prosperino, suck purse; Ignatius Andrade, the saint Loyola I suppose. All for one body. A jester made these documents. Our diplomats aren't so witty."

"They weren't meant to be seen together," Latham was sullen.

"But our lieutenant has done it. It's natural he thinks you're a rebel."

"Sir, I chose the names, but the documents were executed by Frances de Alava, your ambassador to France until last year. My charge is to discover foreign support of your rebels. It is useful to be Tuscan in La Rochelle, a mongrel in Navarre and Paris. It is a lonely life, with the spectre of the rack, manacles, or years in a prison cell only big enough for an eel. Names carry power; they arm the spirit. I sought their protection since I had little other."

"A master of self-pity, too," Don Cristobal laughed. Then he turned serious. He liked the prisoner. "Yet the armour of many identities nearly got you hanged. Why did you leave England? Many Catholics there stay."

Latham explained the choice as he saw it: hell if he stayed, or self-exile. He raced through his past three years then spoke with urgency. "Despite what your scouts say, a foreign army is approaching. As I waste time talking, they get closer. I learned of it in Paris and have exhausted myself outrunning it. Your army's in danger."

"Well, you babble enough to be English," Don Cristobal said. It was so absurd to travel with valid papers in three names, that the Englishman might be telling the truth. "I serve Field Marshal Chiappino Vitelli, so I can hear your intelligence."

He turned to Alvarado. "Lieutenant, your judgment was reasonable. But I want to hear more before allowing execution. Let the surgeon see him. Bring him to my tent in a half hour, with maps. I'll scribe my decision and accept the consequences. And I'd speak to you privately first."

As Latham was led back across the field, he decided he was glad to be alive. It was too late for Genlis to retreat, or turn east and reach William of Orange. So if Don Cristobal acted on his intelligence, he'd be vindicated. He could still shape events. He pondered the mystery that he knew the French army was real and closing, so his heart raced to the beat of this crisis. Hurry, all is urgent. The Spanish commander knew no such thing; his heart beat to the slow rhythm of checking facts, calculating risks, not least to his own career. Yet soon these two rhythms would beat as one, like two separate shadows cast by the morning sun fusing under noon's glare.

Don Cristobal motioned Alvarado to the only chair, while he sat on the bed. He'd cleared the floor for maps; his books, clothes and weapons were piled at the side.

"Lieutenant," he began, "I judge you to be honest, and the taint on the company undeserved. We'll start anew. Brief me on the men's *capacity*. If the spy's credible, can the Eleventh Company fight tomorrow? I know it was established at 250 men, with pike, muskets and cavalry, but is presently at 168."

Alvarado nodded. "The cavalry is too small to charge by itself, but could support others. We have musket and pike that can fight now. Three boy drummers are also crossbowers. I drill them every day." He frowned and continued cautiously, "but not in mixed square. I grew up on Seville's streets. I've seen a lot of action and have my alphabet, but no mathematics."

He's relieved to have a leader, Don Cristobal thought. *Good, no push and pull over old loyalties.* He understood Alvarado's self-confessed limitations. The modern integration of pike and firearms within one square posed technical problems beyond many officers. First, calculating the ratio of pike to gunmen required facility with equations. It had to take into account the spacing of men within and between rows, which was affected by the thickness of armour, the time gunners took to re-load and the range of their guns. The arquebus had a shorter range than the musket, but mixed squares often contained both weapons, and casualties changed the mix. A barely literate veteran like Alvarado would rise no higher than his present rank, whereas a puppy like William Boels, with algebra, could supersede him. Both men knew it, which explained the tension between them.

"Thank you, Lieutenant. Now let's test the prisoner's tale."

Latham was wearing a brown prisoner's robe. Its front stuck to the hardening bandage around his chest, which smelled of rancid fat, egg white, and flour. His wrists were tied in front of him, and a sprained ankle was wrapped in parchment under shackles. His face was red, but he was breathing easily and had stopped coughing.

He's been scorch-washed, Don Cristobal thought. *Steam inhalations; no excuse for lack of plain speaking. Good.*

With the map secured on the floor by books, Alvarado pointed out patrol routes. "One patrol looked for Orange, who's raised twenty thousand Germans. No sign of them. We run constant patrols looking for rebel Sea Beggars coming from the coast. And we go south, close to the French border."

"Well, Hercules Prosperino Ignatius," Don Cristobal said. "Where's your army?"

Latham pointed. "This morning it was two days south-east of Saint-Ghislain. It is led by one of your rebels escaped from Mons, Jean Haguet de Genlis. It formed on the estate of the French Huguenot, Admiral Gaspard de Coligny. It marched through the French king's lands. " He pointed again. "They had right-of-passage…"

"Oh, come on," Don Cristobal was suddenly hostile. "You expect me to believe the French king, a virtuous Catholic, allowed this?"

"I saw the document," Latham said mulishly. "Then they swung back."

Silently, the soldiers studied the map.

Finally, Don Cristobal said, "I did hear Genlis escaped." He turned to Alvarado. "Is it true?"

"It could be, sir. The siege walls aren't closed yet."

Latham cut in. "He came to Paris. Our ambassador begged the French king not to receive him. His Majesty complied, but my informer said Huguenot leader, Admiral Coligny, met him. They fought together in 1567 in a Huguenot army. Genlis raised troops so quickly that King Charles must have approved. The French king wants peace between his religious parties. He'd wink at a Huguenot foreign adventure as long as his role was hidden. If you capture Genlis, I warrant you'll find documents exposing French policy stitched into a seam of his clothing."

Don Cristobal stared at the map, frowning. He could never keep track of French policy. The shifts were unknowable even to the French, he suspected. However, a royal writ of passage for a Huguenot army to invade the Catholic Spanish Netherlands was the last thing he expected. He wasn't surprised scouts hadn't bothered to patrol the border near the French king's lands.

"Is the route plausible?" he asked the cavalry officer.

"Plausible? Yes, sir," the officer replied, his tone sceptical. "But once in our Hainault province, they'd be in territory friendly to us, hostile to them. If they ate off the land, they'll have local enemies."

"What strength?" Don Cristobal asked Latham,

"I observed heavy cavalry about fifteen hundred, six thousand infantry, no pikemen," Latham said. "But they expect one thousand pikemen, already marching from Genlis' lands. I suspect their plan but can't prove it."

Alvarado was torn between his realisation of Genlis' likely goal and his reluctance to concede he'd nearly hanged their agent. But after a moment he said, "Sir, they're after Saint-Ghislain. Take outlier towns and gradually encircle the besiegers; standard tactic. I've heard Saint-Ghislain has rebels ready to open the gates, like Mons. If they take Saint-Ghislain and get pikemen, they'll be of some account."

"Or they could join Orange and not bother us," one of the pikemen said. "I don't believe they'd dare mess with Vitelli. And the Duke of Alva's army will be here soon."

"You're sure about heavy cavalry?" Don Cristobal asked Latham. "How armed?"

"Firearms, mace and lance. I was close to them for days."

"Old-fashioned mace?" Don Cristobal's eyes gleamed at the thought of cavalry using clubs with spiked metal heads against arquebus and pike. "Why?"

"I enticed his courier to blab. He said Orange wrote to Genlis, urging him to combine armies, just as this gentleman said." Latham nodded at the pikeman. "But the courier also spoke of Genlis' grief at the suffering of friends in the city that he'd just escaped, which is Mons. I believe Genlis took what he could get in a hurry, assuming that, with the element of surprise, he could venture something glorious before your siege ring closes."

The soldiers debated, and Latham shuffled over to look at Don Cristobal's books. There were classic texts by Vegetius and Aelian on infantry discipline; a modern Neapolitan book of tables for mixed squares; Latin poetry; a book in Spanish on the money-saving merits of mules over oxen in field ploughing; and what looked like personal journals. *A scholar of war and other things*, Latham thought. If Don Cristobal was concerned about frugal farming, he was of the poor warrior gentry class, whose ancestral estates divided over generations, leaving difficult-to- manage parcels. He picked up the nearest journal.

"Over here, spy," Don Cristobal shouted, furious. "Leave my books."

"Could I ask you a question, sir?" Latham asked, shuffling back, confident his vindication was close. "This tent is far from the tree I was roped to. How did you know to stop my hanging?"

Don Cristobal laughed. "Don't mistake my manners for acceptance. You're not proven friend or foe. Stop or postpone. I'll explain if your merits are established. I'm taking your intelligence to Field Marshal Vitelli. Lieutenant, secure the prisoner until my return."

"So you see, my Lord," Don Cristobal concluded to Field Marshal Vitelli, "we're in a vice. We must decide now whether to act on intelligence from a stranger, or ignore it. Our scouts won't have time to verify this force and get back before the Mons lookouts spot friendly banners. The rebels will send out raiders. We could be engaged on two fronts; even three, if Orange arrives with his bought Germans."

Vitelli nodded, chewing a pear tart. His dinner platters took up most of the table, forcing Don Cristobal to hold up his map and point. One plate with coagulated beef fat; one with quail bones picked clean and a half-eaten fat cheese; a bowl of Spanish oranges and local cherries untouched. Vitelli savoured the tart.

How fat he is; he can't be long for this world, Don Cristobal thought, glancing at a litter on the floor. Vitelli's shoulders and stomach strained the seams of his brocaded doublet. His grey hair was crinkly, with the greasy texture of a man who sweats constantly. He had cut his beard in a horseshoe shape which emphasised, rather than minimised, his obesity. But his eyes were shrewd. He was no buffoon, in high command because of blood. He was Spain's master tactician. Don Cristobal revered him.

"Your spy's ring is genuine," Vitelli said languidly, rolling it in his hand. "It takes me back to simpler times, before religious wars scrambled all our alliances." He sighed.

"My Lord, I'm relieved you authenticate the ring, because I believe the Englishman. He has wit and courage," Don Cristobal said, beaming.

"Wait, you frisk too soon. The ring proves your man's access, not his loyalty," Vitelli snapped. "If Zuniga, our ambassador to France, liked him, he'd have signed the letter, not sent him off with second secretary scribbling. Under normal circumstances, I'd reject your proposal: an impetuous commander urging action before he's met his men, tainted by corruption as I recall…"

"My Lord, may I speak?"

Vitelli frowned. He didn't like interruptions.

"Action could raise morale," Don Cristobal persisted.

Vitelli rang a bell. Two white-gloved servants entered with marzipans, cleared the table and left.

"However," Vitelli said, "because circumstances are *not* normal, I must consider your proposal. Tell me what you know about our situation."

"Dutch rebel pirates, the Sea Beggars, captured the coastal town of Brill in April. Then Mons opened its gates to soldiers of Sea Beggars and Count Louis of Nassau, brother of the rebel leader, Prince William of Orange. We besiege Mons to get it back."

"That's the basic situation," Vitelli agreed. "But you need to know more to understand how abnormal the circumstances are. We've *never* lost a land battle. When our enemies see us coming, they often surrender before fighting, which is wonderfully convenient. But we made a policy mistake last year whose consequences led directly to the nuisance of having to retake Mons. Today, we look foolish, not so terrifying. It's not just Mons we must recapture, but our reputation."

He paused, looking thoughtfully at Don Cristobal.

"What do you know about a plot by England's Duke of Norfolk, a Catholic, to marry Mary, Queen of Scots; topple the Protestant English Queen, Elizabeth; make Mary queen and return England to Catholicism?"

"Little, my Lord. I ready men for battle."

"You should pay attention to politics. If you fight Genlis tomorrow, it is because of Norfolk's dream. King Philip agreed to support him with men and munitions. We moved our cannon and ammunition from Mons to Brill, ready to ship to England on Norfolk's signal. No army escorted the weapons because Brill was quiet. But Elizabeth learned about the plot, and tried and executed Norfolk. Brill was still full of weapons and lightly defended. When the Sea Beggars captured Brill, they got the weapons too. Shorn of heavy weapons, Mons surrendered. The Sea Beggars re-armed Mons with our weapons from Brill. We besiege the town we stripped. Satan is bursting his belly cackling at our folly."

He looks beaten, Don Cristobal thought. "I see the stain on our reputation."

"Good. There is hope for you." Vitelli reached for quill and pen. "I like to draw." He sketched a boy-king face, a light scrawl evoking a first moustache over thin lips. "French King Charles IX. Burgundy used to be French. They yearn for it again."

Then a narrow, watchful female face, Queen Elizabeth: "The Netherlands is our richest tax-harvesting province, *and* England's richest trading partner. Elizabeth misliked our trying to kill her!" He chuckled. "She might dabble here if there's no risk."

Then a round face with an open mouth, next to a sack with coins tumbling out: "Diverse German rulers, feeling poor."

Don Cristobal started to laugh.

"They sell mercenaries to everyone," Vitelli said. "All eyes will be on Genlis. If we rout him and capture incriminating French documents, French Charles and English Elizabeth won't covertly support more action. William of Orange will march his Germans around, but won't fight us. Remember, we've never lost a land battle. If William's men die, he'll have trouble buying more. Genlis must be the fool; not us."

"Sergeant Major, you risk much. We don't know where our governor, the Duke of Alva, is, with his twenty thousand men. But although our forces are thin and we're lamentably ignorant about your spy, for policy reasons I must approve an ambush. You'll lead your new company…"

Action, ambrosia to professional soldiers. Don Cristobal smiled broadly. "Thank you."

"Don't cheer too soon. It Genlis appears unchallenged, my reputation will be tarnished. I can't ignore this intelligence. But if you march and find nothing, that will clap a stopper on your career. You said earlier that *we* are in a vice. *You* are in the vice. This spy is your burden. I won't meet him or assess his merit.

"I'll send four thousand foot and our light cavalry. We'll be vastly outnumbered…" Vitelli looked up, his mouth spreading in a feral grin. "But with a cunning enough plan, we'll win. Frederic of Toledo, the Duke of Alva's son, will command. Do you know this terrain?"

"Regretfully, no, my Lord," Don Cristobal replied.

"No matter," Vitelli continued. "Your officers do." He spread Don Cristobal's map on the table. "Here, a commercial road lined by bushes, woods then farms beyond, bypass tracks good for flanking, leading to Quievrain. This is where Genlis will march his army, if it has more substance than saboteurs' vapours. Genlis' surprise will be ours. I'll place you on the ambush line where he should be. You deserve to take him and his papers. Toledo will move small groups out now, to avoid notice by Mons lookouts. The rest march tonight. Meet your men and send me any you don't need. Well, you've got much to do; so do I."

Don Cristobal sank into a low bow, ready to leave.

"There is a chain of being in policy," Vitelli said, stopping him. "A sound chain rises to heaven, glorious in God's service. But one corroded link breaks the chain. Our rotten link was supporting English Norfolk. Build me a new chain. I like an adventurer, but take care how you give your heart to spies. God be with you tomorrow."

CHAPTER 5
AMBUSH
AT SAINT-
GHISLAIN, A
MOMENT OF
CLARITY

Don Cristobal was wearing light armour when he next met his men. He had two pistols and a sword at his belt, to show that, unlike their last commander Gutierrez, he fought close.

Over one hundred infantrymen stood in the field. About half carried pike, twelve, fifteen or eighteen feet long. The rest carried arquebuses, muskets and pistols. In addition, there were eight youngsters with drums, three also with cross-bows. Forty light cavalrymen stood at the field's side. Both scepticism and eagerness showed in their stares.

There was no prescribed uniform, apart from a patch or sash with company colours. Boots were red, black and brown, high or low. Some gunners wore helmets; others had cloth caps; some pikemen wore armour, others only padded jerkins.

"Men of the Eleventh Company," Don Cristobal cried, "I am your new sergeant-major, Don Cristobal Covarrulejo d'Avila. My authority is advanced one day. My ancestors were crusaders in the Holy Land, and I've been a fighting soldier for fifteen years. We believe a French army approaches Saint-Ghislain. Field Marshal Vitelli has granted my plea to ambush it."

He let a buzz of exclamations roll, then shouted for quiet. "Comrades, a taint of thievery clings to you, but I believe you're more sinned against than sinners. Tomorrow you will confound your detractors. We'll be outnumbered, but that tends to our greater glory. We don't know each other, you and I, but I promise, if we weld our courage to Vitelli's cunning, we'll win a famous victory. I told the field marshal you could fight now. Show me what you can do."

Alvarado led them through drills: target shooting for gunners and crossbowers; cavalry charging pike squares, wheeling and firing as they charged again. Don Cristobal stared with maximum intensity, noting which gunners were quickest to re-load, which pike calmest and strongest. He was pleased that Alvarado had kept their skills up, sparing him the excruciating humiliation of having to tell Vitelli his men weren't ready to fight, after all. He whispered his dispositions to the lieutenant.

When reorganising was done, Don Cristobal explained. "Comrades, Field Marshal Vitelli has granted the Eleventh Company a position close to where the enemy ensign should be. This is because I brought the information about the French army. We're to capture their leader, Jean Haguet de Genlis, alive, with his papers. It's an honour; we must succeed. Cavalry, you manoeuvre well, but this ambush offers no scope for riding. You'll augment Commander Toledo's cavalry. Pikemen with fifteen- and eighteen-foot pike, you'll join Toledo's mixed gun and pike squares, to repel the enemy's heavy cavalry charge. Arquebusiers and musketeers who took two minutes to re-load will fight in the ambush lines. I know who you are. Now, speed is not essential, but accuracy is, and will determine success. I tell you, your greatest challenge tomorrow will be silence. Surprise depends on it. He who shouts or shoots before time will be hanged. All officers are telling this to their men."

He motioned a group holding twelve-foot pikes, and selected gunmen, to stand aside, then finished his address. "Comrades, clean and hone your weapons, eat, rest. See the priest. Make sure your will is in order. We march at moonrise. Carry double rations of water; the wait will be long and hot. You are commoners: farmers, labourers, clerks, blacksmiths, fishermen, fornicators, tender fathers, cut-purses. But tomorrow, Imperial Spain's honour depends on you, not on dukes and barons. You're dismissed."

To those who remained, he explained, "You gunmen re-loaded in one minute. You'll form three small mixed squares, with me, with the short pike. At the right time, we'll force our way through Genlis' guard. He has halberdiers, gunners and swordsmen, no pike. Each gunman will carry an arquebus, sword and brace of pistols."

He drilled his little mixed squares until the sun plopped below the horizon. At the evening officers' briefing, Vitelli's plan elicited whistles of admiration for its astuteness. Don Cristobal's last act before moonrise was to visit Latham, who was sleeping in a hut, under guard.

Latham jerked awake at taps on his hardened bandage. Biting his lips in pain, he stared up at the white teeth gleaming from the stocky figure, made ominous by lantern light.

"You're healing," Don Cristobal said. "We threw dice, and your intelligence came up. In my world of simple soldiering, Sir Edward, a man reaps what he sows; words become action. You come with us. I'll get you a mount. If Genlis arrives, you'll fight him too. If he doesn't, I'll make you answer for your treachery, in advance of my ruin for trusting you."

He turned to leave then came back, his expression softer. "See here," he said, tossing Latham a bag smelling of camphor and crackling with dried leaves. "Coco leaves. Our Indian savages chew them for pain and endurance. Pray God favours you tomorrow."

Late the next morning, Don Cristobal scraped his forehead against the furrowed bark of an ash tree to relieve his itch. Leaves formed a canopy of dusty green, the tiredness of heat long starved of rain. The woods were calm, as if all sensible animals had fled. Occasional plump bees buzzed desultorily at wilted honeysuckle blossoms. The only ebullient life forms were mosquitoes, delirious at the pungent flesh that had intruded into their world in such abundance. Whining, they plunged their suckers into sweating necks and hands, or wriggled under shirts, where the terrain was flat, and safe from grinding thumbs. Don Cristobal had forbidden his men to slap or talk; he heard whispered curses.

In front of him, arquebusiers squatted behind the tangle of bushes separating them from the road. They'd cut holes through foliage for their guns and were playing dice, using hand signals to call bets, piles of leaves signifying winnings. Between groups of arquebusiers, heavier muskets were supported by gun forks, with clearings wide enough for good aim. To deter breaches from the road, stakes had been banged into the earth. The musketeers lounged against trees or checked powder and shot. Deep in the woods, marksmen and crossbowers stood by assigned trees, watching for the signal to scramble up to perches on the branches. All knew their feral stillness was mirrored on the other side of the road.

A large contingent of pikemen and gunners waited in the woods close to Saint-Ghislain, ready to form a square and repel the expected French heavy cavalry charge, while a smaller formation waited at a bypass track. When fighting began, the small square was to attack Genlis' rear, capturing wagons and papers. More pikemen were dispersed among the gunmen, to support the close fighting Vitelli believed would be the battle's final stage.

Don Cristobal had given Latham a padded jerkin before tying him to a tree, under Alvarado's guard. Latham's sword, wheellock pistol and a musket lay near him. If the enemy materialised, Alvarado was to free him and give him a place in the line. Latham's excitement mounted as he absorbed the impatience of soldiers around him.

During the previous afternoon, Vitelli had sent messengers loaded with silver to local peasants, buying right of way for his troops. The hint that plunder could be theirs tomorrow if they stilled their tongues, had fallen on eager ears. Peasants were gathering in barley fields and orchards beyond the woods.

At last, from the direction of Saint-Ghislain, came the sound of hooves chewing up the dry road. The Spanish light cavalry was making its move. Arquebusiers stopped their games; musketeers uncurled from their slouch. As if they were one multi-limbed body, the Eleventh Company stirred. At Don Cristobal's nod of permission, some men scaled trees while others wriggled to the road ditch. When their own cavalry galloped by, carrying pennants with the red diagonal cross on green and white stripes, the men blew kisses at them. Waves of cavalrymen thrust up lances or brandished pistols, grinning at their earthbound comrades. These cavalrymen wore only padded leather, no armour. They were bait.

Hoofbeats faded. Quiet pressed again, and soldiers in the ditch crawled back to their posts to wait. And wait. And resume their war with mosquitoes. Time stretched to eternity. The air became stifling and hostile.

As he walked from group to group, Don Cristobal felt a malevolence more palpable than the heat hit his back. The excited cohesion of last night's march had gone, and his company was dissolving into angry cliques. One man whispered, "Kill the Englishman. He stuck us in this miasma so we'll get the sweats," and was answered by curses of agreement. Without chastising the whisperer, he tripled Latham's guard. Had he been too quick to trust the Englishman? *Our fates are tied*, he thought gloomily, patrolling with a confident smile welded to his face.

Latham saw his doubts. Hands shaking, he crammed the last coco leaves into his mouth.

Another eternity passed.

Finally, harsh honks shattered the quiet. Geese flew above, invisible through leaf canopies, but loud, urgent and many. Masses of sparrows exploded into the air, their *chit chuk, chit chuk* now an agitated *tek tek tek tek*. Birds did scouts' work, trumpeting imminent action.

First, the vibrations: a heaving of the whole earth beneath their feet: stretching, contracting, under the tumult of approaching hooves. Don Cristobal sighed with relief as his men began to smile. Motioning for quiet, he checked his deployments one last time. There was a rustle of bodies easing into position, a clink of muskets on gun forks, the hiss of matches burning, grunts of marksmen and crossbowers shimmying up trees.

Alvarado freed Latham and placed him at a gun fork. "Fire true, Sir No one of Lord Too Many," he rasped. "I'm watching."

They heard the drumming of iron on dirt, the pop-popping of light cavalry pistols, panicked shouts from the fleeing Spanish cavalry. Not far behind were the cracks of arquebus shots and whoops in French. Further away, just audible, were insistent drums and the robust chanting of trudging infantry. Genlis' army existed, after all.

"Help! Thousands of them! Help!" screamed the Spanish horsemen. Peering through the gap made for his gun fork,

Latham recognised Eleventh Company colours on two of the horsemen flying past silent ambushers. He wondered if all of them were acting fearful, or if some were truly terrified by the horde they'd provoked. Once out of range of French shot, the light Spanish cavalry wheeled, trotted back, keeping their mounts turning as they pop-popped pistols or threw lances. Balls slammed the earth and trees around them as they fled again, crying, "Help!" By little and little, they enticed the French cavalry into the ambush.

A rider wearing the Spanish commander Toledo's colours lagged behind his comrades. A lance stuck out of his back, and he fell off his horse, one foot tangled in the stirrup. He screamed as the horse bumped him along the ground. Near Latham, one man rasped, "God's death, Pedro Cortes, I know him." Feeling the collective desperation to attack, Don Cristobal tapped shoulders with his sword, motioning silence. Biting their lips, his men controlled themselves.

Now the enemy light cavalry with their gaudy saddlecloths pounded into view. Banners flying, they were yelling, "Cowering milkmaids! Yellow-livered rooting hogs! On! On!"

The first wave rested the butts of their long guns against leather-covered waists and fired as they rode. The horse dragging Toledo's unlucky cavalryman merged into the enemy's herd. French heavy cavalry followed, riders in armour, brandishing lances and mace, their leader shouting, "Saint-Ghislain! For Louis! The day's ours!" Latham had dodged these horsemen for over a week as they ambled at eight miles a day to this moment. Seeing them at full charge left him strangely bemused.

Behind the bushes Don Cristobal motioned silence; again the men bit their lips. "They think they've frighted us to death," Alvarado whispered to him. "What a caper."

"Vitelli's plan," Don Cristobal whispered back.

At the head of the line, Frederic of Toledo listened, red flag raised. When he judged enough French shot was expended he trumpeted, "Fire!"

His sixteen captains rammed down their flags: "Fire! Fire! Fire!"

Bushes and vines erupted in a thousand stabs of flame, smoke, and flying metal. Released from silence, the Spaniards hollered like banshees as they raked the French with crossfire. The arquebusiers peppered horses with balls that seared skin or slammed bones. Simultaneously, musketeers crashed their heavier shot through armour, into chests and backs.

They took the French totally by surprise. Appalled horses reared and plunged toward the deep ditches, trying to throw their riders. The cavalry charge staggered. On both sides of the road, the ambushers kept up a disciplined rhythm. Behind Latham, Don Cristobal, grinning with wolfish ferocity, directed, yelling at the front row to fire, and slip back to re-load, while the second row moved forward and fired, the rows repeatedly swapping.

Through his gap, Latham saw fallen horses and riders. He hadn't fired yet. He'd aimed, but not touched match to powder pan. Picking up the wheellock pistol, he crawled to the ditch and crouched. Smoke snaked at knee level; dust kicked up by agitated horses swirled; balls whizzed, slamming trees, bodies, the ground. Latham stood, pointed at a cavalryman and pulled the trigger. He couldn't see if he'd hit anything, but the horse threw its heavily armoured rider. Twist or turn, the fallen rider couldn't escape hooves coming down on his head. To Latham, watching in stunned horror, everything moved with glacial slowness. Things sped up when the gunman who'd been next to Latham wriggled out and dragged him back. Latham dropped his pistol and picked up the musket. Seeing two dismounted cavalrymen approaching the bushes, he fired. One clutched his stomach while the other fled down the road. Alvarado nodded approvingly and motioned him to the rear, to re-load.

The acrid smell of gunpowder, the steaming tang of mangled human and animal flesh, terrified the next wave of enemy horses. They refused to ride over the mounds on the road. An officer wearing the insignia of Louis of Nassau, with dashing yellow plumes on his helmet and a yellow cloak over armour, took charge.

"A gauntlet, men," he yelled. "That's all. Clear a path."

He kept his horse moving in a circle, ignoring balls whizzing around him, fired his arquebus at one side of the road, pistol at the other. His men managed to drag enough bodies aside to open a path.

"On!" the officer screamed, and charged forward. His men remounted and followed, defying gunfire that felled several more of them. Their heroic effort advanced them a half mile. Eleventh Company men heard their exultant cheers as they passed the ambushers, riding into an oasis of peace.

The gunfire slackened. Don Cristobal signalled to stop firing; there was no one on the road to shoot at. He grabbed his *looker*, climbed a tree and eased himself onto a branch. The French infantry still hadn't appeared, though the drums and singing were louder. He scrambled down, told Alvarado to take over and ran the half mile along the track, to look at the French cavalry who'd survived the crossfire.

Latham offered his water to the young gunman who'd left the ambush line to drag him back to safety. The man's lips were cracked from reloading powder and balls, his ammunition belt half-empty. Through blackened grime he gave Latham a seraphic smile, rustled under his jerkin and showed Latham a tin locket with a drawing of a young woman; his beloved, Latham assumed. Both men prayed, eyes turned to the leaf canopy. In Latham's heightened alertness, he'd never seen leaf veins so intricately articulated.

Don Cristobal found the yellow-cloaked French officer's remaining riders stopped in a quiet place, between the ambushing gunners and Toledo's hidden pikemen and musketeers. Breathing in ragged gasps, they sipped from their flasks while they waited for more cavalry to join them. When about three hundred had come up, the yellow-plumed officer thrust his sword forward and ordered a new charge. "We've won!" he cried. "We've done it! Saint-Ghislain for Louis."

The horses hadn't even hurtled from trot to canter before they skidded to a halt. There appeared–seemly from nowhere–a bend in the road in front of them, woods on their left and their right, a quick-forming mixed square. The French cavalry charged, but in a single motion the pikemen lowered their weapons. The blades of the eighteen-foot pikes in the second row protruded between the fifteen-foot pikes in the first row, creating a solid wall of steel. Not ready to give up, the French officer tried again, with guns. The cavalry wheeled around, lined up and fired at the Spaniards. Toledo's men crouched as the barrage roared overhead. Then the pikemen stood and pushed forward, three rows of Spanish gunners protected within the square shooting and revolving rows too quickly for the French to re-load.

Some enemy horses headed for the narrow clearings in the bushes, but stopped at the sharp stakes. They backed out, confused, into the road. All the while the pikemen walked forward, taunting as they slashed and chopped. The French cavalry slowly retreated, towards the crossfire they'd just escaped.

Don Cristobal ran back to the Eleventh Company, climbed a tree again and trained his *looker* right, where the French cavalry was bunching in disorderly retreat; and left, where the infantry came into view, and enemy ensigns. He calculated where they'd be in twenty minutes, then slid to the ground shouting, "Fire again!" Across the road, his mirror commander gave the same command.

Terror engulfed the French cavalry. Sounding the trumpet to withdraw, they fled. But obstructing their headlong retreat was their own infantry, which hadn't fought yet. Now the French army fought itself, as the cavalry forced its way through the advancing infantry. Riders trampled and slashed everything in their path, and appalled foot soldiers shot and slashed back.

Seeing this, Spanish officers signalled their men to stop firing. It was quiet in the long ambush lines, as if they were forgotten. Through broken bushes, amazed Spaniards saw enemy foot soldiers dragging riders out of their saddles and stabbing them, cavalry smashing their finally-useful maces down on their own infantry. Genlis' army collapsed into self-cannibalising, fear-maddened bands.

The ambushers laughed with relief. Belly-straining roars of never-ending laughter rolled along both sides of the road, persuading the French who were still upright that Satan himself was behind the bushes. This had been Vitelli's strategy, to get the French army to destroy itself for the convenience of his outnumbered men.

During the respite, Don Cristobal found Alvarado. "Call squares. Time to find Genlis." In a few minutes, the men he'd chosen to capture Genlis assembled. Two had broken arms. Alvarado motioned Latham and Boels to pick up their pikes and join the reserve square. Don Cristobal led the grimy but bright-eyed soldiers along an old deer path towards the point he calculated Genlis would have reached. They trotted over shallow tree roots whose skins were scraped by rushing boots, over crushed vegetation whose musky scent filled their nostrils. The numbing pleasure of coco leaves masked the pain of Latham's bandaged ribs, and he trotted with as much excitement as his mates. The men sang an adaptation of an old Spanish epic.

> Mons may well be joyful, but great should be its grief.
> For Spain will kill its guardian and Orange lose his chief,
> Our gallant soldiers pour like rivers o'er the land,
> To disembowel invaders and bring rebellion's end.

They passed the surgeon's tent, where wounded Spaniards and a few French soldiers waited grimly for sawing and poulticing administered by blood-soaked hands.

Past the medical tent, Don Cristobal paused and peered over blackened bushes. There, a few hundred yards to the left, were two enemy ensigns. The first was a gold lion on blue and yellow, colours of the Dutch rebel Count Louis of Nassau, who was holding Mons. The other was a black cross on white, colours of French Huguenot leader, Admiral Gaspard de Coligny. Genlis was marching under both flags. About fifteen cavalry and thirty infantry guarded them.

Don Cristobal ordered his gunmen to load small shot in the arquebus and balls in their pistols. He led the first square, Alvarado, with their colours, the second, a pikeman the reserve.

"Squares," Don Cristobal yelled, "crouch until their first round of fire, then you pike hack arms and necks, gunmen shoot chests and faces! Square one, attack!"

The first square pushed onto the road. Body by body they forced themselves through Genlis' protectors, disappearing into a mass of enemy fighters. Waiting, Latham was vaguely aware of Spanish horns back up the road ordering a general charge into the remaining French forces. Alvarado led his square onto the road.

Then the reserve square crossed the ditch. Latham was suffused with fear. Somehow, he'd been shuffled into the front line. His knees knocked, his teeth chattered, his hands shook on the pikestaff, which wobbled. This was fighting more exposed yet more hemmed-in than anything he'd known.

"Don't hit me," snarled the man next to him as they inched forward.

Latham lost awareness of his body. His skin felt as if it was dissolving into diffuse sparklets. He didn't know if he even had a skin. He floated forward because the man behind him pushed. He saw his soul looking down from the ether, pitying the fragile frame that tottered into the chaos of clashing swords and gun smoke, coldly reckoning the credits and debits of its brief life.

A feral scream issued from his mouth when his mind finally named the gun pointing at his head as French, the glare of the hating eyes of a killer. His paralysis unlocked. He felt the spirit of Mars lift his pike and chop through his enemy's arm and into his chest. The Frenchman collapsed, his comrades kicked him aside and lurched forward.

My God, like quartering a hen, Latham thought. Filled with a sense of limitlessness and fierce exhilaration, he hacked and pushed. In a few minutes, Don Cristobal's squares linked up, trying to encircle Genlis' guards.

Genlis had dismounted. Next to his flag-bearer, he was fighting fiercely. A tall, saturnine figure, he sidestepped a pike slash and ducked in to ram his sword into his attacker's waist, then leapt back to parry a sword thrust from a Spaniard who stepped in front of the wounded pikeman.

Many of Don Cristobal's pikemen were wounded now. He and his gunmen had no protection but their light armour. Sword in one hand, pistol in the other, Don Cristobal shook sweat from his forehead and peered over chest-high smoke. Just in front of him was the blue ensign. As he lunged for it, he felt a smash on his face. Blood spurted down his neck as a ball nicked his jaw. Cursing, he tripped over a corpse and fell to his knees.

So, so close to victory! As he heaved himself up, pulling out his third pistol, two of Genlis' halberdiers rushed him. Alvarado stepped in front of them, extending his pike. One halberd clanged on the metal blade, the other thudded into the wooden shaft and stuck. Alvarado held his pike steady, his face white as the concussion shot pain from his wrist to his neck.

"Yield, your day is lost!" screamed Don Cristobal at Genlis, scrambling to his feet.

"No!" Genlis shouted.

"Yield or die! Look around you!" Don Cristobal yelled again.

Genlis saw the wrong colours—red on green and white—surrounding him. Taking a great risk, Don Cristobal dropped his pistol and signalled for a pause. Genlis motioned his men to stop fighting. The two leaders faced each other.

Stasis amidst chaos. While the crack of gunfire and the screech of pike on steel went on around them, Don

Cristobal's and Genlis' men stilled like a sculpted frieze, faces black with powder, smoking gun barrels and bloody swords pointed down.

"Captain Genlis," Don Cristobal shouted, "your cavalry slashes your foot, your foot shoots your cavalry. Most of your army is dead. Your flag-bearers stand, but not for long. Stop. I promise you honourable terms. You fought bravely today."

Only five of Genlis' guards were still standing; faces pinched with exhaustion. Shoulders slumping, Genlis bowed and offered his sword. Don Cristobal grabbed both ensigns and handed Genlis to Alvarado, who led him into the woods. Hobbling after them, Don Cristobal called a page to carry the captured ensigns to the Spanish commander, then waved Latham to join him.

About fifteen minutes later, horns began to sound, and shouts came in several languages to stop fighting. The sounds of gunfire and clashing metal became intermittent, then stopped altogether. In the sudden calm, the bells of Saint-Ghislain, the town Genlis had aimed to take, rang out. The great monastery chapel clanged its alert incessantly, a slow, measured toll. But cutting into the decay between these chimes were strange jangles—high-pitched treble bells rung backwards, shrieking a warning to the town's Protestants to flee.

Only a few hundred of Genlis' men were unscathed. Most of them were fleeing into the woods, making for nearby farms. Toledo's trumpeter sounded a stay-in-place order, restraining pursuers. "Let them go. It's arranged. They won't get far," captains told their men.

Meanwhile, Don Cristobal led a gloomy Genlis to Toledo's tent, while Alvarado organised a search for documents at the supply wagons.

Genlis thought he'd surrendered to the devil. The blood on Don Cristobal's neck had clotted, but one side of his head was grossly purple. Soot-soaked sweat covered his sharp-featured face, out of which black eyes glowered, and white teeth grinned in ferocious satisfaction. Nevertheless, he spoke gently. "Captain Genlis, you fought with great courage. But you were undone by our intelligencers and Vitelli's cunning. I assure you we'll treat you befitting your noble rank. Of course, we must look at your papers and ask some questions."

"I'll be your noble adversary as long as I have secrets to give up. Then you'll call me a traitor who deserves death," replied Genlis bitterly. "I know your ways. What about my surviving men?"

"Your officers can retrieve your wounded and bury the dead. Captives we treat according to the customs of war–we're not barbarians –but those who ran for the fields are in God's hands. I believe you lived off the land on your march. The peasants won't love you for taking their grain, maybe killing those who stood in your way."

Genlis shuddered. "Can't something be done? My men enlisted to fight and die for true religion, not to be battered to death by low-born cow-pat eaters."

"A few might get to Mons," Don Cristobal replied, with a trace of pity. "But even we can't stop a mob bent on plunder."

Genlis fell silent. Now he grasped the Spanish tactics: manipulate his men into killing each other and let Dutch peasants finish off the rest. As he walked with Don Cristobal, he saw how vastly his forces had outnumbered the Spaniards. He was shamed.

By now the sun was low in the sky, spewing rays that tinged leaves with shimmering gold. Alvarado and his party returned from their search of supply wagons, leading mules loaded with sacks, which they carried into the command tent. When he emerged, his smile was as close to radiant as his pummeled face would allow. Don Cristobal beckoned him over.

"Official papers," Alvarado reported, "and French gold and silver coins. You judged the Englishman right, sir. I give thanks to the Almighty that you stopped the hanging." Suddenly noticing a grimy Latham, he bowed deeply to him. "It's a blessed day for the Eleventh Company. They were heroes," Alvarado concluded.

Don Cristobal frowned. *Heroic* was too strong, unearned. "They were steady," he temporised. "We were lucky in our adversary. They obliged us by killing each other. Vitelli is today's hero. Bring William Boels here. He saw action for the first time, like Latham."

"Boels, Latham," Don Cristobal said when Alvarado returned. "You need to see war's busy aftermath. It doesn't stop when a defeated general offers the victor his sword, and they get ready to swap war stories over dinner. That moment of clarity is short."

Overhead a hawk drifted lazily, looking for the indiscreet twitch of a rabbit tail. New sounds were coming from nearby farms: the squeak of wagon wheels; the snorts of mules; guttural shouts. Moments later, in the fields abutting the woods, there were pleading male voices in French, abuse in Dutch, many shrieking screams. No need to get a close look to know what was happening.

Latham went white. The spirit of limitless ferocity that had filled him during battle dissipated. He stared into a dark corner of his soul. Feeling confused, he leaned against a pine tree.

William Boels bent over and threw up. Latham thought his features had firmed since yesterday. "They're Flemings, these murderers," Boels muttered over and over.

Alvarado saw Boels in distress. "Best to be on the winning side, Fleming. That's Spain."

Boels nodded. He wiped his mouth, stood and kissed his arm patch with the red diagonal cross on green and white stripes. *I'll cleave to the winning side and rise higher than him*, he promised himself.

Genlis had kept a stony dignity when surrendering, but he was now weeping.

"Wouldn't you have done better to join Orange, as he requested?" Don Cristobal asked, ushering him back into the command tent.

"You know that?" Genlis was astonished. "The letter?"

"We know everything," Don Cristobal replied, unable to keep smugness out of his voice. "I told you our intelligence is excellent." Inwardly he thanked Latham. *He's the best fellow in the whole world. I'm deep in his debt.*

That night, most of the ambushers marched back to camp by torchlight, bringing prisoners and plunder. Latham rode with them, for Alvarado had orders to secure him in the prisoner's hut until Don Cristobal briefed Vitelli. The Spanish commander, Frederic of Toledo, was ecstatic. He'd found a letter with a French royal seal when he slit open a seam of Genlis' doublet. "Crown jewels," he'd told his aides, grinning as he imagined Vitelli's satisfaction. Several officers remained, to direct Spanish and French soldiers in the next day's task, gathering wounded, digging pits and burying the dead.

In the morning, thick clouds closed in over a road full of corpses. There were few wounded to physic. It began to rain, slow drops then a cascading torrent. Water poured down ruts in the parched road, turning it to soupy mud. The living became sodden ghost-like beasts of burden, hardly distinguishable from the mud-spattered dead they dragged into carts pulled by miserable mules. Bodies tumbled into heaps of corpses in burial pits: lowly foot soldiers; proud officers; brown, blue, green, hazel eyes equally vacant. One of the corpses sliding out of a cart onto the quivering mass was a cavalry officer wearing a ripped yellow cloak with Louis of Nassau's insignia. A crossbow bolt stuck out of his chest, and his black-bearded face was frozen in a shocked grimace. Buckets of lime, then topsoil, were hurled onto the piles. Chaplains tried their best. Wind gusts blew up their robes as they prayed, exposing their legs to battering hail, snatching absolutions from their mouths and hurling them at gyrating tree branches. Such were the funeral services for the fallen. Dead horses were pulled into the woods and left for scavengers. Maggots, flies, bears and crows made the most of the battered remains of soldiers the peasants plundered. What was left, peasants dug under, the next dry day.

CHAPTER 6
A BOND

"We routed them, thanks to you, Sir Edward," Don Cristobal began in his bluffest tone. Then he hesitated. Rope burns on Latham's neck embarrassed him. Bowing, he said, "I apologise formally that we nearly hanged you." After dismissing the guard, he unshackled Latham and stood back. "Sir, you can stay or go. When you leave, we'll replace your hired nag. I'll also give you a good horse from my stable."

Latham shook out arms stiff from wielding pike. "I'll wait for instruction," he replied.

"Do you want more coco leaves?" Don Cristobal asked.

"No, thank you." Latham washed his face and hands, then glanced at Don Cristobal. One side of his face was bloated, with yellowing bruises and a livid scar; the other side angular. He looked like a half-painted gargoyle, of the wickedest kind. That both their skins had taken a beating in the same cause, hit them. They laughed and shook hands.

"These wounds bind us," Don Cristobal said, walking Latham to the private tent set up for him. Yesterday seemed a decade away.

"Please call me just Edward, Latham volunteered.

Don Cristobal was startled. "Edward? Not sir? You were gentry yesterday. Are you an impostor? Listen, I swear to lock up your secret and lose the key, so please be honest."

"Of course I'm no impostor," Latham grinned. "That lie could easily be proved. I've been knighted twice, but I don't use the title, except for yesterday, when I was trying to get better odds against the rope."

"I see," Don Cristobal said crisply, as if Latham had said something obvious. But anxiety creasing the intact side of his face showed his confusion.

"You don't see," Latham laughed. "But it is simple. The English queen knighted me to thank my father for supporting her heretical religion. I left her court, preferring to serve a Catholic monarch. Mary, Queen of Scots, knighted me to raise me high enough to represent her in France. So the one who rules I no longer serve, while the one I served no longer rules. Both titles are meaningless."

"Well!" Don Cristobal was astonished by this renunciation. "It shows great delicacy to be plain Edward with two titles honestly bestowed."

Latham frown signalled the end of the subject.

When Don Cristobal praised the integrity of renouncing two knighthoods to Vitelli, the Field Marshal just chuckled. "My dear fellow, which of these queens would most resent your spy calling himself *Sir*?"

After thinking, Don Cristobal replied, "The one who rules: England's Elizabeth."

"So," Vitelli reasoned with weary patience, "he doesn't wish to offer her greater insult than he already has by leaving her court and serving us. A spy must understand his patron's foes, which means some contact with them. Spies live by *quid pro quo*. There's always a *quid* for the *quo*. Don't let quaint chivalry turn you soft." He dismissed Don Cristobal with, "Watch for the *quid*. Ha, ha, ha!"

Don Cristobal ignored him. He wanted a friend, and

Latham had proved his valour. Confiding in any man under his command would undercut his authority; it wouldn't do. But a sworn bond with this spy could soften the loneliness of command, and who knew what glory Latham could put in his way again? Modern armies were tiny compared to ancient hordes, he reasoned, thinking of Attila's million barbarians attacking Aetius's five hundred thousand Romans and allies. Prime weapons today were innovations like his *looker*, and men who knew things. He set about enthusiastically befriending Latham.

During the weeks after the ambush, Vitelli held conferences, after which couriers galloped off, and others arrived. At the end of the third week, the French ambassador came, huddled with Vitelli, then slunk away without Vitelli hosting a dinner for him or reciprocal entertainment by the Frenchman. When his officers asked him what had happened, Vitelli smirked, "At the proper time."

With a frenzy of banging, the siege works were completed, closing remaining gaps. Spain's cannons were assembled and began to roar from morning to night. The Duke of Alva, dressed in his campaign outfit of brilliant blue, arrived with twenty thousand men. They hurried out to meet William of Orange's bought Germans, who'd finally been sighted. True to Vitelli's prediction, Orange wouldn't fight. He marched his mercenaries around, eluding Alva, then went away. *Little against littler*, Don Cristobal thought, nostalgic for the great ancient contests.

In the fourth week, Latham received grudging congratulations from Spain's ambassador to France, Zuniga. "Madrid commends me," he told Don Cristobal, his voice racing. "I'll have a salary and money to recruit my own network. That eel Zuniga's claiming credit for my work, writing that he always saw my merits. Of course, that's false. Somehow, the diplomat who first recruited me heard this and recommended me to Antonio Perez, secretary to King Philip. I'm to meet certain persons here, then return to Paris."

Latham split his time between camp and Saint-Ghislain, where he relished being a guest of the monastery. He also interviewed potential recruits from a list Zuniga had sent him. He rejected them all, deciding to hire informers answerable to him alone, which left him, for the moment, with none.

That soon changed. Although no one said anything publicly about Latham's new status, Eleventh Company soldiers knew he was in favour. William Boels, the Fleming recruit who couldn't shoot straight, tried his luck. He stopped Latham after the Englishman had sweated through a training session with Toledo's sword master.

"Sir," Boels said pompously, as Latham limped to his tent wiping his face. "I'm sorry I misjudged you at first."

Latham laughed. The youth's cheeks hinted at a first wrinkle, but he was still callow. "How could you assess me, for or against, after a week's sentry duty?"

Boels pressed on, unabashed, "The king favours you. I have mathematics and could work cyphers. Decoding is a better use of my talent than hacking with a pike."

Latham shook his head. "Boels, you presume in thinking I have anything to do with cyphering. Further, why would I hire anyone who promises to serve me, yet within weeks chases another post? Follow Don Cristobal in everything. Mathematics will eventually get you officer rank, which I'm sure your family wants."

Boels didn't give up. "If not me, sir, would you meet my uncle and godfather? He's adventurous, like you."

So he did get something from his importunity. After meeting this uncle and godfather, Pieter Boels, a well-travelled buyer's agent, Latham hired Pieter as his first sub-agent, answerable to him alone.

A lean man in his late thirties, Pieter Boels was pure restlessness. He paced as he talked, pumping a fist into his palm. His thinning oiled grey hair smelled of the grain and fur he traded, and threatened to jump from his scalp in agitation. After haranguing his listener almost to insensibility with whatever point he was making, he'd sit, listening, blue eyes candid with empathy. It was a startling change, and Latham could imagine customers rushing to fill the void with confidences, or saying yes to his price. He was committed to Spain's right to rule its Netherlands provinces, and to Catholicism, to the point of fervour. But as a buyer's agent from Poland to northern France, he'd learned the flexibility to trade across schisms and cultures. *With his dishevelled manners, no one will think he's an informer*, Latham thought. A widower without dependents, Pieter could roam. Latham assigned him to monitor anomalous merchant dealings.

When at camp, Latham and Don Cristobal often dined together. Conversations about present conditions went easily, but Don Cristobal discovered Latham was silent about his past. Whenever seemingly innocent topics came up, like a first pony, Latham's listened politely, a vein in his temple throbbing. He never reciprocated.

For his part, Latham envied the simplicity of the Spaniard's life. *To him, God, king and country are one. What can he know about choosing hell or betrayal of one's country, abandoning social degree for a few phrases in the mass?*

Don Cristobal was puzzled by another reticence in his new friend. He offered to treat Latham to the camp girl of his choice, but Latham always refused.

"Our girls are clean," he assured his new friend. "Chaplains tend their souls, physicians answer for their bodies."

"Too young," Latham invariably replied.

"Surely you don't quicken to an old woman," the Spaniard asked, frowning. "Be careful. After the bleeds stop, toxins grow in women's blood and spew out through their eyes. An older barren woman can poison a man with a look. Even kind women can grow vicious with age."

"What about your mother? Did she cast the evil eye?"

"No! She was a saint, of course."

Latham snorted. "You destroyed your own argument. Old women are cankered or mellow, just as old men are foolish or wise. Don't you prefer last season's wine to today's? Last decade's whisky to last season's?"

Both men retreated to private thoughts. For Latham, Eros was a complicated god. His bedmates had been female and male. Mary, Queen of Scots sometimes stalked his dreams, but so did Darnley, with his syphilitic sores and tragic death. Eros, for Latham, brought attachment, a sense of sin, and danger. Toledo's sword master was sending interesting signals, but he hadn't responded. "Older ladies, some high-placed, have seen my merits. I value ripe maturity," was all he offered Don Cristobal.

Eros was not complicated for Don Cristobal. Clean camp girls; a discreet officer's wife on occasion; his own wife, Teresa, when home on leave; all younger. He wondered if his new friend was Greek-minded. Toledo's sword master was known to prefer his own kind. *The idea shrivels my pizzle*, he thought, *but it suited my beloved Achilles and Alexander. Who am I to object? The Church abhors it, but all know priests are busy practitioners.* "Well," he said neutrally, turning to his favourite topic: innovations.

Here their perspectives also differed. Don Cristobal loved anything that worked, while Latham asked a second question: will it increase schism?

For instance, the *looker*. Despite inquiries, no others had been found. Don Cristobal was thrilled with its uniqueness. "It saved your life and found Genlis, so that I could capture him. My secret advantage."

One night they took it into the training field. Latham pointed it at Venus, Mars, and the crescent moon. The heavenly bodies swelled but blurred, white, black and orange shockingly smudged. Latham swallowed back nausea. It was as if the skies were repulsing this assault on their mysteries. "Best for finding lost sheep," he said, handing it back.

"And escaping unwanted house guests. Ha, ha, ha!" Don Cristobal agreed. "But think: if the apothecary ground the glass to get a close view of the stars, Copernicus's thesis that the earth orbits the sun could be tested. We could plot planetary motions precisely."

"His theory upends Catholic cosmology. How is that good?"

"It's good because he's right. Sea captains say his workings are useful," Don Cristobal said absently, cleaning the glass with a cloth.

"But," Latham persisted, startled by his casualness, "Copernicus contradicts Vatican teaching that the earth is the centre of God's universe, and the sun orbits it, which we see daily. People have been burned for less. It will increase schism."

"The Pope hasn't condemned Copernicus, yet. He's published in Spain, though with controlled distribution," Don Cristobal retorted. "Edward, would it be rude of me to suggest you make too much of things? It causes black bile."

Latham glanced at the sky. White, black and orange were unsmudged, as if pleased the *looker* was back in its case. "Black bile," he murmured. "My sister Kathcrine always warned me against it."

Don Cristobal looked at him attentively. A caring sister; the first information Latham had volunteered about his earlier life. He waited, but Latham didn't expand. However, he was cheerful as they walked back across the field.

For his part, Latham learned that Don Cristobal studied war. When finally invited to open his journals, Latham found they weren't personal. Organised into three categories: battles won by tactics (thick); battles won by policy (thin), and battles won by luck (very thin), they recounted historical and modern deployments. The ambush of Genlis was in *Tactics*. Latham took a broader view, and they debated for hours the interplay of policy and tactics. Latham knew classical politics, and Don Cristobal enjoyed being pushed to a fuller sense of events.

One morning, Latham walked into the Spaniard's tent to ask if he could check a point in his journals. A plump glowering trader hurtled through the flaps, almost knocking him over. Don Cristobal was at his desk, head in his hands.

"What's amiss?" Latham asked.

"I'm as bad as Gutierrez, my predecessor embezzler. That rogue practically corrupted me."

"It seems he didn't quite bring it off," Latham said mildly.

"The company's grain vendor. First time I met him. I kicked him out. Listen, on the bill each item was on the left, with a blank space left for cost on the right. On a separate paper, he'd written what he needed to cover costs, with a reasonable profit to feed his family. No problem, I respect that. But he gave me both papers and stood there, eyebrows raised. No words. Meaning I should tell him what to write, paying myself whatever I liked. I raised my eyebrows. No words. Finally, he said, 'This is how Captain Gutierrez does it,' showing me huge sums on yet another page. He named two of my officers being part of it.

"What was terrible was how much I wanted the money. I saw my estate, a bruise on a mountainside, divided over generations, harder and harder to farm, though I love it passionately. I revere my ascetic warrior ancestors, but do I have the right to impose it on my children? With skimming, I could buy city property. That's the thing to do these days, many say. Then I thought of you, giving up your patrimony for religion. I said, 'Write only what you have on the second sheet,' and slapped it hard."

"I'm moved by your compliment," Latham remarked, sitting on the bed. "How did he take it?"

"Outwardly obsequious. 'Sergeant Major,'" Don Cristobal wheedled, "'your courage and incorruptibility are famous.' I confess to relishing the praise! But he would have buffed me if I took the bribe. 'A father devoted to your children;' or if I was a bachelor: 'You don't presume on God's favour, providing for yourself as the parable of the ten talents preaches.' Fellows like this, war or peace, they thrive. We gentry grow poor keeping them safe."

He shuddered to rid his body of the taint. He and Latham laughed. Then he frowned. "I don't want to confront the two officers; they fought well, and morale is high. I must change grain vendors. A new supplier is the only tactful way to restore the company's reputation."

"I'll inquire," Latham promised, making a note to ask Pieter Boels to recommend an honest miller.

Two days before Latham left for Paris, Field Marshal Vitelli broke his silence about Genlis' papers and the frenzied diplomacy that followed.

Eager for Latham's opinion, Don Cristobal hosted a private dinner at a tavern in Saint-Ghislain. The table groaned with roast game bird, beef, cheese, candied pears and apples. Tall candelabras flickered, animating the gold lettering on a Book of Hours he'd bought for Latham.

"Instruction, a gift and feast all in one room. You didn't need to extend yourself," Latham said, embarrassed. "You saved my life. I'm the one under obligation."

"No, Edward. My reputation has soared since your news of Genlis. My men trust me, and Vitelli thinks I'm a natural commander. The obligation is mine."

He stopped, remembering Vitelli saying that spies lived by *quid pro quo*. Obligation was the wrong concept. "But let's not talk of obligation," he pressed on. "Debts are paltry things that can be paid off. Amity is what I mean. It grows as tree bark spreads, season by season. We soldiers of old families adhere to the bonds of chivalry. Tonight I say farewell, I hope briefly, to an oath brother. Let us seal our bond by mingling blood."

Taken aback, Latham stood. They pricked thumbs and drank, arms entwined.

"Call me Cristo," Don Cristobal said, sitting. "My kin do." Flushed with alcohol and beaming with pleasure, he added,

"We're not Palamon and Arcite, sworn ancient knights, to fall out over a virgin maid! Ha, ha, ha!"

Latham almost choked as his wine went down the wrong way.

Don Cristobal had meant to show brotherly acceptance, and that he had the learning to know the tale. Now he wondered if he'd wandered into the murk.

Latham's mind was suddenly back at Oxford and Richard Edwardes' play *Palamon and Arcite*, the royal visit in 1566 when his bond to country and sovereign snapped. Did Cristo mean they wouldn't fight over a woman? The tale offered something darker: the frailty of human bonds. "Well, Cristo, I hope we don't end up like those knights," he said, "but Fortune is unpredictable."

"Oh, I don't contest with Fortune," Don Cristobal said hastily. "Forget poetry. I wanted your opinion of Vitelli's briefing, the aftermath of our ambush."

Glad to be back to policy Latham quipped, "I'm keen to hear it, since I was sulphur to Vitelli's saltpetre."

"Essential compound you certainly were," Don Cristobal shot back, smiling. "Vitelli sent a messenger to Mons inviting rebel leaders to come and hear Genlis' account in person, knowing they hadn't seen the ambush and wouldn't accept our telling of it. Two captains came, and Genlis spoke truthfully about his defeat. Almost all his men were killed; we know that now. Of seven thousand, a hundred reached Mons. Without weapons or food, they're a burden on Mons. We lost eight cavalrymen and one hundred and forty foot, so it was a complete victory. Your prediction about Genlis' papers? More riches than a treasure ship from the Americas."

He paused to drink.

"Don't tease," Latham pleaded. "The papers?"

Don Cristobal grinned. "I can scarcely believe it, even in the retelling. Genlis carried a letter stitched into his doublet from the French king. Valois seal, everything. It promised to aid the rebel leaders, particularly Count Louis at Mons, against us. Under the French king's signature! We were amazed by its blatancy. And other French nobles wrote in the same vein. Vitelli laughed 'til he cried. He sent copies to Paris, originals to Madrid."

Latham whistled.

"See," Don Cristobal continued eagerly, "you grasp what I miss. Vitelli talked about a chain in policy; if one link rotted, the chain broke. He said that when we helped the English Duke of Norfolk rebel against Queen Elizabeth, we made a rotten policy chain that led to our loss of Mons and this siege to retake it. He told me to make a new chain with our ambush."

Surprised that Vitelli was poetical, Latham thought for a moment, then broke a bread loaf into pieces and rolled them in butter. "Helping Norfolk without knowing if Elizabeth knew about his plot was asinine."

He sighed, touching the filigree silver cross that Mary, Queen of Scots had given him. Norfolk had intended to marry Mary and place her on the English throne. Although the plot would have fostered Catholic rule in England, it repulsed him. "I'll show you a new policy chain if you tell me what else Vitelli said," he murmured.

"Well, after we sent copies of the French king's letter to Paris, the French ambassador came cringing: The letter a forgery (we know that's a lie, ha, ha!). Poor young King Charles, surrounded by evildoers stirring up trouble between peace-loving princes, he moaned, face puckering, tears flowing. Sincere friendship desired with his great Spanish neighbour, complete repudiation of Genlis. Blather worthy of the jakes."

"Before I organise my bread," Latham said, "tell me something about war. I've heard that today's offensive weapons and defensive bastions are so balanced that actual fighting victories are unusual. That the power of cannon is mitigated by the angles of fortified bastions, and that sieges are mostly decided by starvation or building tunnels underneath."

"Negotiation ends many sieges," Don Cristobal confirmed. "Most deaths of the besieged come after surrender, hardly chivalrous. Disease dissolves many invading armies

"Then this straightforward rout of Genlis is notable."

"Yes."

"Well, here's your new policy chain." Latham picked up a baked apple and two pears, placing them around his bread pile. "The German Lutheran states, France, and England. Thus," he pointed. He moved his goblet between the bread bits and England. "Because battle victories are rare, your ambush offers a moment of clarity. For the time being, a tale's end."

He tapped a pear representing England. "Elizabeth hates wasting munitions and men. She won't support Genlis' successor." He tapped the apple that was the German Lutheran states. "With her restraint, there's less money for Dutch rebels to buy Germans."

"Are you sure? What a triumph."

"I'm sure. Now, France is interesting." Latham placed bread bits around the pear that was France, some dispersed. After tapping the pear he licked his fingers "Damask rosebud honey," he sighed happily. "You caught the French king red-handed fostering invasion. I'm sure your envoy threatened full-scale war when he showed King Charles his own letter. France can't fight Spain because it's weak from religious civil wars."

"I know. I've fought there," Don Cristobal reminded him.

"Of course, your French is good. King Charles is in an exceedingly difficult position. Gaspard de Coligny, the Huguenot noble whose flag you captured, is allied with the Dutch rebel leader, William of Orange; and William's brother is Count Louis, the general you're besieging in Mons. Coligny is proud and powerful, and now his reputation is damaged. He'll raise troops to avenge Genlis. So French King Charles is pressed by Spain on one side, Huguenot nobles on the other. He's a boy, but not dainty. He *must* control his warlike Huguenots.

"Now, ordinarily, these nobles live dispersed." He pointed to bread piles in different spots on the table. Then he bunched them. "But they're in Paris now, to conclude truce terms, including the marriage of the French king's sister, Marguerite, to Henry of Navarre, the Huguenot prince. Nevertheless, after a generation of conflicts, trust between the parties is nil. This gives Charles his chance. I predict you'll soon hear of Huguenot leaders being arrested."

"So that's policy," Don Cristobal said, looking at greasy bread bits stretching from Mons to Paris, the German states, England. "Ambush on a vast field."

Latham nodded. "There's one more link in your chain." He moved the goblet between France and England. "If Elizabeth sees Charles persecuting her co-religionist Huguenots, she'll stop trusting him. France and England were negotiating a treaty as a bulwark against Spain's dominance, but any unreasonable punishment of Huguenots would make her hold off." He made a new line between Paris and England.

"There," he said, sitting back. "Look at what my intelligence and your trust in me have wrought. King Philip will have time to deal with his rebels without foreign meddling. Who knows? There could even be peace."

"Great possibilities, indeed," Don Cristobal marvelled.

Latham affected modesty. "One question," he resumed. "Does anyone but Vitelli and your men know my role?"

Don Cristobal turned sombre. He'd been putting off this issue all evening. "I fear so. It was one of the reasons I had to see you before you go. Not from my men. Genlis' courier…"

"Albert Braak?" Latham asked in surprise. He saw Braak in a debtor's basket at the clandestine cockfight in Paris, then spilling Genlis' plan to the man he took as his saviour. "I betrayed him."

"He was captured and saw you near Toledo's tent. He knows the name, Edward Latham, swears you betrayed the entire heretic movement."

"Well, at least you have him in custody. Can I beg you not to ransom him?"

Don Cristobal gripped the table. "He escaped."

Latham's eyes went flat and cold. "You let him live?"

"I didn't know about it until long after. Our intelligencers let him go to discover his contacts. They weren't aware of your part. Braak called you *the worst man of all France*. You'll need your many identities."

"And actors' hair dye." Latham started laughing, now more sardonic than angry. "So Braak paid me back for gulling him. I'll have to give Monsieur Hercules Gidon a decent burial. Well, like any man's, my days are borrowed, but at usurious rates." He stood, patting his stomach. "Thank you for the warning, Cristo, your friendship, everything."

"Will you write to me?"

"Yes, of course."

"How will I know letters are genuine?"

"Invent a name for us."

Don Cristobal frowned, then smiled. "Mithridates Midas."

"Ugh," Latham responded.

"It's good: strong man Mithridates and rich man Midas together. You hate it because you didn't think of it. Ha, ha!"

When they left the tavern, the watch was calling out the curfew in one hour.

"Think of me as this siege drags on," Don Cristobal said. "I've been assigned the boring duty of escorting Genlis to Antwerp; I'm one of his jailers."

"It won't last long," Latham responded. "If he gives up what he knows, Alva will have him killed."

Don Cristobal stopped. "But that violates terms I promised when he surrendered!" he protested angrily. "It's against the customs of war."

"War has changed; you said so yourself," Latham answered. "Anyway, whether Genlis lives or dies, Vitelli won't waste you on guard duty. Now, think of brown-haired me, bribing confidences out of palace grooms and ladies-of-the-bedchamber. Thus do I serve my master and push Dame Fortune."

Don Cristobal cried. "Edward, your reach is high. 'Push Fortune?'"

"My reach isn't; ears at walls, seeking conspiracies. No ether-bound soaring for Edward Latham, no-longer knight. But the effect of my work reaches high. The wriggling toes of a spy's foot can direct a glittering royal head. You and I can move events more than you think."

This was the frankest statement Latham had made about his ambitions. Don Cristobal was too stunned to reply.

"Well, adieu, with all my affection," Latham concluded, grinning at Don Cristobal's discomfort.

They embraced and separated.

Humble service, infinite ambitions, Don Cristobal mused as he returned to his billet. *He'll always surprise me.*

Latham was thinking about what was next, instead of what had passed. He packed books, clothes, hair dye, travelling papers and the wheellock pistol.

The next morning, 27th August 1572, two horses were waiting for him. One was a nag to return to the stables in Amiens, to replace the one that had been shot. The other was a sprightly young bay stallion, bred on Cristo's mountain estate for endurance and agility. The label *Surehoof* was attached to his tackle.

Latham left Saint-Ghislain with some traders, stopping at an inn on the outskirts of Amiens at dusk. After securing a private room, he went to check that the stable boy was taking proper care of his horses. A young courier clattered in, accompanied by two guards. Sliding off his horse, the courier shouted for fresh mounts, immediately, any price agreed to. Refusing food and ale, he danced from foot to foot in frenzied impatience, while the inn's ostler looked for suitable replacements. Latham initially thought the courier a joke: acne on his neck, an outsized sword almost toppling him. Until he saw the Hapsburg insignia on his sleeve

"Look at this ring," Latham said, no longer chuckling. He showed the courier the gold ring with Philip II's face. "We serve the same master. What's happening?"

"Who are you?" The courier stopped jiggling.

"Piso Prosperino, servant of King Philip, come from Mons."

The youth studied Latham's ring then pulled him close. He whispered, "Bernardino Gonzales, courier to Zuniga, at your service. I'm going to Mons. All other couriers were engaged, so they sent me. The news is wondrous, urgent, no secret. The evil Huguenot leader Gaspard de Coligny is dead. Dead twice over, his headless body being dragged about the streets by a mob of Paris faithful. Heretics in Paris are being put to the sword. Three days, and no end to it."

"Wait," Latham interrupted. "How can a man be dead twice over?"

Gonzales looked around impatiently; no fresh horses yet. "Laggards. Why so slow? Alright, listen. First, an arquebusier shoots Coligny, bold as you please, from a window in the Duke of Guise's house. 22nd August. The assassin gets away. Coligny is wounded, likely to go gangrenous. So, dead once, see. But the French king visits his sick bed, promises to bring the assassin to justice, leaves Coligny with a guard of fifty arquebusiers. All the other heretic leaders gather around Coligny. So, not only are Satan's minions in one city, they're in one suite. Then before the next dawn, let me see, St. Bartholomew's Eve, 24th August, yes; the bells of that pretty church, Saint-Germain l'Auxerrois, ring and ring after the watch calls four. Now, this from our agent in the Guise household. Henry, Duke of Guise leads the king's mercenaries and kills Coligny; this time cuts off his head, the head is brought to the palace, the body given to the mob. Dead twice over, see? The other Huguenot leaders were killed, too."

"But what about the guards the king left with Coligny?"

"When the duke attacked Coligny, he shouted it was the king's will, so those guards must have stood down or joined in."

Gonzales coughed but waved away Latham's offer of a drink. "Just road dust. It gets better. The Paris Provost locks the city gates, proclaims Guise's shout of the king's will, and faithful Parisians set on every heretic in sight. The English are so terrified that they barricade themselves in their embassy and won't admit a royal delegation, because they believe the king is behind the whole thing. That friendship won't bloom this season. God is *re-arranging* France, my friend, *re-arranging* it all together. Zuniga has written to King Philip, urging a nation-wide prayer station to thank the Almighty. Everywhere I stop I hear of the local killing of thousands more heretics."

At last, the ostler brought fresh horses, and Gonzales mounted. "God be praised for this blessing," he flung back, as he clattered through the gate.

Latham was dazed. He floated upstairs to his room, feeling appalled. The death of Coligny and other Huguenot leaders was an astonishing strike for Philip and the Catholic cause. But a spontaneous nation-wide massacre went far beyond anything he imagined could result from Genlis' small defeat. *We, you and I, move events more than you think,* he'd blithely told Don Cristobal yesterday, playing with the greasy bread bits. How self-preening it sounded now! His talent at finding things out gave him power he now trembled at. Re-arranging France, as Gonzales called it, meant torrents of blood, much of it innocent.

The worst man in all France, Braak called him. If Latham was a marked man earlier, he was triply marked now. He lay on the bed, arms behind his head. He stared at the ceiling, but instead of seeing plaster-moulded twigs and birds, he was in battle, a French gun aimed at his face, its owner a rictus of hate. The spirit of Mars had pulled him over a flimsy human barrier to the destroying joy of the warrior. Was this spirit now rampaging through France in an ecstasy of mob killing? Hours later, he dozed and dreamed.

Huge, disembodied hands, a bracelet of flaxen hair around their wrists, push an arquebus through a window. Latham's hands. A crack, and Gaspard de Coligny clutches his chest. Time is permeable. The same hands, now holding a giant sword, float above the great man's sick bed. A flash of light on steel and Coligny's

*narrow face, with its neat chestnut hair, separates from his torso.
But his eyes still move, following the flaxen-fringed hands as they
place his head on a pewter platter. The blood-spattered ruff frames
the ripped Adam's apple, like a pod cupping a spring bloom,
whose petals flake off, each becoming a little sword that wreaks
its own destruction on the necks of small victims—a boy under six,
a girl of eleven, mothers who have thrown themselves over their
children – while the flaxen-haired hands float the pewter platter
with Coligny's glazed stare to Philip II's private chapel. The great
hands hover over Huguenot strongholds—they know where they
are, of course—and slap. Fields groaning with wheat and barley
flatten and wither…*

Latham woke. He'd fallen asleep on his hands, which were
numb. He shook them. How huge and tingling they felt!
Coligny had been a great man. He, Edward Latham, was the
puppet master of his and other Huguenot leaders' deaths, so
the dream said. Dr Pell had prophesied: *Some live, some die
from your dealings.* Where are the ones who lived? With his
power of finding things out, where would he find virtue?

One thing was certain: he, the hunter, would soon be
hunted. He lit a candle, dyed his hair brown, and burned
Hercules Gidon's papers. Before dawn, he saddled Cristo's gift,
Surehoof, leaving the nag in its stall with a note. He turned
back, to build his network from Brussels, instead of Paris.

PART TWO: DOUBTING

CHAPTER 7
A SEASON OF
SMALL

Brussels, January 1573.

"Ha! Momus, god of irony, rules. They want me to do *what*?" Latham pounded his desk, causing the candle to jump to the floor and fire the rushes. He got up and stamped out the flames. A second reading of the letter left him just as amazed.

It was from his current spymaster, Don Antonio Perez, King Philip's Secretary of State. Both information and assignment were hard to absorb. Perez wrote first that an English exile named Edmund Campion, a celebrated Oxford scholar and former heretic deacon, had seen truth. He had converted to Catholicism and earned a Bachelor of Divinity from the English College in Douai, a seminary founded by dissident Catholic English cardinal, William Allen, and patronised by King Philip.

The irony in this twist of events in itself was enough to stun Latham. It had been Campion's supple debates that had propelled Latham to Scotland. *If intellectuals like Edmund Campion, whom privy councillors call their jewel, are Protestant, Catholics like me will wither.* Yes, I remember thinking that. He's converted? God be praised.

Such a high-level conversion was a propaganda triumph, Perez wrote, but before publicising it, they had to know if it was genuine. There was a warning sign: Philip had offered Campion a teaching post at the College, approximating what he'd enjoyed in Oxford. Campion refused, saying that he intended to make a winter pilgrimage on foot to Rome. It sounded too fantastical. Could he be an English informer? Since Latham's file stated that he'd heard Campion's debates at Oxford, he was the best agent to assess the convert's sincerity, and he should do this in Douai.

Edward Latham, no-longer knight, was being told to judge, for the mightiest Catholic monarch in Christendom, Edmund Campion's soul. This second irony defied the wildest fantasy of how things could turn upside down. Latham would have liked to relish it at leisure, but the dates Perez gave for meeting Campion meant he had to leave in hours.

Could Campion be a spy? Latham wondered. As a debater, he'd manipulated deductive propositions to lavish praise on his sovereign. But that was the job of a queen's debate champion. Treading the murky paths of espionage? Unlikely.

As Latham threw what he needed into his saddlebag, he thought about the day-to-day stresses of his life. He was poorer than he'd expected, given his pension and expense allowances from Philip. Policy caused his constrictions. After Genlis' defeat and the massacre of French Huguenot leaders, it had seemed possible, briefly, that insurgencies in both countries could be quelled, maybe even peace negotiated.

But new Huguenot leaders had quickly emerged in France, while Dutch rebels held land in the north. In the south, King Philip's governor, the Duke of Alva, was militarily successful, but so cruel and heavy-handed with taxes that he alienated even loyal Catholics. Money was short, and vaunted Spanish units were threatening mutiny; they hadn't been paid for months.

Latham adapted, knowing he had to stay relevant at a time when even good intelligence would have little impact. One thing he knew from his courtier days in England was that when little was happening, telling it first was everything. He used only the fastest couriers to send information to Madrid.

That cost gobbled up most of his money, but it was worth it. A run from Brussels to Madrid could take seven to forty-five days; the courier's will more a factor than weather. He lived in one attic room rented from a brewer's widow, paying her kitchen maid and stable boys for cleaning and other services. He ate simply, and kept only one outfit suitable for court. But material comfort wasn't his goal at the moment; a reputation for good intelligence was.

He kept two luxuries. Surehoof, the hardy bay stallion that Cristo had given him, was too essential to his travels to sell. The other luxury was a set of little mirrors he commissioned from Nuremberg that he glued to the brim of his hat. Made of glass backed by reflecting metal, they enabled him to see behind him. When they didn't fog, he could spot followers. He preferred their cool magic to a costly regular servant of unproven loyalty.

He was in less danger in Brussels than in France, but he wasn't safe. Brussels was full of spies: Huguenot, rebel Dutch, English. The Huguenots had put a price on his head because of Genlis' defeat. And despite Latham's agreement with David Hicks and Elizabeth's Secretary of State, Sir William Cecil, he also kept an eye out for English spies. Pope Pius V had excommunicated Elizabeth in 1570, offering a pardon to anyone who killed her. English agents abroad sometimes kidnapped English exiles, and they made mistakes. So Latham was careful as he trawled for information. Did Edmund Campion have the temperament for this life? No, Latham thought. He'd refused the teaching post for some other reason.

Latham had never been to Douai. After three weather-battering days, Surehoof picked his way over compacted snow on a curving cobbled street. Narrow houses supported the shops and residences of generations of artisans, apothecaries, scholars and booksellers. Swaddled pedestrians plodded from shop to shop. A thin stone belfry in the main square soared to the heavens. It was the tallest Latham had ever seen, lending a touch of inspiration to the scene.

A yellow sign for the Fat Cheeses Tavern showed that he'd reached his destination. Black hands on the belfry's dirty white clock face moved to the three o'clock position. All over town, bells clanged. Proud that he was on time, despite rough weather, Latham paid the stable boy to sheathe his horse's hooves in sacking.

Inside, a fug of melting cheeses, warm beer, and smoke from kitchen and room fires. Students stood, sharing flagons; at one bench a stocky workman, two bargemen and a florid priest in a white cope ate. A prostitute trawled, and a dust-coated youth peddled reddish marble remnants from a building site.

At the back of the cavernous room, a long table had been set up. The new graduate, in a Bachelor of Divinity robe, was presiding over raucous chatter. The seminarians had clearly emptied their purses to provide a feast. Edmund Campion was gleefully dismantling his opponents' propositions.

Latham swept off his hat, bowed and introduced himself.

"Sit down, Latham. Eat, drink, throw me an argument," Campion laughed. Two students made room for him and piled venison, turnip and bread on his plate. An esoteric doctrinal dispute raged. Latham listened, but didn't contribute. He felt the magnetic pull Campion exerted on his admirers.

When the argument ran down unresolved, Campion looked around the students with great benevolence, then turned to Latham. "These pugnacious youths are trying to suborn me with a gourmand's indulgence, this soporific fire, and their honed logic. They don't want me to leave. Their devotion moves me, but I intend to go in a few days. I know why you're here; I expected Madrid to send someone."

When the students left, Campion and Latham moved to a private table. Latham put his hat on and looked at the small mirrors. A hard-faced novice was drinking alone. Unaware he was being observed, his face was all angles and aggression, without a hint of spirituality. Latham noted features hard to disguise: ears that stuck out, a square jaw, blue eyes. He felt a jolt of unease.

Campion watched Latham with a bemused smile. "Clever device."

"Yes, and costly. Who's that novice?"

"Who indeed? It gives me infinite joy that I'm not compelled to ask."

"Is he at the College?"

"Yes, but I've only seen him a couple of times."

"Could he be an English agent?"

"I don't know. He speaks clunky Latin. Anyway, if I suspected him, I'd never say. It's not for me to judge a man's journey. Any man can emerge from error to walk with Christ."

They drank ale in silence.

"Why don't you teach here?" Latham finally asked. "King Philip thinks you ungrateful. I heard you at Oxford." He leaned forward, quoting Campion's opening remark. "*I speak in the name of philosophy, the Princess of Letters, before Elizabeth, the lettered Princess.* Students loved you there, and they love you here."

Campion looked down at a knot on the coarse-grained table, gripping his tankard. When he looked up, there were tears in his eyes. "How you hurl a sinner's words at him. I'm surprised you don't understand."

"Please explain."

"When did you take your oath of allegiance to Elizabeth?"

"February 1559."

"Exactly. Before her pestilential sect became the law of England. You sacrificed a courtier's ease in 1566. What did I do? I adapted. For years after I knew the truth, I clutched at glory: the hope of a bishop's palace; the intoxicating power of patronage. I was willfully negligent; I accepted, even helped the spread of heresy. I dithered until constables sought me as a Catholic sympathiser to the Duke of Norfolk's rebellion. Only then did I relinquish ambition, slinking away on a boat to Calais, my sloth of a soul and me. I am utterly ashamed.

"Don't you see," he pressed on, "You exercised the free will God gives us to do good or ill by giving up your birthright when you weren't pursued by the State. I waited until free will disappeared. Like an animal, I ran to save my skin. For the rest of my days, I must physic doubtful souls, try to save them from falling into the crimes I committed. Culpable negligence *is* a crime."

Latham sat back, startled. The last thing he'd expected was that Campion would see virtue in him. The malicious imp in him followed with, "Did you know I left court the day after you debated in front of Elizabeth and the Spanish ambassador? I thought that if scholars like you were Protestant deacons, there was no place in England for a believer like me."

"No! I didn't know that. It compounds my shame." Campion looked stricken.

A bench leg scraped behind Latham as the hard-faced novice stood up. When he passed Campion's table, he stared at them. Cold appraising eyes gave the lie to the curving smile he offered Campion. He left, trailing yeasty garlic breath.

"Well, thanks to God's mercy here we both are," Latham said with a smile, putting aside his concern about the novice.

"Wouldn't you be physicking souls by teaching here? Those lads would inhale anything you gave them."

"They need good teachers, yes," Campion agreed. "But again, I'm amazed you don't see it. Douai belongs to Spain. To teach here, I'd have to swear allegiance to Philip. Why would I swear to any monarch, a mere shadow, when I can swear to the sun that is His Holiness, the Pope? The sun that can excommunicate, cast off any shadow? Suppose I swear to Philip as I did to Elizabeth; what if Philip quarrels with Rome? It's no idle fancy, Latham. Philip's father, Holy Roman Emperor Charles V, counted himself a Christian king. Yet he plundered Rome and held the Pope captive. His men raped and murdered nuns. That was fifty years ago; a minute in the life of the Church. I'm grateful to Philip, but to swear allegiance to him would be venal, soft and chancy. No more shadows. I'll make my pilgrimage to Rome in a penitent's robes and flimsy sandals, begging and walking all the way. I want to be a Jesuit if they'll have me. They serve only the sun."

"Jesuits? Ignatius Loyola founded them, and Philip sponsors them. Both Spaniards," Latham retorted.

"Yes, but Ignatius Loyola said: *if His Holiness names something black, which members of our society see as white, then they must, in like manner, term it black.* He never said that about his temporal sovereign. I long for Loyolan discipline."

Latham stroked his moustache. Where was the nimble thinker melding new science of magnetism to classical astronomy and myth? The one he'd heard at Oxford? "So observation is tossed in the cesspit if the Pope says so?"

"I know it seems strange," Campion replied. "It's because of our pestilential times. After Martin Luther, you're with Christ or the Anti-Christ. You must be altogether within the Roman Church, or you're anathema. It's that simple."

Campion seemed to grow as he spoke. His slender torso elongated, his gaze intensified. He was implacable, happy.

Does he allow any nuance? Latham probed. "What about the Good Samaritan, more beloved by God than His own priests?"

"Ah," Campion smiled. "I love it when a man's argument contains its own contradiction. Those Judaic priests were corrupt. In Luther's time, some of ours were, too. But at the Council of Trent, from 1546 to 1566, the Holy Church reformed itself. From every principality, the lowest parish priests and highest cardinals came. *Every* doctrinal dispute was resolved. After Trent, no heretic can claim that virtue mitigates doubt. Your good man who thieves nothing finds good husbands for his daughters, apprentices his sons well, loves his wife and tends her in sickness, fights for his prince, even endows a school for orphans, but he faces damnation no matter his good works. The hooks may rend his flesh less deep than the murderer's, the fires ebb, flare, spit, offering a second's respite, but his every false word or blasphemous thought mean eternal torment. After Trent, you can't accept Catholic doctrine in general and deny any particular. The only safety is to be wholly within the Church. We're stewards for our brief lives of Christ's living presence in the Eucharist. No tarrying for a shadow. Rome guides me from now on." He sat back, exhaled and drank.

When he's not laughing or looking kindly on his students, he's savage in his certainties, Latham thought when they said goodbye. *Is this what makes a saint?*

The next morning, Latham strolled toward the stables, whistling, but stopped at a colourful marble remnant on the ground. In the enamelled sunlight, its top glistened from the melted ice crust, while its bottom was black from snow-mud. He tossed it from hand to hand, enjoying its myriad hues, thinking about Campion's complex journey of conscience, and what to report. Perez liked granular detail, and he'd get it.

When he reached the stables, there was no one around. Wooden buckets of dung were stacked, ready to be carted to the tavern owner's farm. The stable boys were on a break.

He stepped inside. Some horses were shifting in their stalls. Instinctively Latham knew he wasn't alone. He tensed. As well as smelling hay, horse hair and oiled leather, he smelled garlic. Without breaking pace, he glanced up at the wide beam running the length of the barn, with knobs for tackle. A man could hide on such a beam. Heart racing, he drew his knife.

When he opened Surehoof's stall, he tossed the stone in front of him and stepped back. A hand holding a cudgel smashed down from the beam. It hit air, and the horse surged out of the stall.

Latham grabbed the cudgeler's wrist and pulled. A cursing heap crashed into him, and they fell to the floor, punching and kicking. The novice grabbed Latham's knife wrist and bit, sending the knife flying. Latham kneed him in the groin. The man recoiled, giving Latham a second to chop up with his other hand, bending his attacker's head back. The novice rolled and dived for the knife. Latham felt a sharp punch into his thigh, saw the knife aiming for his eye. He twisted back, and the blade nicked his neck. He jammed his knee into the novice's jaw and broke free.

He threw himself onto Surehoof's bare back and kicked. Blood trickled down his neck and through his hose. Behind him, grunts and a horse rearing.

Latham had the better mount. Surehoof threaded past carts and through throngs of people while Latham yelled, "Way! Make way! King's business!"

Near the city gates, there was a patch of slushy open road. A vegetable cart had overturned, and two farmers were attempting to right it, while a boy scooped up turnips and cabbages. Latham shouted to step back as his horse gathered himself, soared over the cart and landed with a slither. The sacking still on his hooves saved them both. A second later they were through the gates. The novice's horse tried to follow. Latham heard screams and whinnies. He pulled on the mane and turned. The pursuing horse was down, his stunned assailant being helped up. "Thank you for Surehoof, Cristo," Latham muttered, giving his attacker a contemptuous wave.

He soon felt light-headed. Finding cover in a copse of oaks, he thrust threads of wool into his neck wound and bandaged his leg with a strip from his shirt. Was 'garlic-breath' targeting Campion or him, he wondered? If it was him, was he a Huguenot avenging Genlis, or an English agent trying to kidnap him? In the fight he'd only grunted; that was no accident. He had to admit the mirrors hadn't helped. After resting, he rode to the nearest town to find a physician and saddler.

Brussels, January 1573

"I can save you from this: expensive couriers and danger. Mirrors don't draw a sword as a good servant would."

It was Pieter Boels, Latham's sub-agent. Latham had been writing his report on Edmund Campion when he arrived. As usual, he was alternately pacing the room or standing, kneading his hands. Boels' eyes went from his neck sutures to the cane in the corner.

"Oh?" Latham raised his eyebrows. Pieter usually smelled of the grain he traded. Today it was fur. He was back from Poland. "You're going to offer me the Platonic form of the perfect servant," he said in a guarded tone meant to discourage.

"I have another godson…"

"Ah, of course." The inevitable godson. Sub-agents tried to load Spain's payroll with kin who couldn't find work elsewhere. "Your news?" he snapped.

Boels realised that the usually courteous Latham was irritable with pain. "A witch burning in Krasnopol." His eyes had the glint that signified important information.

One had to wait until Boels was ready to disgorge. Latham played along. "Krasnopol," he sniffed. "A remote village of poor fishermen and Jew leather workers. Why were you there?"

"A recent peace agreement re-opened the Russian trade route. I get low prices for leather, fur and gossip."

Latham nodded. Poland's King Sebastian had made regional peace. But he was dead, leaving no blood successor. A strategically placed largely Catholic country was in play. Envoys from Spain and France were in Warsaw, vying to get the Polish magnates to crown their chosen protégé King of Poland. Philip II of Spain wanted his nephew, Archduke Ernst of Austria, to be king; while Charles IX of France pushed his younger brother, Prince Henry of Valois. Polish nobles were terrified of Russia's Tsar Ivan, called "The Terrible," who was cruel and erratic enough to give anyone nightmares. They sought a powerful counterweight in a Spanish or French king.

"Why was the Krasnopol witch burned?" Latham asked.

"For predicting a short reign for the next king of Poland. A country must have a king. Warsaw magnates, who can't agree on France or Spain, are in wild panic."

Latham whistled. He felt the tingle from toes to scalp, presaging major intelligence.

"What else?"

"My godson…"

"Don't bargain with a king's intelligencer. I'm no Krasnopol tanner."

Boels decided to press his godson's cause another day. "They want the new king to share power with them. What to do if whoever they chose reigns a short time? Voila, the provincial witch's prophecy matters. Poland has useful

Protestants and Jews. Jews collect peasant rents for landlords. The magnates ask which prince is the least cruel, comparing the French massacre of thousands of Huguenot civilians on St. Bartholomew's Eve to Spain's Inquisition. They're dizzy with confusion."

Leaning over Latham's desk, Pieter said fervently, "It would be glorious to add Poland to Spain's empire. We could threaten Hamburg's Lutheran bankers who support Dutch rebels. It's a marvellous opportunity. If Philip agrees to the Polish power-sharing terms, he can renounce them as soon as Ernst is crowned."

Latham sat back, caught up in Pieter's enthusiasm. But as he made notes, his conviction grew that Poland was a trap, not an opportunity. His report would have to lay out why he was right, and King Philip's envoys very wrong.

"Good information, Pieter. I'll go to Paris to follow matters there. I don't know who attacked me in Douai, but I might eventually hire a manservant. Tell me about your godson."

Pleased, Boels adopted a confiding tone. "His father despairs over him. Joris Boels speaks very slowly and reads like a savage, but he has an exquisite eye for people and places and draws them, though sometimes backwards."

"Is he cross-eyed?" Latham asked, wincing.

"No, it's some inward muddle. His memory is amazing. He understands what's said in Dutch and French."

"Why isn't he apprenticed to a master painter?" Latham asked.

"He was, but the master sacked him. No one will hire him now."

"Does he steal? Drink too much?" It was getting hard to take Pieter's advocacy seriously.

"No, he's indifferent to coins and jewellery. And wine. The sensory world stimulates him enough. His trouble is choler. No one likes his laboured speech, and he curdles if he's interrupted. His master heard insolence when the lad was just frustrated. He also brawled with other apprentices.

One abused him as a simple; the other insulted a maid he fancied. He's good in a scrap. He broke one boy's finger and blinded the other in one eye, just with two fingers rigid with rage. There was much expense to his father and me settling those affairs."

Latham laughed. "Joris, after his namesake George, the saintly dragon slayer. The army's the place for him, Pieter."

"I wish he could be a soldier, like his cousin and my other godson, William Boels. But he's too restless for standing about. During his apprenticeship, he finished his drawings at lightning speed, regular and reverse image, never sure which was right. Then he'd disappear for days, return stinking of sweat and horse. This maid he fancied was from a heretic family who fled the Inquisition. He might have been looking for her. Once he gives his heart, it stays. Congress with heretics was an intolerable scandal on top of his other troubles. He's silent on the matter, but can't find work."

Latham was now intrigued. He wondered if the youth had something of Pieter in him. "What's the kinship?"

"He's my nephew, cousin of William Boels, the bisono who introduced you to me at Mons. The boys aren't close; William looks down on Joris. But I believe Joris is much cleverer than his algebra-minded cousin." A good salesman, he stopped there.

A loyal brawler who draws well, yet labours at his alphabet. If he betrays me, who'll listen? Latham thought. He did need a servant. "He'd certainly get his fill of loping about, being my courier. He sounds like a puppy," he finally said.

"Exactly," Boels cried eagerly. "He's loyal, has keen senses, is a roamer, and a bit feral. I love him dearly."

"I see that." Latham sighed. "I'll interview him, at least."

Mollified, Boels clattered downstairs. Latham composed a letter to his employer, Secretary of State Don Antonio Perez, about Campion and the trap of Poland.

Madrid, March 1573

Long after courtiers, priests, and the servants who kept a palace functioning snuffed out candles to snatch at sleep, King Philip II worked on. Dressed in a plain white shirt and black doublet, he scrawled sarcastic or approving comments in the margins of dispatches from the Americas, the Two Sicilies, Tuscany, the Netherlands, Savoy, and Catalonia. He rubbed bloodshot eyes over the latest plea for funds from his military commander in the Netherlands, the Duke of Alva. Philip's hand was cramped, but he preferred the solace of lonely nights with quill and paper to face-to-face exchanges, even though the latter were more efficient. There was one more dispatch to read, from a spy in Brussels. He started, raised his eyebrows and reached for his bell.

An hour later, he was berating Secretary Antonio Perez. Kneeling, silk hose touching the floor, plump Perez suppressed a groan.

"Your Brussels spy... presumes is too weak a word," Philip began, looking at a wall tile, not Perez. "Instead of relating facts, which is his *only* duty, he *advises*. Listen. *Please advise His Majesty that his nephew rules his realm, he is a first person... We* know our nephew's rank! He goes on: *Polish magnates envision shared power and making of policy. For your protégé to cede authority decreases his honour, and by extension, His Majesty's honour. Whereas the French prince is only a second person in his realm, younger brother of King Charles, who may never be a king...* He tells me? As if this is news?"

Philip took a breath. He was sitting on a chair by the fire, eyes swivelling left or right. But they fastened on Perez' torso, puffing out a cream satin doublet with gold buttons. "You may sit." Pointing to a grease streak on Perez' sleeve, he said, "Vanity, Don Antonio, cream stains." But you've been travelling hard, no doubt."

Perez had only travelled from his mistress's city mansion, but saw no need to be precise. He took the narrow low chair Philip waved him to, his rump and thighs overflowing its edges. The discomfort kept him alert, which was Philip's intention.

"Your spy goes on: *honour for such a second person is increased by having a state to rule, even if only half-ruled. Further, French Kings have passed edicts of tolerance for heretics, whereas His Majesty never has. Any tolerance His Majesty's nephew extends in Poland completely undercuts the causus belli of His Majesty's quarrel with His Dutch rebels. His Majesty's envoy in Warsaw wants only to beat the French. With respect, he's wrong. Spain is best served by losing to France. Further, a witch prophesied a short reign by the next king. Would His Majesty consign his kin to such a fate?* You see? Presumptuous. Is he any use?" Pained, Philip avoided Perez' eye

"Your Majesty, his report reached you in ten days while you've heard nothing from your envoy. He warned Vitelli about Genlis, reported on Edmund Campion…"

Perez read out: "*Campion's ears stand at a 20 degree angle from his head. His forehead is unlined, unusual for one of his years. His thin lips are set, signifying the fixed purity of his Catholic doctrinal opinions. In another man his mouth would look cruel, but Campion is always pleasant.* No one could impersonate Campion with this description. He says Campion is a true convert."

"That's the same spy?"

"Yes, Your Majesty. About the Krasnopol witch's prophecy?"

"A mystery. My astrologer's chart is not propitious for Poland, but my nephew Ernst and French Prince Henry are long-lived. Your man is appalling, but he makes good points. You may go. Remember, less vanity from you and your spy."

When Latham recovered from the novice's attack in Douai, he rode to Paris in company with members of a goldsmiths' guild. He went to see Hélène Michaud, mistress of the royal laundry. To his surprise, her deputy didn't greet him at the front door. Instead, a pert girl of eight or nine escorted him to her office. Forming a low opinion of the guest's general understanding, she took it upon herself to teach him the building's layout.

"Monsieur Prosperino," she chattered, "the repair room is here. It's the most important room. I sew shirts, petticoats there. Next week I go up to reattaching loose jewels on doublets and overskirts."

A waif and an old woman hauling water buckets were coming the other way. Peremptorily, the girl waved them to stand aside. "Là, Jeanne, old Isabel, make way for Monsieur Prosperino, Mistress Michaud's guest."

Latham laughed. Who was this girl? Undisciplined auburn curls escaped from her embroidered bonnet. She had observant grey eyes and a beanpole chest at odds with a precocious swing of her hips. "Countess," he said, with a bow that thrilled her, "is the repair room the most important because you're in it? What about your mistress's office?'

The girl frowned, considering, then changed the subject. "Did you see that great building outside? It's the kitchen. You can't go there. You're not on the list. If anyone not on the list gets in, the whole staff is dismissed. The king is so scared of poison. I'm on the list. Tomorrow, I buy fish, sugar and molasses with the steward. What do you think of that?"

By now they'd reached Hélène's office, and Latham was spared the need to reply.

"Repair these nightshirts, Marie. Now." Hélène thrust garments at the girl. "Come in," she said to Latham, closing the door. "What joy, Gidon! It's been over a year."

"The joy's mutual, great lady. Who is she?" Latham asked, grinning. "She's got everyone saddled, even you."

"A malapert cousin, Marie Beaumont." Hélène sighed. "I bought an inn in Saint-Denis, The Monk's Brew. Her parents run it—they're decent folk–and the girl learns laundering and provisioning here one month a year. She's actually a hard worker. I'd never hire her–you can see why–but you must stay at the inn when you visit Saint-Denis. What happened to your neck?" His livid scar was noticeable as he bent to kiss her hand.

"Gidon's dead," he protested. "I'm Piso Prosperino now."

"To me, you can only be courtly Hercules Gidon, once in service to my kinsman, Henry, Duke of Guise."

She's signalling that she still informs for Guise, Latham thought.

"But we'll speak softly, softly, if you wish," Hélène lisped through a new gap in her teeth.

As Latham straightened out of his bow, he saw she'd grown more homely. White face powder failed to mask sagging cheeks. *Why did God encase such an engaging mind in such an unprepossessing body?* He wondered. It seemed wantonly cruel. "Mademoiselle, if I weren't affianced elsewhere, I'd carry you off in my golden carriage."

"Ha, ha! There's no golden carriage, you're not affianced, and I'm rotting towards death. Now we've played our little acts, tell me about your neck and what you want to buy today."

He made light of the Douai attacker. "I need information on the negotiations over French Prince Henry becoming King of Poland. But everyone knows Polish envoys are here. I want more, something you won't tell your kinsman, the Duke of Guise."

It was a brazen demand. He laid out coins for her and sweets for the girls. He held back a bolt of magenta damask he'd meant to give Hélène's deputy, as she wasn't around.

Hélène tested each coin before putting them in her pocket. Four testoons. "Prince Henry sulks," she said slowly. "I've seen under King Charles's seal orders for clothes beyond Prince's Henry's purse."

"Then he's going, reluctantly," Latham said.

"He'll sign power-sharing terms and be a little king." She paused, drew a breath, exhaled. "There's something else…"

She was interrupted by a soft knock on the door. The girl entering wasn't malapert Marie. Putting two baskets on Hélène's desk, she curtsied and left.

"I need more," Latham persisted.

"Wait," Helene said.

Latham watched her sort through the baskets. One contained fabric scraps and loose threads. The other had coins, buttons, scraps of paper with writing, a locket with a broken chain with a lock of hair inside, along with notations of whose clothes these items had fallen from.

With a distracted air, Hélène put the fabric scraps, threads and coins in one pile, for resale. Latham could see she was turning over the "something else" in her mind.

She inspected items from the second basket, snorting with amusement. "Young love always shows itself, while old illicit love burrows for cover," she said, waving bits of paper and the locket at him. "It advances no one's fortunes to keep these clues to a multitude of betrayals." She rang for an assistant, instructing her to return them to their owners, mentioning discreetly how Hélène cared for their peace of mind.

Latham burst out laughing. "What an enterpriser you are."

Helene smiled as she sat. "I know something I could never say. I can put you in the way of seeing it yourself, but you must reward me commensurately."

Latham thought for a few minutes. "What if I help you keep your freedom, riches, even your life?"

"God in heaven, how ominous. What do you mean?"

"Your kinship to Henry, Duke of Guise has served you well. You think that what has been will be, because it is. You're dangerously complacent."

"Guises have fought Valois battles for generations. French kings are nothing without their Guise warriors."

"That's the past, not the future. Prince Henry won Poland because he'll tolerate heretics, which Spain doesn't. Guises don't either. One day, your Guise kin will join Spain and fight the French royal family. That endangers you."

Latham thought he saw fear flit across her face.

"A gentleman from the king's bedchamber tried to dismiss me recently," she conceded.

"So," exclaimed Latham triumphantly. "What happened?"

"The Duke, my kinsman, protested, so he gave up."

"Why did the king's man move against you?"

"You'll understand if I show you. What's this offer to save me?"

"I'll warn you before a lethal quarrel between your kin and the French king occurs. If I'm alive, I'll know. You can record it in your unofficial ledger as an obligation, if you like."

"Oh, come. An uncollateralised bond? You're an enterpriser yourself, weaselling secrets out of a poor old woman for a mere promise."

Nevertheless, she wrote the bond, which Latham initialled P.P. Then she picked up a ring of heavy keys, and some candles. Latham followed. They walked along an empty passageway to a small room whose door had three strong locks. When they were inside, Hélène lit the candles. "I say nothing, nothing, nothing." She left him alone.

The shelves were full of sumptuous clothes. Latham held the candle up and inspected five-layer ruffs that needed cleaning; detachable embroidered sleeves with diamonds, pearls or rubies coming loose and in need of stitching; dirty breeches with crinkled ties; velvet doublets with silver and gold thread that needed airing and brushing; sweat-stained hose; and three white silk shirts that needed cleaning. On the table was a wardrobe book of items with an embroidered fleur-de-lis on the cover.

The king's clothes looked normal. What did Hélène expect him to see? He rubbed his cheek against plush velvets, luxuriating in their thick softness; he ran his finger along shimmering satins and silks. Then he studied the shirts. Oddly, they'd already been cleaned.

He spread them on the table. Three clean shirts, with cuts to be repaired. The edges of the cuts were neat; they weren't accidental tears. The cleaning was horribly unprofessional. There were streaks of soap on the sleeves where they'd been hastily rinsed. Why clean shirts badly then damage them, in order for them to be properly cleaned and repaired?

He peered at the shirt fronts. Then he saw it. Some threads around the pearl buttons and buttons ties were faintly pink. He lifted one shirt to his nose. Through the uric acid, he thought he could smell blood. He picked at a reddish flake embedded in a button tie and put it on his tongue. Yes, maybe it was blood.

Latham put his hands on his own shirt at places where Charles's shirt was stained. He leaned back against a wall and coughed convulsively the way he'd seen in consumptives. A gobbet of spit landed on the back of his hand. He did it again with the same result. So the French king had a bad cough that his bedchamber servants tried to conceal. If he was coughing blood, he had consumption. Young King Charles IX was dying, and keeping it secret. That was why his man had tried to fire Hélène.

Suddenly the Krasnopol witch's prophecy made brilliant sense. She'd prophesied a short reign for the next King of Poland, which wasn't the same as foretelling his death. The panicked Polish nobles had conflated the two. There would be a royal death in France, which would *cause* a short reign by Poland's king. No wonder Hélène kept it from her Guise kin. To speak it was a capital crime. The newly crowned King of Poland,

Prince Henry Valois, was heir to the French crown. He'd leave Poland and rush back to secure it. That was the short reign.

Latham gasped with excitement. He glimpsed the future. Yes, yes, yes! Poland would have to find another king; a new Valois king who'd signed terms tolerating heretics in Poland would rule France. Guise/Valois tensions would flare. This was truly important.

He put the shirts back on the shelves and returned to Hélène's office. "Shirts," he said. "Sad."

"Only I handle them. His deaf-mute brings them. I'm sworn to secrecy," she answered.

"Does Prince Henry know? He's next in line to be French king."

"I don't think so. Remember, I told you nothing. Knowing this is a terrible burden. I'm relieved to share it."

Latham said goodbye to her in a state of preoccupied excitement. Pert Marie materialised to walk him out. "You must be careful, Monsieur. Outside the city walls are bandits, and inside lots of pickpockets." She'd decided to like him.

Latham inclined his head. "Thank you for warning me, Countess. I would never have thought of it." He gave her the bolt of magenta damask meant for Hélène's deputy.

She was ecstatic, fanning it out, then expertly folding it. "I'll make this a dress for the opening. Come to our inn, Monsieur. Now tomorrow…" She reminded him she'd be shopping for food with the steward for the Louvre Palace's kitchen, which the Monsieur had no permit to enter.

Latham took an amused breath when he saw the last of her, and turned his mind back to the French king's illness. This intelligence was too sensitive to entrust to any courier. It had to be delivered personally. He sent instructions to Pieter Boels to return to Warsaw and watch events, then joined the next relay of couriers to Madrid. For several nights he rode pillion, slumped dozing against the back of night couriers.

He reached Madrid in nine days, close to the record of seven. Exultant, he hoped to get an audience with King

Philip. Instead, he was directed to Secretary Perez' private mansion. Perez dismayed him: Don Antonio's gross appetites and preening ambition were overwhelmingly apparent in his shape, clothes, jewels and words. The secretary debriefed him carefully, intending to use Latham's astuteness to elevate his own position at court. That the mystery of the Krasnopol witch's prophecy could now be explained was a triumph. Perez showered money on Latham, and ordered him back to Brussels on the next day's relay.

When the French king died on 30th May of the next year, 1574, Pieter Boels, who'd stayed close to Prince Henry and the Polish court, gave Latham early notice of his night escape to claim France's crown. Latham got that news expeditiously to Perez, and Latham's reputation soared. Perez sent him a bonus that enabled him to rent a house in elegant upper town Brussels. He was no longer poor, and he owed Pieter an interview with his odd nephew.

CHAPTER 8
A SERVANT
AND A LETTER

September 1574

Pieter Boels ushered a gangly youth of about sixteen into Latham's receiving room. Holding his cap in big, rough hands, Joris Boels stood braced in utmost opposition, young mouth set in pinched angry lines. Apart from this extreme mood, his looks were ordinary: light brown eyes, straight brown hair, a moderate nose in a face free of pockmarks, moles or freckles. *Easily forgotten*, Latham thought approvingly, *if he could relax*.

"I hear you draw well," Latham began. The youth nodded sullenly. Latham dismissed Pieter and handed Joris paper, quill and black ink.

"A man attacked me last year," Latham continued.

A flicker in the noncommittal eyes.

"I don't know who he was, but listen and draw." Latham described the Douai novice's square jaw, the angle of his ears, his cold blue eyes, his build, his walk, everything he remembered, including garlic breath and grunts.

Joris sat and looked at the ceiling then bent to the paper. His scraped-knuckle left hand became a delicate instrument, making tiny movements to fix facial details and sweeping ones to capture the attacker's aggression. He brought the Douai novice to life, first full-faced, facing left, then right.

"It's very like him," Latham exclaimed in astonishment.

A faint smile spread the boy's lips. "Eng——el," he attempted.

Latham interrupted. "Engelsman?"

The boy's momentary openness slammed shut. He glared.

"You think he's English?" Latham tried again. "Why?"

Joris shrugged.

"No matter." Latham was angry with himself. Pieter had warned him about condescending, yet he'd fallen into it right away. He handed Joris more paper and coloured inks. "He could disguise himself, so make him an artisan, a wounded veteran, a liveried servant, a physician."

The novice became these characters.

"Would you recognise him anywhere?" Latham asked, settling in to wait as long as it took for the answer.

Joris focused on the ceiling. "Mm-INE!"

He was saying that he now owned this man. Latham was intrigued because it was a subtle concept. Perhaps Pieter was right about his virtues. He took Joris to the window, pointed to a building and a carriage with ornate decoration. Then he closed the shutters and asked him to draw them. The result was accurate.

"Very good, Master Boels. One of your duties would be to follow my followers, draw them and map where they stay. Now, your uncle says you can fight."

Joris nodded. Flexing his hands, he ambled after Latham to the courtyard, where a hired pugilist waited. Joris's sword-work was slow, but he parried well enough to defend against a common bandit. As a fist fighter, he was more dangerous. Following no rules, he landed kicks on the pugilist's groin and ankles, a punch to his throat. The pugilist laid him flat eventually, but it was hard to tell who was the more exhausted.

"Well, Master Boels," Latham said, "I'll hire you as my courier and manservant. On trial, you understand, for three months."

To his surprise, Joris sank in an elegant bow, the kind of obsequy a mercantile family would teach its sons. Of course, Joris came from such a family. Latham began to suspect that behind his speech confusions, an energetic brain was at work. Pieter had also said Joris had puppy-like loyalty. Latham resolved to watch for an opportunity to cultivate it.

For Joris, carrying messages and payments to Latham's far-flung informers suited his nomadic soul, while scouring Brussels for a thug following Latham satisfied his aggression. In time, he uncovered two skulking but timid Flemings trailing after Latham as he came and went from Coudenberg Palace, the administrative centre. And once, with his weapon of choice, a crowbar, he broke the leg of a tousled-haired man he'd seen twice watching the house. His sketch resembled Albert Braak, the courier Latham had fooled into betraying Genlis. When Joris reported that all three Flemings, who appeared to be one cell, had left Brussels, Latham heaved a sigh of relief.

Being thanked for disabling Braak gave Joris confidence. His angry face began to relax, and his kindness showed. He collected injured wild animals, nursing them until they could be released. Through the door of his attic room, Latham often heard the rumble of a pigeon with a splinted wing, or the squeaky bark of a malnourished squirrel gored by some predator. Some of Joris's rescues didn't survive; he was no apothecary. He buried these corpses near the vegetable garden, chanting mangled Latin funeral prayers.

Joris stayed clam-shut about his inner thoughts. But Latham noticed he wore the same threadbare breeches, jerkin and boots, despite a decent salary. One afternoon, he followed his servant to the central market and saw him give a packet to a herring merchant. Latham paid to retrieve it. In addition to half of Joris's monthly earnings, it contained drawings a child would love: jugglers, acrobats, great nobles and ladies, and the misshapen motley citizens crowding any great city. He whistled. Pieter had said Joris wanted to marry a heretic girl, which shamed his parents. Perhaps this was for her. He tripled the money and gave the packet to the merchant next market day.

Two months later Joris came in, poring over a note in big capital letters thanking him for more money than he'd sent. He scratched his head in perplexity. Latham grinned knowingly. This unspoken understanding won Joris's devotion.

One May morning in 1576, Joris brought Latham a letter that a foreign messenger had delivered. "U-cron," he said, extending his index finger. It seemed to make him extremely happy.

Latham was writing to Perez, reaching for a tenuous insight linking two seemingly unconnected events. With the interruption, he lost it. He surrendered to the sadistic imp that seized him when Joris's speech defects overstretched his patience. "Read it out," he snapped.

Joris broke the seal and grunted in horror at patterns dancing on the page. He looked up, humiliated.

"Wait, give it to me." Ashamed, Latham snatched the letter and dismissed him. The calligraphy was elegant, paper and embroidered linen tie expensive, the broken seal of royal quality. First, he looked at the linen tie. *U...cron*, with an extended finger. Unicorns. Of course, the mythical animal would enchant Joris. He pressed the letter's edges together and stared at the ruptured seal. He sucked in his breath, turned and rummaged in a box, and pulled out a tracing made of this seal eight years ago. It matched.

No! Praise God. No! His emotions churned from joy to fear. Unicorns, the reverse side of Mary, Queen of Scots' seal, were embroidered on the tie. And two halves of a female seated on a throne had closed the letter. Could Mary, Queen of Scots have written to him?

He opened and flattened the pages. There were several. He tried to recall her script. It certainly resembled what he was looking at. The first page was in clear text, the remaining three in code.

Despite being confined to an English castle, Mary knew his address and alias. That was startling. He started reading and found the opening sentence equally unexpected. With the peremptory affection of a still-powerful sovereign, Mary wrote that she required the services of her former envoy. Her assumption that she was still his liege lady convinced Latham that the letter was genuine.

He delayed decoding the rest. All night he struggled. Should he reply that he couldn't undertake any service before getting approval from Perez? Could he ignore the letter? If he decoded it–obviously it contained secrets–could he refuse the service, having learned it? A young man's curiosity grabbed him one moment; mature foreboding restrained him the next. What he kept coming back to through that thought-scrambling night was what he'd explained to David Hicks years ago in Paris: his obligation to Mary for protecting him when she herself was at risk.

The next morning, he threw open the shutters and rubbed eyes gritty from sleeplessness. Voices floated up, braying mules, the squeal of metal as shops opened, a pleasant background for concentration. He worked to break the code. Curiosity had won; circumspection lost

To find the key, he did what he'd done with Alava's letter to the Duke of Guise, his first decoding. He looked to the sign-off. Mary was less formal than other monarchs. They typically signed, *Your loving sovereign.* Mary wrote, *Mistress, Friend,* either of the *dear* or *best* variety, *Mary R.* When he was staring bemusedly at *Your old kind mistress and best friend, Mary R,* he had the key

Right trusty envoy,

I make no doubt you will adhere to the promise you made to serve me, which I thought sincere when I knighted you. I assure you today you will never have a better friend than myself. I am well advertised how virtuously you serve my good brother, King Philip. I rejoiced that your good works gained advantage for the faith in routing Genlis and ending Coligny's evil doings and the evil of thousands of rebellious Huguenots. That they reckon you the worst man in all France is notoriety to cherish.

I know you will never forget whose commendation caused you to be saved by my Guise cousins after the treachery of my Protestant nobles. Now I ask that you fulfil my present commission, concerning matrimony and money. I beg you to divert, for a short time, your labours on behalf of Spain. Remember, my good friend, the truest trial of a servant is when service might not seem convenient.

For eight years, I, an anointed Queen, have been a prisoner. Malicious machinations of my unfriends have poisoned the mind of my good sister, Queen Elizabeth, with forged proofs I compassed my husband's murder and other evils. I entreated Elizabeth to allow me to answer in person for my innocency, wherein I am sure she could not have resisted me, such meeting being her duty, as any Prince is bound to assist another of equal degree. But she conceived that meeting an alleged murderess before acquittal at trial would dishonour her. But trial of an anointed Queen she deemed not meet at all. It was never held. No acquittal, no meeting. No trial, no acquittal. All left fog-shrouded, a condition pleasing to her but casting me into despair.

'When I was deposed in Scotland this same good sister Elizabeth threatened war on the usurpers if they harmed me. They dared not. These good offices led me to love her friendship above all others. So when I escaped, I went to England. That turned

out to be a different case. Despite my pleas and affirmations she will not allow me to come to France to raise an army, nor return to Scotland where I have supporters. I am moved from castle to castle, each shift further from them who'd risk all for me.

It is time to put these matters right, for, as seasons flow, valiant friends age, ail or die. I have a remedy. Marriage. My good brother, King Philip, has a natural half-brother, John, a warrior who slaughtered rebellious Moors in Granada, and will soon be appointed Captain-General of the Army of Flanders, Governor of the benighted Netherlands....

Latham stopped, sat back and whistled. The current governor, Don Luis de Requesens, had recently died of fever, but his replacement hadn't been announced. Latham knew from Perez, but most in Brussels didn't. Mary's network was formidable. He turned back to the letter.

My friends in Madrid write that this gallant wants to fight the Dutch rebels, while King Philip, starved for funds, needs a truce. John will be eager to venture greater things. My marriage to him will help both of us. When he tires of the accursed Netherlanders, he can spirit me out of this place to Scotland, where I can get rid of my enemies and help my subjects correct the errors their heretic government has led them into....

What? Latham got up, paced the room, laughing then crying. This was a dream borne of frantic isolation. Mary's letter then described Don John's lineage, which he knew, of course: son of Philip's father, Holy Roman Emperor Charles V, by his last mistress, Barbara Blomberg, a German knight's daughter. She had a divine singing voice, but a reputation for choler and looseness. She'd been married off to one of the Emperor's bodyguards, and John taken from her and raised in Madrid. And now he would govern the Netherlands.

Latham had no idea what all this had to do with him.

He learned.

This concubine of meagre rank and dubious virtue is to be allowed to meet her son in Brussels for the first time since separation. I require you to become acquainted with the said

Lady, conduct the suit on my behalf with your most obliging manners. Your love of music and handsome face will endear you to the Lady. If she shows a mother's anxiety for her son's union with one reputed to be a husband killer, you, above all others, can relieve her doubts, because you were with me when we heard the explosion and knew not what it could be. You witnessed my shocked innocency. This marriage will bring honour to her son, a bastard no how my equal, and to her, who must have a mother's ambition for her whelp to gain a kingdom. In better times I would not wed a natural son, but the Almighty, in His infinite wisdom, has seen fit to subject me to the trials of a Job, and Don John is said to be comely.

Say no word to anyone of this except the said Lady, and in your dealings confuse the watchers, who are many. You will gain glory as a Sovereign-restorer and protector of souls.

After you have secured the mother's agreement, I wish you to go to Florence and raise a loan for me from Francesco, Grand Duke of Tuscany. Debased French coinage has lowered my income, and I need ten thousand pounds to reward my supporters. All funds you need for the commission get from my Paris agent, Thomas Morgan, but mention only the loan to him, not marriage, for Elizabeth's spies watch him. Send assurance by the messenger that you will help me. I place my whole trust in you. Be a queen-restorer, have a care for endangered Scottish souls, or you will have all the blame.

I pray God keep you in his Holy keeping, as He has me, for without His love my miseries would be unbearable. Know that I would rather lose all in this venture than stay in the same case.

Your old kind mistress and best friend, Mary R.

Conduct the suit with your most obliging manners… Latham got up, breathing hard. She was whoring him, demanding he be ready to romance Barbara Blomberg into supporting Mary's marriage to her son. How much did she know about his erotic adventures in Scotland? Probably a lot more than he realised at the time, given the quality of her information network now.

Could he do this? There were greater matters than personal inclinations here.

He drank a goblet of wine and paced the room. Twelve paces, by fourteen, and back. Many times. Another drink. He did respond to some women, particularly older. In the end, he believed Mary was wrongly deposed, a blow to social order. Whether her plot was likely to succeed wasn't the point.

His network was functioning well; he'd proven his value to Spain; the location, Brussels, was convenient. He saw no compelling reason not to try. Scotland was in play, and the knight in him longed for a quest after several quiet months. He replied: *Yes, Piso Prosperino.* If he heard Dr Pell murmuring, "Presumption, dear boy, is your greatest flaw," he ignored it.

CHAPTER 9
HUBRIS

Brussels, October 1576

Brussels was blazing with autumn yellows and reds when Latham finally clattered through the white stone archway of the Hotel Ravennais to begin Mary's suit. In addition to rooms at Coudenberg Palace, Lady Barbara Blomberg maintained a suite in the elegant Burgundian manor. Close to the palace, Hotel Ravennais housed military officers, courtiers, and patricians with business at court. Built early in the century, the hotel consisted of two red brick buildings, gardens and stables.

Brussel's Upper Town vibrated with the pomp of imperial life. But it was a façade, a brittle gaiety Latham marvelled at because mayhem was not far away. A mutiny in July by Spanish troops in Holland had caused the loss of the province; the Dutch rebellion seemed entrenched, and elites loyal to Spain were deeply anxious. Nevertheless, Upper Town carried on as if God was blessing its every day.

Writing as Piso Prosperino, Latham had requested a meeting with Barbara Blomberg, saying he had an important private matter to unfold. Weeks later, she'd agreed. As he stabled his horse, he reviewed what he knew about her.

She'd been just eighteen when a jaded Emperor Charles V fell for her voice. It had begun accidentally: she was pretending to be a boy substituting for a famous chorister who had fallen sick just before a command performance. The solace the Emperor sought from repeated musical performances became sexual, resulting in the illegitimate Don John. Emperor Charles had married her off to an imperial knight, Hieronymus Kegel. This union was said to be unhappy, although they had three children, now grown and dispersed. Kegel had died in 1569. There were rumours that during her marriage Blomberg's voice had sickened; if so, it had recovered with the freedom of widowhood. She lived on a modest pension from Philip, occasionally performing for guests. Her invitations were prized by those for whom probity wasn't everything.

Now, twenty minutes early, lute in hand and heart thumping, Latham walked across the courtyard. Squelching fallen chestnuts underfoot, he passed the lower building, glancing at the spired turret and white stone framing the upper floors. He opened the door to the main building and climbed to the first-floor landing. He was blocked from getting further by a knot of officers and townsmen. She was rehearsing; male voices and a solo soprano floating down, accompanied by a spinet. The uninvited locals were eavesdropping.

It was the motet *Grief hath besieged me*. Basses and tenors interwove like hemp rope being plaited, while the silken soprano soared above, in phrases so long that they seemed to defy the gross need to breathe. The imperceptible change of texture when breath did occur imbued the sound with otherworldliness, arousing the listener's profound yearning, a soul stretching to its Maker.

This is what Emperor Charles had to own, Latham realised. Too soon, the motet ended. The eavesdroppers exchanged glances, but didn't move. The music began again, the soft sections more inward, an intimation of sound, yet fully present. Then swelling at *Call, cease not to call, And I say, what shall I say?* The soprano adopted a different hue for different characters, and the male voices finished with pelting affirmation: *In thee, Lord, do I put my trust.*

It was over. The door opened, and five men trooped out, chatting eagerly until they saw the listeners. "Get out knaves, or pay us!" Done with spirituality, they pushed the eavesdroppers downstairs. Latham waited until everyone had left, then returned to the landing, as a viol de gamba and cornet were tuning up.

Secular songs began: a troubadour love song; a sarcastic ditty on a miserable marriage; a martial ballad of Spain routing Moors. The soprano duetted with fast instrumental lines. Latham had never heard the style before; she must have invented it. Demanding great virtuosity, at one moment her voice was liquid gold pouring from high to low when following the cornet; a string of shimmering diamonds tossed in the air when imitating plucked spinet scales; low with urgency when improvising with the viol de gamba. She made the instruments sound all wood, brass and gut, compared with the vibrating resonance that was her body. Latham's blood tingled, his own body travelling to very far places.

But she'd had pushed her accompanists too hard. Into this glorious cosmos, foul notes from the spinet, a staggering inability to keep up, a jagged tailing to silence.

"Turd-fingers, muse-murderer, dung-sucker! Get out of my sight. You're dismissed! Out! Out! Out!" The voice down from the ether: violent, guttural. Pottery breaking, the clang and jangle of metal hitting a keyboard. The door banged open, and a man backed out, clutching his bleeding forehead. A sheepish cornetist and gamba player followed him.

Latham ran upstairs and walked in. He came face to face with a middle-aged woman bent over, face flushed, her chest heaving with incandescent fury.

"Lady Barbara, I am enchanted," he cried, sweeping off his hat and bowing. Straightening up, he thought: *I'm to conduct this suit with my most obliging manners. How do I begin?*

Blomberg's ferocity subsided as she, too, stood. Smoothing dishevelled hair, she said, "Ecstasy and rage vibrate as one string, don't you think?" Flat-toned, as if her life-force had drained away.

"No, lady. Angels do not brush me, as they do you."

She smiled slightly and rang for a servant to clean up the mess.

"Signor Piso Prosperino? You look Saxon, not Tuscan. A mystery. Well, we're finished here. This private talk will have to be short because I must find a new spinet player for tomorrow."

A homely lady-in-waiting embroidering cushions in the window recess bobbed a curtsy and left.

Alone, Latham and Blomberg appraised each other.

Latham looked down at a well-proportioned full-breasted woman of about fifty, with luxuriant, greying fair hair escaping a string net infused with malachite. Her eyes were intensely blue, her features classic and her skin pale. Petulance etched her mouth, and her eyes were framed by fine crows' feet. She extended a large bare hand to be kissed. Latham felt calluses on her fingertips from lute strings. A musician in every piece of her body, he thought.

Her clothes were a cry of taste amidst constraint. Over a narrow farthingale, she was wearing a cream woollen dress fastened with malachite buttons, with an embroidered blue and green hem and matching bands all the way up. She had green velvet shoulder puffers and attached woollen sleeves. These malachites yearn to be emeralds, her dress said, wool deserves to be satin or summer velvet, except this world is cruel.

Clothed in Tuscan fashion, Latham was wearing a white cambric shirt with blackwork at cuff and collar, a black velvet doublet with vertical and horizontal slashes showing russet satin, which brought a tawny glow to his hazel eyes; matching upper stocks with slashes over russet and black hose. With no puffers or padded codpiece, the contours of his physique were visible.

She waved him to the window recess. "Well, what is this important private matter, Signor Prosperino? I've never heard of you."

Latham decided that directness was the only way to proceed with a woman of such temperament. He made a brief account of his life, then showed her the page of Mary's letter concerning her son, Don John. The veins in her neck throbbed as she sat up; her eyes gleamed, then dulled. Latham guessed that she was visualising her son wearing the Scottish crown, then recalling Darnley's murder. He waited.

"I like your plain speaking. Reminds me of my poor Kegel," she said, leaning against the window frame. "But you're reckless, with yourself and others. Kegel was timid, in his drunken way. To be king consort and breed royal heirs fits my son's merits, but that queen is ill-starred. Even though I'm poor and ill-thought-of, I hear the gossip. Your Mary married the man who murdered her consort, Lord Darnley, and many say she plotted the regicide. Her first husband, young King Francis II of France, died of a strange disease some call poison; her third husband, the murderer of her second, fled Scotland and lies in chains in a Danish prison; her intended fourth husband, the English Duke of Norfolk, plotted with her against the English queen, and was executed. How could any loving mother favour this match?"

"My lady, you say you like plain speaking. I give you more. No Queen enjoying Fortune's smile would marry a natural son. This is your son's only path to a throne. Tell me: are all the tales about you as true as you assume the tales about Queen Mary are?"

She blushed.

"Aha," he went on. "I don't expect you to love this suit at first. As you see from the letter, Her Majesty commends your fears, being an anxious mother herself. All she asks is that you write to her. I can get letters back and forth. I warrant your reservations will turn to favour."

"And while letters ride back and forth, you are to make watchers guess what you're about? How amusing."

She got up without agreeing or refusing. Instead, she eyed his lute.

"You came ready to play. I must replace that foul keyboard thumper and the spinet. The goblet I threw ruined it. Let's see if, with two lutes, you and I can play the spinet parts. It will save me time and money if you're good enough."

She sang softly and slowly, playing the upper parts on her lute, allowing Latham to take the bass and tenor lines. She gradually increased the pace. He felt he was treading a rope strung between church spires, hundreds of feet in the air, petrified to think or look at the music, finding his way by instinct, swept where he needed to go by her force. Miraculously he played true, finding the right chords, fingering the scales perfectly. It was only later, when he was hundreds of miles away, recalling the afternoon with the clarity of time and distance, that he realised she'd divined his abilities from how he had tuned his lute. She'd paced herself to let him succeed.

At the time, she just inclined her head and said, "Not too horrible, Piso Prosperino, who isn't. Let me show you a trick." She re-tuned his lute, tightening the strings, then adjusted her own. The pitches rang out higher now, piercingly plaintive. She sang higher, a brassy gloss in her sound. Latham was laughing with delight, this sublime brilliance new to him. He began to think her beyond human.

But during their second run through, her voice cracked. With stricken horror, she clutched her throat, croaked a few foul notes, odd ugly honks. She whispered, "The muse left me. I must rest. Get out."

She was entirely human. Latham now understood her rage at the spinet player. She couldn't bear weakness in others because of her own fragility. The unreliability of her virtuosity was the reason she was still poor. Because of her tantrum and his visit, she'd sung for longer than she'd intended.

At her concert the next night, she was at her best, though with a short programme. Latham accompanied her creditably enough to avoid censure. And so their acquaintance began. He escorted her on hunts and to court balls, tossing her higher in the volta than was fashionable in Brussels, ruled by ascetic Philip II. But it was how he remembered it from his English courtier days, and Lady Barbara relished it.

The first time Latham met Lady Barbara, he'd seen her at her most vulnerable, dignity shredded and in naked terror when her voice cracked. Physical nakedness meant less to her. As letters between Mary and Barbara travelled, she signalled that she wanted more from Latham, and he felt the same. He liked her neck wrinkles, and other physical evidence of years lived, mistakes made and lesson learned. Her vibrant longevity aroused him.

After a good rehearsal, followed by a provocative political argument, they migrated to her bed, a large four-poster with luxurious linens. She stood, lounging in the unmistakable posture of beckoning him to kiss her. He stood, Tuscan clothed, half-paralysed. He glanced around the room. With her high temperament, the rage or ecstasy she'd dumped on the spinet player and spinet, was she the kind of dominant character who needed to administer, or suffer, whips and chains? That, he couldn't do.

She read his thoughts, chuckling with rich sensuality. "Relax, you fool, it's only sex! There are no devices on hooks or in the dresser."

Coupling didn't engage the extreme reaches of Lady Barbara's temperament. Choler never intruded on physical intimacy. She wanted languorous play: warm clove oil gently spread on skin, the hot breath of a near-kiss, then full moist kissing, bringing to aching hunger every inch of her desiring body. When arousing him, she added bracing turmeric to the oil. She also liked variety. He became a planner of bed strategy, arriving with poses on twisted pieces of paper, which he selected at random. He felt burdened, periodically taking aphrodisiacal sarsaparilla root to perform, but his affection for her steadily deepened. What he had no mental space left for at all was the condition of the world.

As Joris took letters to Mary's factor in Paris and brought back answers, Latham hired a substitute manservant from a list at Coudenberg Palace. He didn't vet him. If the man spread rumours about him and Lady Barbara, he'd be confusing the watchers, as Mary had instructed.

Hiring an informer manservant was a situation he'd set up, and thought he controlled. But in the drama of knowing Barbara Blomberg, he forgot Madrid. He paid no attention to the absence of notes from his employer, Secretary Antonio Perez. It didn't occur to him that Perez's status could change. He took the absence of Perez's nagging verbosity as a sign that the Almighty favoured his mission.

In early March 1577, Latham was walking home after seeing Lady Barbara. Outside his front gate, he stopped, startled. Tied to a post was a splendid black gelding nibbling the early grasses thrusting through the street surface. Its saddle cloth had a diagonal red cross on green and white stripes.

"Eleventh Company. Cristo!" Latham ran up the steps and into his receiving room. There he found a frowning Don Cristobal dressed for travel, pacing.

Don Cristobal's frown dissolved into a beaming smile. "Edward." He folded Latham in a hug, "what joy to see you."

"What brings you? Can you stay for supper, or several days?"

"No. I leave within the hour, for Sicily. I wanted to see you, for pleasure of course, but also to report some things."

The servant brought bread, cheese and wine, and left. While Don Cristobal drank, Latham looked at him. He was as imposing as ever, but his cheek lines turned down with dug-in frustration.

"Cristo, you're melancholy."

"Yes," Don Cristobal agreed. He dabbed his lips with the napkin.

Latham knew he was trying to decide how much to say. "You can speak freely. You know my discretion."

"Ah, freely then." Don Cristobal thumped the napkin down. "You know I love God, king, kin, and country. My life is a simple duty. But we wasted the chance we had after routing Genlis. Remember our last dinner? All those yellow greasy bread bits stretching from Mons to France to England—I'll never forget your new chain of policy favouring our cause—and it was for naught. Our enemies were confused, but we made more bad policy. The Duke of Alva was too cruel, his successors ineffective."

"Where were you last year?" Latham asked. "I got no answer to my letter."

"I'm sorry. I was a brooding hermit. I found out that Alva murdered Genlis. Night strangulation of a chained man. It made a mockery of my promise to him when he gave me his sword: treatment according to customs of war. I wrote a protest, and was sent home on leave. We had a new baby boy. *Be fruitful and multiply*, as the Bible says."

"Cristo, I give you joy in your son."

"It pleased Teresa mightily."

"Not you?"

"It's not enough. I want victory. With our repeated mistakes, this war could go on for generations. What joy are boy heirs if they must bleed in the same battles as their father? I returned to the Netherlands when Governor Requesens died. He wasted from an ague, but not before presiding over a mutiny in the north by our soldiers, which cost us the loss of all of Holland. It broke my heart. I told you at Mons that today's armies dissolve through disease or lack of pay. I never thought to see it in ours. We've never lost a land battle, but this mutiny and loss of Holland trumpets our Achilles heel: stop our money and we'll attack ourselves, just like Genlis' hapless rogues! Our new governor is hopeless, for all he's the king's natural half-brother: handsome Don John, son of the king's emperor father, by Lady Barbara Blomberg. I call him the *ceramic knight*. Privately of course." He looked anxious. "You won't repeat this to any man, or....woman?"

"Of course not." Latham patted his sleeve. Cristo had heard about his acquaintance with Lady Barbara. For Mary's sake, he wanted a professional assessment of her son. "Didn't your *ceramic knight* crush Moriscos in Granada?" he asked.

Don Cristobal flicked a breadcrumb off his sleeve. "That's different. A few rebels hid in caves. Don John's men fired the caves then cut down fleeing survivors. Breaching our own fortified bastions here requires true ability. Don John neither negotiates well nor fights, but adores dressing up for both. He's a bright-painted hollow pot. There, I said it."

Don John, Mary's saviour, Latham thought sadly. "Still," he said, "treasure ships from the Americas will bring money. This is surely just a pause. Is the whole company leaving?"

"Yes, except William Boels, who got a promotion. More of him in a minute. Listen, Edward; there are things I must tell you. First, this you must keep secret. My written orders for Sicily came from Madrid. But when Don John gave them to me, he patted my shoulder, winked, and whispered I should tarry in Genoa."

"So he means to recall you? Break the king's, his brother's, truce?"

"I'd never circumvent a written order for the *ceramic knight*. I just want you to know that Madrid and Brussels aren't aligned. This stinks of bad politics."

Latham felt a sudden foreboding. "Did Antonio Perez or his clerk sign it?"

"Someone else. No one's heard from Perez recently. I must leave, but there's something else I wanted to tell you. William Boels…"

Nerves shrieking, the last thing Latham wanted to hear about was young William Boels. How could he have missed Perez's' fall from favour? But he willed himself to pay attention. "Oh yes, William shot at my horse at the Mons siege, the day we met, and missed. His uncle is my sub-agent, and I hired his cousin, Joris, as courier. What about William?"

"He's now logistics clerk at Coudenberg Palace for the Royal Guard, because of his mathematics. You can't imagine how puffed up he is. Thick codpieces, peacock hat feathers, black velvet doublets with silver thread he can't afford. He walks around with a nosegay to ward off unwholesome air. He's made big by serving 'the empire on which the sun never sets,' as he puts it, kisses our king's face on the gold escudos he counts. I tell you this because he's a rising man; you might need his help someday. He passed on gossip about you…." Don Cristobal looked down, embarrassed. "You know how I feel about older women, the risk of the evil eye. Dear friend, a certain German lady is not altogether safe. Now, I embrace you with a brother's love and say goodbye."

In London, Sir Francis Walsingham, England's chief spymaster, winced. He was trying to keep up with his sovereign, Elizabeth, who was striding along a paved path in her privy garden at Whitehall. Early warmth had seduced crocuses, hyacinths and daffodils into bloom. But frost followed, and the blooms had a shocked, near-dead look. A gust of wind made Walsingham grab his hat, while Elizabeth spread her arms, gulping in the bracing freshness. Her guard and ladies-in-waiting withdrew to allow private conversation.

Elizabeth turned in front of a gilded heraldic falcon on top of a striped pole. She eyed her spymaster without sympathy "Dour thoughts, Master Moor. Is hatred of this Dutch/Spanish truce braiding your gut? You'll have to stop shrewing me to send English troops, the perils of which you won't see."

"Your Majesty, I fear I must report a marriage."

At the word "marriage," Elizabeth lowered her arms, becoming attentive and hostile.

"None of your relatives, Ma'am," Walsingham added quickly. "Naught touching crown or succession."

She relaxed.

"It isn't illegal, but you'll be displeased," Walsingham persisted.

"Who's the fool this time?" she asked. "One of my arthritic old bishops plucking a nubile maid? How his flock will snigger. Must I hear this? I was enjoying the morning."

Walsingham chewed his lip.

This time Elizabeth showed concern. She didn't like him but knew his value.

"Moor, you need rest. Take my chickweed. It's good for gut pain."

Walsingham loathed herbs, but couldn't refuse a queen's remedies. "Thank you, Ma'am," he replied cautiously. "I'm sure it will cure me."

Elizabeth cast him a broad smile, knowing he'd throw her remedy away. "So, who wed?'

"No bishop. At least, not today. You former papist courtier, Sir Edward Latham."

"Latham? Do I remember him?" Chewing her thumbnail, she frowned at the gilded falcon, looking for an answer in its blank painted eyes. She thought back to early courtiers. "Flaxen hair, unsatisfied hazel eyes. Tall. Yes, he left us to serve

Darnley, and now Philip. A papist through and through. Who did he marry? I hardly think I'd care."

"Lady Barbara Blomberg."

"What?" Elizabeth was flabbergasted. "Old Emperor Charles's mistress? The one with the voice?" She was speechless, then snorted a laugh. "She must be much older than he is.'

"Ma'am, some fifteen years."

"Well, that's admirable, now I think on it."

Walsingham was appalled. "Ma'am, Blomberg and Latham both receive pensions from Philip. This marriage raises the spectre of Spanish pensions being paid to English nobles partial to the Pope. It's dangerous."

Elizabeth was irritated. Just because she'd had a moment's fun, he thought he had to teach her the implications of the match. "Moor, I demanded a list of pension recipients from the Spanish ambassador the day I became queen. I stopped the pensions long before you came to court. The marriage is against our interests, of course. Does Philip approve?"

"I haven't heard."

"Was there a ceremony?"

"No reports, but my agents watch them. They are often alone."

"You don't know much, do you? S'wounds, what a stupid cur Latham is."

Cheeks reddening with anger, she strode inside. "You did well to tell me, Moor. I reserved the right to confiscate Latham lands. I won't touch his kin; they've done nothing. But stop his income. Now, this marriage touches Philip much more than me, Blomberg being the mother of his half-brother. We're not at war with Spain, and there's a pause in the fighting between Spain and our Dutch friends. Send word to Philip by our Paris embassy about this ill-judged coupling. Let him sort it out."

Madrid, late March 1577

"In the matter of Poland, that spy advised above his station. Now he *acts!* She's no better. I pay them both pensions! Well, what would I expect from Perez' man? Was there a ceremony?"

In his study, Philip II drummed his fingers while an aide scrambled through reports. "Your Majesty, not a public one. But they comported themselves in a manner only marriage could excuse. Our informer is Latham's manservant. Courtiers in Brussels corroborate companionship, and the English ambassador to France told us they find reports of a marriage credible."

"I wouldn't have approved the marriage, if asked. It dishonours the Hapsburg name. That English ambassador is a heretic, but an unimaginative truth-teller. He couldn't invent this tale. Banish Latham from Spanish lands and stop his salary. She…" He was so angry, he had to stop to think what to do with her. "She goes to a severe Castilian convent. I'll decide which one after prayer. Use troops."

Brussels, April 1577

Lady Barbara pulled Latham into her receiving room and slammed the door. She was dressed in just a blue smock. Her bodice and farthingale were on the window sill, while her sleeves lay on the floor, their stiffened open shoulders gaping.

Some new drama, Latham thought. He reached for a twisted paper. "Bed frolics?"

He'd misinterpreted her signal.

She leapt up, "Bed frolics? No! It's time for plain speaking. You rut like a clock. Tick tock, tick, tock. Do you think I haven't tasted sarsaparilla on your tongue? How else do indifferent men who want my voice jig? And I know when a man's mind draws David as his body plunges into soft, yielding Aphrodite."

"Soft, lady? Yielding?" They were both red-faced. "You have no yielding in you. You don't insult me. It's a compliment. I exult that my will can order my body to the herculean task of pleasing you. If my rutting is like a clock, then your cunny chimed the hours merrily enough. When not touched by Orpheus, you have a dried-out heart. You sold your soul, like Faustus, to sing. When the thread tying your throat to Mephisto frays, you croak like a frog. Ours is a friendship of policy, and you just shredded its foundation: discretion."

He strode to the door and bent to the keyhole. The back of a skirt scurried away. "See," he said angrily. "Your servant heard. One more tavern tale about you. Now, tell me what ails you. Some new thing does."

She pulled him to the fire, sat him on cushions and whispered, "My son agreed to the match with Mary. But he told me for the first time that King Philip instructed him last year to pretend to court the other one, the English Queen…"

"What?" Latham gasped.

"Not only that. Someone tried to poison his chief military aide while the aide was in Madrid. Please make the union with Mary happen quickly."

"How? After months of 'No, maybe, slowly?'"

She slumped, looking old. "Edward, forgive my harsh words. I didn't mean them, at least not much. I'm as fond of you as what you call my dried-up heart can manage. I'm in a panic. Because of the king's suspicion of my son, his natural brother; because of his lack of plain dealing with me."

They stared into the fire. Latham's mind whirled. Cristo had warned him that Don John might break Philip's truce with the Dutch, which almost constituted rebellion.

"John says Don Antonio Perez, who encouraged him, is out of favour." Lady Barbara broke the silence. "He's afraid. He's the baby of my womb, Edward; I see the pattern of me in his face but know nothing of his heart. I dreamed such felicities would come from our reunion."

Latham didn't reply.

She tugged his sleeve. "What are you thinking?"

"I was surprised at not hearing from Perez. Now I understand."

"Understand? This isn't the time for puzzle-solving."

"It's always the time for puzzle-solving. Listen, dear. Many people suspected your son might not honour King Philip's truce. Don John has been playing a dangerous game. When a councillor like Perez loses favour, the monarch immediately cuts him off from his foreign agents. That's the puzzle I now understand. Your son said someone tried to poison his aide. Philip won't attack his half-brother, his blood; but he's sending a signal. Mary will be delighted. We need to be prudent, meet only when there's a plan.

"I also spoke far too harshly. Unlike many men, I relish a lived-in body, with the tales life has scribed on it..." His tongue formed around the words *I love you*, his mouth opened to say them. It was the truth. Then he shut it. "This labour of Hercules has been an unforgettable privilege."

As Latham left, he heard her tuning her lute. He stopped on the landing. He'd miss her terribly.

They were too late. Soldiers came that night. Torches flaring, boots ringing on cobblestones, they brought neighbourhood dogs to frenzied barking. Candles flared at windows, eyes peered out, drew back in relief as halberds and swords passed their house. Eight men went to Latham's house; six to Lady Barbara's rooms.

"What am I charged with?" Latham demanded, as men splintered his door and read out orders banishing him from Spanish lands, and ordering for him to be taken over the French border.

"Marriage above your degree," the corporal announced.

"*My* marriage?" Latham started laughing. Confuse the watchers, Mary had written. Well, they had. What irony, he mused as he packed. He'd achieved the near-impossible in getting Don John to agree to Mary's suit, yet nothing would change! Would his network, six years in the making, survive his banishment? He was middle-aged–thirty-three–must make a third beginning. Three; three; three. He kept laughing an amazed, forlorn laugh.

"It doesn't do to offend the king," the corporal said sympathetically. "Now you have no lady, no salary, no country, no status."

"No status? Fellow, you're wrong," Latham chuckled, clapping the mystified corporal on the shoulder. "I have so *much* status that Dame Fortune has to chasten me from time to time. What will happen to Lady Barbara?"

"A rigorous convent in Castile."

Latham sighed. With her passionate temperament, she'd

suffer more than he would. He, at least, was on the move. He grieved for her, willing himself not to visualise the constrictions of her future hours.

Joris knew Mary's commission included raising a loan for her in Florence. But the only decent thing to do was to release him from service. Latham asked the corporal to deliver his severance letter to William Boels, at Coudenberg Palace. William also got custody of Surehoof, the stallion Don Cristobal had given Latham, until Cristo could take the horse back. In the stall, Surehoof gazed at Latham, eager for adventure. But he was too beautiful a beast to waste on an uncertain future.

What have I learned, Latham asked, as he followed his captors to the road. He'd missed Perez' fall, a terrible mistake for a spy. Would his effort to raise loans for Mary also be ill-starred? He'd allowed the drama of being with Lady Barbara to blind him to political shifts. Hubris, and now he was punished. Never again would he allow personal entanglements to distract him in this way. *I might not be quite apt for marriage, he mused. Being with my own kind is easier, but female striving touches me. Now I'm prepared.*

Florence, September 1577.

Open windows and three servants waving fans didn't dispel the stink of fumes filling the chemistry laboratory, where Latham waited to be acknowledged by Francesco, Grand Duke of Tuscany. He stared as the thickly-gloved duke held a glass container with tongs over four bricks. The substance in the bottle was sizzling and spilt onto the bricks, where it dissolved them.

The duke sprang back. "Good. I have the right mix."

His face, as he turned to invite Latham's bow, was coldly affable. "I invented this compound, combining a smelting mineral first described in 1530 with vitriol. It burns armour joints. And flesh."

He paused, letting the words sink in, then inclined his head toward the corner of the room. Latham followed his movement and clutched his mouth. He wanted to vomit. Beneath a blanket were seared hind legs. The duke had tested his vitriol on a dog.

"Now," Francesco mused, as if talking to himself, "if I could find a receptacle that could resist its poison, I could hose down enemy walls and hordes. Then we'd be mighty, indeed. But what would that resistant substance be? That's the mystery."

Focusing on Latham, he said: "Sir Edward Latham, eh? Confounder of Genlis. Yes, I heard about that; a neat piece of espionage. I understand you request a loan for Mary, Queen of Scots. She wrote to my wife, did you know? Proposing our daughter marry her son. I see your surprise; you didn't know! I warned my wife not to tell you. Good. She obeyed. Your Queen Mary weaves many tapestries. No one can keep track of all her yellows, reds and greens. Remember that, Latham. We don't think to marry cold, remote Scotland when we can marry France. Besides, Mary can't dispose of her son. He's a king and will make his own union. So, no to marriage. The loan's another matter. We'll consider it if you perform a service for me."

He motioned Latham to a bench, waved the servants out and sat beside him. "Constantinople, Latham, 'the Sublime Porte,' as many call it. There are rumours that the new Sultan, Murad III, will change trade policy, upending generations of privileges. I'm a Medici. I love our banks. I'm determined they'll prosper by favouring whoever the Sultan favours. Who is that? Will the French keep the monopolies of their 1535 treaty? Will Spain get advantages with a truce, that would favour *us*, as Spain's treaty ally? Or will the sultan favour our rivals, the Genoese? Or your upstart birth country? I need an Englishman of rank there, even as low as yours. You turned up fortuitously. It doesn't matter that you left Elizabeth's court; you'll serve me. I'll make travelling papers for you as Sir Edward Latham. Find proof of who Murad favours, and Mary gets her money. Constantinople's an interesting place, I'm told; prey to hazards of nature and man. I have a Venetian's travel diary in my library, with helpful pointers. You can have it for a few hours. Sir, you may withdraw."

Latham bowed himself out. Alone in the corridor, he leaned against a door, wiping his sweating forehead. As his breathing slowed, he looked around. There were portraits in the new realistic style on the walls, so vibrant that he expected a draping fur to fall onto the stairs, an outstretched hand to pluck his sleeve, or a pink tongue-tip to kiss him. Their tactile warmth was a stark contrast to the cold brilliance of the man who'd commissioned them.

When he got to his assigned room at the Palazzo Vecchio, a slim volume lay on his bed. He paged through illustrations of official robes and turbans; a dazzling variety. Like England's sumptuary laws, Latham assumed, but bewildering to his untutored eye. There was an impalement gallows with hooks, an ornate royal processional, and a page on romantic courtship rituals involving pistachio nuts and pillows, a play on two Turkish words: *fistik* for pistachio, and *yastik* for pillow. Latham had no intention of seeking romance; evidently the Venetian had. Next morning, a clerk retrieved the book. Despite making notes, Latham hadn't absorbed much.

He wrote to Mary's factor in Paris, explaining the delay in obtaining her loan, but predicting success. He enclosed a coded letter to Mary, recounting events in Brussels. *We kept the watchers guessing, as you instructed. Gracious Sovereign, they guessed we married each other.* Was that too harsh? He wondered. No. He'd tried to help her and was now ruined. His last letter was to Don Cristobal in Sicily, saying he was going to Constantinople for the Duke of Tuscany, and that Surehoof was at the Coudenberg Palace stables, in the care of William Boels. He added a sentence asking Cristo to get a message to Lady Barbara, then crossed it out. Dr Pell's chart reading came back to him: *Love, yes, but fleeting.*

His destiny wasn't between bed sheets. How strange, he thought as he sealed his letters, that the first royal travelling papers in his birth name would be provided by this terrifying Medici. The challenge of functioning in Constantinople was certainly better than staying here under the Duke's menacing eye.

Two days later he was preparing to join merchants riding to Belgrade, the first stage in the long overland trek to Constantinople. A guard rushed up to him. "An urchin says he knows you, Signor. He won't go away."

To Latham's amazement, Joris Boels was in the Piazza. Mouth agape, he was drawing Michelangelo's statue of David.

"Joris, why are you here? I'm leaving today. Yes, let him in," he reassured the guard as Joris ran to the gate. "He was my courier in Brussels."

Two guard dogs hurtled over, growling. When they got to the gate, their aggression dissipated, and they let Joris fondle their ears. "Dogs...like," Joris muttered, his half-moon grin huge. "Let... me come, wh...erever"

Latham was stunned and moved. The best trial of a servant was when service wasn't convenient, Mary had written. Crossing the Alps to follow a disgraced master wasn't at all convenient.

"But I can't pay you, Joris. I need my salary for bribes."

"Work…food." Joris put away his paper and showed Latham a pack of marked cards and loaded dice.

Latham roared with laughter, visualising travellers taking Joris for an idiot—merchants, carters, artisans, farmers—getting fleeced from Brussels to Florence. "Then swear to my conditions," he conceded. "First, when we reach Ottoman lands, stop cheating. They impale thieves. Second, you'll go to a physician I choose to treat your speech malady."

Scowling, Joris clenched his fists and swore. On the month-long ride, he spoke little. He hoped Latham would forget; surely in Constantinople, so foreign, he could just draw, not talk at all.

CHAPTER 10
IN THE CITY OF
SAFFRON

Constantinople, September 1577

On the walkway of the soaring Tower of Galata, Latham rotated his shoulders to ease the pain of his bruises. The brawl two nights ago had been good sport, but as the envoy of the Duke of Tuscany, he couldn't repeat it. Inadvertently, he'd got caught in a night-time fight between Muslim sects. He hadn't been scared, just surprised; because the melee exposed more disorder in the capital of the Ottoman Empire than he'd expected. Now, from his vantage point, he gazed over the distant market district near the royal palace, trying to place the street where cudgelers and dagger-wielding opponents met.

The sun blazed on white marble mosques with their gold-tipped spires. Its rays bounced back, hitting Latham's eyes with painful intensity. Beyond the city walls and aqueduct, the Sea of Marmara glittered white. Between Constantinople and Galata, where he was, the Golden Horn looked enticingly blue before dumping rubbish and grey sludge on Galata's stony shore. Glory and filth, coexisting

An official patrolled the terrace, watching for fires. In addition, two pig-tailed Asians in embroidered black robes and a sable-cloaked Slav with a clerk were staring at the harbour, waiting for their sails to come into view. The thick Slav pointed excitedly at two cogs; he and his clerk clattered downstairs. The two Asians talked in sing-song intonation, looking anxious. Latham heard the Latin word *praedonum*, pirates. They left too, their foreheads creased with worry.

Three Janissary soldiers were also on the walkway, watching the watchers. Black-moustached men in red jackets over loose blue trousers, they were frowning under their beige turbans. Latham frowned in turn. Was this the same outfit worn by the soldiers who'd joined the brawl? He was still unfamiliar with the language of official robes.

Latham looked again for the dervish lodge and coffee house where the brawl had erupted. The street was beyond a slave market and caravanserai. But with such a winding mishmash, he couldn't tell one street from another. Which is why he'd got lost.

He and Joris had reached Constantinople in the third week of August. On his second day, Latham had rented a house with servants in the European quarter of Petra and sent Joris to map the docks and warehouses, and to draw ship flags on both sides of the channel. The Duke of Tuscany wanted him to find out about Ottoman trade policy, and understanding the docks was the first step.

The same day, Latham had followed a *clap clap* of wood on wood to St Peter's and St Paul's Church. Bells were prohibited here; wood on wood or iron were the sounds allowed Christian institutions, a pathetic utterance overwhelmed by the sinuous muezzin calls to prayer that marked time in the Sublime Porte.

Latham had let himself into the enclosed church courtyard and met the chief priest. Father Jerome was a morbidly pessimistic clergyman, having developed arithmetic for *Revelations* that proved Judgment Day was near. But the approaching end of the world didn't preclude him getting commissions for referrals. He recommended a French physician to treat Joris's speech defect. Latham meant to hold his servant to the oath he'd sworn in Florence.

It took a few weeks for Latham to get his household set up and supplies ordered, present his credentials to the palace, and interview the physician that Father Jerome had recommended for Joris. But finally, he found himself with an unscheduled day, and decided to wander, for fun and education. He started with the famous market in the old city, an exhausting sprawl of shops jamming sixty-seven short roads. After tiring of textile and luxury goods shops, he watched a slave auction in a small square. Clearly, slaves were expensive, because only wealthy-looking merchants and servants to high officials were bidding on European galley rowers, captives from conquered provincial towns, experienced slaves re-sold by families who'd suffered financial reverses.

But poorer spectators milled about, enchanted by some entertainment close to the ground. Latham joined them, noticing a dwarf with a wizened face and the high cheekbones of a Slav. His grey beard reached his knees, while his matted grey hair was cut to shoulder-length to show his bare torso. A huge sea monster filled his back, cut and inked into his skin. The monster's tail was on one shoulder blade, its bloody fangs on the other. The dwarf danced, twisting his face into a semblance of sardonic bliss. As if alive, the monster on his back danced with him.

It wasn't just fun. Pint-sized pickpockets were at work. After several thefts, the dwarf with the monster on his back signalled them to stop, and the gang scampered through the courtyard of a caravanserai into a warren of streets.

Intrigued, Latham followed them but soon lost his bearings. He could see the top of the Egyptian obelisk, but not how to get there. He could have asked directions by gesture while it was still light, but some spell had been cast on him, keeping him meandering.

Thus he was lost, at night, with no lantern. After traipsing several cul-de-sacs full of what smelled like burned-out abandoned houses, he saw a dim lamp at a street corner. He shouted, but only a mangy dog came.

Turning that corner, he saw more light and heard voices. Hand on his dagger, he strode toward them. Muffled howling of a horrid excitement came from a closed building on one side of the street; laughter from a shop on the other.

A bitter smell, along with that of caramelised sugar, suggested he was at one of Constantinople's coffee houses. He looked in at customers talking animatedly, obviously at ease with each other. A being of unclear gender, with a white-painted face and rouged pursed lips, stood by a board picturing a woman, a peasant, and a lion nosing into the edge of the frame; presumably characters in a story about to be performed.

Latham was debating whether to go in when he heard tramping boots and shouts. A swarm of bobbing torches eddied closer. He slipped into the muddy alley by the coffee house.

About thirty men in long robes that looked blue in the torchlight stormed the building with the howlers, and dragged out dazed-looking men in white scarves; Latham counted eighteen. The howlers had scarred scabbed faces. "Allah Akbar!" hurtled back and forth, the dazed men frothing with as much hate as their attackers. Latham didn't need to understand the words to recognise religious schism. The blue-robes cudgelled, the dazed men met them with daggers, then fled. The mob of blue robes surged back into the building and came out with whips, red-glowing braziers and knives. *The howlers were a self-hurting sect*, Latham concluded.

Five men in short jackets and loose trousers, hefting scimitars, arrived and accepted the plunder from the blue-robes. *Janissaries*, Latham realised. *This is official.* The five soldiers boarded up the lodge and marched away, leaving the blue robes standing around. The Venetian, whose travel diary he'd read in Florence, hadn't described fights like this; Latham was thrilled by his first-hand witnessing of internal Ottoman conflict.

Someone had doused the coffee house lights. Hoping the fight was over, Latham found the back door and eased into the kitchen. He drew his sword, picked up a skillet, and waited. The front door splintered and there was a tumult of breaking pottery, splitting wood and screams. Torches roved everywhere. Terrified customers tumbled into the kitchen, blue-robes chasing. Seeing Latham, the mob's leader yelled "Frank!", the universal epithet for Europeans, and charged. Latham fought his way back to the alley, collecting several blows on his shoulder. There were no Janissaries around; they'd given the night to the blue-robes.

Mercifully, no one followed. Eventually, the crashing glass stopped, and the torches swarmed away. Latham forced himself to stand quietly while some animal nibbled his boot ties.

After what seemed a long time, soft, tentative footsteps made him draw his sword.

"Ho there, Frank. I mean no harm," a husky voice said in a mixture of French and Latin that Latham understood. The man reached for Latham's hand and pulled it to his lips. Latham felt gooey paste making a round mouth out of a long thin one. It was the storyteller.

"What did the howlers shout?" Latham whispered.

"Mosque and tavern are one," the storyteller answered, "the supreme insult. The word was, coffee houses were safe tonight. You can't tell these days. The blue-robes are orthodox, out of Damascus Sunni sects, while the self-cutting mystics are a sect of dervishes, Persian Sufi Shiite sects. One of our ancient sultans brought the Shiites in and revered them; today, not so much. It's a muddle. Persian culture—painting, poetry, stories—are loved, but Persia is hated."

Latham was silent; this old sectarian conflict didn't seem relevant to trade policy.

"Why are you in Constantinople?" the storyteller asked.

It was such a strange night that Latham decided openness was the best policy. "I represent the Duke of Tuscany, to inquire about the Sultan's trade policy."

The storyteller chuckled. "May Allah have mercy on your suffering. You'll need a proper friend. Have you heard of the Selim paradox?"

"No," Latham murmured.

The husky voice intoned, "Selim II, called '*Sot*' by you Franks, was a drunk." The storyteller seemed to be swelling, bulging his eyes. "Islam forbids alcohol. A paradox. Selim built a bath decorated with the most beauteous tiles ever. It was empty, awaiting his final approval. Being in his cups, he dived in and died of a cracked skull. Final approval." He staggered, made a diving motion, wailing as his pretend head hit the ground. Then got up and leaned against the wall, shrinking to his former size.

Latham laughed. "Who are you?" he asked.

"I am the tales I tell, nothing beyond them."

At first light, the storyteller's features were revealed. He was a thin, nondescript man with cropped grey hair and cheek stubble. Latham shook his hand and bade him farewell then took a boat back to Galata. He was bemused and sore.

On the Tower walkway, Latham pulled his eyes away from the mishmash of streets where he'd got lost, and his mind back from the melee of two nights ago. He glanced at a hilltop overlooking the European quarter. Ant-sized men were whipping oxen hauling brick-filled carts to the summit. The Sultan's white marble astronomical observatory was near completion, cart drivers rushing as if to meet an imminent galactic deadline. Natural philosophy was co-existing with cudgelling sects; glorious official complexes were juxtaposed with burned rotting streets. Joris expressed Constantinople's paradox by writing the exquisite Arabic calligraphy for *Hope* in the air with his left hand, pinching his nostrils shut with his right hand. Joris was on a Golden Horn wherry now, coming to meet the physician who was supposed to treat his speech.

As Latham twisted down the tower's winding stone staircase, he wondered if he'd ever master this place from which he must wrest a political secret. The storyteller had told him to find a proper friend, but how?

A few weeks later, on a Saturday morning, Latham was sitting on a stone bench in the Royal Park, in a section opened to the public for the day. Picnickers were eating kebabs and dates, while jugglers, fabric peddlers and water-carriers hustled, crying their wares.

Latham's bench faced a grove bordered by linden trees in full yellow glory. There was a tall swing with a triangular seat attached by ropes to the top, leather straps to secure three or four riders per trip. Pushed by two dark-skinned operators, with features Latham had learned were typically Egyptian, it whooshed ever higher, its excited occupants urging the operators to shorten the ropes and push harder.

Older riders worked the swing themselves. They soared to the height of the transverse pole, screaming with delight, propelling the seat over the top in a violent, bucketing arc. Then operators would grab the ropes and slow the swing.

A second swing had been set up for younger riders, of up to about eight years of age. A horizontal cartwheel with eight wooden buckets, it was cranked around at great speed. Long lines of restless children waited their turn.

These little riders faced Latham during their rotation, and when they came level with him, they pointed and tittered, his blondness setting them off. He was amused at first, then pierced by loneliness. *I don't understand their words,* he thought, *but this is the first honest reaction I've found in Constantinople.*

He'd never worked in a city where he didn't know the principal language. He could talk to Ottoman officials in the Latin, Italian or French they used with Europeans. However, without Arabic, used for religion and law; Turkish, used in ordinary life; or Persian, used in international trade; a European was unable to grab the sotto voce murmurs, often the critical part of communication. Latham feared he was on a fool's quest.

It took him a while to realise the difficulty. His Ducal papers got him into the outer courtyards of the palace. After morning prayers, accredited visitors like him could tie their horses to posts outside the Gate of Salutation and enter the First Courtyard. The architecture was familiar: a curved arch of thick stone framed by two Gothic towers fitted with archers' slits. The inscription: *There is but one God, and Mohammed is His prophet*, was unfamiliar, but that was to be expected.

He was amused at first by the latticed pavilion on top of the Gothic wall. Guarded by eunuchs, it housed harem concubines tittering at the foreigners below. Ottoman rules required visitors to wear native dress, so promiscuously dazzling varieties of outfits surged forward when permitted, as urgent Europeans, Arabs, Persians and Serbs tried advancing their projects. He'd giggle too, he thought, if he was a bored concubine.

The Ducal travelling papers also got him into the Second Courtyard. Its walkways passed a cistern in the middle, separating a huge kitchen complex from Divan Tower, the administrative centre. The kitchen had been destroyed by fire and was being rebuilt. Three gleaming new chimneys had been completed. Every time Latham came, he saw a green-robed, white-bearded man with an animated face appraising the progress, accompanied by adoring workmen. The soft white folds of the man's turban, fastened by a ruby brooch topped by a peacock feather, marked him as an artisan of high rank.

"He's Mirar Sinan, the royal architect. A great man," a guard told Latham, his tone reverent. "He's building ten kitchens where there were two. Each will have its own chimney and dome, so there can never again be a fire that engulfs everything at once."

But that's as far as Latham got: making his way daily under laughing concubines; drinking pure cistern water; dutifully admiring the royal architect. He didn't have permission to enter the palace proper. He introduced himself to green-robed secretaries to the vizier, red-robed clerks and interpreters in the chamberlain's office. All were polite but vague. He distributed gifts, gave a splendid dinner in his rented house. But Ottoman trade policy remained as hidden behind platitudes as the faces of concubines behind lattice frames and muslin veils.

Latham had also met merchants and artisans in the public baths and markets. Three invited him home to dinner. Their hospitality was generous, but when he asked about trade policy, he met the same opaqueness he'd encountered at the palace.

Joris has done better than I have, he thought morosely, as the children whooped at the swings. Joris had discovered that Jews farmed customs duties for the Treasury by following them to the Jewish quarter, where he'd seen them enter their synagogue. That was interesting, but not helpful on the question of trade policy. He'd drawn docks on both sides of the Horn, mapped principal warehouses, and recorded the flags of ships bringing in spices, coffee, Persian or Chinese silks, Chinese porcelain, English tin, and Venetian fabrics.

What was more intriguing, was a consignment of iron-framed boxes unloaded from one English galleon but treated differently from the rest of the cargo. These boxes weren't released to the Jewish customs officials. Instead, they were taken to a separate guarded warehouse, where Treasury clerks signed for them. Latham's instincts told him that seeing the contents of these boxes would reveal something about Ottoman trade preferences, but he had no idea how to get at them.

The horizontal swing came to rest. Nine children tumbled out of their seats and ran at him. It was hard to tell girls from boys; both wore caps and skirts over trousers. Their high-pitched jabbering eluded him, although he recognised the Turkish word for "flour." Four remonstrating veiled women followed the children, and the entire group was escorted by a swarthy male carriage driver. Judging by the way the children waved off the adults, Latham concluded that the youngsters were from wealthy families, and the adults were house servants. The women stood behind their charges, eyes lowered, but not so low that they couldn't appraise him. He didn't look away in the polite Turkish manner, but stared back, noting two pairs of brown eyes in tight young skin, a pair of hazel eyes under a freckled forehead, and tired blue eyes framed by wrinkled skin.

One forward child reached for Latham's hand. Latham rolled up his doublet and shirt sleeve, grinning as he exhibited his pale skin and hair. This provoked more chatter, and the other children edged closer.

Behind Latham, something new cast a shadow. The women curtsied, and the children froze. He turned and found himself looking up at a tall, lean man wearing the olive-green robe, white turban, and olive-green fez that signified the Bureau of Diplomats. The scent of sandalwood soap wafted up Latham's nostrils.

With a shock, he realised he'd seen this man before, near the Divan Tower, the royal administrative centre. The man had watched him, looking amused as Latham had scurried around with his questions. Latham had also seen him in the market. After the brawl, Latham had left nights to the Sultan's subjects and wore his mirrored hat during the day. He'd seen this man outside a ceramic tile shop, with the look of savouring a joke. He seemed amused today, too; black eyes dancing in a dark face, framed by a bushy black beard.

"Would you like me to translate?" the Bureau of Diplomats official asked Latham in Latin, his voice was deep and mellow.

Latham stood and bowed. A surge of attraction made him too discombobulated to reply.

The Ottoman took silence as consent. "They say Allah pickled you in cider vinegar, and sprinkled you with white flour. They've never seen such a pale Frank."

Latham's retort ripped off his tongue before he could stop it. "That's the first honest remark I've heard here."

The Ottoman laughed, revealing uneven white teeth. "Here's the second: I am Ibrahim, assistant to the Secretary of the Bureau of Diplomats."

"And I am Edward Latham, an Englishman serving Francesco, Grand Duke of Tuscany."

"I'm honoured to meet you, Sir Edward." Ibrahim's expression was knowing.

Sir? Latham was startled. Of course, his bureau would examine his papers, but did he know his history?

"I don't use that title, Effendi," he replied. *Is this the right way to address him? He's probably a slave.* He touched his fingers to his forehead in the Turkish way.

The Ottoman grinned. "Lips as well as forehead, and right hand only," Ibrahim corrected. "But I accept the intent. I'll address you as you wish, of course. But why? Franks usually trumpet their degree."

Having lost their fear, the children were babbling again.

"It's an old story." Latham sighed. The Ottoman might be testing his truthfulness. "I've been knighted twice, Effendi. First, by the English Queen, Elizabeth, to reward my father for taking the oath of allegiance to her heretical religion. As a committed Catholic, I left England to serve Mary, Queen of Scots. She knighted me for services I performed for her in

Scotland and France until she was deposed. Both of my titles are meaningless. After Queen Mary's fall, I served King Philip, and now I represent the Grand Duke of Tuscany, Francesco."

Ibrahim raised his eyebrows. "Abjuring two knighthoods is a sacrifice worthy of ancient chivalry. These children don't see your virtues. They say Allah pickled you then forgot you, leaving you so pale the sun couldn't bake you wholesome brown. They pity you."

"Oh no," Latham said, leaning toward the child who'd clutched his arm, "I was born dark like you. But in England, an island in the cold northern seas, clouds are jealous of dark skin. They eat light, hide the sun, and pour rain for months. So we get paler and paler."

As Ibrahim put this into Turkish, the children's eyes widened, while the visible part of one woman's brows pulled into frowns.

"Such nonsense," Ibrahim translated the blue-eyed old woman's mutterings.

"No, good lady." Latham squatted, removed his hat and pointed to the crown of his head. Remnants of the brown hair dye he'd applied in France remained. This brought exclamations and more chatter.

"This girl says English clouds are lazy. They forgot your eyes, too; Frankish devils have blue eyes," Ibrahim said.

"How wise she is," Latham agreed. "There's always more work for the clouds to do." He was having more fun than he'd had for years. *Maybe I could marry,* he thought. Then he looked at the Ottoman, and his lips moistened. He suspected the Ottoman had been stalking him, but why? Could this be the friend the storyteller said he needed? He had an odd feeling of being part of someone's tale.

Ibrahim pulled out an asper and pointed to a kiosk at the city wall. "Buy sherbets then take your charges home," he told the carriage driver.

"These children are forward," Latham said, as they scurried off and he and the Ottoman sat. "We Franks learn courtesies by their age."

"Yes, I remember bowing and grave phrases. I was born an Armenian Christian, before being taken into the Sultan's service.

"Why are you here, on a Saturday?" Latham asked.

"I'm looking for runaways from the Sultan's school. The Janissaries take clever Christian boys with strong physique from the villages. They bring them here to become elite administrative slaves. It is a brilliant but hard education. The boys sometimes sneak away, looking for peddlers at the fairs to smuggle them home. I know their tricks because I tried them myself. Happily, none came today; the punishment is a public foot-beating."

"Are you a slave?" Latham asked curiously.

"Yes. My life is at the Sultan's disposal, without what you call a trial; the time of my death is inscribed by Allah. Meanwhile, my earthly condition is as interesting as my abilities make it. Now to you, honoured visitor..."

Eyes lowered, Ibrahim brushed Latham's fingers. Meeting no recoil, he pressed Latham's hand. Latham pressed back. "I know who you are," Ibrahim continued, still looking down. "It's not by chance I meet you here. I come with a gift."

Latham saw no package or purse. "What do you mean?"

"Call back your boy, who looks simple but isn't. He might slink around unnoticed in Europe, but not here. He stares too carefully, draws too much, sees things he shouldn't. His labours will spoil our acquaintance."

He let go of Latham's hand. The separation of their flesh felt clammy-cool; Latham ran his tongue over his lips but said nothing.

"I know about your difficulties," the Ottoman said. "Your duke gave you a hard duty. However, crude Frankish haste guarantees failure. Let's move. The swing masters need customers; if they don't prosper, we cannot tax them."

Indeed, while Latham and Ibrahim were talking, servants shepherding children had come into the grove, and shown intense disappointment when swing operators waved them away.

Ibrahim led them down a flight of steep steps to the sea wall. They walked along an empty pier, gulls screeching, fighting over scuttling crabs.

Latham decided to play out the encounter. He was excited by the sexual tension but felt he'd been put down by a slave, which he didn't like it. "Yes, my position is difficult," he confirmed. "The English envoy and trader, William Harborne, shuns me. He's Protestant, and I'm Catholic. He knows I left England to serve Catholic rulers and sees me as an opponent." He pointed to his silver cross.

Ibrahim examined it with tapering brown fingers. "A fine piece. French, I believe."

"You're astute, Effendi. It is French. Mary, Queen of Scots, gave it to me when I became her envoy in Paris. I had great positions in her court—Master of the Horse, envoy to France; I was no slave." He was so busy massaging his wounded pride, his impotence in the face of weeks of Ottoman opaqueness, that he was oblivious to his appalling crassness until Ibrahim flinched.

"You're not superior to me." The Ottoman was angry. "You courtiers abase yourselves on trembling knees, begging for favours. Your society isn't better than ours. You Franks chew your own flesh, as the saying goes, with your burning, burying alive, cutting to pieces the ones you call heretics. But who is heretic depends on which sect governs in a season. You shred your society's fabric, thread by thread, with murderous intolerance. We are wiser, mixing complementary ingredients into a nourishing whole."

Latham couldn't rebut the indictment. The conversation had gone horribly wrong. He hadn't meant to insult Ibrahim, and his clumsiness also betrayed his employer. The duke might be a tyrant, but he deserved competent diplomacy. In a welter of embarrassment, Latham scudded a stone into white-capped waves, trying to think of how to retrieve the situation.

Ibrahim clenched his teeth and folded his arms into his capacious sleeves, a big green oyster slamming its shell shut. He was miserable, too.

Latham wondered if he'd felt frisson between them. "Effendi, I apologise for my barbaric crudeness. I'll abase myself on my knee. Or do you prefer to give me a foot-beating? You only have to say. You've been kind to me, beyond my merits." He knelt, hoping humour would diffuse the tension.

Ibrahim unfolded his arms and laughed. "Franks have primitive irony," he conceded. "I won't hold against you what you can't help, any more than the cat can be taught to turn from the mouse. Now, your difficulties: having served King Philip of Spain, our nemesis, is a disadvantage, and your duke is Span's ally. We have a truce with Spain, but we believe King Philip's peacefulness comes only from his current lack of funds."

Policy seemed to be comfortable ground. Latham expanded: "The Spanish envoy won't talk to me because King Philip banished me from Spain's lands. His Majesty resented something he believed I'd done. I was innocent of that act, but honour to another prevented me from saying it."

"More chivalry? Touching." Ibrahim's expression was softer than his tart words.

"Genoese and Venetian envoys won't talk to me," Latham continued. "They compete with Florence. The only prattler is the priest at St Peter's and St Paul's, who hears my confessions. He's useless. By his own invented arithmetic of *Revelations*, he says Armageddon will destroy us next year. Whatever he's heard about trade he forgets, since the world will soon end. Your merchants are uninformed, or discreet."

"Our men of business have the sense to be discreet," Ibrahim said flatly.

"The Duke of Tuscany simply wishes to favour the Europeans your Sultan prefers," Latham offered hopefully. "There are rumours that the great French monopolies will be changed. We're on the same side. How do we befriend your friends? A simple question."

"Not simple," Ibrahim retorted. "Friendship flowering between states is delicate. A premature March petal can withers in April frosts, while a May bloom unfurls fully in season. You don't want to be a March petal. You'll find what you seek at the right time. Meanwhile, would you like to dine at my house? See a slave's condition? "

To Latham's astonishment, he pulled a pistachio from his pocket. "Fistik?" Ibrahim asked nervously. He nibbled half and gave the rest to Latham.

Latham's mind raced back to the Venetian's travel diary entry on courting rituals. *Fistik*, pistachio, rhymed in Turkish with *yastik*, pillow, and referred to a Turkish love song: *Ikmize bir yasrik* (Let us share the same pillow). This Ottoman official was courting him. Heart pounding, he swallowed the half pistachio.

Shoulders sagging in relief, Ibrahim hailed a boat.

A few hours later, they lay on a quilt in a satiated doze, cocooned in mingled sweat. They were in the garden pavilion of Ibrahim's mansion. Latham opened one eye and looked at the decorative wall tiles. Until he came to Constantinople, he'd never thought dancing angles and curlicues could be dynamic. To his surprise, he found them fully satisfying. *I don't miss flesh and robes,* he thought.

The two men were still entwined. As Ibrahim exhaled, Latham drew that breath into his nostrils. He touched his moustache and licked his finger, tasting cloves, saffron and sandalwood. His rose oil clung to Ibrahim's beard.

If the windows of the pavilion were open, Latham knew he'd see the Golden Horn, for the estate Ibrahim occupied was on prime coastal land on the Constantinople side. But discretion required shutters. Late afternoon rays hit them through wooden slats, forming copper bands on Ibrahim's skin, alabaster on Latham's paleness. Ibrahim's love-making encompassed the human condition: tenderness, near-ruthless teasing, roughness, generosity.

He had never known such contentment. Yet he was

also outside the moment. As it came awake, his inner spy whispered: *Policy. He knows what's in the boxes at the separate warehouse.* He wouldn't get lost in this affair as he had with Lady Barbara.

"The Romans pushed out; we Ottomans pull in," Ibrahim said emphatically, sitting up. They untwined.

"What do you mean?" Latham realised Ibrahim had a political agenda, too.

The Ottoman got up to fetch water and towels, and explained: "When the Romans conquered lands, they sent Roman rulers out to impose Roman ways; pushing out. Spaniards do the same. But our sultans pull in: Egyptians, Jews, Asians, all sorts of Christians. *Gathering*, it's called. You've seen the Egyptian obelisks, the German architecture at the palace. Our officials can be Greek, Armenians, Arabs, Serbs. They know they're subjugated, they pay higher taxes, but their talents are rewarded. We tolerate differences. The royal architect, Mirar Siran, was Christian. Most Janissaries were Christian. And I know that you know Jews collect customs duties."

"But," Latham said as they began to dress, "in this mix of people you boast about, where are Turkish nobles? Your own kind?"

"Dispersed," Ibrahim said excitedly. "Frankish kings depend on nobles of their own kind for subsidies and musters. It leads to rebellions and deposing of monarchs like your Queen Mary. Our sultans find safety, which means peace in the realm, by appointing Turkish nobles to rule provinces, while the sultan rules the capital and Empire through learned slaves and subjects who know their inferiority. Upon accession, each new sultan has his brothers garrotted, so there's no challenge from one of equal blood. When a sultan dies, the successor is uncertain. Shrewdness in building factions as well as blood determines who rules. Princes of the blood accept the result as Allah's will, as long as the killing cord is silk. The sacrifice of the losing siblings brings stability. These strangled princes are saints, in a way."

Latham was unwilling to credit saintliness to losers in a royal power struggle. Besides, he wanted to know about the special crates. He shook his head. "There are limits to the benefit of pulling in: confusion about wine or no wine, coffee houses or no coffee houses. I've seen it." He described the brawl and destruction of the coffee house. "Your officials look perplexed; your sects are thugs; your alliances are opaque, which hurts trade."

"Our small eruptions are nothing like your Catholic and Protestant armies carving up your lands," Ibrahim argued. "I know what you want; I can't discuss shifting policy. Control Frankish haste." He laughed as he ruffled Latham's hair, with its brown patch of hair dye. "Egret-magpie, will we see each other again? I must join my servants when the muezzin calls, but my boatman will take you back. He's Christian."

Latham settled in a small boat with a yellow lantern at its prow. The oarsman, a blue-eyed Circassian, pulled away from shore. The darkening channel bobbed with myriad lights, while the air rang with the calls of oarsmen, ship bells, and the undulating call to prayer. *Ibrahim has some goal too*, Latham mused. For his own reasons, he needed this Frank egret-magpie to learn what he sought.

"I have a new friend in the Bureau of Diplomats," Latham said happily, back in his house. Joris was behind him, waiting to take his cloak. "He warned me to stop you from drawing any more warehouses." Oblivious of the rigidity of Joris's stance, he babbled on. "It makes me even more certain that the consignments you saw taken to that separate warehouse are the key to Murad's trade policy. But you must stop. Draw caravanserai, mosques, markets, be a tourist. I'll find a way to get His Grace's espials. I'm close."

As he turned into heavy silence, he met a face mulish with fury. The knuckles of the large hands holding his cloak had fresh scrapes. Latham's good mood deflated. "Who now?"

"D...d...doc..ct...or. B...B...broke...n...n...n...ose."

Joris had never been a stutterer. His speech was worse since Dr Gaspard Antonin started treating him. Physician to the best French and Venetian families, he started by bleeding and purging Joris. It didn't help. He put him on a diet of vegetables and sugared violet water for melancholy, made him speak with a mouth full of pebbles—Demosthenes had sworn by this practice—no improvement. He elevated Joris's tongue with a spoon then depressed it, no change. He even took Joris to the steepest of Galata's serpentine streets, a twister so precipitous it ended in steps. He made Joris run up this street declaiming *The Lord's Prayer*. Shopkeepers and residents loved this entertainment: the puffing, the incomprehensible half-syllables, the patient's growing rage. They looked for a violent denouement. Dr Antonin resented failure; it threatened his reputation.

Joris handed Latham the doctor's note. *Your servant cleaves to his malady with the willfulness of a possessed brute. In ancient times, Aetius of Byzantium cured Emperor Justinian's stutter by dividing his tongue. I will read about the surgery and perform it next week.*

Terror of the knife had provoked Joris into attacking the doctor.

Latham sighed as he led Joris into the men's receiving. "You're getting worse, not better. I won't allow this cutting, of course. But you didn't have to break his nose. He won't call you out to a duel, your rank's too low, but his manservant might. I can't have fighting. You must apologise. He's scared of losing customers. Admit to being obdurate about your defect; it will let him save face. I'll find a new physician. You swore to improve your speech. That oath holds."

Wiles of francolin, spirit of hawk, quickness of magpie,
Splendour of osprey, hair like egret—attainable as…. Air.

With poems in the Persian style and gifts, Ibrahim courted Latham, and Latham answered with French love songs, which he sang, accompanying himself on his lute.

As leaves fell in October, and a November sun angled lower in the sky, Latham made his way to Ibrahim's mansion, hat pulled down and cloak fastened against squalls. Their couplings remained intense but didn't deepen into intellectual intimacy. But nor did they tire of each other.

Joris began to realise what the sandalwood scent on Latham's clothes meant. He recoiled at first, becoming as distant as a servant could be without being insolent. Terrified that this liking of man for man was contagious, he turned to brothels; as if jasmine and the fabric sheaths he left on his bed to be seen by the servants could ward off a catamite taint to his intense loyalty to Latham. But as his desires remained wholly directed to soft breasts and vaginas, he relaxed. One afternoon, after visiting the Royal Zoo, he drew two male lions copulating. "B…both…k…kings," he said. Latham kept his face neutral, unwilling to let Joris see how moved he was.

Ibrahim was both open and secretive. He showed Latham much of his house: the kitchen, library, screened women servants' quarters. But every time they were together at noon, he'd disappear for over an hour. When Latham asked where he was, he smiled and said it was his little folly. Latham had noticed a separate domed building with its own courtyard screened by cypress trees. He assumed Ibrahim went there, but something in his manner discouraged direct questions. Ibrahim was skilled at signalling what could be asked and what couldn't. *A slave wouldn't attain his position without commanding subtle arts of authority*, Latham thought.

The household was well-managed. All served with grave courtesy, except for one lithe youth with caramel-coloured skin, who cleaned and folded Ibrahim's turbans. Whenever this boy came into his master's presence, fury showed in his pouting lips. He wondered if he'd replaced the boy as a bedmate.

Ibrahim introduced Latham to coffee. Latham had heard about the miraculous beans but avoided coffee houses after the brawl. At lunch one day, a servant brought a pile of beans on a wooden platter. Ibrahim pounded them with a stone, pestled them into a coarse powder, soaked them in steaming, honey-sweetened water, then invited Latham to drink the sludge. Latham recoiled at the bitterness. But after a few sips, thin hot wires snaked through his veins, his fingertips tingled, and his brain curled into a scythe. *There's no mystery beyond this tonic*, he thought. Laughing, he drank two more dishes. It wasn't as powerful as the coco leaves Cristo had given him at Mons, which removed pain and made him a warrior for a day, but it was marvellously stimulating. After that, Ibrahim sent him beans regularly.

All the while, Latham was seeking a new physician for Joris. After rejecting several, he asked Ibrahim for help, describing how Dr Antonin had made Joris worse. Ibrahim looked through a box of papers and said thoughtfully, "If you insist on holding this poor boy to his oath, Dr Alfonso Gomes has learning and imagination."

"Is he Portuguese? Father Jerome never mentioned him."

"He wouldn't. Gomes is what Spaniards call a converso. His birth name was Abraham Ben Lev. Working in the Bureau of Diplomats allows me to know these things."

Gomes was a stooping man with penetrating brown eyes and an expression of quizzical inquiry under wispy grey hair. Latham hired him but soon questioned his decision. Gomes's first examination of Joris consisted of studying his drawings. During the following expensive weeks, he found them playing chess or card games. Gomes didn't seem to mind Joris's marked cards. His tricks just elicited an upward turn of amused lips. This wasn't treatment Latham had ever heard of. He wondered if Ibrahim was playing him for a fool

"We play for chicken bones, not money," Gomes assured Latham. One day, Latham came in toward the end of a chess game. He could see that Joris would checkmate Gomes in five moves. Gomes held a bishop to his lips then jerked his knee, upsetting the board. The pieces tumbled to the ground.

"Replace them as they were and replay the game backwards," Gomes ordered. With intense focus, Joris did.

"What remedy is this?" Latham was angry. "He doesn't say a word. What am I paying you for?"

"Why does the expense worry you? Your Father Jerome prophesies Armageddon next year," Gomes retorted. "Your coins are of no use. Better I have them."

"Father Jerome confesses me, but I don't accept his arithmetic of Armageddon. With God's grace, we'll all be here in 1579. In truth, I can't waste money belonging to the Duke of Tuscany. I have none of my own."

"If we talk privately, I'll explain," Gomes said, with a smile. A few minutes later they were sitting in Latham's study.

"Well," Latham demanded, frowning.

"Joris has been badly treated for a stutter he didn't have," Gomes began. His voice was tight with contempt. "He has no physical impairment; his tongue is normally sized, his urine is robustly coloured and textured, and his humours balanced, though he's of marked choleric temperament. He suffers from a muddle in seeing sequences of letters, which he imports to stumbling speech. You know better than anyone his native cleverness, or you wouldn't bother looking for a cure. I'm devising games of vision and memory using his native abilities. It's not easy to play an unfinished chess game backwards. I can make his speech comprehensible soon, although you must expect pauses."

A few weeks later, Joris greeted Latham in the stables with a courtly bow, a pause, an upward gaze, then, "Horses shod today."

Latham looked at him, astonished. "Very good. What did it cost?"

Joris gazed at the roof again, licked his lips then rushed out with, "Smith charged one English...shilling for English iron..." another stare at the roof. "I flatten him half..." Pause, an upward gaze, "in local coin."

"Joris, this is progress. What do you see when you look up?"

"Dancing...pictures."

Latham had thought Joris's infirmities were God's will. He'd hoped for just enough improvement to relieve his own irritation at living with him day in and day out. Joris's temper and lack of appeal to other employers were useful to Latham; his brilliance something only he and Pieter Boels understood. He had set conditions for bringing Joris to Constantinople. Now that his conditions were being met, he wasn't sure he liked it. This was too much progress.

"Dr Gomes," he asked after the physician's next visit. "You have powerful arts. Joris is improving remarkably. But could he also speak in the old bad way?"

Gomes laughed, pulling his wispy beard with a bony hand. "Triple my fee. Yes, he could speak both ways. Appearing simple disarms people, doesn't it? Useful to a master who's a fisher of secrets." He glanced at Latham shrewdly.

Of course, Latham thought. A physician would learn many things, perhaps report them. And he'd seen Joris's drawings of warehouses. "I like a secret as much as any man," he responded. "You'll find great appreciation from me on behalf of my master, the Grand Duke of Tuscany." He felt a surge of hope.

"Ah," Gomes, replied frowning, "a misunderstanding. Tuscan bait doesn't tempt me."

"Because you're Abraham Ben Lev?"

Gomes sighed, his face ageing a generation. "My blood sings with the expulsions, false accusations and persecutions of centuries. You, a papist, can't imagine what being Ben Lev is like. My great-grandfather, a converse, served his king faithfully. He was still burned by the Inquisition. Your Tuscan duke is a client of Spain, isn't he?"

"Yes."

Silence. Gomes appeared to be waiting for nuance. He got none.

"So, Doctor," Latham said, ushering Gomes out, "let it be as if no word of this passed."

Later, he pulled out his coded book of contacts. He wrote: *Converso Alfonso Gomes, physician, fished the fisherman. Did my English name confuse him about my allegiance? He may report to the Turk, the English, both.* He listed Gomes' address, description and birth name. Next, he wrote: *Ibrahim, assistant to the Secretary of the Bureau of Diplomats, my very great friend. He'll show me what I need to know. But when? In the name of Jesus Christ, when?*

CHAPTER 11
WOBBLING
CERTAINTIES

Constantinople, December 1577

That year, the month-long Ramadan began in December. The road to Ibrahim's estate became snow over iced mud, causing him to spend nights at his rooms in the Divan Tower, or in the new astronomical observatory, where he was a keen follower of Tariq-El-Din, the Sultan's chief astronomer and astrologer. He met Latham at the Englishman's house. Latham learned that graduates of the Sultan's elite slave school were expected to excel at some hobby: a craft, natural philosophy, gardening, hand-to-hand combat. Ibrahim's avocation was measuring instruments.

To honour Ibrahim's request that he keep being his egret-magpie, he dutifully daubed black dye in his hair. But this got him no pillow confidences about trade policy. If Ibrahim said one more time: "Like you, egret-magpie, royal policy is *as attainable as air*," Latham knew anxiety would burst his skull. He diverted himself by reading about Ottoman law and customs, learning about everything but trade policy. Joris resumed watching the separate warehouse that had accepted crates from an English ship, and saw another delivery. This time Ibrahim didn't warn him off. Either he didn't know or didn't care.

Latham got three letters from Europe. Mary's factor in Paris thanked him effusively for securing the duke's loan, which he said would alleviate the conditions of Mary's continued confinement in English castles. The letter's date showed that the loan had been approved before Latham had even left Florence; Mary's money hadn't depended on Latham's success in Constantinople at all! And here he was, struggling to wrest intelligence from this infuriatingly opaque society. *Francesco gulled me*, Latham concluded, shaking his head ruefully. He was thrilled to see Cristo's handwriting, but that letter was just a great moan: *All is awry in the Netherlands. My men carouse under the Sicilian sun, skills rotting. When will I see action again?* Pieter Boels' coded letter said that part of Latham's network was still functioning; ineffective Don John, Lady Barbara's son, had captured a few towns, but only those that had raised the white flag, and all was awry in the Netherlands. Latham thought of Lady Barbara with a pang, hoping she was coping with convent life. Mercifully, the duke seemed to have forgotten him. *Nothing changes*, Latham thought, burning his letters.

How wrong he was! On the first night of Ramadan, as a blood-orange sun fell below the horizon, the muezzin called the fast's end. As if answering invocations from thousands of minarets, a giant star with multi-pronged tails thrust into shocking visibility, its tails tapering across half the sky. It lay beyond a crescent moon, humping Sagittarius, whose own heavenly bodies flared in sympathy. The comet bathed hills and sharp-edged buildings with a light that made them seem alive, pulsating, ready to lurch about and wrench the ground open.

Latham, Joris, and the house servants climbed to the roof. Latham grabbed a glimpse, and closed his eyes. How could he forget his childhood nurse warning him to never look at a comet? "The Almighty will no longer hear your prayers," she'd warned, wagging a finger at him as she recounted blighted lives from her village, all because of staring at a wicked comet.

Latham ached to know if it was oppressing England or Sicily. What was his sister, Katherine, telling her children? Would it sober Cristo's men? He looked directly at the long tails. He thought he'd outgrown superstition, but crossed himself and prayed. His Muslim servants were on their knees, foreheads to the ground, while the Christian stable boy worked his rosary as he crept back to the comfort of a dark stall. Horses whickered nervously, turning in their wooden confines. Joris tried to draw the sky, but his hand shook, as if recording it was blasphemy.

When day broke, the comet was still there, pale and ponderous. It hung from a shocked sky, a gross goitre framed by vomit-coloured clouds. It seemed to challenge the sun to dare go about its business; the sun did, timidly, and human dealings eventually began. It was Ramadan, and Constantinople required an evening feast. City gates clanked open, cartwheels screeched, and the town roused itself.

The Sultan's sleep-deprived subjects whispered as they went about their routines, as if the comet was eavesdropping. Some imams proclaimed Allah was foretelling Divine punishment. Father Jerome was smug: the comet's arrival near Christmas proved Armageddon was near. The circle of Christ's birth and the annihilation of the human race he sacrificed himself to redeem, was closing. The Sultan's astrologers took a different view. The heavenly body's arrival during Ramadan was a portent of glory: the fulfilment of royal ambitions. They cast a new chart for Murad.

Late that first afternoon, Ibrahim invited Latham to the observatory to break the fast and watch the night sky. "Oh, come," he snorted derisively when Latham cited his childhood nurse's warnings. "You stared as a child and are still here, with sound physique and intellects. You looked last night–don't tell me you didn't–and you're intact."

Blushing, Latham agreed to go with him. At the observatory, there were two buildings, in addition to the stables. "The library and sleeping cells are there, and we can eat whenever you like," Ibrahim said, waving at the larger building. Smoke curling from the chimney smelled enticingly of grilling meat and stewing fruit.

They went inside. A long table groaned with food, with fennel and orchid tea, and coffee to drink. The feast was traditional, but its consumers were not. There were no rows of cushions, just stools here and there. No groups sat chatting companionably. Tariq-El-Din's followers ate standing then rushed outside to gape. Ibrahim jostled Latham to do the same. In truth, they broke the fast slightly ahead of the muezzin's calls.

"This is the important place," Ibrahim said excitedly, ushering Latham into the smaller building. He swallowed a last piece of chicken kebab while Latham sucked on halvah. "Measuring goes on here."

In the main room, astronomical instruments were laid out on shelves and labelled: armillary spheres; astrolabes; mural quadrants; sextants. "Obsolete," Ibrahim chuckled. "Tariq-El-Din has invented better instruments." An apprentice bent over a table, inking pricks on a blank chart. On another table, an old chart of the motion of stars and planets was spread out. The apprentice went from table to table, comparing positions.

"He's using last night's measurements. You'll be surprised what they show," Ibrahim said, clapping the boy approvingly on the shoulder.

Outside, the view was wonderfully clear, better than from the Tower of Galata. Snow contoured hills and buildings. It reflected the pink/orange/purple of sunset so dazzlingly that sky and earth hummed as one. Latham gulped in transcendence.

Seemingly oblivious to the glories bathing him, El-Din hunched over a sextant. An assistant hovered, holding a clock with three dials and three hands. El-Din's silent intensity seemed premature because the moon and constellations were mere hints as yet. Still, quiet appeared to be the rule.

Latham pointed and held up three fingers to Ibrahim.

"Hours, minutes and seconds for accurately capturing the ascension of the stars," Ibrahim mouthed in his ear. "There are twelve seconds to a minute. Nothing as exact has been done."

Latham recalled Cristo's *looker*. If the Dutch apothecary had made it for distance instead of a half mile, it could settle the movement of planets and stars better than El-Din's instruments. It could rip away the veils shrouding the secrets of the heavens. Latham opened his mouth to describe the tubes, as a point of Frankish pride. Then he hesitated, wondering: Should man breach heaven's mysteries? The more knowledge, the more powerful the sin, and the more vicious the schisms. He decided to say nothing.

The sky blackened, and constellations and moon blazed. Now El-Din allowed talk. Three astronomers murmured in Arabic, which Ibrahim translated for Latham.

"Our tables show that planets move in an ellipse, not a circle," one said.

"And the comet's position above the moon challenges Aristotle, maybe Ptolemy," another agreed.

"We live in dazzling times," the third man said. "But we must be careful not to offend the imams. What are the common people saying?" he asked Ibrahim.

Ibrahim's task was to monitor popular opinion about the comet's visitation. He laughed. "My boy, Ahmet Gul of Adrianopolis, he's a clever little linguist, heard these versions: God's trebuchet hurling missiles across the sky; headless generals in cloth of gold treading the heavens. A sailor says Satan grabbed the monster squid of the deep and hurled it into the sky. Its tentacles will sweep us into its pointy mouth, and it will chew us to a pulp. Women say doves are silent;

water is metallic to taste; babes are born with two heads."

"Has anyone seen the babes?" the third astronomer asked.

"No, Gul says. But many believe in it."

El-Din ignored the chatter.

"It's nonsense," the first astronomer said. "Other comets never ended the world.

I've heard the Sultan's new chart augurs '*glory and wellbeing*' for our Empire."

The comet hugged the sky for forty days then vanished as suddenly as it had come. Its absence gave the exhausted populace a sense of divine reprieve.

One afternoon, Ibrahim brought Latham into his rooms in the Divan Tower, then left him alone. It was the first time Latham had been in Constantinople's administrative centre. He opened two scrolls on the table. One was in Turkish, the other in Latin. It was a truce between Philip II and Murad III for one year, with possible extensions, unsigned.

"Thank you," Latham said when Ibrahim returned. "But they're unsigned. I can't report on an unsigned, unsealed text. There could be changes."

"It will be, with no amendments," Ibrahim said irritably, locking the documents away. "I promised you'd learn what you needed to in season. I took a big risk, showing you this. You must choose between being first with this intelligence for your duke, or laggardly. When it's signed, everyone will know."

Latham needed more. Did this truce alter trade policy? Since 1535, French middlemen had a monopoly facilitating trade between the Ottoman Empire and European states. The French loved their treaty and guarded it jealously, while it was costly to everyone else. When Murad III took power, he'd hinted at change. Latham's job was to get the details. Logically, an Ottoman/Spanish truce should benefit Spain's ally, Tuscany, in trade, but the crates Joris had drawn being taken to a separate warehouse came from an English ship - although a crate unloaded from an English ship didn't necessarily mean its contents were English.

"Does this mean that Spain and my Tuscan duke will have equal preferences to the French?" he asked.

"Don't push," Ibrahim snapped. "There are layers, layers still. This truce results from the Sultan's new chart, which predicts '*wellbeing in the Empire and the conquest of Persia.*' Murad is delighted. He has wanted to settle accounts with Persia for years. But to do so, he needs peace in the Mediterranean. Philip needs the same, to put down his Dutch rebels. Murad got the better bargain. We Ottoman always do."

The last sentence piqued Latham's interest. "The better bargain? How?"

"We will expand our lands—the prophecy is clear—while the best Philip can hope for is to get back his lost territories, and he might fail in that." Ibrahim's smile was wolfish.

"What do you know about Spain being thwarted again in the Netherlands?" Latham demanded.

Ibrahim folded his hands into his sleeves. "I've said more than I should. The text I showed you is all you can report to your Medici duke."

Latham had to be content. He repeated the wording of the truce, adding observations on conditions of Constantinople society. He paid a huge fee for both a land and sea courier, but there was no response from Florence.

Soon, preparations for war were visible everywhere. Tin and iron imports arrived in the ports. In the city, the blacksmith's quarter rang with the hammering of armour and swords, carts of fodder and food rumbled toward military warehouses, and on every day but Friday, a colourful crush of infantry and cavalry in a dizzying variety of uniforms clogged the streets.

They marched off, leaving the city quieter and in suspense. Reports from the distant front were positive, but as winter gave way to spring, Ibrahim's mood changed. He laughed less, and when he did, it was long after Latham's joke. It was as if he had to travel from one end of a convoy to the other to retrieve a witticism that had passed him. Their couplings decreased, then stopped. Latham wondered if Ibrahim was eating opium. But his eyes were dull, not dilated, and he was as fastidious as ever. Latham concluded he was melancholic, deeply oppressed by black bile. He'd noticed similar lowness in some officials at the palace. No one, of course, offered to explain.

One morning, Ibrahim and Latham were lounging on a divan in Ibrahim's receiving room. Neither had touched the dates and oranges on a side table.

Ibrahim broke a long silence. "How are your inquiries for your Tuscan lord going?" He sounded at once detached and urgent.

"What gambit is this?" Latham snorted. "You know I get nowhere. I've spent all the money I have on bribes, to no avail. The duke will dissolve me in his vitriol if I return as ignorant as I left."

"What did you expect?" Ibrahim said wearily. "We have no treaty of friendship with Florence. They're Spain's client. Our truce with Spain is tactical." He smiled faintly. "But don't repent of your generosity to our officials. Your gifts pleased the recipients, I assure you."

He leaned forward and grabbed Latham's hand, whispering, "Egret-magpie, I'll give you everything you want today."

Latham was alarmed by Ibrahim's volatility, almost desperation. "Why now? Listen, my affection goes beyond information I need. What I said about the duke's vitriol was phrase-making. I'm not afraid of him. My astrologer, Dr Pell, predicted a long life for me."

"My chart differs," Ibrahim replied slowly. "As the Persian poet, Jajarmi, writes: *With the Moon in Pisces, study learning and theology, Make requests from ministers and judges. This is the end of the tale,"*

"The end? What do you mean? My friend, surely you don't believe in Father Jerome's Armageddon."

"Oh no, something far less important than the world's destruction. Portents have turned ugly. Tell me, how do officials look these days? Triumphant? Did you notice paper glued to city gates?"

Latham thought. "The Janissaries look triumphant, but many others do look as if they've chewed mouldy lemon rind. And yes, two days ago I saw a paper fastened to Adrianople Gate. It was a list. Three lines in Turkish. It's gone now."

"There you have it. You looked, but didn't see."

Ibrahim reached for a date, then pulled his hand back, empty. He sighed. "No appetite. Do you remember the first day we met? I said Roman conquerors pushed out, dominating the culture of those they subjugated, while we Ottomans pull in, absorbing influences from those we defeat? There's been, perhaps, too much pulling in. The orthodox imams rage. Some people will pay.

"Militarily, we've taken two Persian towns, so the Janissaries strut. But the cost in men and treasure has been appalling. I've seen the accounts. When Murad does, he'll be furious. Janissaries won't crow for long. Worse, there's disease in the provinces. Spring plague is a particular calamity: too few peasants to plant and harvest mean widespread famine, fever, and the lumps sweeping a city crammed with hungry, weakened subjects. It may already have reached here. That list on Adrianople Gate names dead citizens taken beyond the walls for burial. It's plague, my friend, not the '*well being and glory*' El-Din prophesied. His followers like me will be punished. But I cannot die without helping my egret-magpie. I'll give you what you need for the dread Francesco, then you must leave."

Latham leapt up, overturning the table. "No, Ibrahim! This can't be."

Ibrahim pulled him down. "The dates; you dirtied the dates." He gave a wan smile. "Listen. The Persian couplet I spoke is exact: *Study learning and theology;* that's our Sultan, who closets himself with his Grand Mufti, chief of the enraged imams. *Make requests from ministers;* that's you with your endless questions. *This is the end of the tale.* My end"

Devastated, Latham protested, "But you serve your Sultan devotedly. Any examination of the facts must exonerate you." He reached to embrace Ibrahim.

The Ottoman pushed him away. "That's what you Franks call a trial. Our procedures are different. Out of favour, I know too much."

"Then come with me to Florence. Let me save your life."

"Impossible. Don't dare tempt me to interfere with Allah's will. Here's how it will go. The whole problem is Tariq-El-Din's glory-prophesying chart. Now, the Sultan meets his Grand Mufti, as the poem says. Murad will pose his suspicions of evil service as a riddle or dream. It will show El-Din's followers using the new instruments and observatory Murad paid for not for mathematics, but to lust after angels. Orthodox imams have accused us of measuring their noble chests, touching ourselves all the while, gyrating our hips and pumping our erect manhoods in lewd fancies of copulating in the super-lunary sphere, forgetting service to our Sultan. Too much *pulling in* they say, and look, plague! Allah is displeased. Murad won't name individuals because he recounts a riddle or dream. But when the Grand Mufti, who's Syrian, interprets the vision as Murad wants to hear it, the fate of some is sealed. The Grand Mufti will exempt Tariq-El-Din, a Syrian compatriot. The scourge falls on his followers. My time is short. You'll learn what you seek, but it comes with things you may wish not to know. To start, you've wondered where I go at noon. Let me show you."

He got up. In a churn of emotion, Latham followed him into the domed building screened by cypress trees. Its main room was full of clocks of various sizes, timepieces and hourglasses.

"Ibrahim, you have a reckless avocation," Latham protested. "Public clocks are banned." He had to shout over chimes, bells, tinkles, clicks, and the whoosh of sand falling through the neck of the hourglasses. Each device told a different time. Two slave boys stood by, surly but attentive, waiting to wind clocks and turn hourglasses as they ran down. Latham hated this madhouse. He picked up a German clock, put it down, then did the same with a French timepiece.

"Mine aren't public," Ibrahim shouted back. "Look!" He pointed to four timepieces with tiny silver falcons on top. "I made these. The falcon is my mark." He smiled, momentarily his old self.

"You're a superb craftsman. I didn't know," Latham said, running his finger pad over the fine silver work.

"Which time-teller has the truth, Edward?" Ibrahim asked, with intensity.

"What?" Latham tried to estimate how long they'd been there. A quarter hour? The varied times offered by the clocks made the concept seem wobbly. He strode to a squat, gold-topped clock with a border of rubies around its large, black face. Uncertain, he looked toward the window.

"Yes, look outside," Ibrahim said with a trace of amusement.

A sundial lay in the centre of the courtyard. A boy stood, holding a horn. When the sun cast the noon shadow, he blew it. The two boys in the room rushed to examine the timepieces and make marks in a book.

"My daily ritual," Ibrahim said. From a nearby minaret, they heard the call to prayer. While Ibrahim and his servants prayed, Latham studied the book. It documented which clocks were correct on which days. Few bore any marks signifying accuracy, and only two had been marked more than once.

Noon prayers done, Ibrahim dismissed the boys. "You see," he said, flipping through the book, "we try to capture the truth of God's heavens by clumsy devices of our own making. Which is true, which false, changes constantly. If one timepiece snatches truth, as you can see from the book, it isn't often. I gave the best ones to El-Din. Alas, none of my own devices is among them."

"That must be frustrating," Latham responded, shaking his head to relieve discomfort from the clock noise, "but what does it have to do with trade policy? You promised." Carefully, he put the falcon-topped clock back on its shelf. According to the sundial, it was seven minutes slow.

"Think. We make untruthful measurements of time. Why would our manufactured theologies be any more a perfect reflection of God's word? Muslims bend foreheads to the ground, always facing Mecca." He shouted over more chimes, clicks and whooshes. "Jews mumble, rocking back and forth, looking down. Is Yahweh under the earth? Christians kneel, fingers and face extended to the sky. Is your Holy Spirit up there? Dervishes whirl, finding the Spirit in manic circlings; men from India sit cross-legged, eyes swivelled into their sockets, finding the Spirit in their own sinews. Who is your prating pope to say which is God's sanctioned pose?"

Latham was stunned. True religion was Catholic liturgy, divinity expressed in Catholicism's soaring Gothic spires and arches, the noble tolling of their mighty bells. Other doctrines were primitive, misguided or deliberate heresies. Ibrahim was implying that no doctrine was better than another; all as defective as the timepieces that began another series of jangles. Doctrinal relativism, an odious philosophy. But was he being too generous to Ibrahim in calling this relativism? What kind of man would construct this din of confusion, visiting it daily to wallow in its Babel-like muddle? Only an atheist. Loving across skin colour, faith, social rank and culture had stretched Latham. Embracing an unbeliever was inconceivable.

"You are whitely silent," Ibrahim said. "So tight-wound in your doctrines that you walk through life in swaddling cloths like an infant."

Latham flushed. "No, I pity you. You converted from Christianity, though of a misguided sect, to Islam, for earthly advancement. These swaddling cloths of mine, they… fit… snug. Do you even acknowledge God?" He was too disoriented to keep in focus that Ibrahim had been sold into slavery, and was walking to his inscribed death.

"I answer to no man on that," Ibrahim said sadly. He could see Latham was shocked beyond sympathy. "However," he continued, "one of my boys saw the clocks the way you do. He told the imams."

Latham wondered if the pouting caramel-coloured turban cleaner, once Ibrahim's bedfellow, had betrayed him.

"Don't ask who," Ibrahim said. "It's unimportant. Well, there's no more to do here." He waved Latham out of the room.

Confusion gripped Latham. Featureless Muslims, Dervishes, Christians, Jews and Hindus twisted in frenzied rituals. Their imagined chants roared inside him, mingling with door-muffled timepiece chimes. His eyes blurred, he felt his bones dissolving. He leaned against a wall, heaving for breath. Ibrahim watched dispassionately. After a few moments, Latham disengaged from the wall, and they walked back to the house in silence.

Soon they were on the divan again, dates and oranges untouched. "What do defective clocks have to do with trade policy?" Latham asked in a chilly voice.

"A lot. Come to the library."

There, Ibrahim pulled a flat box from a shelf and opened it. "You need to understand our context. These are copies of portraits made by a Venetian painter twenty years ago."

He showed Latham a sheet. A beguiling young woman with pale skin, sharp cheekbones and luxuriant braided red hair gazed at them. Her eyes were steady, brazen. "This is our Sultan's grandmother, Roxanne. She was a concubine to Suleiman the Magnificent. He loved her so much he made her Empress. Yes, she was a whey-faced red-haired Slav. Doesn't she resemble the whey-faced red-haired Queen of England? The one who says your silly Frankish doctrinal quarrels are a '*dispute over trifles?*' Further, she doesn't make windows into men's souls? She fines those who don't attend her official services, a kind of tax. Just like us."

Latham was beginning to understand: Murad thought Elizabethan governance, with regard to religion, was like his; and that England's queen resembled his grandmother. "Your Roxanne doesn't look like Elizabeth at all, but your meaning is clear. That's enough to give England trade preferences?"

"They don't look alike?" Ibrahim asked, raising his eyebrows. He was genuinely astonished. "But Harborne, the English ambassador, said they could be sisters. He came with a portrait of his queen."

"Harborne probably never met Elizabeth. He'd say what you want to hear," Latham retorted. He was beginning to recapture his mind. "I served her for six years. She's compelling, but not in Roxanne's way."

"It doesn't matter now," Ibrahim considered. "Sultan Selim II, Murad's father, said they look alike. Selim revered his mother because Roxanne secured the succession for him, no certain thing. You remember that princes who don't accede are strangled? Roxanne's plots against Selim's father's other children saved Selim's life. His son, Murad, reveres his grandmother for the same reason. You know Selim loved wine?"

Latham nodded. "He died of a cracked head after diving into an empty bath when he was drunk."

"Murad doesn't like alcohol. He's a rutting Sultan, loves women. A red-haired Frank queen who's ruled unmarried for fifteen years? He'll imbue her with infinite longings, prefer her politically unless she does ill by him, which she hasn't. Harborne says she doesn't burn religious dissidents, unlike Catholic rulers. Murad says she's Ottoman at heart."

Latham laughed, more a short-lived brittle bark than a laugh of amusement, but he touched Ibrahim's sleeve affectionately. "Ibrahim, Elizabeth isn't tolerant in the way you mean. She's a heretic with a gift for choosing clever envoys. What about your imams' fear of too much pulling in? There's nothing more chaotic than the mushrooming heretical

Christian sects."

"Does Elizabeth burn or fine Catholics?"

"She fines them. That much is true."

"That's enough, egret-magpie. We don't expect a Frank to be as civilised as we are. Our trade policy will soon favour the English. Their tin, iron and steel will be much cheaper if we cut out French middlemen. With the war not going well, that matters. You must keep it close, for the new arrangement will infuriate the French. So there's your answer. Advise your Tuscan lord to like the English better. And take it as my dying gift to you. You loathe my words and clocks because they challenge your doctrines and wobble your certainties. But I had a dream long ago that you will perform actions that turn the affairs of Frankish states, and those turns favour us. I have always seen that power in you. Like my death, our meeting was preordained. One day you will step from your swaddling cloths and think with subtlety. Then you'll look kindly on today."

Ibrahim put the picture away while Latham tried to shrink his passions to manageable intensity. He was revolted by Ibrahim's blasphemies, and grief-stricken at his imminent death; he felt the cold fingers of loneliness closing around his throat. But he was an intelligencer. A Venetian portrait of a Sultan's Slav Empress; a verbal report of an English alliance; Persian couplets. Back in Europe, he'd never have accepted these hints as reportable. His work demanded proof.

"Ibrahim, I'm grateful for your help. I have no words for my grief at your situation. But I need more specific information. A few months ago, my servant saw crates taken to a separate warehouse, bypassing the regular customs agents. I must examine the contents. We both know they are the proof of Ottoman foreign and trade policy."

"You ask the impossible," Ibrahim's voice was harsh with alarm. "I'm not in the department that stores them."

"I insist," Latham pressed. "What further harm can come to you than what is already written?" His customary excitement at grabbing facts was beginning to return.

"The method," Ibrahim said bleakly. "Impalement is worse than beheading."

"That can't happen. Show me the crates and come to Florence. I'll manage it."

"Impossible."

Ibrahim thought, *wiles of francolin; spirit of hawk, as I dreamed*. "I wouldn't have respected the hawk in you if you hadn't pressed," he said after a pause. "Practically speaking, it's impossible."

"Why?"

"Firstly, the consignments are no longer there."

"Others will arrive."

Ibrahim smiled. "Yes," he conceded, "next week. However, the guards are mutes; tongues cut out. They can't tell you anything. They're fiercely protective of the warehouse, so you can take nothing out. Secondly, I have a code of honour. If you describe the contents of those crates to your beloved Tuscan lord, some whom we like could be endangered. I refuse to stoop to that."

"I serve the Tuscan lord, but don't love him. He's too cruel. I pray daily for the Almighty to grant me a better master. If I swear to keep what I see in these crates secret; if I use the knowledge only to be certain that what you've shown me is solid truth in my report on Murad's policy, will you help?"

"Oaths aside," Ibrahim considered, "you can't get in to take anything out. It would take the cunning of a Trojan horse to accomplish it."

Latham had met Ibrahim's moral worries, and they were now considering the problem together. His confidence grew. The cunning of a Trojan horse, Ibrahim had said. After a moment, Latham whooped. "I've got it. No Trojan horse, my moon and sun. A Trojan camel! You say these brutes let nothing out; very good. I don't want to take anything out. Listen, their job is to let consignments in. I'll make a delivery. There's a life-sized, two-humped camel skin at St Peter's and Paul's church, used in Christmas pageants. It's made of real camel hide, stiffened with wire and plaster. It stinks like the old beasts around the caravanserais. Two men can operate it, to bring crates in. On a cloudy night, we'll evade discovery as we make the delivery. Once inside, all I need is to look into the crates. No one will know you had anything to do with adding inventory."

Despite himself, Ibrahim was captivated by Latham's enthusiasm. As they made plans, they ate the dates and oranges, savouring every bite.

Five nights later, there was a new moon. Starlight stabbed through banked clouds, creating a tracery of blue patterns on blue. A tall two-humped Bactrian camel with a thick neck lurched awkwardly up a hill to the warehouse Joris had drawn months earlier. An embroidered rug was draped over the humps, supporting a board on which a wooden box was attached by a rope. A young camel driver thumped the beast's right foreleg rhythmically with the handle of his whip. At every blow, the beast shuffled forward. A stooped man wearing the olive robe of the Bureau of Diplomats escorted the driver. His grey hair and wrinkled face were belied by bright, darting eyes. Ibrahim had enlisted two boys he trusted from his household to help Latham. The camel driver was Mustafa of Tikrit, a swordsman in training, and the clerk was Ahmet Gul of Adrianapolis, a mathematician and linguist. Ibrahim had provided robes and delivery documents. The boys were nervous and excited.

Inside the camel, Latham and Joris were miserable. Each stooped at a horrible angle under a hump, camel skin legs pinned around their own legs, their arms jammed at their sides. Their shoulders were bruised by the box pressing on them, and old camel hair and dried tissue, stinking of blood, dander, and curing chemicals, made them lightheaded and desperate to sneeze. In addition, Latham had doused the camel with ox piss, hoping to discourage scrutiny by the deaf-mute guards that Ibrahim said were fastidious. The wires shaping the camel cut their skin through their shirts, and their shoes were unspeakably filthy. They were loosely roped at the waist to each other, so when Mustafa rapped Latham's thigh, his step jerked Joris into motion.

An ingenious system of wires and curved wood worked the neck. Mustafa's bang on the front hump signalled that Latham should make a camel-like movement for a night watchman. Slowly, over what felt like hours, they approached their destination. During the Christmas pageant of the *Three Kings*, Latham had watched this camel weave a sinuous path through the streets of Galata. He'd never thought about how it was done. Now he was filled with admiration for the skill of the men who worked this awful contraption with a semblance of elegance.

A thump on the neck; Latham halted. Unaware of the signal, Joris kneed him. The humps shivered, wobbling the load. Latham began to panic as he heard heavy footsteps (it sounded like two pairs) and strange vocalising: hawking phlegm deep in a throat followed by a spit and high whine. Were these challengers? As Latham and Joris pushed their shoulders up, they felt Mustafa grab the box and stabilise it. Mustafa chattered rapidly in Turkish. Guttural grunts replied; more chatter from Mustafa, another whine. Some feet clumped away.

"Two mutes," Ahmet whispered to the humps. "One went behind the warehouse with Mustafa; the other stepped away from your reek to sneeze."

Then Latham heard Ahmet's cultivated voice, raised to cover the sound of any scuffle. A few seconds later, there was a surprised shout of alarm from a voice that sounded like Mustafa, then several cracks in succession, a feral moan, a few thuds, a clinking of metal and the squeak of doors opening. A final thump on the camel and they were inside the warehouse.

"How did you do it?" Latham asked Mustafa when he and Joris had disentangled themselves. They gulped the woody miasma of the warehouse as if it was pure mountain air. Ahmet's little horned lantern shed enough light for them to get their bearings.

"I told them I had to piss and went around the corner," Mustafa said cheerfully. "I shouted I'd seen a bandit, cudgelled the brute with me, then crept back and cudgelled the other one while he was stooping to read Ahmet's document. Now I have to make sure they don't wake up too soon. What sport!" He was grinning as he and Ahmet went outside, leaving Latham and Joris alone.

Joris levered open two crates. When Latham saw the bills of sale taped to the lid he asked Joris to go outside. He wanted to be the only one to view the contents. Against each item, the price was crossed out. In elegant English capital letters, it read "NO CHARGE." There was no signature.

A cloth bag protected each piece. Latham pulled out gold, silver and brass candlesticks of different sizes. Some were simple, some ornate. There were many brass chalices, crucifixes, incense thuribles, statues of the Madonna. They were artefacts for Catholic mass.

He opened the second crate. It was full of small caskets: gold, silver, brass. Many had once had precious gemstones embedded in them, for holes gaped where the stones had been pried out. Latham knew they were relic caskets from monasteries dissolved by Elizabeth's father, Henry VIII, like the gaping ruined priory he passed when he visited his mother's grave.

Revolted and intrigued, he squatted. This had to have come from Elizabeth herself; only the Tower would have such valuables. Most people assumed that when Henry VIII closed the monasteries in the 1530s, all useable metal had been melted down or sold for his wars. Here was evidence that some remained. What was Elizabeth up to?

He imagined the issue from her point of view. He could see her in the Tower, pondering the artefacts. It was against her frugal nature to make no use of what, to her, were superfluous objects. She was too canny to be seen selling them or having them melted down herself; that would alienate her Catholic subjects. But keeping them opened her to pressure from her radicals to use them for the Dutch rebels. That would alienate Spain. What was more strategic than giving them to an infidel who needed brass for weapons, silver and gold for coinage, to fight a different infidel? The Ottoman Sultan was Spain's enemy and well-disposed to the red-haired queen who, he insisted, resembled his grandmother. Latham had to admit that her deployment of the artefacts was elegant.

She'd want something in return, of course. The agreement between Murad and Elizabeth probably went beyond preferential trade tariffs, he reasoned. This gift would make the most sense in the context of an offensive-defensive understanding. If Philip were to attack England, Murad might threaten to attack Spanish lands in the Mediterranean, or actually do so. The threat alone could make Philip split his forces.

Suddenly Latham understood Ibrahim's hint that Spain might not be able to vanquish the Dutch rebels, despite the Ottoman-Spanish truce. English merchants who traded in the Orient would profit greatly with lower Ottoman tariffs, an arrangement greased by this brass. Many of them, like Ambassador Harborne, were fervent Protestants, and now they'd have more funds to give their Dutch friends.

He listed each item with its price crossed out, and copied the various makers' marks. Then he re-packed and closed the boxes.

He stood, rubbing his back. This was a great piece of intelligence, but he couldn't use it directly. If he blabbed, Elizabeth would be hurt at home and abroad, and he intended to keep his promise to Ibrahim not to reveal what he saw. There was also no signature on the bills. Elizabeth had sent them, but he couldn't prove it.

Much suspected of me,
Nothing proved can be.

The young Elizabeth had scratched that couplet on her prison window, when under investigation for plotting against her sister, Queen Mary. She hadn't changed. Latham suspected that any military understandings were informal. He could only use these Catholic mass artefacts to be confident in advising Francesco that the Sultan favoured England.

He'd been alone in the warehouse for an hour, judging by the flickering lantern. When he got outside, Mustafa was standing over the prone guards, tapping the end of his cudgel against his palm thoughtfully. Joris and Ahmet were a few yards away, Ahmet talking quickly, Joris using hand gestures and disjointed words. They'd made friends. *Why not?* Latham thought. *Little Ahmet is odd-looking, with an oversized head; Joris has speech defects. Both elicit scorn from society, and both are clever.*

"Thank you, gentlemen," he said, bowing. "A good night." He and Joris wriggled into the camel, and the boys led them back without incident. After returning the beast to the church, Joris and Latham tumbled into their beds at dawn.

Latham sent a note thanking Ibrahim, then slept for two days. His dreams were jumbled: slow burning in hell, assaulted by clocks ticking and chiming until he voided from stress. When awake, he was too distraught to eat. His certainties wobbled unbearably. He returned Ibrahim's poems and gifts, while railing against the loss of love. He went to mass daily, blocking his ears at muezzin calls, allowing himself to hear only the wood-on-wood or iron announcing Christian services

Joris had no such confusions. He went to see Ahmet Gul several times, coming back one day with a book he said was Gul's gift. It was a riot of pressed flowers: orchids, roses, cyclamen, crocuses, and pages of strange bowl-shaped blooms labelled *Tulips.*

"Gul... hobby. Says... import." He pointed to the bowl-like flowers.

"You're not licensed," Latham replied.

"Y...Yet," Joris muttered.

The servants were looking forward, Latham thought, while he and Ibrahim felt the end of things.

One night, at about 4.00 a.m., there was a hammering on his door. His servant admitted Gul, who was carrying a small clock with a silver falcon on top. His eyes were bloodshot and swollen from crying.

"No," Latham pleaded.

"Yes, sir, I'm sorry."

"How?" His stomach clenched, terrified that the next word would be impalement.

"Beheading. El-Din was spared, but followers weren't. Their heads will be displayed outside the Imperial gate tomorrow. Murad has placed cannons at the observatory. If the Persian war doesn't go better, he'll blow up the buildings to appease Allah."

A shattered priory near his mother's grave, a bombarded astronomical observatory; odd tangent, his thoughts rattled. Gul was still talking, and Latham forced his mind back.

"My master made this clock. There's a lock of his hair in a false top under the falcon. He thought you'd want it. I took it before the executioners smashed the others."

Latham turned the exquisite timepiece in his hands, gulping at the smell of sandalwood soap. "Why are the hands at 2.00?"

"The hour of his death, sir. I'll start it if you like."

"No, I cherish it as it is. The hands will always point thus. I loved him."

"I know. I'll be sold tomorrow, after the furniture."

"Are you afraid?"

Gul shifted uneasily. For the first time, Latham really studied him. He was about fourteen, with pale blue eyes under a forehead already dented by daily prayers. The way he cocked his oversized sharp-boned head gave him a prematurely wise look. No wonder he played the old Treasury clerk so well at the warehouse. His skin was pale, hair black, eyelids slanted. *A brew of races*, Latham thought, *remnants of Genghis Khan, Alexander, Byzantine monks, the Constantinople mishmash. How will the grown man look?*

"Yes... no." Customs of centuries brought a puzzled frown to Gul's face. "I'm a linguist, mathematician and gardener. I could be a house slave, be taken into the Sultan's service and rise to secretary, be an aide to a diplomat. It's Allah's will. I didn't betray Ibrahim, nor did Mustafa. He was a good master..."

"Mustafa the cudgeler," Latham interrupted. "Will the Janissaries take him?"

"No, they want Christians. He's Arab. A provincial noble will buy him. Sir, plague spreads. Ibrahim cancelled your permit to stay and booked you and Joris on a Venetian ship. It leaves tomorrow. Here's the paper. I must go."

He slipped away. Latham inhaled the clock's sandalwood scent. "Oh, Ibrahim," he murmured. "How I wish things could have been different."

CHAPTER 12
DANGLING
DAYS

Florence, August 1578 to
Boulogne, May 1580

It was the death of another man, not Ibrahim, that determined Latham's next year. Within a few months of his return to Florence, that death reinstated him as a spy for the Spanish Catholic cause in Europe. The same death, in October 1578, liberated or trapped everyone who'd been involved in Mary, Queen of Scots' quest to free herself from confinement in England by marrying Don John of Austria. For Don John, Governor-General of the Spanish Netherlands, Lady Barbara's son and Philip II's half-brother, died of typhus.

Philip had long been dissatisfied with his half-brother's incompetence and penchant for conspiracy. In Philip's world, he was the only plotter. He'd approved the murder of Don John's aide, an ominous sign. Philip wasn't Cain; he wouldn't kill a brother, but his grief was shallow. After the required ceremonies, he was delighted to appoint a better replacement. Alexander Farnese, later Duke of Parma, was Philip's nephew by his sister, Margaret of Parma. Farnese was a good soldier, understood military engineering and had diplomatic finesse. Philip also made another decision. Declaring that he no longer believed Lady Barbara had married Edward Latham, he freed her from the convent and re-hired Latham.

Lady Barbara was devastated by her son's death. Meeting the grown man she hadn't seen since he was two years old had been a tumult of love, pride and anguish. He was a stranger to her, and now he was gone. The loss put her into a prayerful frame of mind. Still, she was thrilled to be free of convent life. She didn't return to Brussels, with its charged memories, but bought a house in Spain far from Madrid. In Ambrosero, a northern mountain town in Cantabria near the harbour, she lived without scandal. She might have wanted to write to Latham but didn't have an address.

Don Cristobal was ecstatic. Don John was no longer ruining everything. Cristo's letter reached Latham in Florence, just before Latham left for France.

Mithridates Midas, my dear oath brother,

How I longed for this news! The ceramic knight has died of fever. His Majesty has shown marvellous wisdom in appointing his nephew, Alexander Farnese, to command the Army of Flanders. Being Italian, he has subtle arts of strategy, like Vitelli (may his great soul rest in peace), and is equally aggressive. His mother, Margaret of Parma, was Regent of the Netherlands, so he knows the evil stubbornness of our rebels.

To my joy, he recalled the Eleventh Company. In a few days, we leave Sicily to fight a winter campaign; no waiting for sun and soft breezes. This is all I know for certain. But I thought you'd want to hear about a certain German lady who caused your recent inconvenience. A captain who came from Madrid said she'd left the convent. His niece is in the same order and wrote about the old cankered woman with the angelic voice and devil's temper who came and went. When will we see each other again? It must be soon.

Affectionately, Cristo

Latham snorted at Cristo's words. He couldn't let the issue of older women go. For a man who ran into gunfire and clashing metal, he quaked at female wrinkles. Still, he wished him luck.

Mary, Queen of Scots, was depressed by Don John's death. Bereft of her saviour, she remained Elizabeth's prisoner. But she didn't give up hope. Her thoughts turned to her son James, King of Scotland. Regents still controlled the twelve-year-old king, but he'd come of age soon. He would be her saviour; a son would naturally help his mother, and she developed proposals for joint rule of Scotland. She convinced herself that James, who hadn't seen her since he was a few months old, when he finally took control and ruled as one, would see his honour *increased* by ruling as half, because that half birthed him.

Elizabeth saw nothing good about Don John's death. She didn't know about Mary's plot to marry him, or Latham's role in it. If she had, she might have been so relieved to be rid of Mary that certain critical guards might have been absent the night of the escape. As it was, she was used to Don John, alternately negotiating with him or allowing English volunteers to help the Dutch rebels. His incompetence kept Philip's attention on the Netherlands and off England. She didn't know much about Farnese, but any better man than Don John endangered her realm.

As for Latham, he lived dangling weeks in Florence until Don John died. When he arrived, he was grieving Ibrahim's death and still feeling the shock of Constantinople. He'd see, hear or smell one thing, but call it another. He often woke at night, sweating from dreams of a summer Constantinople day. He'd put a hand out for Ibrahim's shoulder, recoiling when it fell on an empty sheet. He'd light a candle and stare at Ibrahim's clock set at 2.00. And weep. His days were also confusing. When his fleshly ear welcomed tolling church bells, his memory's ear heard only the wooden clack-clack of St Peter's and St Paul's Church in Galata.

But gradually he did heal.

Latham's job for the duke had been to learn which European state the Ottoman Sultan favoured in trade policy, so Francesco's Medici kin could get richer. "Like the English better," was the message Latham brought back. When he conveyed this to the suave adviser Francesco sent to interview him, the adviser showed far more delight than Latham would have expected from an official of Spain's client state, Tuscany. Giovanni Figliazzi, Knight of Malta, accompanied by a handsome and imperturbable aide named Benedetto Landolfi, remarked, "The English queen repays her loans, which can't be said for our glorious patron, King Philip. Well done, Latham. I sense we'll work together in the future."

Latham wasn't in the mood to be charmed by malleability, as he was just recovering his equilibrium. *One knee bends to Mammon, the other to the Defender of Christendom,* he wrote sourly, naming them in his code book.

A few weeks after Don John's death, in the third week of November 1578, a clerk from the Spanish Embassy brought Latham's reinstatement letter. Don Juan de Idiaquez, Philip's Secretary of State replacing Antonio Perez, sent orders to go to Boulogne and report on French Huguenot support for the Dutch rebels, and French internal power struggles between Philip's ally, the Guises, and the French crown.

It took a few stunned moments for Latham to grasp that he was being given a second chance to serve Philip. He resolved to do great service to redeem his confusions in Constantinople. There were risks; he'd be back in the fray. Malleable Florentines like Figliazzi would report his restoration to the English, who might tell their Huguenot allies, and Huguenots had a price on his head for betraying Genlis in 1572. Still, he was eager to begin.

He and Joris left for Genoa in late November, to sail to

Marseilles. Latham planned to go overland to Boulogne, reactivating his network. On the sea voyage, Joris got into serious trouble for cheating at cards. Using Dr Gomes's methods, he'd improved his speech a little. It had advantages and disadvantages. People stopped being repulsed by his defects and noticed him. He loved that. But when a wealthy passenger accused him of unfair dealing, the disadvantage of normalcy was clear. The victim didn't indulge him as a simple, but threatened to throw him overboard or cut this throat. In an old cargo-laden caravel, there was no hiding place. Latham paid several florins to settle the quarrel.

Afterwards, he snapped, "You're useless to me if people remember you. Dr Gomes said you could talk straight to me, and the old way in public. Do so, or go back to the Netherlands."

After a truculent pause, Joris conceded. "Yes…Until I meet….her."

"Her?" Latham asked. He assumed it was the girl from a heretic family that had fled the Brussels Inquisition. "That lady you sent packets and money to? Is the child yours?"

Joris flushed. "No. Inquisitor… raped her. I pledged… she… marry another. She NOT *her*." He looked irritated at having to explain something so obvious.

The story was out at last: the girl's Protestant family arrested, goods forfeited to the Church; the Inquisitor helps himself to the girl; her belly swells and the family is allowed to flee, for silence. Joris to the rescue offers marriage, but his beloved rejects him.

"That evil Inquisitor will answer on Judgment Day," Latham assured him. "If she's not the right *her*, then which she *is* her?" He felt he was in some upside down comedic farce.

Joris pulled a crumpled drawing from his pocket. This *Her* had long blond hair, puppy-fat cheeks and blue eyes decorously lowered over bulging early breasts that overflowed a tight bodice. Her expression was of puzzlement, at an internal blooming she didn't understand. Madonna/whore, every man's fantasy. Latham wondered if she was one of the "virgins" that brothels advertised. "Where did you see her?" he asked.

"She... somewhere," Joris replied.

"A nowhere maid."

Joris shook his head, stubborn. "Somewhere. Your travels... bring her."

With the understanding that Joris would talk badly in public until Latham's travels put *her* at his feet, and Latham chuckling at the unlikelihood of *her* materialising in the foreseeable future, they reached Boulogne in April, without friction.

Entering through Porte Neuve, they clattered along the crowded Rue de Lille to the main square, then turned into a side street where Latham had arranged rooms. Joris worked the harbour, trying to identify boats infiltrating supporters of the Dutch rebels. It was a sedentary time for Latham; a few nuggets of intelligence came by mail, but the main actions were happening far away. Soon he felt like a parsnip stored too long in the cellar, only fit for compost.

Hélène, mistress of the royal laundry, wrote in her crude code about the French king, Henry III (Valois), formerly King of Poland for a few months. His effort to make peace between Huguenots and Catholics was infuriating Hélène's kin, the ideologically fervent Guises. *The king cavorts exclusively with pretty boys, dressed in skirts over farthingales, pearls around his neck, then walks next day in breeches and shirt to church, whipping his back until it's bloody. Despite his marriage, diplomats write home that there's small hope of an heir. As the cleaner of royal clothes, I know there's no hope of an heir at all.*

Latham whistled. The certainty that the French king wouldn't produce an heir was important intelligence. Spain would want to ensure that a strong Catholic succeeded him. Hélène added: *the King's and Duke of Guise's favourites duel over trivial disputes. King Henry's minions look winsome, but they're lethal.*

Modern royal courts forbade duels, so these were a proxy test, the beginning of a Valois/Guise rupture. It became his first report to Idiaquez.

He warned Hélène, as Guise kin, to be careful. Knowing that she would love Ottoman dress, he sent her a book of watercolour drawings. He laughed as he imagined her poring over the turbans, calculating where a secret invitation to assignations would skulk amidst the folds.

He did get a letter from his sister, Katherine. Dated September 1579, he got it in November, addressed to Piso Prosperino. He was ecstatic to rub his finger over her neat script and the cheap paper she always favoured. But just when he'd reached a reassuring clarity of outlook, it reawakened his conflict between kin, faith and country.

My beloved little brother, by now you must have lost teeth but gained aching joints and unwanted flesh, as I have. How I wish we could play our childhood games again. Sadly, childish Irish Catholics are raising rebellion. Suspicion of supporting them falls on innocent Catholics here. We Lathams quake particularly because of your dealings for the Spaniard. We're always first to be questioned. Any jar by a Catholic and thump thump goes our door; arrogant poundings with no respect for our rank. The queen looks away from private worship, but care for my family's safety made me give up mass. What will be my fate if my breath gives out before a priest shrives me? It's a strange journey, dear brother, this sagging of flesh while the soul brightens, striving for heaven.

Your old friend from court, David Hicks, was joyful at first to join his name to a Latham, the Protestant branch, and he dotes on his five children. He intercedes for us. But he gets haggard with the stress. He's in Walsingham's service, ferreting out plots and priests. If I thought you were settled in Boulogne, I'd live out my days with you in a Catholic town. Can you say, yes? No, you're a roamer. I don't complain. I love you forever.

Katherine

Yes, he was a roamer; he couldn't even say that he'd be in Boulogne next week. He started having nightmares. They weren't precise, more perversions of nature: waterfalls pounding up a mountain rock face instead of down, Latham slithering on ice as he tried to outrun them; the Constantinople comet pointing directly at him then plunging to earth, levelling whole cities; the moon never setting, bringing floods across vast lands. These visions were terrifying, but never clear. Meaning occasionally teased him, but dawn invariably tore it away. One dream was a visitation: his astrologer, Dr Pell, waved a brass key at him with 'misunderstand' inscribed on it, but when Latham reached for the key it crumbled to sand. When he woke, exhausted, he wondered if he was displeasing the Almighty by doing too little, or the wrong thing.

That same month, he heard from Don Cristobal. It was well known that the Army of Flanders was besieging the Dutch rebel city of Maastricht. As Latham had walked around Boulogne's ancient walls, noting damage from Henry VIII's siege in 1544, he'd often thought of Cristo. Was he on a ladder against a Maastricht wall, dodging boiling oil? In a tunnel? At last, he got word.

Esteemed Mithridates Midas,

We took Maastricht after a hard siege, many losses and a sad reduction of that elegant place. What strange times God has granted me to live through. After the surrender, we expected our brilliant commander, Alexander Farnese, to besiege other cities.

Instead, he made a witch's paper called the Treaty of Arras. I'm off to Milan on furlough. Not for any failing, but for being too good at my job! A victorious army leaves the field entirely in November, in return for three Dutch provinces bending to Philip's rule. Not in any of my war journals did a winning army run away when the campaign achieved a tenth of its mission. Is that policy, tactics, or luck? How do I write up our conquest of Maastricht? But I am well, thanks to Almighty God.

In frustration, with loving hopes that your life is simpler,
Cristo

What with a troubled oath brother and sister, and his own disturbed sleep, it was a red-eyed Latham who opened orders in March 1580, from Idiaquez: meet expatriate English Jesuits in Calais. They planned to infiltrate England to give private sacraments to faithful nobles.

Trusty Signor Prosperino,

Your earlier report on Edmund Campion makes you the best agent to send. You will meet four men: Edmund Campion, Robert Persons, Ralph Sherwin and Ralph Emerson before they embark in June or July for England. His Majesty desires them to be discreet with private masses, to avoid angering the English Government, as we are sending a Papal/Spanish expedition to support the Irish Catholic rebels. I will send jewels and local contacts by separate courier, but only give it to them if you judge them discreet.

In the service of Almighty God,

Don Juan de Idiaquez

Madrid, March 1580

Campion! *How our feet tangle,* Latham thought, thoroughly awake. The meeting wasn't until June, so he had time to write to Pieter Boels to see if he'd heard of the Jesuits. The answer came as he was about to leave. Pieter wrote three pages about Dutch merchants, how they viewed the Treaty of Arras, which, as Cristo had written, expelled the Spanish army in return for obedience to Spain; and who was pro- or anti-Spanish. Only the last sentence mentioned Jesuits. Boels had heard from a Genevan clockmaker that fifteen Jesuits had gone to Geneva, where Calvinist leader, Theodore Beza, had his headquarters. A Father Campion had challenged Beza to a public debate, the loser to be burned at the stake.

In the courtyard, Latham tapped his boot with his whip, disturbed. Blatancy was the opposite of the discretion Idiaquez wanted. But it was just an anecdote. Despite Latham's instinctive forebodings, Boels hadn't mentioned a burning. He decided to make up his mind in Calais. Foot in the stirrup, he was mounting when Joris ran up with a sack.

"Let... me come. *Her...* might be there," he begged.

"Only priests, spies and fishermen are in Calais. What's in the sack?"

"Coffee beans."

Latham whistled and dismounted. "Where did you get them?"

"Buy... from Dr Gomes... For you."

"But you write poorly."

"S...Scribe."

Joris must have spent most of his salary to import from Constantinople something Latham craved. This was devotion. Joris's enterprise also surprised him. He'd kept contact with Dr Gomes, the physician who'd improved his speech. He was about to let him come when a shape slithered out of the boy's shirt and wound around his neck. Its dark eyes glared, then it gave a sighing hiss as it wound down the other side of the shirt. A local red milk snake; one of its vertebrae bulged through its scales. Joris pointed to the sack.

Cramming beans into his mouth, Latham said, "Thank you, Joris. But stay here. If *her* is in Calais, would she love a fellow wrapped in sick serpents?" Amused, he cantered out of the city gate under a caressing, normal June sun, coffee enlivening his mood.

CHAPTER 13
A HOLY MAN?

Calais, June 1580.

"Where are the others," Latham asked the neatly-dressed man at the dock. "I have jewels for four."

"One changed his mind about going. Another is a lay supporter. The third sailed already," his companion answered with a gentle smile, avoiding names and places.

Latham nodded, keeping his expression neutral. "Let's talk in the cemetery," he said. "It's cooler." They were both sweating. Latham had assumed the gait and clothes of a wounded veteran with scuffed boots and a weather-beaten cap. He wore a dirty sling on one arm, and his hair was grey. Edmund Campion was dressed as a merchant, his white collar hidden.

They walked past white-blossomed Tamarix shrubs dotting the salt marshes and entered Rue de Quatre Coins, where poplar trees offered some shelter. The street was full of shops, taverns, excited sailors and their whores. Both men grinned at the hubbub of languages, as vendors hustled to sell charms to ward off evil boat spirits; food; cheap tooth-drawing; leather and wool goods; and money changing services. Sand clung to their boot soles, rasping cobblestones as they entered a residential area.

The flora changed. Myricaria bushes with pink flowers stood in front of houses while fence vines sprouted yellow or fiery red berries. They turned right into a gravelled street and reached the whitewashed stone church. Two sailors came out, stared at them and turned towards the harbour. Latham raised his eyebrows. Campion shrugged. "Calais is full of spies. I can't tell a watcher from a seeker of God's mercy." He smiled. "Perhaps a man can be both."

The staring sailors hadn't alerted Latham's instincts; he wondered if he was out of practice. His past year had been sedentary, a matter of reporting on letters he received.

The cemetery was deserted. They wandered around graves, reading headstones that mourned French and English citizens, the legacy of the town's shifting sovereignty. Then they sat on a bench under a plane tree. Latham spoke the text Idiaquez had sent him.

"Father Edmund, King Philip grieves the misery of great English Catholic families, who pay ruinous fines if they don't attend weekly heretic services. He wants to help them keep their lands intact for a more hopeful day in the future, when armies of the virtuous restore the true faith in England. I'm to tell you that time hasn't come. You must be discreet."

Campion nodded.

"What about your forward colleague, the one who sailed? Will you tell him?"

"I might not see him again; we scuttle in shadows. But Persons is very careful of his person." Campion smiled at his own pun. "Emerson took fright and bolted to Prague."

They were silent for a few moments.

"We must talk about the problem of Ireland," Latham muttered.

Campion frowned, chewing his lower lip.

Idiaquez had informed Latham about a planned Papal/Spanish expedition to support Irish Catholic rebels against Elizabeth. Because of that venture, Philip thought it was particularly important for Jesuits infiltrating England proper this year to keep a low profile. Campion had quoted Loyola, founder of the Jesuits, to Latham in Douai seven years ago. 'If His Holiness names something black, which members of our society see as white, then they must, in like fashion, term it black.' Campion's expression told Latham he couldn't quite term white as black with respect to the Irish expedition.

"That venture will just nip the governing weasel, turning it rabid," he said.

"Exactly," Latham agreed. "His Majesty favours quiet in England. I have money and contacts for you provided that your mission is discreet. As patron of the Douai Seminary and Society of Jesus, the king can expect your agreement."

Campion smiled. "We Jesuits are eternally grateful for His Majesty's sponsorship. There's no conflict between Vatican, crown and cross. I'm to comfort distressed Catholics in the privacy of their own homes and to avoid challenging state policy once in England."

At this assurance, Latham gave him two of the four bags of jewels. "For you, for the Catholic nobles that you help, and for Persons."

Campion opened one bag. Seeing paper as well as jewels, he looked up, inquiringly.

"Contacts of friends for if you need to get out. Commit to your memory and destroy," Latham said grimly.

He paused. Katherine's fear came to him: *I've given up mass out of fear for the family. What will be my fate if my breath gives out before a priest shrives me?* "I add one name for confession and absolution, someone I love tenderly: my sister." He gave Campion Katherine's name and address.

The church door opened, and a priest and two nuns stepped out with fresh flowers. They blessed the wounded veteran and his companion, then tidied two large headstones. Just two.

"Expecting donor relatives," Campion smiled. He and Latham walked to the last row of headstones, neglected ones. Latham stopped in front of one and muttered a prayer. Campion read: Genevieve Belleau, 1512-1531.

"She died birthing my current landlady," Latham explained. "The good woman never saw the one who gave her life, but still grieves." He couldn't help thinking of his mother's grave and the shattered priory he passed whenever he visited it. Campion prayed for Genevieve's soul.

When the nuns and priest had gone back in, Latham picked up roses from one grave, lilies from the other, and placed them at Genevieve's grave.

Campion grinned. "Our Lord would like that."

"Yet you're to succour mostly English nobles," Latham remarked, as they returned to the plane tree.

"Saving those souls first speeds opportunity for the rest, is the theory," Campion said defensively.

"Private, you said?" Latham asked.

"One at a time; the progress of an ant." Campion laughed. "In the new directive, Pope Gregory XIII lifted the yoke of mandatory rebellion from Elizabeth's subjects. They can live within the constrictions of their misguided government without fear of eternal damnation."

"Such a mission is survivable under present conditions," agreed Latham. "The priests who were executed called for Elizabeth's death. Years ago, I swore not to act directly against her. I've stuck to it."

"I won't call for rebellion. The directive's peaceable, apt for the night-slinking mole."

Latham sensed divergence between Campion's modest mission and his inner drive. Where was the implacable purist he'd met in Douai? "I wish you obscurity," he began, "but I heard that in Geneva you challenged the Calvinist leader Beza to a public debate, the loser to be burnt at the stake. Not knowing the source, I wouldn't tell Idiaquez before asking you.

Now Campion laughed frankly and fully. "Your source was right. We had a merry time. Persons actually issued the challenge, but you know I love disputations. Here was our argument."

He tugging Latham's arm, eyes sparkling. "Firstly: the English queen rules her church with a strict hierarchy. Secondly: Calvinism considers church hierarchy anathema. Therefore, thirdly: the English queen is a heretic to Protestants as well as Catholics. It's unbreakable. The chance to publicly debate the leader of the Calvinist heretics was irresistible! Our superiors didn't say to avoid challenging Elizabeth everywhere; just in her own lands. Geneva's not England. It was a great caper. How could we lose?"

He released Latham and leaned against the tree, laughing. "We had logic on our side. Tactics favoured us, too. If Beza refused our challenge, he'd be shamed in front of his students, a beaten dog slinking into shadow. If he took the challenge and we won, smoke would have risen over Satan's greatest ally since Martin Luther! Elizabeth's lustre tarnished, whatever the verdict. And if we lost, then we weren't worthy messengers of God. He would have clasped three cleansed souls to His merciful bosom.

"As you must know from your source, Beza's wife clapped a stopper on the whole thing. What kind of holy man hides behind a woman? We had him cornered until she came. He was in the courtyard, all uncertain. I told him I simply wished to understand how he could excuse Elizabeth from heresy, given the differences between her church and his. He muttered, no doubt clinking English silver in his pocket, that the differences weren't great. I pressed him for one example; he didn't even try.

"Then she ran out, the wife, carrying piles of paper, shouting he had work to do. She bodily dragged him in, and how we laughed. He sent two students to meet us at a tavern, and we debated all night. They weren't bad fellows, but they were just students, so we didn't press a burning. Once

I touch English soil, I'll preach giving Elizabeth her due in temporal matters."

"You're naïve," Latham snapped, alarmed that Pieter Boels' report was true. He wished he could take back Katherine's address. But how could he? How could he possibly get between her and her soul? She thirsted for a priest like Campion, and he'd left England over the same issue.

"If I've heard the story, " Latham said acidly, "so has the English privy council. With a Papal/Spanish attack on English territories in Ireland, they won't distinguish between challenging Elizabeth outside and inside their borders."

"Do you have a report saying privy councillors know about Geneva?" Campion pressed.

"No," Latham conceded.

"Then trust in God's infinite goodness, friend."

"But if they have heard," Latham continued, "and catch you, how are you going to answer the so-called 'Bloody Question'? 'If Catholic forces invade England, who will you support, queen or pope?' It's red-hot with this Irish business."

"Set your mind at rest," Campion urged. "We're prepared to counter it. As I said, Pope Gregory says English Catholics can now live within the constrictions of their misguided government without fear of damnation. Look, I agree we weren't prudent in Geneva. I've also heard my arrival is expected by those who want it and those who abhor it. I confess to fear; I'm just a scared sinner like everyone else. I'd prefer to continue making converts on this side of the Channel; I did well in Prague. But my orders are to minister to the faithful and educate the willing in England, which is the Church's greatest need. There's been a generation of quiet under Elizabeth. As Catholics die, theology is forgotten. A nation slumbers unaware towards perdition. I must do what I can to turn its fate.

"His Holiness says we may urge English Catholics to give Caesar, Elizabeth, her due in temporal matters, to obey her until the Vatican directs otherwise. What could the privy council object to now, that's not purely doctrinal?" Campion's eyes glowed. "I can offer such comfort that I ache to begin, including to your sister."

Latham sighed. "Gregory's neutral directive justifies my handing you the jewels and contacts. My task is done. But listen to what you've said. Think about how Elizabeth will interpret it. The Vatican's not compromising; it's playing for time. English Catholics shouldn't rebel now, all passion and no plan. No. They should wait for orders, presumably given when missionary priests like you have converted enough of the nobility to papal allegiance to be able to defeat the government. It's not *whether* to rebel, it's *when*. You ask what the privy council could object to. Gregory aims to nurse opposition into viable life. *That's* what they'll object to. Your tautology is gossamer."

Campion was listening intently.

"Think on it another way," Latham said. "If you were a man who sowed your fields, walking up and down the muddy furrows, dropping the seeds into the hungry earth, watering your seeds if times were dry, spreading the richest dung to help them grow; and your brother, with a stronger back, harvests, aren't you both equally engaged in bringing ripe crops to market?"

"Your argument is faulty," Campion countered. "Your season is an earthly metaphor. In the work I'm called to, maturation is in God's hand, as are our lives. The evidence of your error is here, in the headstones: a man dead at sixty-three; a girl at three. It's God's will; naught to do with named months, days, or seasons. I appreciate your concern, but since my mission is spiritual succour, I have a chance to survive. Elizabeth is riddled with the sin of pride. Her principal brag is that she's too enlightened to kill for the sake of religion, that in this, she's superior to Catholic rulers.

"But if I'm wrong about her, I embrace my destiny, though it may bring me to an executioner's eager knife. We all must die. The manner of death matters not a whit when eternity lies beyond. And if that queen killed me over religion, she would be exposed as a hypocrite. Don't trouble yourself in my case."

He took a breath. "But I'm troubled in your case," he pressed on. "I have no doubts, and I sleep well, but doubts beset you, good man. I'll pray for you, and seal this conversation as if it was in the confessional. God bless you."

Latham's last glimpse of Campion was his back, as he bent to pick wildflowers from a roadside ditch. The Jesuit whistled cheerfully as he straightened up, then strolled to the harbour to find a boat to Dover. Latham walked the other way, to a stable at the zig-zag walls. He mounted his horse, but paused to look out to sea. In the haze, the cliffs of his native land, just twenty miles away, were hidden.

On the ride back, Latham pondered Campion's words: "Doubts beset you." The priest had seen his nightmares. Had he fallen into heresy? No, he had no doctrinal doubts. But some aspect of his life was displeasing the Almighty, or he'd feel certainty, like Campion.

Back at his lodgings, he greeted his landlady. "Madame, there were fresh roses and lilies on Genevieve's grave."

"Oh Signor, someone prays for her besides me. It helps me feel less alone." Wiping tears from her cheeks, she gave him a letter.

He opened it in his rooms. Short and coded, it was from Pieter Boels. Latham's initial reaction was that it described a small stir of smaller importance. But as he considered its implications, his excitement grew. At last, he was holding information he could use to shape events. He was sure he was alone in seeing how to leverage this incident to alter policy in the Netherlands. He believed Philip II had the anointed right to govern his own legally inherited Netherlands. The rebellion was simply wrong. Working to right it, he thought, might also banish his nightmares.

The decoded message read:

Heretic rebel bandits crossed the northern border. Vandalised churches, fired merchant warehouses, costly losses. Several raids.

Walloon merchants met for secret debate to petition Farnese for Spanish army return. Most local merchants want the Army of Flanders back, all worry. But one influential Hansa merchant, A.D., forced postponement of vote. PB

Latham pulled out Pieter's list of pro- and anti-Spanish merchants, which he'd received before meeting Campion. The Hansa merchant had a diverse, international enterprise: his interests weren't the same as those of local traders, and strong Spanish rule could hurt him. Latham paced the room: this way four paces, back four paces, pulse racing.

Six months after the withdrawal of Spanish troops from the Walloon provinces, per the treaty that sent Don Cristobal on furlough, the rebels were becoming frisky. Walloon notables had been delighted to get rid of the detested Army of Flanders. But the loss of merchandise worried them enough to consider bringing the Spanish soldiers back.

If there were no more raids, they'd do nothing. But with bigger incidents, they'd seek the army's protection. How to create such incidents was the question. Getting Spain's army invited back to the Netherlands would be a major service to Philip. Cristo could mount the right raids, but would he violate a treaty? There was one way to find out. Latham picked up his quill and wrote: *Cristo, I will write when I'm in Milan. Would you meet me for important news? It will be a joy to see the living man again. Yours, Mithridates Midas.*

CHAPTER 14
SECOND
CHANCE

Boulogne, July 1580 to Milan,
August 1581

C lever plans fail for many reasons. For Latham, it was a cough. He started for Milan with Joris after writing to Don Cristobal. But they'd only got to Saint-Denis, near Paris, when he got sick. He was staying at the Monk's Brew Inn, which Hélène Michaud, his informer at the Louvre Palace laundry, owned with her cousins, the Beaumonts. Latham had met the Beaumont's pert daughter, Marie, at the laundry. He was curious about seeing her again.

Patronising Hélène's inns was one of the ways he paid her. He intended to stay one or two nights at The Monk's Brew Inn and get fresh horses. It was a welcoming place, with a sign featuring a jolly monk holding a tankard of frothing ale. Marie's father, Auguste, was thick-boned and vivid, with a loud guffaw and an addiction to bad jokes. Sporting an unruly auburn beard, he enfolded guests in chest-crushing hugs, asking them repeatedly if the hospitality was all they wished. Latham soon realised his flamboyance covered illiteracy. His quiet wife, Jeanne, who was Hélène's cousin, did the accounts. However, anything beyond simple texts reduced her to breathless blushing. Marie seemed to adore her father, but was wary around her mother.

Now a long-legged twelve-year-old, Marie seemed pleased to see him. She offered a tutored greeting: "Monsieur, I give thanks to God for preserving you in your long journeys." She lowered her eyes dutifully, but he caught a whiff of disdain. It had been a point of pride for her four years ago in Paris that she was on the approved list to enter the Louvre Palace kitchen, while he wasn't.

Repressing a grin, he gave her a ceramic tile featuring Arabic calligraphy. It was exquisite. "I got it in their market, which is huge. The shops fill sixty-seven roads! The writing means *hope*."

She looked sceptical. "There's no picture. You paid for something with no picture? Monsieur, how they fooled you." Still, she took it.

Latham noted a supreme indifference between Marie and Joris. They looked through each other as if each was an inanimate accessory to their employer's possessions: a rope securing a bag to saddle, a sprig of lavender keeping clothes fresh. Knowing how exceptional they both were, he was disappointed. A niggling notion that Marie could one day be Joris's ideal "*her*" capered around his mind, then he snuffed it out. *Preference is whimsical*, he concluded.

Instead of resting, he coughed all night and ended up in the monastery infirmary. By the time he was fully recovered, the weather had turned foul. He and Joris returned to Boulogne until spring.

During the lost months of winter, Pieter Boels reported more raids on northern merchants, but the Hansa merchant still opposed inviting the Army of Flanders back. Joris resumed courier work for Latham or drew ships at the harbour. In February 1581, Latham got another letter from Katherine. There was no mention of Campion, but there was a hint that they'd met, and a revelation that made him very pensive.

My beloved little brother,

Your letter assuring me of your robust health thrilled me. I thank the Lord for protecting you. And I thank Him and you for another kindness, if you take my meaning. Lunacy gripped the foreign Catholic army that dared to seize Ireland's Smerwick. Thump, thump on our doors again! Never was the search so violent, the questioning so long and repetitive. I lost my wits and had a palsy. David Hicks again interceded, this time as a questioner. Our army took Smerwick and Dingle Bay back, massacring them who surrendered. No survivors, we hear. The public mood is calm, for now.

Because God will take me at His pleasure, I must relate events we kept from you when you were a boy. You were so young, you grieved our mother and were comforted by your faith, we protected you from learning what happened in our older brother Nicholas's household, and in too many others. He won't speak of it, so I must. Nicholas loved his long-time servants, John and Anne Somers. Late in the reign of Queen Mary, shortly before she died and Elizabeth became queen, John and Anne were tortured, convicted of heresy and sentenced to burn. Anne recanted, perhaps for the sake of her four little ones. The law said recanting can save you, but this was the year Queen Mary ignored recantations. Anne burned. She went to the stake first. Nicholas was there. It was a terrible death. The faggots were green, and the gunpowder in the bag they tied around her neck to kill her quickly when the flames reached that high, was defective. John was also scheduled to burn, but Queen Mary died before releasing the signed warrant. Elizabeth immediately spared him, although law and religion hadn't yet changed. Our family swore to give our new sovereign a chance. Nicholas settled in Ireland, as you know. He found a wholly Catholic place. Only the local dialect and Latin are spoken, and few can read. After one letter where he described the simple, orderly life of bells, prayer and farming, he cut off contact with us. There are no heresy trials there because there's no dissent. He lives as if before the printing press and Martin Luther.

None of us turned heretic, but I hope this helps you understand why we bend to royal law. It's a question of birth year. Being older than you, we remember Henry VIII's persecution of Catholics or Reformers at whim; Edward VI's rough Protestantism for six years; Mary's burnings for five years. Papa is frail but is still Justice of the Peace. He speaks fondly of you.

Your devoted sister, Katherine

Latham was shaken up by this account, so different from his childhood memories. He couldn't reply immediately. But at least Campion and Persons seemed to be conducting themselves discreetly in England.

In April 1581 he set off again, this time leaving Joris in Boulogne. He finally embraced Cristo on an August market day in Milan. Laughter, shoulder clapping, a step back, variants of: "So hard to believe after all these years." A pinch of cloth and kissed cheeks then "Yes, the real Edward/ the breathing Cristo." Finally, a serious step back to appraise each other, and mutual recognition that times hadn't been easy on either of them.

They joined a jostling line for a pie vendor at the market's entrance.

"What happened last year?" Cristo began. "I get a letter: *Meet me for important news.* Leaves yellowed, winter rains rotted my cloaks, buds bloomed. Nothing. Then last week, an imminent date that had me scrambling into my saddle within half an hour. *I return a favour,* you wrote. *Dress for cold like the sheep farmer you are at home.* Why? It's cursed hot."

Latham laughed. "The sheep-skin cloak becomes you. I'm sorry it's out-of-season. You know I can't write why. For this meeting, I didn't want to be seen near military colours. You'll understand soon. I was sick last year; then I waited until I was sure I could get here."

Don Cristobal nodded. "I see from your skin that the years have tried you."

"I had no money when King Philip banished me. That's why I went to Constantinople. I'm back in favour now; Idiaquez pays me."

Don Cristobal wanted to say, "I told you the German lady wasn't safe," but contented himself with a knowing smile. "You could have asked me for funds."

"Thank you; I managed. More later," Latham murmured. He pulled down his hat brim and peered at the mirror.

"Are you being followed?" Don Cristobal asked.

"No, but you are, by the cleverest street thief in Milan. In a few seconds, he'll have his knife through your sheep farmer's belt."

Cristo listened for the rustle of metal leaving fabric, then whirled and grabbed a little ear.

"Got you, brat!"

He gazed into furious green eyes in a prematurely wizened face. Yowling, a scrawny boy waved frantically at Latham.

"Kick his arse and let him go," Latham said. "I pay him to watch for followers. Joris stayed in Boulogne."

Don Cristobal released his hold, and the boy bolted away.

"Look for me here, later," Latham called after him.

They bought meat pies and sat to eat them on a piazza bench, where the sun warmed them. Dominating the view was the unfinished cathedral.

Don Cristobal swallowed his last mouthful and said, "I saw furloughed soldiers going into the market, prime men lazing instead of fighting the Dutch. I wanted to weep. At times, I think the king's counsellors are a parcel of petticoats."

"You speak bitterly. Be careful," Latham cautioned, looking around.

"That cathedral's shadow is a black shroud, the Almighty frowning at our defects in advance of our deaths," Cristo added portentously.

"Come, Cristo, you're a man of science. You know that at this time of day, the sun casts shadows in the opposite direction," Latham retorted. "It's your black bile speaking. Any shrouding shadow is oppressing some melancholic on the other side of the building."

"You're right, of course." Don Cristobal stood, massaging his rump, while Latham worked on his second pie. "About the shadow. It's wasted opportunities that grind me down. As I said to you in Brussels long ago, what joy are boy heirs if they must fight for the same grass and battlements their father did?" He sighed.

"What grieves you? The Treaty of Arras?" Latham asked.

"Yes." Cristo chewed his lower lip. "And something else. Do you remember that the Eleventh Company's captain before me was jailed for embezzlement? The contempt I had for him, and how I stopped all corruption in provisioning? Well, when Teresa birthed our latest son, I walked our land and despaired. It will be divided on my death. I was disgusted by Alva ordering Genlis to be strangled, against all customs of war, and frustrated by the king's bad policy in the Netherlands, so I started taking bribes. I wanted city properties for my heirs. I confess to our priest but never feel clean. Always, I prided myself on the integrity my warrior ancestors bequeathed me. I'm not proud now."

Latham pulled him down to sit. "You're not an island, Cristo. Society is disordered; it plagues us all."

"Perhaps." Don Cristobal shrugged. "As to military conditions and the treaty, Alexander Farnese is the general the king needs to win, but Madrid isn't supporting him. That's what I meant about the councillors being petticoats. It's horrible to be a fighting man, knowing with the hard clarity of a corpse counter, that he wins each tactical battle, but sees no progress in the larger war.

"Truces just prolong things. Get the fighting over with, or compromise and make peace. Let me tell you about Maastricht. I say this as the victor; it was awful. The siege took months. I lost mates to boiling water thrown over the walls, crawled through a smoke-filled tunnel exploding with fire, waited for a new tunnel to be built, then crawled through again in the first night assault. We caught the rebels asleep. After their surrender, there were three days of looting, fires and rape, and the trials and executions of remaining rebels. Farnese was as cruel as the Duke of Alva. Then, a liberal treaty; not like Alva. You know its terms?"

Latham nodded. "Farnese got three compliant Walloon provinces without firing another shot or losing any more of your friends. That seems successful."

"Oh, you don't know what happened!" Don Cristobal cried. "He expected more. I can see how one city for three provinces looks good to the distant eye, but Dutch negotiators implied that many states would return to obedience to Spain. That was false. Not even all the south reconciled; just three Walloon provinces. And the rebel leader, William of Orange, refused to talk. They call him "Silent William." Ha, ha! I suppose there's dark comedy in it. Anyway, Farnese adhered to the treaty. We trudged back over the Alps. I'm now an expert in Alpine crossings. He's Governor General, a pretty title, but he sits on a patch, mute without his army. The Dutch run their affairs with their customary arrogance. The army can't return unless it's invited. I can't bear the thought that one day my sons might have to take Maastricht again. What a stinking mess."

He spat.

"The stinking mess," Latham assured him, "is why I asked you to meet me. I have intelligence that could alter this treaty and bring you rewards. But it's risky."

"Let's go to the cathedral roof. We'll be safe from skulkers during the midday break," Don Cristobal said, his voice tight with anticipation.

After crossing a canal bridge and a wide congested road, they reached the cathedral, its towering exterior forbiddingly plain. A plate on the front claimed it was the tallest church ever built. Engineers had devised new supports to elevate the dome to its present height, and the central spire, now a stump, would soar higher still.

Cristo whistled with admiration, his natural ebullience coming back.

They passed scaffolding around two buttresses. Masons were winching up heavy stones, encouraging each other under the watchful eye of the head mason. The decorative framing of the first window had begun. The filigreed stone carving was lacey, a delicate contrast to the blunt might of the walls.

As they walked to the external staircase, there were clicks and whirrs; then the air exploded with noon bells and chimes. Midday was counted as the eighteenth hour in Milan, which meant eighteen tolls from unsynchronised churches. Workmen clambered off scaffolds, thrusting fingers in their ears when they reached the ground. Latham and Don Cristobal climbed to the roof and leaned against a parapet, gasping for breath. They were alone, except for a guard watching the tools.

Below them lay a jumble of canals, bridges, curving streets and churches. They could see the original city wall, a burgeoning outgrowth of houses, new Spanish bastions beyond. The bells had stopped. Human and animal noises were distilled in the sweet air.

"Your news?" Don Cristobal prompted. "Nothing could make me happier than getting rid of this treaty."

They climbed onto the workman's platform on the spire stump and gazed at snow-capped mountains dividing Italy from Savoy and France. Don Cristobal pointed. "Before you start, that's Moncenisio. Some say Hannibal hauled his elephants over it. Have you crossed there?"

"Once," Latham answered curtly. It had been his journey from Brussels to Florence when Philip banished him, not a happy memory. "I prefer to sail, Marseilles to Genoa."

"Of course, islanders like Neptune," Don Cristobal went on. "Our army uses Moncenisio because the trail isn't too steep, and as you've seen, an industry of carriers helps. It descends to Savoy, our client-state. Do you remember my *looker*, that saved you from hanging?"

"Of course, the magnifying tubes," Latham replied.

Cristo pulled the device out of his bag. "I paid a spectacle-maker to grind glass for distance. Let's try." He put two tubes together, swivelled at the mountains, then down at the streets. Frowning, he tried again. Face crumpling with disappointment, he muttered, "A waste of money."

When Latham tried it, he said, "It's better than what you had at Mons, but no good for mountains. They don't have *lookers* in Constantinople. I was in the Sultan's observatory, and your device is still unique."

Cristo smiled as he put his tubes away. "Better equipped than the infidel Sultan! Wonderful." He pointed to the tallest peak. "Monte Viso is the shortest route. It's precipitous, and much feared. Engineers hewed a tunnel through it last century. A miracle! Saluzzo and France were at peace and wanted to trade. During the wars of the 1520s, they closed it, but I've heard it can open, for bribes. Landslides have to be cleared, and smugglers don't love company. We avoid it because descending into France now is politically impossible for a Spanish army. Well, your news?"

"You'll cross the Alps again, Cristo. Here's what I know. Several leading Walloon merchants are debating inviting your Army of Flanders back."

Don Cristobal jerked to face Latham, black eyes boring into Latham. "I'm astonished. They want us back? Are you sure?"

The watchman approached.

"I'm sure of the debates," Latham said softly. "Not

the result."

Cristo lowered his voice. "Why are they even debating it?"

"There have been raids by rebel heretics across the northern borders."

"I didn't know that."

"It's been kept quiet," Latham said.

"What kinds of raids?"

"Vandalising churches; thieving and burning merchandise. Northern merchants raised funds for border guards. But it's made merchants everywhere nervous; they're terrified of another eruption of violence and destruction like the worst days of the rebellion of 1566. My sub-agent wrote that some merchants proposed bringing you all back."

"I'm stunned. The hens want the fox to guard them because of a mouse nip?"

"Unless there's a crisis they'll do nothing because each merchant would have to give up some local privilege to submit to Philip. They know that if Farnese gets his army back, his nominal rule will grow absolute."

"I've always thought those local autonomies absurd," Don Cristobal mused, as he tried to take in Latham's news. "Different weights and measures for each town, an army of inky clerks keeping tables. When they dispute, brigades of lawyers run to the courts, putting the profits in their own purses. Everyone but the lawyers would be richer with centralised rules."

"Merchants profit greatly from local patronage," Latham said wryly. "Alteration for the better will seem worse unless the pain is significant."

A flock of geese wheeled around the spire stump, calling as they headed for the ducal park. The wind shifted, bringing an Alpine chill. They climbed down to the parapet.

"You said a crisis could move them," Don Cristobal said, "but if local guards contain the incursions, there is no crisis."

"You could make one."

Don Cristobal went still. "Ah. So that's it. How?"

"Raid the south. Hit merchant convoys in the Walloon provinces."

"Pretending to be Martinists."

"And other sects. Anabaptists are always good for a fright."

Don Cristobal whistled. "What wicked notions you have. Farnese won't break the treaty."

"I agree. Local notables will have to petition him. If raids spread south, the merchants will tear up their treaty to get army protection. A little lever, cunningly applied, can shift a boulder."

"Hmm." Don Cristobal drummed his fingers on the parapet wall. "The risk is legal; I'd be violating my king's treaty. There could be casualties."

"Cristo, this service will favour Spain and the Church. I'm offering you this intelligence before sending it to Secretary of State Idiaquez, my employer in Madrid, which I must do. Eventually, the southern provinces will invite the army back. They're mostly Catholic, and it's in the nature of things that they bend to their rightful sovereign. But if you're not the catalyst, you'll gain nothing. As to the legal risk, yes, there is some. But you said there was a lack of plain dealing in the treaty's formation; that the Dutch implied many provinces would reconcile. The treaty could be defective. I believe Farnese will see your incursion more as an unseasonable storm than a crime. You saved me from hanging; this is my reciprocation."

"If Farnese credits me privately, he'll promote me. Then I could end my skimming."

"If he gets his army back, he'll protect you. But act within a moon. As I said, I must tell Madrid, but I can choose my couriers. If you decide to act, I'll use laggards."

Don Cristobal's eyes settled longingly on the precipitous Monte Viso. *Thirty to forty would do, Eleventh Company, others recruited here. Good disguises. Get there for holiday fairs, disclose plan details only on reaching the Netherlands*, he thought. "I could do it, but…"

He frowned. His oath brother was pushing him out on a branch. There were many reasons to decline. Turning to Latham, he said, "This isn't easy. Act within a moon? I'll have to think on it. But if I do it, I have funds this year. Our wool was ample, and I sold horses."

"I have funds," Latham said, thinking of jewels he had left over from his meeting with Campion in Calais. Idiaquez had sent four bags, for three Jesuit priests infiltrating England with Campion. But Latham had only met Campion. One priest had fled to Prague, and a second wasn't ordained. So he'd given one bag to Campion for his own use, and a second for him to give Father Robert Persons, who'd sailed for Dover already. There was plenty of money left for an enterprise favouring Spain.

"If you go through the Monte Viso tunnel," he assured Cristo, "I'll pay the bribes and come with you. Descending to France suits me; I need to see sub-agents in Paris. I assume smugglers use the tunnel; my street thief will know who to talk to. Listen, while you think on this, I'll go back to the market, in case he has something to tell me."

Within a moon, forty-five men assembled in a field outside the village of Crissolo, in the Po Valley, along with horses, mules, goats, caged chickens and provision carts. William Boels, Joris's condescending cousin and Pieter Boels' nephew and godson, was there, vibrating with excitement as he checked provision carts. He greeted Latham with a half-bow. The last time Latham had heard of William he had been a logistics clerk in Brussels. He must have decided that this venture offered advancement. Juan Alvarado, who had tried to hang Latham at Mons, was also there, doing his best to avoid Boels, whom he'd always resented. Alvarado embraced

Latham warmly, blushing at the memory of his mistake years ago. Then he turned to organising recruits for Don Cristobal's inspection. Furloughed soldiers and a couple of sailors had joined, as well as out of work labourers, and a red-haired chorister who'd lost his job when his voice broke and needed to support his widowed mother and two sisters. Latham's companion was his street thief's uncle, a smuggler who'd agreed to go as far as the tunnel to negotiate their entrance.

Don Cristobal studied his recruits. Their faces had been alive with enthusiasm and avarice when they'd signed his contract. Now they were tinged with anxiety. Looming over the grassy field kissed by a September sun, Monte Viso intimated danger. The assembled men glanced at it apprehensively.

Having grown up in the mountains, Don Cristobal was familiar with sudden weather changes, precipitous trails, air that seared lungs, and dank caves with creatures that bit or stung. He was excited about the climb, intending to use it to shape this improvised band into a tough, disciplined group. Their job would be to terrify and humiliate their victims, not kill them. He wanted no mayhem. Dead merchants couldn't petition for the army's return. So discipline was first on his in mind as he walked the rows. Smelling wine on the breath of seven men, he dismissed them. "The contract says you drink alcohol only when an officer hands it out," he barked, taking back their signing bonuses. With that peremptory cut, the march began.

Latham had never climbed a mountain as severe as Monte Viso, but he'd made many arduous and shocking journeys. As they ascended the foothills, he saw amazement on faces as the once-kind breeze whipped from autumn caresses to winter claw. Men used to fecund fruit orchards and meadows filled with wildflowers now gazed, amazed, at dried-out star plants separated by quartz rocks, and tall black stalks topped by dark petals growing out of boulders, spurning soil.

The men's dubiousness turned to fear as a red sun set. Grey twilight leached the life out of everything. Stalk flowers became spiked clubs on boulders; boulders became petrified monsters. In this near-black world, an owl's hoot bouncing from rock to rock became the screams of a nether-world flock, while loose stones tumbling into the rocky creek beside their trail were pagan gods' thunderclaps.

They made their first camp by a glacial lake. Latham, on watch, woke Don Cristobal before dawn, whispering that four recruits were deserting. Don Cristobal got up in one smooth movement and strode quietly to the trail. He waved at the scurrying backs. "Let them go, Edward," he said grimly. "I don't want them. Didn't you see the cow herders watching us yesterday, marking the weaklings? Our deserters won't get far before losing everything; they'll be lucky to live."

Faint cries for help were carrying up from below when the convoy set off again. Don Cristobal said nothing, as if the deserters had never existed. Scree fields were the next challenge: feet plunged through fluffy to compacted snow, leaden-weight legs treading, ankles in danger of twisting. Don Cristobal went from man to man, showing each one how to manoeuvre. "Here the thick-armed pikeman is weaker than the rigging-scaling sailor," he told them gently. "Move as I do."

They went higher still the next day, on switchback trails with sheer drops into a roiling gorge. Thin air seared the men's tired lungs, muddling their thoughts. The poor red-haired chorister had hummed all night instead of sleeping. Staggering along in a daze of exhaustion, he slipped on badly-hacked ice and slithered toward the precipice. He grabbed the cloak of a freckle-faced sailor, who grabbed the reins of their mule. Amidst gasps, yells, a futile reaching of arms and a rope thrown too short, the men, mule, cart, and two tethered goats plunged to the gorge's bottom, shrieking. The rock-filled river silenced them. One goat shook itself gingerly and minced slowly back up and up, to the trail.

The convoy stopped. The street thief's uncle made crosses, and Don Cristobal read a funeral service. Afterwards, William

Boels inventoried the remaining carts. Don Cristobal was relieved that the fallen cart wasn't the one with false bottoms concealing swords, muskets, ammunition, forged heretical tracts, and the vital schedule of Dutch merchant convoys that Latham had got them. Instead, it was a food cart. Boels redistributed the remaining supplies between carts, and the convoy trudged on.

Soon they achieved a plateau above low streaming clouds, the sun beaming innocently. They couldn't see the trail they'd just climbed. Don Cristobal decided to split his force into two groups temporarily. He chose ten, who'd been deft in manoeuvring the scree fields, to take the summit path with Alvarado, a veteran of Montcenisio crossings. He led the remaining twenty-four men, with the carts and animals, to Monte Viso tunnel.

A few hundred yards from the entrance, the convoy had to pull up. Some of the men, mules and carts were strung down the trail, and began braying and cursing. Five men armed with swords, crowbars and muskets stood in front of boulders blocking the tunnel entrance. Latham bowed. He approached with the street thief's uncle and handed over one purse. After hectoring, bargaining, hands on sword hilts, and a lot of posturing, everyone nodded. One of the armed men bit each coin. He nodded again, and the boulders were hauled away. Latham handed over a second purse. The man bit each coin again. Business done, Latham said goodbye to the street thief's smuggler uncle. With a cheerful wave, the smuggler turned back down the trail.

The mouth of the Monte Viso tunnel yawed. Once in, the glaring light of the plateau dimmed and disappeared in musky gloom. William Boels hastily lit lanterns, while several men dragged back horses and mules that were trying to get to the light plateau with its spindly grass. The men gazed at the rock face blackened and chipped from ancient firing and wedging. A small, grimy statue of the Virgin Mary was nestled in an alcove. Her lips drooped as her downcast eyes fixed on the grey-swaddled infant in her arms. Hundreds of candles lay at her feet: some recent, others nibbled and ancient.

"Pray for safe passage," Don Cristobal ordered. "A hundred years ago, miners fired and wedged, robbing this mountain of its implacable height. It took ten years, and many died. Because of their sacrifice, we're spared the summit. Give thanks to the miners whose ghosts smile on us. Beg Our Lady's mercy."

He led the convoy, placing William Boels with an Eleventh Company pikeman in the middle, and Latham in the rear, to keep order. They inched forward. Wicker frames had been attached to parts of the walls, but stone shards broke free, periodically clicking against the dry wood and plopping onto the soggy walkway. Mules and horses bucked and swivelled when hooves punched through rotting planks. Thick dank air coated men's throats, turning them into gasping, staggering knots.

Deep in the mountain, a furry ball hit one man's ear, scraped his face and fell. He shrieked, pulling his sword. Clouds of bats whirred, narrowly missing heads. They hit the roof and swirled into invisible crevices. Latham, Boels, and the pikeman used the flat of their swords to stop the men's chaotic retreat.

"Quiet!" Don Cristobal yelled, incongruously. "It's just bats. We're in their bedchamber. Keep moving."

The convoy plodded on. A few minutes later, Cristo and several men behind him grunted. Their lanterns veered right and downward, almost disappearing.

"Where am I?"

"No, here!"

"Help!"

Their panicked cries got the mules and horses kicking again. Dodging nimbly to avoid being hit, Latham went from animal to animal with apples, calming them.

Cristo roared, "No harm! Each man hold onto the man in front, and back up slowly; the rest of you wait!" Backsides, then lanterns reappeared. Cristo called for calm, and said,

"Don't move until I return." He disappeared, returned, and went back to the bats' bedchamber and returned again.

"Men, this was my fault. There's a flaw in the tunnelling. The miners hacked from both ends, France and Saluzzo. Their arithmetic wasn't perfect in the joining, but the deviation was clearly marked. The bats distracted us, a useful lesson."

Further in, and the walls themselves heaved to monstrous life, as colonies of grubs undulated, feasting on bat guano. In the garish lantern light the grubs were translucent, their pale intestinal shafts pulsing. Two men cried out that they'd been led to hell.

Latham twisted up to Don Cristobal and whispered, "Let me play a game. It'll distract them and teach them observation."

Cristo nodded; he was sceptical.

Latham shone his lantern on a busy mound of grubs. "Are you petticoats or soldiers?" he boomed. By now everyone realised they'd come too far to go back. "They're just bugs, fat and good to eat if a man is hungry enough. God's creatures, like all else on earth, and the Lord gave man dominion over all the animals."

He grinned. "When you signed your contract, Don Cristobal told you that your service would demand courage, endurance and observation. Now, which of you has the courage, endurance and observation to do what I do?"

He scraped a bug from the wall. Intensely curious, men stopped cursing and crowded around. Latham brought the bug and hand to his mouth, and his Adam's apple bobbed. He swallowed.

In the stunned silence, someone threw up.

"Is there gold in it?" a former sailor yelled.

"A ducat," Latham promised, "for the man who does as I did."

"Can't be worse than ship fare." The sailor scraped off a bug, thrust it into his mouth, chewed once and swallowed. His face crumpled in dismay. He spat and spat again.

"Well, master sailor…" Latham announced.

Don Cristobal, who'd seen the trick, roared with laughter.

"…you have the courage and endurance our commander demands, but not the observation. You didn't do as I did. I pulled off the bug with my thumb and index finger, but put my fourth and fifth finger in my mouth. You pulled off the bug with your thumb and index finger, put your thumb and index finger in your mouth, and ate." He opened his hand, showed them the squirming bug, and tossed it away. "No ducat. I'm sorry."

"But extra wine when we reach Guil Valley," Don Cristobal promised. "The lesson, comrades, is this: things are not as they seem. I haven't told you the details of this enterprise, but you will work a jest on our quarry. To them, things will not be as they seem. The seeming will count for more than brute fighting."

The men, including the sailor, laughed. Tension fell away, and they plodded on. Eventually, a pinprick of light, another grimy little Mary, visible chipping and wedging in the rock face, and the escape to the brilliant sunshine of France. Men gulped sweet air with manic relief,

They waited for Alvarado's summit party. It arrived an hour later; faces strained with terror and shock pouring out in broken phrases what happened. On the small flat summit, thick piles of white clouds blotted out all below. All was an infinity of white snow-capped mountaintops and crevices. The light dazzled. They could have been alone in the universe; could stretch their fingertips to tickle the ether. The view was miraculous to any who hadn't climbed a summit before. They were numb, too stunned to name what they were seeing or where they were. One was more befuddled than the rest. Brainsick, he proclaimed the clouds angels' pillows. Before anyone could get the energy to stop him, he'd staggered to the edge, yelling, "I'm the angel." He launched himself at the thickest cloud, arms spread. "Free! Free!" were his last words.

They made another cross. Don Cristobal said, "Let's

pray for God's love for the souls of our fallen. Pay homage to Ricardo, a chorister supporting his widowed mother; Benedetto, the sailor who went down with Ricardo; Afonso, who hurled himself onto angels' pillows. All young, cut down before their characters could be scribed."

He allowed time to mourn then roused them. "Pruning. It's a tough thing, comrades," he said, as gently as a hardened soldier could. "But polling the tops off sick blossoms helps the plant grow stronger. You are that hardy plant. We have days of hiking and training ahead."

Their descent was long and tricky. Everyone was observant, and there were no more accidents. Winter ice gave way to autumn grass, distant sheep pens, and a curious shepherd who they bribed to silence.

It was time for Latham and Don Cristobal to separate.

"I need to collect my salary in Paris," Latham reminded Cristo. "I'll be in Saint-Denis in January, at the Monks Brew Inn. Write to Piso Prosperino as my devoted godchild."

They embraced, wishing each other good luck and God's mercy. Latham watched the forest close around Cristo's men, unaware that this was the peak of their friendship. He walked back to the shepherd, palms open to show he meant no harm, and asked directions to the nearest religious house. After an hour he found a small monastery, the fifteen monks were overworked but welcoming. He slept the moment he closed his eyes, but badly.

He was riding the courier horse that had carried him to Mons years ago. Hurry, stay ahead of Genlis, he urged. Raindrops plopped onto dusty tree leaves. But, as if ruing the world they'd landed in, the drops spurted back into a dappled sky. 'Oh no, the place that isn't,' groaned Latham. He'd been here before and come back; could he again? With his shot pincers of dread in his stomach, he hauled on the reins.

The horse ignored him. When he pulled again, its gait changed, taking him by surprise. Its tail rose, peacock-proud, while its neck flopped. Two hind legs and one front leg rose then crashed down, as the two front legs rose and the rump surged forward. The pattern repeated, familiar yet strange.

'God save me, it's cantering backwards!' whimpered Latham. He swivelled to face the direction the horse was going, but the horse adjusted. To Latham's amazement, now he saw the Milan Duomo. 'Milan, not Mons? I'm brainsick.' Mons, his first urgent intelligence for Spain; Milan, his recent service. The road itself began to move. Rising, it smothered the Duomo and its tolling bells.

Latham slid off the horse. When he looked up the road was empty. Heart pounding, he ran at gnarled roadside trees that looked like his favourite childhood oak, but they waddled backwards. One turned into a twisted knight in medieval armour, then another. 'You're false, Palamon,' Arcite shrieked. 'You betrayed our lifelong tryst,' Palamon stormed back. Both tree-knights had Latham's flaxen moustache. Groaning, he leapt for a branch... and connected with the cold stone floor of the guest hall. Murmuring, "God forgive me, I have sinned; though I know not how," he rolled over and got up.

"Did you have a visitation?" the traveller in the next cot asked warily.

"I often do," Latham replied, running his fingers through his hair. "But wakefulness takes meaning away."

The traveller edged to the wall, hunching against it for the rest of the night.

Afraid that he was possessed, Latham confessed after Lauds the next morning. He admitted his doubts of Campion; his fornications; his confusion in Constantinople. Adding old sins, he kept the monk behind his latticed screen for over two hours.

"To make such an account shows you're not possessed," the monk said when Latham ran down. Fervently wishing longwindedness was a punishable sin, the weary cleric imposed only mild penalties. It was a cleansed penitent who started for Paris. Latham still sensed there was something off in his dealings, but knew not what.

CHAPTER 15
SPY'S
RECKONING

Paris, early January 1582

When Latham picked up his salary at his Paris banker's office, an ink-spotted clerk handed him two letters. As it was a sleeting morning, he took his letters into a tavern, called for wine and a candle, and opened them. They weren't from Cristo or Pieter Boels, but two informers in the Walloon provinces. He started reading, and whistled. In clear text, they described raids on merchant convoys by diverse heretic gangs.

Twenty pikemen wearing the blue and yellow sashes of Louis of Nassau, brother of the rebel leader, William of Orange, had forced merchants on their way to Cambrai to strip naked and walk eight miles in sleet, wearing only shoes and Calvinist tracts covering their private parts. The bandits destroyed cart and merchandise.

The same informer described a substitution of cargoes near Valenciennes. Two pilgrims had joined a convoy for protection, paying a fee. That night, their servants drugged the stable boys and merchants' servants with opium in wine, and switched cargoes of fine lace and jewellery with rubbish. At the bottom of each cart, an Anabaptist tract repudiated private ownership.

The second informer recounted two more raids. *Esteemed Signor Prosperino, I was a hired guard for a large convoy travelling on the old Roman road to Cateau Cambresis. Mounted Sea Beggars, banners with gold coins on red flying, charged us just before curfew, yelling 'Vive les Gueux! Long live the Beggars.' They took the carts into the woods. We chased them, but the devils had strung wire between trees. In the dusk, one guard broke his ankle, another cut his neck. I am unhurt, God be praised. All the cargoes were stolen.*

He ended with his priest cousin's account of an ambush by Lutherans two miles out of Vitry-en-Artois. A substantial convoy protected by three mounted German mercenaries had set off before dawn to get ahead of farmers, but the bandits knew. Two crossbowers in white shirts rose from the roadside ditch, shouted 'Gott fur Martin!' and shot the mercenaries' horses, pinning the Germans on the ground. The merchants had swords, but there were twenty-five bandits. They smashed fine glass, burned wool and silk, and stripped the valuables off everyone, even taking the maids' earrings. No bandits had been caught, despite the hue and cry. Opinion was that such disorders could not go on. All were stunned that the raids in the north had spread south so quickly, but it is God's will that they have.

"No, it is Cristo's will, based on my idea," Latham murmured, putting his letters away. Cristo had acted with finesse, but these reports didn't mention that a vote to get Spain's army back had been scheduled. He'd have to wait to for letters from Pieter Boels and Cristo. Leaving the tavern with his cloak pulled around him, he decided to leave for Saint-Denis in a few days.

Le Plaisir du Roi Inn, formerly The Monk's Brew Inn, Saint-Denis, France.

Tap. Tap.

Boom, Latham dreamed. *Crack. The building collapses, villagers fleeing the spiteful cannon are lacerated by stone shards and metal. He watches from the edge of a lush green field. Three headless clothed bodies are roped to a spreading oak tree. He jams Don Cristobal's looker to his eye, knows he climbed this tree as a child. Aghast, he runs to it, keeping bush cover between himself and the guns.*

Tap.

Latham swam towards the day, listening. It was quiet. He dozed.

He's in the lush field, and now doesn't need the looker to name the dead: in anguish, his father's ring; his sister Katherine's apricot-coloured overskirt; his brother Edward's olive leather boots. Soldiers wearing a red diagonal cross on green and white stripes, the Eleventh Company colours, carouse around a fire. Spain is in Latham's county of Surrey and his kin are dead.

Bang. Bang. Robust now.

"Monsieur, washing water and breakfast," a light voice trilled. He opened his eyes. Like painted scenery being towed offstage, soldiers and corpses slowly disappeared from view. Groaning with relief, Latham sat up. He was in Saint-Denis; Farnese and Cristo were in the Netherlands; and his father, brother and sister were alive in England. "Horrible," he muttered weakly, "but at least I see it." His sense of approaching understanding was both ominous and relieving.

"Letters!" The peremptory voice belonged to Marie, daughter of inn owners, Auguste and Jeanne Beaumont. He hadn't seen her since he arrived.

"Wait!" he yelled. He threw off his covers, to be blasted by cold air. "Merde," he cursed. He'd let the fire go out. He threw his cloak over his shoulders, thrust his feet into slippers and opened the door. Smiling mischievously, Marie bustled in with a tray of cider, bread and cheese, and a basin of water.

"About time, the cider's getting cold." She deposited the tray on his table, knocking his lute to the floor. Protesting twangs united Latham with the day. He washed his face and hands, then smiled at her.

"Tut, Monsieur," Marie chided, taking the moist towel. She looked around. A clock topped with a silver falcon stood on the mantelpiece, its hands at 2.00. "You let the fire go out, and your clock stopped. You need a servant to do for you. Where's your man, barely-speaking Joris?"

"He's in Paris, if it's any business of yours, you pert shrew," Latham retorted, falling into a familiar banter with her. "I keep the clock that way."

Marie went to the fireplace. *He's alone*, she thought, as she re-stoked the fire. Soon it was sucking chill from the air. Latham opened the curtains to let in the dawn light. He lit a candle, and the room became cosy.

"Marie, my letters?"

"You must search for them."

Latham stared at her. *She's growing up,* he realised with a shock. Her chest sprouted two bulges that pushed over a pinching bodice. Her auburn hair was even more undisciplined, tendrils escaping an embroidered bonnet. There was a new glow on her skin. *First menses*, Latham thought. A thin packet poked out of her bodice. Her parents would hate this cat-in-heat display.

He sighed. Ordinarily, he'd give her a bauble and promise to tell her travel stories another time. But this morning he wanted to ask about the new inn sign. The Monk's Brew had become Le Plaisir du Roi Inn, featuring France's Valois king, Henry III.

Latham bent and kissed Marie's hand, his flaxen beard brushing her fingertips. Then he went down on one knee. "Marie, my baroness, grant me one boon."

"A boon, you common trader?" Marie squeaked, leaning over him.

"Preserve your virtue for one more worthy than I, a good young fellow here. I'm old and battered by the world, a rough stone that rolls downhill yet finds no resting place in any valley. I'm no man for you. Instead of flirting with you, let me teach you a new dance step."

Marie pouted. "I know too many dance steps already, and the boys in this town are either louts or monks. Not dancers."

"Come, Marie. As a caterpillar becomes a gorgeous butterfly, some of these boys will become handsome men. Your February revulsions will become July urgencies, soothed only by the marriage bed. A suitable alliance will please your parents. Meanwhile, we're friends. Come, share my breakfast."

He drank his cider, wondering if she grasped his metaphors.

She did. "This town's caterpillars will never be butterflies," she stormed. "And if I did marry, there would be my loutish husband all the nights and all the days, pawing me 'til I rot from childbirth fever." Tears flowed down her cheeks.

"Relax, dear Baroness. You're eager but afraid. You want a man who travels, who'll be with you less," Latham said. "I promise if I find one acceptable to your parents for his substance, and to you by his absence, I'll make the introduction."

Still standing, Marie tore off a hunk of bread. After a few moments, she sat beside him. Their steady chewing became companionable.

"The letters came a half hour ago," she said at last. "The roads have just become passable."

Latham went to the window. A pale disk edged the horizon; it would be a clear day at last. Snow and freezing rain had obliterated the previous two days; most people had stayed indoors, hunched over their fires. Roads had frozen into icy ruts, and the inn's yard was slippery. The courier must have been under pressure to brave delivery.

Marie was still talking. "I ran out when I heard the horse. He was weighed down with dispatches for the abbey. I took the letters for everyone here. I wanted to stop him waking Papa, so I could bring you yours myself. Aren't you going to search for them?"

"In my own good time. Look, let's play a game. For every question I ask you, you can ask me one about my travels."

Marie couldn't resist this idea. Other guests never talked seriously with her. Not even Mama or Papa appreciated how much she knew and saw.

"Why did your father change the inn's name?" Latham began.

"Baronesses go first."

"Oh, of course," Latham conceded, biting back a smile.

Marie considered. "What did the ugliest naked man you ever saw look like, and where was he?"

Latham roared with laughter. "Let me think. Constantinople, a dwarf entertaining a crowd at the slave market."

"We don't have slaves. France is civilised."

"Well…" Latham hesitated, glancing at Ibrahim's clock. He had an urge to push her to think. "So say many. But French pirates steal slaves bought by Spaniards in Africa. They sell them to the Portuguese, lend their profits to French nobles here, and those funds are esteemed."

"That's different," she retorted.

"Is it? A lawyer would agree; a good priest wouldn't," Latham argued. "Three steps: French pirates steal and sell slaves; they lend money to French nobles for high interest; the nobles endow monasteries to ensure prayers for their souls. Well?"

This was too much philosophy. "It's still my turn. The naked dwarf? I told you about the letters." She tugged his arm like a nagging dog.

"Alright, the dwarf. He was less than four foot, with a wrinkled face, the high cheekbones of northern Slav tribes, and a long grey beard that reached below his knees, covering his front. He had a huge sea monster on his back. The monster's tail was on one shoulder blade and its snout on the other. When he danced, the monster gyrated as if it were alive. He danced like a dervish; like this."

He jumped up and circled, head angled and arms spread.

Marie's eyes widened. "Ugh. What colour was the monster painted?" Marie asked.

"It wasn't paint. A permanent decoration was etched under his skin with needles and ink, something done in Slav lands, not here."

"What else?"

"His skin was olive-hued."

"Black or green olives, or nasty brown-grey?"

How observant, he mused. "You're clever," he said.

"None think so," she replied, her eyes tearing again.

"Then they're fools. To answer your question, none of those. By olive-hued we usually mean tawny yellow. As a northern man, his natural hue was white, so he might have suffered yellow fever or drinker's poison."

"Then you should have said burnt-butter hued, like Beurre, my dog," rejoined Marie.

"I beg your forgiveness for my sloppy story-telling," Latham joked. "While everyone was entranced by his monster-back, he had pint-sized accomplices picking the pockets of the laughing crowd. When they got their haul, they scampered into a caravanserai and got away. Now, it's your turn. Why did your papa change the inn sign? How did a jolly monk with a tankard of ale become your king, crudely rendered?"

"It's a good story about the dwarf, but you cheated with his beard. What if he was caught stealing?"

"You don't want to know. That's a second question you haven't merited. You're the cheat today."

She nodded reluctantly. "Mademoiselle Michaud sold Papa the inn last year, and Papa just sold it to some grand gentlemen. They changed the sign. We'll train their servants, then leave. They gave Papa some money, and he bought a small farm. They'll pay Papa and Mama forever something called an anny...." Her voice trailed off as she searched for the unfamiliar word. She brightened. "And I get a dowry."

She frowned. "Except, I don't want to marry. Some foreigners came, jabbering not in our tongue or Latin, and a cardinal once. And smelly old scar-faces, who cursed when the priests weren't around. Soldiers, I think."

Again, Latham was impressed by her cleverness. Saint-Denis was a key place for a spy like him to understand. Its cathedral housed royal tombs dating back to the eighth century, and it had hosted coronations for centuries. That suggested allegiance to the crown. But since Luther, its preferences were more ambiguous. Huguenots had occupied Saint-Denis in the 1560s, horrifying clerics; they favoured the militant Guises over a king they thought too soft on heretics. In Saint-Denis, Latham could sense shifts in the power struggle between Spain's protégé, the Guises, and the French monarchy.

He returned to the inn's sale. "Dear Baroness, an *anny*, as you call it, is a promise of timed payments. The proper word is *annuity*."

"Ann-u-it-y." Marie repeated, sealing it in her memory.

"Did these gentlemen give your papa a document?" Latham continued.

"Oh, yes, with a seal. They signed, and Papa put his mark on it. He doesn't read. Mama and I mostly know numbers. What about my next question?"

"I'll show you a trick first. Close your eyes."

Marie complied. Latham whisked the letters out of her bodice with a smooth flick of his knife tip. When the package brushed her skin, she snorted. "You cheated, you dung-chewing trader."

"Language, Baroness. That's not how great ladies talks. I told you I'd search in my own time. Now, let's be serious. I can read in many languages and your papa can't, even in his own tongue. Show me the contract, and I'll tell you if it's sound. This property is his life's work. He's exchanged it mostly for a promise on paper. I'd grieve to see you robbed."

Marie became pensive, knowing her dowry was at stake. Latham ached to see the buyer's name.

"Alright, they're sleeping. I'll get it."

She ran out, returning in minutes.

"Here. They also brought a big flat box, which they hid."

"How do you know about it if they hid it?"

"I see things, Monsieur. Will you promise not to tell my secret?"

"May the devil take me if I fail you," Latham said, putting his hand on his heart.

"I have a peephole above the servants' stairs. Most nights Jean and Yvette rub up against each other on the landing and pant. Ugh. But one night, after they went away, two of the new owners crept upstairs. One was a grand personage carrying a candle, and his servant had the box. They put it in the storage room off the landing. They were there a while, so they were hiding it. Then they locked the room. I'm sure Papa doesn't know, although he has the only other key."

"Are you sure they didn't see your candle?"

"Yes. They didn't look up."

"That's a dull matter, to be sure. You'd do better getting your beauty sleep." Latham affected indifference to conceal his interest. He'd have to open this box before leaving Saint-Denis, and without Marie seeing him. A night-time peephole! She was enterprising as well as observant. He put his hand out for the document.

It was a traditional arrangement: a small advance of cash, then an annuity for Papa and Mama's lifetime and a dowry for Marie. He stared at the signature–Francois Lamont, avocat, acting for–here his eyes widened in amazement - His Grace, Henry, Duke of Guise. So Guise bought out this distant kin. This was strange. Why would Henry, Duke of Guise, buy this inn, and put up a sign picturing King Henry III, with whom he competed for influence? Marie had mentioned foreigners and old soldiers. It smelled of conspiracy.

"This contract looks sound," he said, stroking his flaxen moustache. "God grant you a happy life. You're my special friend. Perhaps I can visit your farm. Where is it?"

She told him: near a village five miles away. "I'll be pleased if you visit, Monsieur. You're not dull." It was her supreme compliment.

Latham smiled. "I'm going to mass this morning. When are you going?"

"Mama and I are going at four," she responded. "Papa's taking the servants at midday while I go to the market with Yvette."

She ran downstairs humming. The story about the dwarf was good. She'd tell Jean, but make the beard shorter. Jean would kiss her. He'd practised enough on Yvette.

Latham looked at his two letters. He rubbed the seals with the pad of his fourth finger. Unbroken. The second seal had a faint 12, signifying a coded note from Pieter Boels. The first letter was from Don Cristobal.

Signor Piso,

Things run apace. The master steward guessed the origin of my fable and caned me, five light lashes, for opening a gift before times, but never told Papa. Notwithstanding, my labour was successful, and I thank you eternally for telling me the story. From it, I composed a one-act play about fat chickens harried by the fox, squawking then inviting a pride of lions to frighten the fox! The elders will perform it. The steward dressed my toy soldiers in new costumes. They will guard the chickens. I will soon work for Santa of the Sea. Am I not clever at this kind of writing?

Your loving godson, Cristo.

So the raids had succeeded; Walloon merchants had invited the Army of Flanders to return. Latham pictured Don Cristobal scratching his curls as he invented his prattle. In fact, he was good at it; it said a lot. Farnese (master steward) had guessed who was behind them, but concealed Don Cristobal's violation of the Treaty of Arras from Philip II (Papa), merely reprimanding (caning) him. *As I predicted,* Latham thought.

However, Cristo wasn't unscathed. The phrase *dressed my toy soldiers in new costumes* suggested Farnese had taken Cristo's men and dispersed them to other commands. Sending Cristo to serve *Santa of the Sea*, Spain's Admiral Santa Cruz in Lisbon, was a great promotion and made him someone else's responsibility. Farnese was astute.

He decoded the letter from Pieter Boels, which added to Cristo's news. The merchants had petitioned Farnese for the Spanish army's return. Local cloth and leather merchants had received contracts from Farnese to supply the Spanish army, and were pleased. But Pieter expected the Hansa merchant, who opposed the Spaniards' return, to be pressured by Farnese to use his influence at the Lubeck Hansa Council to get high tariffs on English goods throughout the Hanseatic League, to punish English merchants for supporting Dutch rebels.

This nugget got Latham drumming his fingers on the table, thinking. The Hanseatic League was a centuries-old association of towns governed by merchants, across state borders. It offered partial independence from princes, backed by its own ships, which it used to enforce its trade privileges. If Farnese meant to bend league policy to Spain's will, then Spain's opponents would eventually push back. This introduced a new element into European conflicts. He made a note to pay attention to Hansa dealings.

As he burned his letters, he went over what he'd learned.

Firstly: the sale of the inn to Henry, Duke of Guise, with foreigners, clerics and soldiers coming and going, suggesting an international plot.

Secondly: The Army of Flanders would return to the Netherlands.

There was a saying that favours and blows come in threes. He already had two good pieces of intelligence. Was a third waiting outside? He was going to mass at the cathedral, in any case.

As he dressed, he thought about the nature of power. The little lever of Cristo's raids would bring Spain's army back to the Netherlands. If there were unforeseen consequences, could he influence that? He couldn't forget his morning's nightmare.

This was nerve-wracking, so he went over the day's tasks. He had to break into the storage room to look inside the hidden box. That would be tonight. Before he tried, he needed to attach some kind of noisemaker to Marie's peephole, so he'd be warned if she was there. He'd do that when Marie and her mother were at the four o'clock Mass. When the servants were at midday mass, he'd check that his picks could open the storage-room lock.

His day organised, he started downstairs. On the landing, he heard from the communal sleeping room the lilt of a morning prayer, a slap at a bedbug, mutters. The guests were stirring. On the main floor, he stepped aside to let the harried servants rush to the dining room, carrying platters of steaming bread, melted cheese and twice cooked sausage.

Outside, he studied the inn's new sign with fresh eyes. The winter sun gave it a clarity it had lacked on previous storm shrouded days.

Le Plaisir du Roi Inn was in bold black script. King Henry III's velvet cap was set at a jaunty angle on his purple-tinted hair, his thin eyebrows arching, as if he was startled.

These perturbed eyebrows framed dull, brown eyes in puffy sockets. The long Valois nose presided disapprovingly over a sensual, twisted mouth, under which his receding chin slunk quietly into his neck. The paint was vivid, pearls rimming his cap almost palpable in their gleaming grey-white, while his earrings, heavy with emeralds and diamonds, distended his earlobes, giving him a pixie-like look. In each corner, brilliant blue and gold fleur-de-lis, the coat of arms of the Valois dynasty, were exquisitely detailed, the leaves extended–contrasting the nobility of the king's symbol with the grossness of the man himself.

Latham saw that the fleur-de-lis were slightly crooked. When the sign swayed in the breeze, they looked as if they would fall, tumbling into the mud below. It was a subtle effect,

A clever insult, Latham thought; a public hint that a challenge to the king was coming. Details like the earrings and purple hair were taken from a notorious ball that Henry had recently hosted. Its decadence had horrified sober citizens in his famine-struck country. The portrait wasn't quite enough of a caricature to be called treason, but it mocked. There was no strength or grace in the dissipated face leering at Latham. He shook his head and started for the cathedral, avoiding black ice. The Beaumonts deserved better than being caught in a Guise/Valois contest. He was glad they'd soon leave.

CHAPTER 16
SPY'S
QUANDARY

Le Plaisir du Roi Inn squatted in a short, diagonal street that served the needs of tourists and residents. Latham passed two apothecary shops, a bookseller, and a jeweller who crafted pendants and brooches featuring the saints whose faces were carved into the cathedral's stone decorations. At the corner, there was a barber shop whose red and white striped pole trumpeted hair cutting and bloodletting. Above the stores, the top floors of residential houses jutted out, windows almost meeting over the ancient cobblestones.

Latham looked behind him, seeking tails, but he only saw village life stirring. Apprentices were unbolting store doors, while house servants opened shutters on upper floors. At the far end of the street, a gong farmer, shoulders bowed under a pole with two full buckets of excrement, trudged toward his cart. A chambermaid flung a pot of waste from a second-floor window. She aimed for the sewer drain in the centre of the street but missed.

The gong farmer cursed as he lurched to avoid the steaming mess. He shook his fist at her.

"Pardonnez-moi," the maid apologised, quickly closing the shutters.

The gong farmer eased the pole off his shoulders, picked up his spade, and shovelled up the waste. He emptied the buckets into his cart, rang a tinkling bell, and trundled to the next street.

The street's private drayman followed, nodding as he passed Latham. As he gathered broken wood, shattered lanterns and other rubbish, he rasped a popular ditty:

> *My gloves, my face, my hat, my boots,*
> *Gauzy veiled with shit, with soot.*

Latham relaxed; no one was following him. He turned into Rue de Boulangerie, a curving street leading to Cathedral Square. As its name suggested, it housed bakeries licensed by the abbey. The scent of warm crusts pursued him as he walked. Although the young sun grazed him with embryonic warmth, it was still cold. He tied the cords of his cloak and pulled it around him. As he leaned against the bakery wall, his mind was on his letters and the inn's new owner.

Then he noticed a crowd forming in the square. He straightened up to get a better look. As it was market day, he wondered what could have induced people to abandon trade for even a few minutes. Peasant women had stopped lugging turnip-filled carts and were standing around; farmers had left bleating goats tethered to posts; vendors had left closed sacks of food on their stalls; maidservants tarried, their baskets empty.

Latham strode forward. He had to stand at the back of the crowd, but he was tall enough to see that the distraction was a ballad singer. Swarthy and short, the singer wore a dun-coloured doublet over dun breeches, minimally enlivened by dull red thigh ribbons and a faded red felt cap. *Down on his luck*, Latham thought. While the singer stood on a box, his apprentice beckoned the crowd closer, to hear the latest fashionable love songs.

The ballad singer strummed chords on his lute. Then he looked up at the belfry and handed the instrument to his apprentice. He put his hands under his armpits to warm them and waited. Nothing would happen until the bells had chimed eight o'clock, Latham realised.

Soon enough the bells rang out in a descending scale, obliterating all chatter. The deep tenor bell created a humming undertone, below its actual pitch, then its booming bong crashed into the peals of the lighter bells ahead of its time, driving the rhythm faster and faster. Bell cut off bell in a joyful cacophony: tune, counter-tune; a boisterous banter, though always with the powerful tenor harmonies anchoring the riffs of the lighter bells.

This tenor bell ringer is bold, Latham chuckled, remembering his bell-ringer bedfellow at Oxford. He pictured empty ale jugs rolling on the belfry floor, and laughed again. He had often joined his friend in the belfry, eyes agog as the bells were swung full around, the giant metal bowls crashing onto metal clappers. After high holy days, lead ringers and senior clerics often took a holiday. Free of supervision, the students would drink and improvise. It was a universal habit, Latham's friend had told him; the most inventive bell ringing could be heard off-season.

That seemed to be happening now. This first peal was English style, where a short pattern, rather than a tune, drove the piece. In this style, permutations of the pattern were exploited in fast shifts tantalisingly close to chaos.

The peal lasted over a minute, then came to an abrupt end. Latham clapped his hands, feeling young and innocent again. Next to him, a tradesman smelling of leather and a peasant woman swathed in a hay-streaked cloak edged away, thinking him brain-touched.

There was a long silence from the belfry. A faint "ooww!" floated down. Now the people around Latham were laughing. The ballad singer looked up, surprised. Conversation started again, a few birds chirped. Carrying a stuffed satchel and loose papers, two monks hurried up to the ballad singer and seemed to be cajoling him. The singer nodded as they put their papers on the box, and walked back to the monastery.

A second peal began. This one was in the French style, a chant setting of the Credo, full of gravity. During the silence, a monk must have chastised, perhaps beaten, the ringers.

After the second peal, there was a short silence. A treble bell began a soft dirge, clappers muffled by leather, a slow, steady peal. Three soft bells. Pause. Three soft bells. Pause. Three soft bells. Three: mystical number. Three times the pattern of three. Another silence. Then the pattern repeated.

Someone has died, Latham realised, and the news is fresh, the bells proclaimed. Not royalty, for the dirge bell would have been the great tenor. But someone of religious importance, because the preceding peal had been a Credo.

Latham recalled Marie's chatter about the messenger weighed down with dispatches for the abbey. Could there be a connection between a courier braving icy roads to get here, the sudden change in the peals, and the satchel the monks gave the ballad singer?

The ballad singer whispered to his apprentice, and the boy called, "Come hear a tale of martyrdom! Come hear, come see. Broadsheets two billons."

The fourth peal drowned him out. It was a triumphant Gloria. Like the first peal, it was brilliant, but disciplined, collapsing into the piercing toll of a single bell. Well-spaced strokes proclaimed eight o'clock, although the hour by now was a few minutes old.

As soon as the vibrations dissipated, the ballad singer began. The crowd had grown, the townspeople brought out by the promise of news. Latham recognised the tune from the Grand Duke of Tuscany's court's court, a poignant ballad about unrequited love. The composer, John Thompson, was a Catholic expatriate like Latham. He wrote boldly, piling dissonant chords on top of each other, pushing to the edges of harmony before resolving their exquisite tensions. In this tune, his phrases also rose in pitch, until the membranes of the heart ached with pain. Strange fare for a market-day crowd, Latham thought. Yet the audience was leaning in to catch each syllable.

A servant woman in front of him with a young girl in tow muttered in dismay and dragged her charge out of the crowd. When Latham took her place, he realised the tune had new lyrics. It wasn't about love at all.

Voyez son mort si triste.

Mark his doleful end, the ballad singer crooned.

Instead of a thwarted lover's laments, it was a chronicle of gory death.

The ballad singer repeated his first verse.

Regardez Campion doux,
Voyez son mort si triste, he carolled.
(Behold kind Campion,
And mark his doleful end.)

Latham was punched with a shock so sharp that he gasped. Edmund Campion! Since leaving to meet Cristo in Milan, he'd heard nothing from Katherine, or about the Jesuits. He'd assumed they were still safe, and being discreet.

Behold kind Campion, and mark his doleful end
In heathen England, by a cruel Queen's hand.
He hangs from gallows as great bells chase the hour,
The crowd sighs tears as his youthful sap doth sour.
Birds still their song, rough clouds paint out the sun,
And thus he lived, and thus his life be done.

The ballad singer paused to re-tune, knowing he had control of his audience. Having established a martyr's death at royal hands, none would leave before hearing how and why.

Latham's mind swirled. How had Campion been caught? Bad luck? Betrayal? If Campion was dead, what about Katherine, his beloved sister, whose name Latham had given him? In his head, he started raging at Joris, imagining that reports about Campion were waiting for him in Boulogne. He checked himself. He hadn't told Joris he knew Campion, so how would Joris, whose reading was still laboured, know that a tale about him should be sent on? No, he couldn't blame Joris. His heart pounded as his morning nightmare flashed before him. Had he got the danger to his kin right, but the source wrong? The persecutors were English, not Spanish?

With a few plucks, the ballad singer signalled the second verse. Latham pulled himself together, determined to extract facts from the lyrics. He soothed his anxiety by giving himself over to the sweet baritone of the ballad singer, who sang fervently, peering at the sheet the monks had thrust at him.

> *Behold sweet Campion, and bless his learning's power;*
> *He walked that land, and faith came yet to flower.*
> *Though heathen prelates rose, and brought him to dispute,*
> *His perfect arguments did strike them all stark mute.*
> *He opened God's truths, NOWELL's sureties he stung!*
> *And thus he sang, and thus his life be sung.*

The facts in this verse appalled Latham. Campion had actively challenged state policy by demanding to debate with Alexander Nowell, Dean of St. Paul's. This wasn't bringing covert Catholics relief, explaining privately that English Catholics could attend the mandated heretical Elizabethan liturgy without endangering their souls. Public prating was a form of betrayal. What had happened? How many did Campion take down with him?

Latham had left his inn room this morning having learned two pieces of intelligence, and thinking, smugly, that a third awaited him outside. Well, he had it, and it was devastating. He'd kept his emotions shackled in the cellar of his heart all this time, while his mind stitched facts and names into tapestries of plots against his Catholic patrons. Now his emotions burst their constraints and rampaged through him.

His first emotion was contempt, at the stupid English government for killing Campion. Crone Contempt skipped, shaking a gnarled finger at the English queen. Next came hatred, for Jesuit provocateurs—for that's what they were—making religious co-existence impossible. An armour-plated dragon, Hatred spewed fire on Crone Contempt. Then came fear for Katherine and the Latham family, for the lush green fields, bustling cities and vigorous universities of his birth country. Campion's execution might bring civil war and invasion. A giant worm, Fear slithered over Contempt and Hatred, secreting vitriol that dissolved them both. Edward Latham, the slick spy of many aliases, shed his past fifteen years. Beneath was an ordinary man, desperately worried about kin, and a country he belatedly realised he loved.

The ballad singer drove to the song's climax, while the crowd pressed in, muttering against heretics.

> *Behold brave Campion, a traitor's death he dies.*
> *Cut down while trussed and limp, they hold his racked frame high;*
> *Then drag his entrails out, his manhood scythe away,*
> *And quarter him in course, his poor sweet face display.*
> *A dew mist of his blood baptises souls new sprung,*
> *And thus he wrought, thus England be undone.*

The crowd began shouting:
"Curse all English."
"War, war! Kill the heretics."
An old monk yelled, "Campion disputed with Nowell, laid him flat and dry as last year's bread."
The ballad singer began the song for the second time. Higher and higher the pitches went, as he grabbed the top notes of Thompson's aching lover's pleas.

His apprentice went to work. "Two billons for the ballad," he cried, waving broadsheets. Several tradesmen threw coins in the box and grabbed a sheet. Latham bought one. Beneath a crucifix, the words of the ballad were printed in large letters. The ballad singer played a popular dance tune while sheets were sold.

The crowd dispersed, peasant women pulling vegetable carts to the market and farmers lugging their livestock out of the square. Food vendors lit their braziers and started hawking chestnuts and game pies.

The apprentice ran around, crying, "A grisly execution of a holy martyr! Hear the tale! Come hear the tale. The evil English Jezebel draws and quarters a true Christian! Here's the whole tale in a song to make you weep!" A fresh crowd formed.

Latham grabbed the ballad singer's sleeve. "I've bought your broadsheet. What's in the satchel the monks put on your box?"

"The whole history, Monsieur. The martyr's own words, this song, and much else. But it's only for them that can pay silver."

"Show me," Latham challenged. The singer opened the satchel and pulled out a bound booklet with gold lettering: *Ballad for the Most Holy Catholic Martyr, the Jesuit, Edmund Campion.* There were also two pamphlets. A few merchants read over Latham's shoulder as he flicked through them.

"Here! Pay to read," the apprentice protested. "This is no library." Two merchants laughed at him, bought the broadsheet and strolled to the cathedral.

The booklet's frontispiece featured a woodcut. Queen Elizabeth, eyes narrowed, glared down from its upper right quadrant, while Campion, looking up at her, occupied its lower left quadrant. The priest's dark hair was brushed neatly off his forehead, his white collar visible and eyes wide open. His expression was gentle yet defiant, his mouth yielding and sad. A hurdle with a body strapped to it took up the middle of the woodcut.

A good likeness to Campion, Latham thought, while Elizabeth had been caricatured. Her aquiline nose had been enlarged, while her curly hair, rendered in violent tightness, sprang in all directions. Her thin lips formed a feral snarl, and her jewelled earrings sported scimitars, an indictment of the recent trade agreement between England and the Ottomans, which cut out French middlemen. This caricature looked nothing like the vibrant woman Latham remembered.

The second page consisted of the ballad, words and music, while the third page had names of ancient Christian martyrs. In a section entitled *English Martyrs*, Cuthbert Mayne's name appeared first, executed in 1577 for a plot against Elizabeth. Campion's name was second, December 11, 1581, along with four other priests. There was no mention of Robert Persons. Latham remembered Campion saying in Calais, "Persons is careful of his person." Latham wondered if Persons had egged Campion on, while keeping himself safe. There was an ominous space below, for more English martyrs. The fourth page was filled with prayers for salvation, while the final page extolled devout Henry, Duke of Guise.

Latham's emotions stirred, but he suppressed them. The analytical man re-asserted himself. It was a clever and expensive production, and proof that the Guises and some monks at Saint-Denis were collaborating. The hint of intrigue he'd gleaned from Marie now had a clearer outline. Were the Guises preparing to challenge both Henry III and Elizabeth? If so, they'd need foreign support. Marie had mentioned foreigners, but who were they? Papal envoys? Spaniards? If Spaniards, did they represent Philip or some independent adventurer?

He tapped the pamphlet as he thought.

"Give them back if you can't pay," the ballad singer snapped, "because I'm ready to sing again." His fingers strummed randomly. Latham handed over a testoon, a vast overpayment, as the singer began the ballad again, hurrying to finish before the bell tolled the quarter hour.

Latham put the booklet and papers in his breeches pocket. He opened the gate to a tiny courtyard, crossing it with two long steps. He bowed to the conical rows of stone-carved saints around the oak front door. Was it his fevered fancy, or did the saints gazing sideways, down and across at him change, becoming his sister, the English Queen, Philip II and Campion, and nod sardonically at him? Saints, devils. Not simple. Was he sure which was which?

Confused, he walked inside. His churning conflicts receded as the mystical spirit of the building pulled him to the long nave. Tall, multi-pronged shafts rose uninterrupted to support the springing arches. The conical stained-glass windows on the cathedral's three levels pulled in light from the bright sun. Glazed stone, seemingly as thin as membranes, separated the windows. The stone picked up light refracted through the reds, blues, greens and yellows of saints' images until it, too, was luminous, framing the windows which shone like gigantic lanterns. Glass, stone, reciprocally alive with the fire of revelation.

A foretaste of heaven on a patch of earth. How could sin-ridden man create such a place if not inspired by God through his one true Church of St Peter? The ghosts of right-thinking Catholics soothed his doubts, murmuring, "It *is* that simple."

He walked the nave, treading softly so as not to disturb worshippers placing votive candles at side chapels. He entered the south-west aisle. It was lit by large windows filled with plain, green-tinted glass, which focused the light on cold, rectangular stones. Latham basked in the warmth for a few moments.

He pulled out his papers, but the words danced on the page. So he shoved them away, reflecting on the supreme irony, for him personally, of Campion's death as a Catholic martyr. As Elizabeth's debate champion at Oxford sixteen years ago, the suppleness of Campion's arguments had convinced the young, conflicted Latham that there was no place in England for a doctrinally committed Catholic like him. He'd been astonished by Campion's conversion to Catholicism. When they had met in Douai, they had been on the same side of the greatest issue of the day.

But in a further irony, when they had met in Calais, before Campion infiltrated England as a missionary Jesuit, their paths had been diverging again. Latham had been beset by nightmares he didn't understand. Campion had named them as doctrinal doubts, and had absolved him. For his part, Latham had found Campion's purity implacable and dangerous.

His mind a jumble, Latham sighed. Who was saint, sinner, martyr, nuanced pragmatist? As if to argue Campion's case, the cathedral beckoned him. He walked up the main nave, noting the delicate carvings on top of pillars holding up the arch supports. The design was the fleur-de-lis, coat of arms of Henry III's long-reigning Valois dynasty. Royals were buried here. King, Church, the foundation of social order.

He looked at altarpieces, with their incalculable wealth of gold and silver. The cathedral's architect, saintly Abbe Suger, had seen no conflict between gold and grace. He had embraced opulence as a visual tool for spiritual persuasion, particularly for those who couldn't read. But the church's dominant aesthetic was infinity.

Abbe Suger was cunning, Latham mused. While he'd accommodated the ostentation demanded by his royal patrons, he'd ensured, by the sheer magnitude of the cathedral's dimensions, that his structure would dwarf the grossest human pretensions. Latham craned his neck at the ceiling, an arch thrusting so close to the sky that there seemed to be only stiffened grey silk between man and his Maker.

He slaked his soul's thirst on the atmosphere, returned to the outer aisle and pulled out his papers.

This time he could concentrate. He ordered them according to dates. First, the ballad was January 1582; current. Next, the booklet, dating Campion's execution to December 1581; also current. He put broadsheet and booklet on the window recess: his urgent interest was the time between his meeting Campion in Calais and the priest's capture, a gap of more than a year.

He examined the thinner of the two pamphlets. It was a letter, purportedly by Campion and published in 1580. There was an explanatory preface written by a priest from the Duke of Guise's household. The preface began by celebrating a wondrous portent that preceded Campion's arrival in England. The bells of Westminster Abbey, bereft of human agency, had rung out in crashing peals. *What could this be but God trumpeting the reclamation of a land benighted by sin and heresy?* the writer asked. He explained that Campion had written this text at the request of Catholic gentlemen imprisoned at Marshalsea. They were allowed to go free by day, the writer noted. The feebleness of their punishment showed the weakness of the heretic regime, its ripeness for toppling, given a little help by the militant faithful. Campion had sent his letter to Europe, where it was printed. Titled *Campion's Brag*, it was smuggled back into England and circulated widely, bringing its author instant fame.

As Latham read the *Brag*, his face reddened with anger. After explaining that his mission was to *cry alarm spiritual against foul vice and proud ignorance* besetting his co-nationals, Campion threw down a gauntlet to the Elizabethan establishment. He demanded public debates on theology in front of the *Lords in Council* and the *Heads of both Houses of Parliament*, in which he would prove England had a faulty relationship between Church and State; at both Oxford and Cambridge Universities, where he promised to prove the truth of the Catholic faith; and in front of the *Courts Spiritual and Temporal*, where he would justify primary allegiance to Pope over Crown. Moving to the top of the hierarchy, he demanded an audience with Elizabeth, to correct her misguided beliefs. He issued this challenge, justifying prime allegiance to Rome while a Papal/Spanish army of six hundred men had taken Smerwick, an English fortress on Irish territory ruled by

England, and an English force was trying to take it back. So much for private absolutions, Latham muttered angrily.

The Duke of Guise's cleric recounted the next ten months. *Feeble corrupt sinners in high places would answer the good priest with silly printed words. But none dared face him; none could brave his perfect arguments. Their depraved Parliament invented false laws to trap him, but their soldiers couldn't find him, except as he wished to be found. Edmund Campion ventured in and out of London, a den of iniquity, where he received fresh inspiration from his superiors. Still they didn't catch him. Almighty God nurtured his path to martyrdom.*

Retrieving reality from hyperbole, Latham concluded that the English government had rebutted the *Brag* with published argument, despite what must have been their fury at this challenge. Still, Campion wasn't preaching rebellion. He was demanding to argue doctrine to a conclusion. There were legal precedents for changing religious law after public debate; Elizabeth's church had been created by Parliament after several debates. It was a rigged result, because three key Catholic bishops had been manipulated into breaking procedural rules, and thus were imprisoned until after the vote. But it was a freely elected Parliament, free speech respected during the disputations; a known process. Campion must have thought he'd found his legal loophole. But his radical intent was abundantly clear, his timing appalling, hence new laws.

Latham looked at the date of the final pamphlet: June 1581, nine months later. After the *Brag*, Campion had evidently retreated to the covert Catholic network. *Did he stay with Katherine?* he wondered, feeling goose bumps on his arms despite his warm clothes. Her last letter had hinted they'd met.

The second pamphlet's title was *Ten Reasons*; ten proofs of Protestant heresy. The Guise writer explained that it was published in England, on a secret printing press. The *fresh inspiration* Campion received during his London visit must have encouraged him to escalate.

He certainly did. He arranged to put this tract on the seats of St Mary's Hall, Oxford, before graduation ceremonies for four hundred degree recipients. Many of these youths were going into government, due to take the oath of allegiance to Elizabeth, an oath they couldn't take if they accepted Campion's logic. After arguing that Protestant theology was self-contradictory, he insisted that Heaven couldn't hold both Calvinist and Catholic monarchs. On top of the *Brag's* 'cry alarm spiritual against foul vice and proud ignorance' besetting English citizens, he was implying that they were in danger of damnation. And by putting his tract in the hands of new graduates, he was demanding of them choices that he hadn't made at their age.

Latham's temple throbbed. "No overt challenge" was what Campion had promised Latham, and through him, Philip II. His mind was a cauldron of colliding visions: Campion a saint, an angel floating in the ether; Campion a subversive warrior, armed hordes following in his wake; a red-wigged queen grimly giving the nod to torturers; a pope in the white vestments of purity, conniving with assassins before or after blessing all God's creations. He began to sweat.

"Are you sick?" a voice asked him in accented French. "I can call the monks. Their remedies are excellent."

Latham turned to see a thin man with olive skin and black eyes peering at him. His doublet and breeches were cheap copies of the latest fashion in Madrid; clothes that a councillor's third secretary would wear. The questioner had a small wart on his chin, partly covered by his curly beard.

"Thank you, I'll be all right," Latham replied, mopping his face with his shirt cuffs.

"You've been reading the pamphlets," the Spaniard said. "I bought them too. A shocking martyrdom; five executions in one day. The beginning of the end for those heretics."

The spy in Latham awoke. "Do you know these monks well?"

"I'm their guest for two days. Then I return to Spain."

"Ah. Beautiful country around here isn't it? Although there's not much to see under the snow. Perhaps you could return in a gentler season."

The Spaniard smiled complacently. "My purpose was to go to the Hôtel de Guise in Paris, then here."

Latham switched to Spanish. "Not the Loire valley as well? The Loire is mildest in winter, more benign for one from your climate."

"No time to play tourist," the Spaniard replied, startled.

"Well." Latham chewed his lip as he considered the stranger's unsolicited disclosure. King Henry III wintered in the Loire valley, so this visit to the Hôtel de Guise and Saint-Denis was being concealed from him. This stupid clerk had confirmed Spanish collusion with the Guises.

The Spaniard looked into Latham's hazel eyes. With a start, he realised that Latham's flaxen beard and moustache deceptively softened a hard face. His mouth formed a question then he thought better of it, bowed and left.

Alone, Latham fell back into reverie. He pictured that summer morning of 27th June 1581, at St. Mary's Hall in Oxford. Graduation day. The night before, shadowy figures slowly, slowly, inching the heavy carved oak door open, flinching as it creaked, glancing everywhere but no one stirring, the watch at the other edge of his route. Creeping to the benches and placing Campion's *Ten Reasons* on each seat. He imagined the young graduates the next morning, hearts filled to bursting at the solemnity of the day, blue hoods of the bachelor degree draped over black gowns. For sons of the wealthy, bought for the occasion and close fitted; for the scholarship boys, rented, too long or too short, threadbare on the seat. Both rich and poor scoured clean, the edges of their caps biting their temples.

One, then another, seeing the pamphlet, lifting it up, reading. A titter, several titters, nervous then growing in volume until a collective roar of laughter rolls around the echoey chapel, like a pride of lions in a cave. Gouty administrators limping in, brown cloaks flapping, faces white with rage; red-coated beadles pounding their staffs, arresting anyone with the wrong expression. Then family members coming in for the ceremonies and finding the hall sealed, their pride cruelly punctured by hostile constables questioning everybody. "Names, give us names. Your son. What has he read, written? Who are his friends? Who are yours?"

A messenger loaded with copies of *Ten Reasons* for the Privy Council galloping off on the muddy road to London. A day of nervous quiet. Then the tramping of soldiers' feet, the clinking of armour, midnight raps on residential doors, weary inhabitants in nightshirts, holding a sputtering candle, opening the door, fear twisting their guts. Men brandishing halberds and swords rushing in. Rough searches of the houses of known Catholics: chests upturned, pictures thrown from the walls, clothes and books tossed around. Then more delicate fingers, probing, probing like a tender lover, stroking panelled walls and stairwells, seducing the polished wood to give up the secret of the priest holes. And with a sigh, the wood sometimes giving in. Candlesticks, statues of the Virgin Mary extracted, smashed and burnt; a priest or two dragged out by the hair. Ruinous fines levied. Sketches of Campion shown everywhere. And one morning, Campion taken at last.

Heaven couldn't hold both Calvinists and Catholic monarchs, Campion asserted. No strong monarch would let this challenge go. Campion had gone from a survivable mission to one that was brazen and doomed. Latham believed that Campion had told him the truth in Calais about his instructions, but he must have been encouraged to go public after the *Brag's* success. Private conversion was tame; lacking the ferocity that could ignite a movement. The Jesuits must have decided to use willing English priests to escalate religious conflict.

Elizabeth and her stupid regime would take the bait, obliging them with martyrs aplenty. Not burning. The stake wasn't for a pragmatist like Elizabeth, who'd dismissed doctrinal differences as a '*dispute over trifles*.' Instead, a traitor's death: hanging, drawing and quartering.

Latham's bladder summoned him. He walked outside to relieve himself. Back at the front door, he stood aside to let worshippers surge into the nave and make for side chapels. He returned to the outer window recess, to wrestle with the implications of Campion's death.

CHAPTER 17
SPY RESOLVED

Time passed quickly in the sunny window recess as Latham considered how Campion's execution was being used to whip up anti-English propaganda. He was rocked by Campion's public challenge but had to admit in hindsight that his escalation was predictable. Despite Campion's promise in Calais not to challenge Elizabeth on English soil, his wounds of shame must have reopened when he had inhaled the familiar smells and sights of England. *For years after I knew the truth, I clutched at glory, helping to spread heresy,* he'd told Latham in Douai. He hadn't lied to Latham in Calais; he'd intended to perform a discreet mission. But his essence flowed to a great public destiny commensurate with his shame. The Campion who'd dared Calvinist leader, Theodore Beza, to debate to the death in Geneva, the loser to be burnt at the stake, was the Campion who was hanged, drawn and quartered in London.

And what about Latham? He loved Catholic doctrine without reservation, but he abhorred the notion of dismembering his birth country. Hell or treason, treason or hell. That had been the choice when he had left England in

1566. Now the choice had returned. Could he reconcile the irreconcilable?

Half-hour bells tolled, then three-quarter hour bells, then the full complement of nine o'clock mass. Latham walked up the main nave, watching townsfolk organise themselves according to class: merchants and their servants standing in front, farmers and peasants at the back. The choir entered from a side door, followed by tonsured monks and fidgety novices. Latham saw the Spaniard who'd spoken to him earlier. He came in with the monks and sat on a bench facing the altar.

Cloaks rustled, feet shuffled, as the crowd turned to the back of the nave. A sub-abbot led the procession. Tall, large-boned and plump, his dazzling white alb was embroidered with a large cross of gold thread under a cope of cloth of gold. Behind him walked the archdeacon and deacon. They undulated up the nave, sub-abbot with the lighted taper, deacon swinging the incense thurible. The choir chanted while burning gum sent tendrils of cloying smoke into the damp air, the taper's dancing light complementing the altar candles' flickering. Inspired rituals, magic and mysticism.

"Kyrie Eleison." The tenors began, boy sopranos soaring above them, then the basses entered. Bass tones as long as a slowly exhaled breath, the other voices weaving around each other. As one breath expired, another interposed, all coming together in an abrupt minor cadence. A slow Kyrie. Now the Christie Eleison. This time in unison and full-throated, but trailing off into the same minor cadence. Dorian mode: soulful, sad. The Gloria faster, with a triumphant unison climax. This was emotional music, designed to excite the soul. The composer was the new star of Spanish liturgical musicians, the Jesuit Tomás Luis de Victoria.

Victoria! How surprising, Latham thought. There was no disputing his ability to arouse fervour. But why was Victoria being performed next to the tombs of French monarchs? He'd never be the French king's choice, or that of his mother, Catherine de' Medici. They favoured the serenity of Giovanni Pierluigi da Palestrina, or France's own Claudin de Sermisy.

Symbols mattered. A political point was being made for those willing to see it. Latham looked at the clerics, the Spaniard, the worshippers. Some had knowing expressions, and a few choristers looked uncomfortable. Did the French king's spies know what was happening here?

By now, the processional was at the gold-plated carved chancel. Standing high on a thin base, it gave the impression it was hovering in the air as it presided over marble floor tiles. The tiles' decorations looked as if they were oscillating as the sun broke through or hid behind the clouds.

The deacon read the lesson, followed by Victoria's Credo. As Latham lowered himself in an obeisance, his knee touched cold stone. An upper layer of incense-infused air gave way to dead grass in loam. In its wake, a more pungent smell flooded him so vividly that he pinched himself to make sure that he wasn't there, with this other smell. A musty, rancid smell of cooking flesh; fire spitting as goblets of fat melted and ran into the smoke, provoking more wild-beast flames, maddened with desire at the first touch of prey. The animal stench was made more complex by damp clothes, greasy hair infused with prison filth, and the sweet, sappy young wood used to make a fire burn slowly. The fire that was cleansing the souls of heretics at the stake.

Latham had never witnessed a burning. His sister, Katherine, had written to him in Boulogne about how the family had shielded him from the burnings ordered by Elizabeth's Catholic predecessor, Mary. But his brother, Nicholas, ten years older, had been devastated when his beloved childhood servant was burned. Latham's senses today were saying it was time to stare the practice, in all its cruelty, in the face.

In Saint-Denis Cathedral this morning, his ears followed his nose. Piercing the choir's silken tones, he heard the voices of the condemned: defiant prayers, then feral screams, moans, whispers. Finally, silence.

Latham knew the Inquisition wasn't monolithic. Its ferocity was determined by local circumstances. Like gout: at times too painful to bear, forcing suspension of ordinary life; at others, a dull irritant susceptible to salves—in the Inquisition's case, bribes. Its rationale was to barricade against anarchy. But this morning, for Latham, cloying incense became burning faggots, rendering mute the heavenly music of the choir.

Numbers. He turned to counting. How many heretics had been massacred and burnt since mid-century? Tens of thousands? Yet this English queen, who could only be blamed for five, perhaps six, cruel executions of Catholic priests, was being bruited as the evil one.

In the year such and such, so many Protestants, so many Catholics. Did Jews count? Forget them. What about the savages of Africa or the Americas? Forget them, too. Only count Christians. His mind raced, faster than a bird could fly, across borders and through time. No matter how he counted, it was a few thousand Catholic dead against many, many thousands of dissenters. He remembered a bishop in Cambrai remarking, as he surveyed his smashed vestry, "Protestants are fonder of breaking apart things than men."

Who was right? Centuries of divine inspiration manifestly favoured the Catholic Church. Take Saint-Denis Cathedral, for example, and hundreds of equal beauty, how did they stand without the help of God Almighty? He'd read of the numbers governing the proportions of cathedrals at Oxford. The nave twice as large as the transepts, the tower half or twice as high as the nave was long - 2:1:3 or 2:1:4. Weren't these numbers divinely inspired? Catholics had read the mystery of numbers to make their houses of worship most pleasing to God. They'd erected soaring buildings as had no others. Not Jews, with their low-slung synagogues; certainly not Protestants, who made dour greyness of all they touched; not Musselmen or misguided Byzantine Christians, with their domes.

Then there were the numbers of music. Sheep gut to viol string. What a miracle of mathematical perfection the scale was: the octave in a half relationship with the octave above it, the fifth half of that. And then the overtone series: sixteen partial tones vibrating sympathetically when the gut-string was plucked. Sixteen ascending tones that became progressively closer, yet each named note within the series recurred only at a mathematical doubling, no matter where you started: 1, 2, 4, 8, 16; 3, 6, 12; 5, 10; 7, 14. Harmonies of nature, God's harmony. Greeks first described this phenomenon, but only Catholic composers put it to proper use, offering to God glorious thanks for what He'd given the world. Music was at its apex: Palestrina, Victoria, Canova, Tallis, Claudin. Nothing better could possibly be imagined, Latham told himself.

What had Protestants created? Fat farting nothing! Ranting tomes, simple-minded monodic hymns, the destruction of sacred artefacts. Absolution denied. An arid, reductive spirit.

But, his dissenting voice nagged, *aren't human numbers important? Did the number of God's creations killed count for more or less than the numbers governing shape and sound?*

Was it possible, he asked himself, that a false theology could be more virtuous in its application than a cruelly implemented true faith?

"My children…"

The plump sub-abbot overflowed the lectern. He was beginning his sermon.

Latham listened.

"We grieve the earthly end of martyr, Edmund Campion. But we also celebrate the ascent to heaven of a true child of God. He and four other priests with him were cruelly executed across the sea in England, a nation that once followed our Church. But this arrogant land has embraced heresy, and wallows in depravity. Our beloved ally of centuries past, Scotland, has also been infected by heresy. Fourteen years ago, treasonous Calvinist nobles ejected their anointed Catholic queen, Mary Stuart, niece of our gracious duke, Henry of

Guise. Scotland declared itself Protestant. An entire island won by Satan, its citizens blindly tripping to damnation.

"Last year, Almighty God called our brother, Edmund Campion, to rescue them. He took as his inspiration Paul, who said, 'We know that the whole creation has been groaning as in the pains of childbirth.' Think about Paul's ancient cry. Isn't it true today? Who among you can deny the misery of our present age?

"Think on the meteors slashing night skies, foretelling our punishments because we're obdurate in our sins. Aren't we suffering? Aren't our crops shrivelling, making beggars of us all?"

Latham winced at the largeness behind the lectern aligning himself with beggars. Having read the Duke of Guise's pamphlets, he knew this was a rhetorical pivot.

"But let me tell you of a hopeful portent. When Edmund Campion sailed to Dover to conquer heresy, the great bells of Westminster spontaneously pealed, by themselves. No human hand touched them…"

He paused to savour gasps from the audience. Raising his arm, he shrilled, "I say, no man whatsoever touched those great bells before their crashing rings. The heretics say the ground buckled, making the bells jangle, but none I know there felt it. I tell you, Almighty God was trumpeting to the faithful of His re-consecration of His ancient abbey. England will be reclaimed with the help of martyrs like Campion, and our own land must be cleansed of heresy and filth.

"Listen: at no time has our Church been in greater danger. Remember our history. Ancient martyrs in Rome braved gnawing by jungle beasts for the entertainment of hordes. Their sacrifices united us. We survived. We grew strong. But as soon as the rod of persecution stilled, the flock became unruly, some claiming inspiration not granted by God. We survived that too. How? Because we acted as great Constantine prescribed, by casting out Satan-infected doubters, and exterminating them when we had to. For they sought not reform, but to enfeeble us by schism.

"Conformity yields strength. Look at this building, the fruit of firmness in the face of perfidy. How could it stand if one mason placed his stone lengthwise and another diagonal? Or if one stone had the strength of limestone, the next the brittleness of terracotta? You smile, masons and carvers, but you know that only conformity makes us strong."

He leaned over the lectern, his voice low yet crisp. "But Satan was never vanquished. He grew subtle. He uses the abuses of a few sinners among our priests to turn you towards him. Through the forked tongues of heretics, he simpers: *Take Church property to help the sick, the poor, the ignorant.* His seductive name for this theft is *common good.*

"Common good? Our church does this already! How subtle modern Satan is. What is the result of common good? Satan strides unimpeded across our beloved earth. You've seen his insults to our theology, his trashing of sacred artefacts, the wasting of your farms by mercenaries marching for heretic nobles here in France.

"Let's examine this devilish invention, the common good. It was first propagated by an excommunicant, the gross, wife-killing tyrant, Henry VIII of England, who broke from Rome to marry a whore. He dissolved monasteries, taking their wealth. Now, what did he do with his new gains? Help the sick, the poor, the ignorant? You know better than that. They're worse off than before! He mustered an army and attacked Boulogne, which had offered him no insult whatsoever. So much for the common good.

"Now, Elizabeth, bastard daughter of Henry and his whore, accused Edmund Campion of being a traitor. You heard the song this morning. This Jezebel's executioners hanged him, sliced out his entrails, boiled his limbs and stuck pieces on spikes around London. But how can he be a traitor to an illegitimate, heretical queen?

"Think on his death and weep. But then rejoice. Edmund Campion said, 'the expense is reckoned; the enterprise is begun; it is of God: it cannot be withstood. So the faith was planted. So it must be restored.'

"I call on you to renew your service to your God, who weeps at what Satan has wrought. Heed Campion today. Not tomorrow, next week, after the harvest. Today. You didn't know him. I did. He was a gentle man, a merry man. He knew there is life beyond the flesh, the transcendent reality of the Spirit. He embraced his martyrdom. By shedding bone, muscle and hair, fleshly vestments that decay by the day, he's been saved. Salvation awaits you too, if you serve with a pure heart…"

As the sermon wound to its climactic call to arms, Latham turned inward. He realised that his nightmares were expressing his old contest between God, kin and country. He envied Cristo, who lived comfortably without conflict; or David Hicks, his old court friend, partisan for the queen and her false church. But Latham's conflicts pulled him in opposite directions. Could he ever reconcile them?

"God bless you and preserve you for His service. Edmund Campion has shown you how to be free."

The sub-abbot had finished.

There was profound silence. Boots scraped as penitents lined up to take communion. Latham remained on his knees, praying for guidance. There was none in the rabble-rousing he'd just heard. What you're called *to*, or what you yourself call *for*–how to distinguish? He rose to the Agnes Dei and followed worshippers into the sunlight.

A new crowd pressed around the ballad singer. Latham bought a salted eel pie and took a bite, but it turned to plaster in his mouth. He threw it away and walked around the monastery abutting the cathedral. Poor and maimed people, four deep, shuffled into the refectory for free food and physick. A monk walked among them, inquiring of their woes, a protective hand on the shoulder. He kneeled in front of the children, seeking in dull, malnourished eyes a spirit to nurture. *There is the grace of my religion*, thought Latham. Without wealth, there wouldn't be charity. Henry VIII, destroyer of monasteries, never replaced the services the church provided.

The shattered priory Latham passed on the way to his mother's grave had been destroyed to free up grazing land for its new owner. On that point, the sub-abbot spoke true.

After handing a few billons to the monk, he stopped at the corner of the square before returning to the inn. How long it seemed since he saw the ballad singer warming his hands in his armpits. Now people were coming and going from the market, and broadsheets were selling well.

He lounged against the wall, seeing Campion's joy in debate and love for his students. But that image was superseded by the Jesuit's ferocious, bloody-minded dogmatism, which had probably endangered Katherine and countless others. It was a day for truth. He regretted the suffering of the executed Jesuits, but his abiding emotion was anger at them.

A day for truth: was he as devoted to Catholicism as he'd always believed, and never tired of telling others? Why not vow vengeance against his birth country, and exult in the hatred the executions aroused here? Was he already taken by Satan? *There is not room in Heaven for both Calvinist and Catholic monarchs*, Campion had proclaimed. Was it that simple? Had Latham lost his faith in priestly certitudes, or had priestly certitudes lost their virtue?

He'd left England to live under Catholic governance. But he'd seen too many depredations by Catholic rulers to believe they should rule more than they did. Greed and cruelty were just wearing a new fabric: theology.

Constantinople's Ibrahim hovered over him. "Someday, egret-magpie, you'll think with subtlety." Was this the day? Ibrahim had used inaccurate clocks as a metaphor for the fallibility of human theology. *No*, Latham protested inwardly. *Catholicism has the truth. But this isn't its time to rule Europe. We are so sin-poxed that only the parity of opposing force will allow the earthly world to survive.*

A balance of power; that's what he believed in! He straightened up, staring unseeingly at the bustling Cathedral Square, shocked at the revelation.

But if he valued a balance of power, his actions hadn't supported it. He'd sent Cristo on a guerrilla mission to secure the return of Philip's army to the Netherlands, immeasurably strengthening Spain's hand; and he'd helped Campion infiltrate England. Because he'd never conspired directly against England, he hadn't considered how his actions could affect his kin and country. Now, the rabble-rousing call to arms by the sub-abbot showed what could happen if Guise or Philip prevailed.

He thought about his brother, Nicholas. Katherine had finally revealed how devastated he had been when his beloved servant, Anne Somers, was burnt at the stake. Pious, Catholic Queen Mary had ordered her burning, despite Anne's recantation of heresy, despite Anne having four young children. Anne's husband, John, had also been condemned, but Queen Mary had died before releasing her signed warrant. It was Elizabeth who'd spared John in the first hours of her reign. Elizabeth had tolerated the covert Catholicism of the Latham family. Their lives weren't open or pleasant–he couldn't have borne it–but if they followed the rules, they had a tolerably strong likelihood of safety and moderate prosperity. Latham realised he'd taken this stability for granted as he roamed the world. And so far, a balance of power had taken care of itself.

But Campion's execution had changed things. Jesuits would send more martyrs, and English cruelty, if not moderated, would unite the world against it.

Is it quite true–*deal honestly*, he admonished himself–that Protestants have created a fat, farting nothing? What about living numbers? England had grown strong under Elizabeth. Surely this couldn't have happened if it wasn't God's intent. Had he misunderstood God's will when he'd left? His dreams said yes. He believed England would one day return to true religion. But the Almighty must mean it to do so when strong, not wracked by civil war, like France and the Netherlands. If God wished to use a lettered heretic to further His design before consigning her to hell, no mortal like Edward Latham should question it. Elizabeth said she'd studied divinity for years; she had chosen her path.

The Almighty had guided her to remain a virgin, to abjure from breeding more troublesome Tudors. Despite Catholic plots to assassinate her and put Mary, Queen of Scots on the throne, Elizabeth hadn't yet removed Mary from the English succession. There would be a Stuart succession: Catholic Mary or her son James, who was said to be open to the true faith. England's return to the true faith would be peaceful. It was wrong for anyone to dismember his country, as contrary to God's will as it was for heretics to vandalise Catholic icons, kill priests, mute their choirs or maul liturgy.

He was called to help the Elizabethan government survive by becoming a double agent, using his access to urge both English and Spanish rulers to deal more moderately. Maybe the Almighty would grant His foolish servant, Edward Latham, long enough life to see a Stuart on the English throne.

Irreconcilables could be reconciled! His brain was sharp, and he was filled with a strange excitement as he returned to the inn. He had seen the two chambers of Campion's soul: the formal room of public martyrdom, the tiny room of individual absolutions. Now he saw his own heart. It was cleaved clean in two. Each riven side beat strong: one for his faith, one for his country. It was no longer hell or treason, but a course full of untasted perils and confusions.

Back in his room, he sat on the windowsill and looked down at the yard. A few hens were scratching at seeds. Guests strode to the stables, tipped the stable boy and trotted into the street. Normal life.

Sixteen years ago, Latham had heard Campion debate at St. Mary's Hall in Oxford, the same hall where he'd placed his *Ten Reasons*. How more closed could a circle be?

He recalled a child's swing in Constantinople. Riders secured by leather straps had propelled the seat higher, until it had soared over the transverse pole in a bucking arc. Elizabeth, Edmund, Edward. They'd all been in the wild swing seat in

1566. Then Edward had spun off into the orbit of Mary, Queen of Scots. Elizabeth and Edmund had swung high a few more years. Then Edmund had spun into the Society of Jesus, and had now spun off the earth into the ether. Now Edward would leap back into the seat with Elizabeth. May God show him how to slow the contraption if seat straps got tangled.

Life as a double agent would be like drawing through a camera obscura. The Douai attacker might be his protector; devoted Pieter Boels a man to be careful around. And Cristo, his oath-brother? Would they be Palamon and Arcite, falling out over a virgin royal? His dream said so. Was this thinking subtly, as Ibrahim had urged? And what kind of priest could hear his confessions?

Uncurling, he rubbed circulation into stiff legs. He picked up his lute and tuned it. He plucked a few chords and sang the first verse of Thompson's ballad. He stopped, screwed the tuning pegs tighter, raising the pitch of the strings. It was the trick Lady Barbara Blomberg had shown him, to bring more brilliance to his sound. The lute string was most poignantly beautiful when stretched tautly, she'd said, just before it broke.

He tightened the pegs, waited for the strings to adjust, tightened once more. He played the ballad again. Thompson's fearless ascending phrases rang out, each note pinging with desperate clarity, the tortured strings shaking in their yearning for release. Latham crooned:

Behold kind Campion,
And mark his doleful end.

As he sang, his voice was breaking with anguish. Twang. One string broke. He shifted his fingering, sang a few more phrases. Twaaaanng. The second string broke. He sang the ballad again. The third string broke. He put the instrument down.

Lute strings were most beautiful just before they broke. So it was with his bond with his church. Catholic rituals were at their most beautiful that morning, during Victoria's fervent mass setting in one of the noblest cathedrals in Europe. But the strings of Latham's heart had been wound too tight.

He'd go to the English Embassy in Paris and offer himself into his country's service.

CHAPTER 18
EPÉE DE
FEU AND A
KIDNAPPING

After a night in the storage room examining the box that Marie had told him about, Latham padded back to his room as the moon was setting. A tap on his door woke him. Judging by the angled light, he must have slept several hours.

He opened it to a giggling Marie. "Monsieur, why were you wailing yesterday? You were singing the ballad singer's song, but he sang prettily, and you yowled like a strangled cat. You broke your lute." She eyed the dangling strings disapprovingly.

"Listen, Baroness, take my lute as a gift. It will support you if the scar-faces and jabbering foreigners make problems. They're bad people."

She shook the lute and pulled out a purse with silver coins he'd put inside it. Eyes widening, she understood.

"Now, my little friend,' he said, wagging his finger. "In the future, please call me Signor Prosperino, not Monsieur.

I'm leaving. You misunderstand your age. You're far too old to ask men to take letters from your bodice, and far too young for peepholes, even if woodrot on the staircase invites you."

Blushing, she promised to heed him, then left, carrying the lute carefully.

He didn't know yet how to get the English Embassy without arousing Spanish suspicions. But as he packed, he went over the previous night. He certainly had a tale for whoever interviewed him.

The hidden box contained a different sign for Le Plaisir du Roi Inn. Instead of King Henry III, it was Henry, Duke of Guise. Unlike the dissipated French king, whose chin slunk into his neck, the duke had a sculpted jaw and frontal stare under pink-blond hair. Above all, he was manly. The sign itself was innocuous; but knowing there had to be a reason for all the secrecy, Latham poked and rubbed the surfaces. Eventually, he felt anomalous wood nails in moustache and jaw. On his knees, he levered them out and pulled papers from the gaping hole in Henry's face. One line in simple substitution code read: *At the password 'epée de feu' instruct sign painter Auguste Remaille of Saint-Denis to inscribe this sign on both sides King, by the grace of God.* François Lamont, avocat for the duke's purchase of *The Monk's Brew Inn*, had signed, with the Guise seal.

A second paper named partners, and they encompassed three countries. Next to a unicorn, Mary, Queen of Scots' symbol, was the name *Crichton*, a Scots priest, liaison to Mary for Scottish affairs. Latham's heart raced at two other names, scions of ancient English families. Like many noble dynasties split apart by the dizzying changes in religious laws after Henry VIII broke from Rome, one branch of the Pagets and Throckmortons served the government, while another seemed to be bent on rebellion.

Treason, with a global reach. Shaking with excitement, Latham sat down hard, the resulting dust making him sneeze.

The plot's scope was so broad–France, Scotland, England–that it was more dreams than plan, he thought, wiping his nose with his shirt sleeve. He made copies, reinserted them in the sign's hole, and closed it. The originals he took.

When he reached his rented rooms on the Petit Pont late afternoon, he was musing on Guise's limitless ambitions. He still had no idea how to get to the English Embassy uncompromised. Turning his mind to the problem, he opened the bedroom window and looked out at swaying clotheslines strung between buildings and boats plying the river.

His mouth was curving into a smile at the solution when Joris clomped in, waving papers. Back from watching for followers, Joris jabbed his finger at the top sketch. And there were the protruding ears and cold eyes of Latham's Douai novice attacker. Now he was a physician with black robe and staff. The iron gates of the two-storey building he entered featured the Tudor arms.

"We have him," Latham said. "You always guessed he was English."

Joris glowed as he warmed his hands at the fire.

Latham turned to his other drawings. Piles of bricks and stones on mud next to the English Embassy showed it was in the Marais district, where marshes were being drained for urban expansion.

He whistled at the next face.

"Wh….Who?" Joris asked.

"No matter," Latham said curtly. Joris clenched his teeth in resentment. If Latham had to describe the silence as sound, he'd have said the air crackled. But he had more urgent concerns. Was it good or bad that David Hicks was here? Now kin by marriage, would Hicks's connection to Latham make him a harder or softer interrogator?

David had graduated from a silver earring in one ear to a gold one, and his muscular torso was fuller. His fingernails, formerly buffed, had a chewed look. It was sharp of Joris to note that; he must have got close. *Stress eats at all of us*, Latham thought. The third Englishman man was new to him: young, slender and short, a neat dresser, his pockmarked face sporting a blond beard. At the Spanish Embassy, there was a stocky guard Latham hadn't seen before.

Still not talking much–his mind was too full–he wrote letters for Joris to deliver. The closest was to Hélène Michaud at the royal laundry, warning her of an imminent rupture between Guise and the French king, reminding her of her vulnerability as Guise kin. The others were far-flung, keeping Joris out of Paris for a few weeks. "If I'm not here when you return, please give the Spanish ambassador this drawing of the Douai attacker. Say he took me."

Incredulous, Joris stood, his face a stew of concern, hurt and rage.

"Don't worry," Latham called as his manservant catapulted out. "My astrologer predicted a long life for me. Say naught to anyone. I'll explain when you get back. God give you safe journeys."

Dressed ostentatiously five days later, in a magenta doublet with turquoise satin-slashed sleeves under a black cloak, Latham trotted his hired horse along the Petit Pont to the Left Bank. He was putting his plan to get to the English Embassy into motion, and expected to be noticed. At the second road, Rue de la Rondelle, he turned right, reining in at

Galerie Henri, one of the street's bookseller/ printers. Produce, spice and fabric carts rumbled the other way through snowy slush to shops on the bridge, while students, professionals and clerics hunching in cloaks looked at bookshop windows. Water carriers bustled in and out of printing houses, while an occasional apprentice loaded books into customers' bags.

It had taken a while for Latham to figure out how to talk to Hicks, and whoever the pock-marked blond man was, without arousing Spanish suspicions. Sending a note, or meeting at any public place, was out of the question. But after a couple of nights spent tossing and turning, he found his strategy. Both sides knew he'd served Guise; both sides knew he was a thorough papist; the Spaniards, at least, knew he'd helped Campion. It was plausible that he'd disseminate Guise's publications on Edmund Campion in Paris. His plan was to print and distribute them, hoping to manipulate the English into kidnapping him under the eyes of Spanish agents.

After visiting the printers' guild and looking at shop lease records, he'd chosen Galerie Henri. A specialist in Catholic tracts, Monsieur Henri had apprenticed with the Duke of Guise's printer and had permission to use the name Henri. His printer's mark was a unicorn, also the coat of arms of Mary, Queen of Scots, Guise's cousin. Finally, Monsieur Henri needed money. His lease required reinforcement of the first floor to bear the weight of the presses. In debt, he was unlikely to refuse the job, despite its controversial nature.

The press room was light and buzzed with activity, smells and noise. Three journeymen manned each of four presses, while apprentices worked at long tables wetting sheets of paper or cleaning used letters. Shouts came from everywhere of "Care!"

A man with black hair, stubble around his beard and a worried frown bustled to Latham. Offering a smile, he said, "Signor, I am Henri. I got your letter. What do you need?"

Inclining his head, Latham handed him the publications from Saint-Denis.

Henri studied the ballad, music, woodcut of Campion gazing serenely at a feral Elizabeth, the booklet chronicling Campion's mission and execution. A muscle throbbed in his temple as he studied the woodcut–official French policy was friendship with England–but he relaxed when he saw Guise's cleric's name. "Well," he said, "text, music, tricky woodcut, the meaning lost if faces aren't differentiated. You've come to the right place for craft. But certain foreigners won't like it."

"My payment will offset any inconvenience," Latham assured him.

Henri struggled mentally, then nodded. After settling on paper and binding, Latham handed Henri half of a very generous price. Delighted not to have to haggle, the printer promised speed.

A dew mist of his blood
Baptises souls new sprung.

Pure young voices, cracked old baritones. Soon the ballad of Campion's execution could be heard at markets, in church squares, at the colleges of the Sorbonne, outside the main hospital and in taverns.

After a week, Latham saw the Douai-attacker-turned-physician through his mirrored hat. Behind the fake physician was the stocky guard from the Spanish Embassy. Latham started dining at the Yellow Cock's Spur Tavern, paying singers from there. One evening, he'd just hired a new one when the Spanish guard came in. Latham saw no other followers.

"I need to piss, but they've taken the pots for emptying," the singer said. "Rough wine does in an old bladder."

Latham agreed: his bladder wasn't young, either. In the muddy alleyway a puny cone of orange light thrust through a window, but beyond its tiny authority, it was dark. They smelled their way to the cesspit, sidestepping rubbish.

On the way back, a snout poked Latham's codpiece, depositing vegetable peel on it. "Get away, pig," Latham hissed.

When the pig backed off, the singer whistled. Multiple feet thumped. From behind, a burlap sack tumbled over Latham's head. Something hit his head, and he lost consciousness to the singer's laugh. When he came to, he was lying face-down in a cart, gagged. The sack was still over his head, a small hole for breathing. He felt an insect bite on his ear. He tried to wriggle to the side to rub it. A knee crashed into his back, and a knife nicked his neck. Blood seeped out, warming his chilled skin. Garlic-breath made him retch. "Douai," Latham grunted through his gag.

"Evil-willer." The Douai attacker's voice sounded French. *At last, I hear him talk*, Latham thought with languid detachment.

"Don't move or squeak," his attacker went on, "I'd disembowel you, but some want to talk to you. I'm Gerard Martin, of Guernsey. I know you've wondered. French grandmother of the old faith, but I'd do *anything* for Her Majesty."

Latham lay still as Martin searched him and took his knife.

"Hurry," Martin urged the others, "curfew soon." He smacked the cart. The pressure on Latham's back eased as the knee lifted. The donkey lurched forward and stopped, the driver cursing at a feral squeal. The pig was back, angrily determined to reach its rubbish. Latham heard whip cracks as the driver lashed both animals.

New footsteps thumped out of the tavern, and a voice shouted in Spanish to stop. The driver and singer jumped the Spaniard. Martin's knife was back at Latham's neck, warning him. Latham heard a stifled cry, grunts, the thump of a solid body hitting mud.

The cart rocked and turned left onto gravel. At last, a street. It gathered speed. Latham felt another turn and the clatter of wheels on cobblestones. Distant horns called an hour before curfew.

It was Saturday night. Latham soon sensed space. The air was cold and clear, but he detected a tang of blood through burlap sack fibres. *Place Maubert market*, he thought. Cattle, chickens, goats slaughtered today. The cart turned left. Between church bells, he picked out river sounds. The stones under the cart became flat, paving stones. Quite close, men sang in several languages as they slung sacks from barge to quay.

Nearby, watchmen's shouts and clanging hooves, a splash in the river; they were after someone else. The cart rattled onto a road with heavy traffic. Latham flinched as a carriage step going in the opposite direction grazed the cart side. Another cart passed on the other side. Three lanes. He made out dancing lights, pedestrians holding lanterns coming out of restaurants. He longed for his room on the Petit Pont. In a minute they passed it, taking him from the known shabbiness of yesterday into a terrifying newness.

Over another bridge, which Latham guessed was Pont Notre-Dame. Then they turned right. Latham coughed at a new smell, dye chemicals. *Place de Greve*, Latham guessed. Martin's knee slammed into his back. Soon it became quiet, occasional measured footsteps of watchmen calling "All's well."

The cart turned onto a curved cobblestoned street. Now there were human sounds, only the heaving of the donkey, the squeak of wheels, and behind them the clop-clop of his captors' horses. Church bells from the left were faint; none came from the right.

"This place gives me nightmares," the cart driver muttered.

"Just a cemetery," Martin scoffed. "Peaceful souls at rest."

"No," the driver insisted, "I've heard angry shades caper here, planning mischief."

"You see ghosts everywhere, Billy." Martin was impatient. "Stop your mouth. You don't want our prisoner to think you're a coward. He might venture something."

Latham realised with a shock that he'd had to strain to follow the banter. He was hearing English spoken fast and continuously for the first time in years. *Then how have I dreamed? Spanish, French, English, Latin?* He reeled back visitations, but couldn't attach language. He wondered if his

English would be adequate for probing interrogation.

The cart stopped. A multitude of French voices chattered beyond an archway, coin-clinking hordes jostling to pay guards to let them in before city gates shut. Then the cart was through.

With the old city receding fast, the air sweetened. It was quiet in a different way. A wolf howled, another answered. Nervous cows lowed, an owl hooted. *The Marais*, thought Latham, smelling marsh mud. His senses acutely heightened, he was mapping by sound and smell, through the tickling sack fibres, the interlude between his old and new life. He was curiously detached: he could be taken to England and convicted of treason; or plunge into being a double agent; or make a narrow trade of his sister Katherine's safety for the Duke of Guise's plots.

Brick dust tickled his nostrils. They were close. The Marais was more affordable than the old city, which Elizabeth would like, and was safer from uncontrolled massacres of Protestants. Physically safer, but prey to summer marsh diseases. He hoped that Martin, pretend physician, wasn't the only doctor there.

"Who goes there?"

The cart stopped.

"Gerard Martin, for Master Thomas Phelippes."

"Password?"

"Doubting Thomas."

There was laughter and back-slapping at some shared joke as the gate was dragged open. *Doubting Thomas?* Was he the pockmarked youth Joris had drawn? He must be an important newcomer.

The cart rolled to a sucking stop in mud at the back of the mansion. The men dragged Latham out and removed the sack. He felt woozy, the ears and the cold blue eyes of the Douai attacker fuzzed. But his brazenness was intact. He gave Martin his third finger, "Who caught who tonight, Martin?"

His captors pushed him through the servants' entrance, up steps into a corridor, past pantries and a kitchen. Up to a warm main and first floor, then the second floor, colder and dank. Two gold right earrings and four chipped teeth danced in front of Latham's wool brain.

"How did it come to this?" David Hicks asked. "Or must I ask in Spanish?"

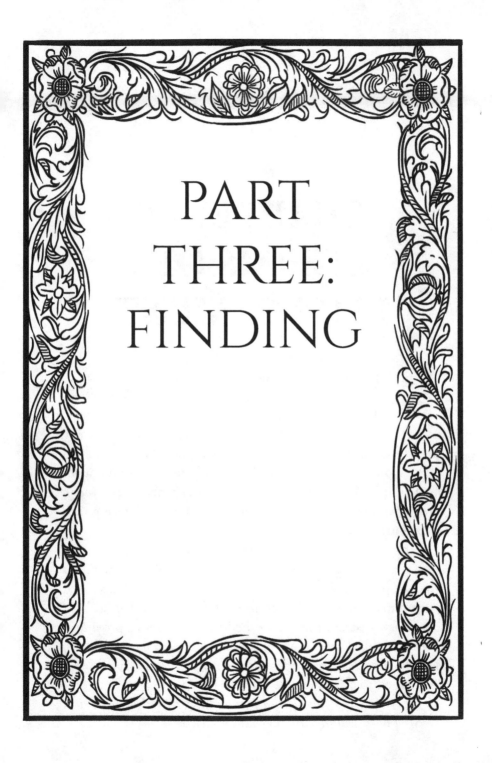

PART THREE: FINDING

CHAPTER 19
TERMS OF
EMPLOYMENT

H icks opened a door for Latham's kidnappers to throw him onto a straw pallet. Locks clicked, keys jangled. He heard shoes clattering away, leaving one pair of boots phlegmatically plodding outside. Cautiously optimistic, Latham pulled his cloak around him. The Spanish tail had seen him kidnapped, as he'd planned. *I've made it here with flea bites and a headache; nothing a day won't heal,* he thought, sinking into a dreamless sleep.

The next morning, in a windowless room smelling of new plaster, Latham looked up from his low stool at Hicks and the pockmarked youth from Joris's drawing. Hicks asked interminable questions. Not about Latham—that would have been easy. Instead, they concerned the affinities of provincial French nobles. The youth, introduced as Thomas Phelippes, said nothing as he made notes or handed papers to Hicks. Yet he seemed to be dominant.

They're testing how deep my knowledge is; if I even merit a meeting with Walsingham, Latham realised.

Hicks worried a thumbnail as he turned a page. "And Collumbiers?" he asked about a Normandy noble. "We assess him as a sympathiser. His wife is Huguenot."

"And his mistress is Catholic. Whose cunny is sweeter?" Latham's crassness masked his astonishment at their deep familiarity with the French governing class. Giving them anything of value would be a challenge. He'd hidden information they couldn't possibly know in the sole of his boot, which he intended to give only to Walsingham. He was glad he'd had the foresight to prepare it.

Hicks got up to leave, not meeting Latham's eye. "You know enough. Thank God Almighty," he flung over his shoulder. Clearly, the marital connection was awkward for him.

Left with the young man, Latham blurted out, "Spare me your clichéd 'You bowed to the setting rather than the rising sun in serving the Queen of Scots.'"

"Boring, I agree," Phelippes said, playing with a quill feather, "especially for a man who engineered his own kidnapping. I'm a code-breaker. You started your career breaking code. Do you know which puzzles rob my sleep? It's when a writer botches his own tongue. Would you like to compete to break a code we intercepted last night? Have some sport while we're at it? First to find the key gets double breakfast."

Rubbing his temple, Latham agreed. He wished he'd eaten some coffee beans before this interview. Phelippes opened a sealed parchment. Side by side at the desk, they tackled the numbers. By the time Latham determined the text was Latin, Phelippes whooped. He had the key. "Sorry, Latham, bread and ale for you, game bird and sausages for me."

A few minutes later, Latham was back in his second-floor prison.

The next morning, Phelippes led the interview. "We must know if you married Emperor Charles's concubine, Lady Barbara Blomberg. You played her witch's tomcat in Brussels. A gentleman would have tied the knot."

"There was no marriage," Latham said flatly.

"Your proof?"

"How do I prove a negative? Is that why they call you 'Doubting Thomas?' Search the records in Brussels."

Phelippes smiled.

The door opened. Hicks came in and leaned against the wall.

"You did, and found nothing," Latham snapped. "Lady Barbara and I were banished separately, escorted by armed guards. There are no records outside Brussels, either. Besides, you know from your various spies that I'm not the most apt-for-marriage man."

Hicks exhaled. "Enough, Tom."

There was a silence; Phelippes looked apologetically at Hicks.

"Your problem is bigger than my connection with Lady Barbara," Latham began. "*A dew mist of his blood, baptises souls new-sprung.* Executing Campion and the other priests as traitors have united Europe against you."

"Edward," Hicks said, "we need you to list the principal intelligence you gave the Spaniards. You have two hours." He left, this time inclining his head at his cousin-in-law. Latham concluded that he'd passed the first test.

He sat at the desk, fingering his moustache. The principal intelligence he'd given Philip II amounted to four things. Item: The Queen of Navarre used her jewels as collateral to fund Dutch rebels; Item: Genlis was leading an army to ambush the Army of Flanders besieging Mons; Item: Early advice that the French king, Charles IX, was sick and would soon die; Item: Walloon merchants could be "persuaded" to petition the Governor General of the Netherlands to bring back the Spanish army for protection. A thirteen-year slice of his life. Strange to see it on one page, Latham mused, adding dates but not sources.

He gave it to Phelippes. "A spy's foot can direct a royal head. In your fevered dreams, doubting Thomas, you crave it too."

"No. In my fevered dreams, I unlock code," Phelippes laughed.

Three near-sleepless nights followed, due to constant noise outside his room. It was the gentlest of tortures. Finally, he faced Elizabeth's spymaster in a pleasant library. He contemplated the narrow face that terrified Elizabeth's enemies. Walsingham had a long nose and chin, framed by a neat beard and ruthlessly cropped hair. His eyes gave the impression of boring down through Latham's chest to the floor rushes.

With a wintry smile, Walsingham pushed a list titled *Persons provided by Edmund Campion and arrested* at Latham. Katherine Latham was there. In parentheses were the letters *L, M, R2*, in light charcoal. "Edmund Campion gave these persons up," Walsingham began. "Do you understand the initials?"

"They can be rubbed out, so it's something you can deny." Suffused with dread, Latham stared at Walsingham, who steadily returned his gaze. "*L* means Little Ease," Latham guessed, "the tiny cell that cramps an adult to foetal size; *M* means manacles; *R2* means two rackings. You haven't subjected my sister to these rigours?" He jumped up. "S'wounds, I'll kill you!"

Two guards approached, but Walsingham waved them away. "Will you, indeed? So let's trade." He smudged the letters with his thumb.

Latham believed he could obtain Katherine's safety for explaining the fake heretic raids that persuaded Dutch merchants to invite the Spanish army back, and the Guise plot. He showed Walsingham the papers and names he'd taken in Saint-Denis.

Walsingham leaned back with a smirk. "Well, Latham, I think we can work together. I'm not surprised by the English names. We had suspicions. I need time to corroborate your information and obtain Her Majesty's approval. I'm puzzled on one point. How, so soon after you helped get the Spanish army invited back to the Netherlands, did you discover your errors and return to true religion?"

"Sir Francis, I *am* Catholic!" Latham shouted. "I'm not here because I've fallen into your heresies. I'm here to save my kin, and because I can't bear to see my birth country dismembered. Cutting up priests is appalling, but Catholic rulers are no better. I now believe the power of the parties must remain balanced."

Walsingham raised his eyebrows. "Well, you've hurt our interests in the past year. The consequences of the Army of Flanders being back in the Netherlands are inimical to any balance of power."

"I know, and will help you. Here's something to encourage you to deal straight with me and my kin." Latham untwisted the heel of his boot and pulled out the list of Catholic artefacts he'd made in the Constantinople warehouse.

Walsingham pored over the makers' marks, the notation of them as a gift, the royal origin obvious. He was dumbfounded. "What! Where?" he demanded.

"Elizabeth gave them secretly to Sultan Murad III four years ago, for weapons."

"I didn't realise mass artefacts survived Henry VIII's dissolution."

"His daughter did."

"If I'd known, we could have melted them down to support our Dutch brethren."

"That's why Elizabeth sent them to an infidel sultan. She didn't want to anger her loyal Catholic subjects by desecrating our sacred artefacts herself, or let you do it. If this gift becomes public, you and Elizabeth will be damaged. There are copies. If my kin or I am harmed, they'll be published."

Walsingham drummed his fingers on the table. "Latham, you're very free with unsolicited opinions. You can leave. We'll give you a good disguise and send word when you should return. Meanwhile, we'll watch you, for your protection." He left the library, and the guards took Latham back to his prison.

In the corridor, Hicks saw Walsingham shaking his head, looking stunned and amused. "Sir, did you...." he began to ask.

"Your traitorous cousin-in-law can go. We need to confirm his information and consult Her Majesty. No, Master Hicks, I didn't tell him that all the papists on my list had been released with no charges. You're not to tell him, either. I got three pieces of intelligence for nothing! In that sense, we won. However, he has something in the way of leverage, so he also has the sense of winning. He thinks he's Atlas, holding Catholic states on one shoulder, our states of the true religion on the other, keeping power balanced. As you know, I'm fascinated by motive. This is a new one!"

"Atlas?" Hicks was amazed. "What self-opinion. Can we trust him?"

"Grandiosity will keep him honest. Yes. He reports to you."

Walsingham walked to his office laughing, and Hicks sagged with relief.

A few hours later, the servants' entrance to the English Embassy opened, and Phelippes escorted an elderly woman to a mule. She was tall, stooping under the weight of a pole with two baskets. A faded blue kerchief covered her shoulders and grey, stringy hair. She had a scratch on a pale chin and three warts. She wore a grey wool undershirt; a brown wool cloak, buttons tied by scuffed leather strips across sagging breasts. But if the woman's posture suggested defeat, the scents from her baskets were robust: fresh herbal concoctions for ague, indigestion, insomnia, migraine, snakebite, cuts, impotence.

Latham was now a gipsy herbalist, a disguise for travels between his rooms and the English Embassy. With Phelippes following, he rode to the Petit Pont. When he saw the stocky Spanish guard, watching the bridge for the man called Piso Prosperino, he tested his disguise.

When Latham waddled up, wheedling, "Would the gentleman buy my puissant powder of acorns and pomegranate blossoms, guaranteed to soothe a sore head?" the guard drew his sword. Phelippes waved and left.

It was four weeks before Latham returned. Hicks outlined his terms of employment: payment per confirmed intelligence item, minus costs. Latham frowned, disturbing a wart. Impatiently, he brushed off the paint flake. "There's no provision for bribes. I'll lose each time."

"That's right," Hicks agreed. "Your Spanish pension subsidises work for us. Her Majesty said, *'It is just that Spanish Philip, who has tried to kill us and raise havoc in our realm, should pay our intelligencers to thwart his practices.'* Stay out of England; your value is your foreign contacts. We guarantee your family's safety if you and they stay loyal. There's something else: Mary's son, James, has come of age and rules Scotland as king. Mary is proposing a joint Scottish monarchy with him. As you are aware, she's been our trials of Job for fourteen years. We've told her we'll listen if James is eager. She's confident. But, as you informed Walsingham, her cousin, Henry, Duke of Guise, is developing a concurrent plan to attacks us and put Mary on the English throne. Consider that duality when you leave here."

Latham tried to get his mind around the possibility that Mary could be released to James, yet had a parallel plot going. He was re-hearing the Duke of Tuscany's words–"No one can keep track of all the yellow, red and green threads in the conspiratorial tapestries she weaves"–when Phelippes burst in with papers, banishing further thought of her.

"Good morning, Mistress Gipsy. Sir Francis got a note from the Spanish Embassy, asking delicately after your health. Are you ready for the confusions that go with changing allegiance? Double agents can't be single again."

"I'll have to report to Idiaquez that you kidnapped me and tried to turn me." Latham was surprised by a softer side in Phelippes.

"Of course." Phelippes snorted.

"Otherwise, how will you make Spanish subsidies work for us? Ha, ha, ha!" Hicks added. It was his first laugh since their strained reunion. Latham gave him a wan smile.

Phelippes tapped a paper. "We need reports from Boulogne on Spanish activity. Philip's new commander, Alexander Farnese, is formidable."

Latham nodded. "Idiaquez will also want me in Boulogne."

Approving, Hicks went to the door. "To keep your cover, write to us as if you're Catholic," he flung back as he exited.

Latham got up, flinging his arms wide in frustration. "David, I *am* Catholic."

After two days of learning codes, and the location of a safe house in Wimille near Boulogne, Latham was ready to leave in his own clothes, sporting a false flaxen beard.

"Get results," Phelippes urged.

In the courtyard, Hick folded him in an embrace. "Ear-wax brain!"

"Wool-droop cock," Latham retorted.

"I'm so relieved it turned out all right," Hicks said, embarrassed by tears filling his eyes.

"Don't forget to write as if you're really a Catholic," Phelippes warned.

They're all ear-wax brains, Latham mused as he rode back to his rooms. *Like the English better, Ibrahim said. Dear friend, I'll try.*

When he opened his door, Joris was rummaging through the gipsy's herbs. He stared amazed at the wool skirt and scarf Latham had slung over his shoulder. Throwing himself at Latham's knees, he cried, "God... mercy...s...safe! T..told Spanish... Embassy."

"I know. That swarthy fellow, their man, refused my remedies. Get up. I need to tell you something."

"Trojan… woman. Ha, ha, ha!" Joris sat on a stool and leaned forward. "I…say it." His hands shaped images as he ran through what must have been an exercise Dr Gomes had given him. "Dust…to stone to plant to tree… knight to baron… servant to master. Degree…"

Medieval hierarchy, Latham sighed.

"Only… moral …trumptude … can break it!" Joris finished triumphantly.

"Turpitude, not trumptude, Joris. But who but God can judge it?"

Joris frowned. That hadn't been part of the exercise. A wet nose poked from his pocket, and he pulled out a rabbit with a scabbed flank. Joris bathed the scar and matted fur with wine and put it in a cage. After bumping its restraints, the rabbit gave its captors a reproachful look and slept. "Degree," he persisted. "You… to English queen…I to you."

Latham got it: Joris was reaffirming loyalty, no matter who his master served. "Joris, I'm still Catholic."

"I…too. Spain different. That girl….Inquisitor raped. Spain…all turpitude, Gomes says."

"You can't tell your godfather Pieter."

Joris nodded.

"Listen, Joris, to help that queen, I must keep working for Spain," Latham said.

"I…don't care. I chose… serve you."For Joris, the matter was closed.

That night Latham stared at the ceiling, reckoning the dangers of being a double agent: manacles, the rack, hanging, drawing and quartering if Elizabeth decided his prime loyalty was to Philip; manacles, the rack, and burning at the stake if Philip decided he served Elizabeth. Those were the extreme perils. The lesser ones were the confusions Phelippes asked if he was ready for. He didn't know. But his sleep was dreamless.

CHAPTER 20
CLOSING
CIRCLES

The Beaumont farm near Épinay,
August 1583

"**M**adame Beaumont, I was desolate to see your inn boarded up. I've come straight from Saint-Denis," Latham said. In shock, he glanced at Auguste Beaumont, an inert lump slumping in a chair in the farmhouse's parlour.

"Auguste stares at the wall all day," Marie's mother told Latham, twisting her apron ties. Jeanne Beaumont looked at her lap, embarrassed that a former patron was seeing their reduced circumstances. "He doesn't weep or ask for anything. Where's the strong man I married? The bad jokes, the embraces?"

Latham bowed to Auguste, saying loudly that his house was solid and the soil rich. The lump didn't react.

"Terrible black bile," Latham murmured. *The wages for double-dealing,* he thought. This wasn't some distant, abstract blow, but the granular reality of people he'd hurt; the confusion Phelippes asked if he was ready for.

"My darling Auguste didn't understand this place," Jeanne explained. "We rushed to buy because that wicked lawyer representing the Duke of Guise, Lamont, pushed us. You've heard about the duke's trouble?"

Latham nodded. Walsingham had informed the French king about Guise's busy little plots, and the king had confronted Guise, forcing him to back off.

"Lamont's vanished and Remaille, the sign painter, was hanged," Jeanne continued.

"The inn was shamed by association. With the duke out of favour, our annuity doesn't come. Auguste despairs that he let us down."

"The acreage is small, but you can support yourselves, surely?" Latham offered.

"Auguste thought so at first. Then we learned the great problem."

"What problem, Madame?"

"Everything's the problem! Auguste doesn't read, nor do I much, nor Marie. He didn't understand local laws. The seigneur's grandfather reclaimed common grazing land for his grain crops because grain prices go up and up. The town made a law limiting the livestock that small farmers could own, since they must graze on their own land. No one wants starving herds, and the officials come counting."

"I see." Latham sighed. "Few animals means sparse manure, growing poorer grain that you can't sell profitably."

"Exactly. We own half of what we need to support ourselves."

Her voice droned as if she was bored with enumerating someone else's pain. But it was her family's sufferings.

"We have meat now because Marie found some money, we don't know how. But next year we'll have to buy it, and meat prices go up and up. We can get fish and frogs in our stream, and there are rabbits. In the seigneur's woods, game is plentiful. Marie says we should hunt, but that's poaching. So Auguste broods, while Marie, Yvette, and the stable boy work the fields. I work the house. We pray daily for God's mercy."

Latham pressed her hand to his lips. "Dear lady, maybe I can do something for you." He had had to stop Guise's treachery, but alleviating the consequences to the innocent Beaumonts was now a new imperative. He cast a mortified glance at inert Auguste.

The door banged, and Marie ran in with onions and lettuce. Her hands had always been scratched from sewing, but now they were covered by the grime of farming. She deposited her haul on the table and embraced her father. He shivered to life for a second, then slumped again.

"He only responds to her," Jeanne said sadly. "You remember Signor Prosperino, Marie? He's kind to visit us." Her tone warned her pert daughter against giving offence.

"I'm sure he's an excellent gentleman."

As Latham bowed, she gave him a knowing look.

She's changed, he realised. Her mischievous grey eyes were determined and steady, while her skin's nubile glow was tinged with the pallor of work. Her breasts, once restrained by her bodice, now lived comfortably under a loose work dress. There was an ethereal charisma to the devoted fifteen-year-old woman she'd become. But if their lives didn't improve, her determined eyes would grow desperate, her grace canker; a terrible waste of an exceptional person just not meant for sainthood.

He asked her to walk him to the stable to check his horse. On the way back, they sat on a pitted stone bench. Elderberry bushes divided the house from the two working fields, where the sun gleamed on bobbing wheat grass. The very smallness of the crop made the labour of harvesting it achingly palpable to Latham.

"You used the money I gave you eighteen months ago to buy meat. Sensible," he said.

"Yes, thank you. I also sold the lute. Grand gentlemen came after you left, and the yapping foreigners. They were doing something awful against King Henry. I can't wish they succeeded. I understand enough to know that if they'd won, there would only be dreadful killing. It's no small matter, getting rid of a king."

Latham stared at her, impressed. Was she absolving him in taking this broad view?

"Mostly, I worry for Papa. I could have married the bookseller's fourth son, but he's one of those Saint-Denis caterpillars who'll never be a butterfly. Ugh."

Latham laughed, remembering their banter. "You want a husband who'll be absent, while Mama and Papa need a man with substance. The bookseller's son lacked both."

Marie laughed with him, her mischievousness returning.

During a companionable silence, he studied the house. About three centuries old, it had additions in different periods and styles. Holly bushes screened a closed-up archway over a space in which ancient farmers and livestock cohabited. The property had been substantial, but inheritance divisions had shrunk it beyond viability, attractive only to a naïve townsman.

"It's pretty, but just not enough," he said.

"Antoine and Yvette stay for board. If they leave, the work will be too hard. Papa can do nothing. It will kill us in the end. I know it's proper to accept God's purpose, but why, why, why?" The wail started in her gut; she flung it at the world.

"Marie, be patient one season. I told your Mama I'd do something for you. Your father will recover if I can accomplish it. Melancholy ails him."

A summer storm set in. When they went inside, Jeanne insisted that Latham stay the night. Almost as an afterthought, she gave him a packet addressed to Signor Prosperino, care of The Plaisir du Roi Inn.

After a supper of laboured cheerfulness, Latham retreated to a spare room clammy from too few hands caring for too much space. Olive-green mould smeared part of the ceiling. He lit a candle and opened the packet. From sunny Lisbon, it was from Cristo, now serving the Spanish admiral, Santa Cruz. After affectionate greetings, Cristo described his enclosure: a study ordered by Santa Cruz of past invasions of England, whose ignorant errors he hoped his oath-brother would correct. He called it, ominously, *Old Tilts at Albion*.

Latham groaned. Cristo had no idea that Latham's allegiances had changed. God, king, kin and country were one to the Spaniard, and he'd never had the sensitivity to imagine what living with conflicted loyalties was like. More of the confusions Phelippes predicted.

Cristo had analysed invasions from the Norman conquest of 1066 to the failed attack on Smerwick, Ireland, in 1580. He'd obviously remembered Latham's lessons on politics—the buttered bread bits Latham had spread across the table at their Saint-Ghislain dinner—because Cristo related the outcome of each invasion attempt to the internal weakness or strength of the English ruler in question. He'd produced a thorough preparatory paper to a modern invasion plan. Without criticising Philip II directly, he had excoriated under-resourced attacks. Not only were there no errors, but Latham learned details he didn't know. That made him wonder if there was a pro-Spanish spy in the English admiralty, who'd informed some expert Cristo consulted. He copied out the relevant part for Walsingham.

'The most recent folly had been in July 1545. French King François I's armada had reached the Solent, his 200 ships facing Henry VIII's 80. Guns had been fired, but were too distant to hit their targets, or if they did, the balls' force had been spent. Small French galleys had got close, but their shot had barely dented English hulls. 200 modern ships couldn't overwhelm 80. One galleon of each side had been wrecked, only by accidents of their own side. Eventually, the French had gone home to harvest, ending what had been wasteful gaming, not war.'

I copy part of a Spanish officer's study to ask if someone near you is Spain's agent, Latham wrote. *Note the unpublished details. If you weren't imbuing your cause with viciousness, turning moderate Catholic princes against you, you'd have allies beyond the miserable Dutch. Now the burden of defending your shores falls square on you.*

He slept fitfully. When he woke, he was unable to move his limbs right away, transfixed by the ceiling mould, whose colours were enriched by sunlight broken up by window dust. Brown rims edged the green fuzz, making his mind leap backwards to a childhood memory: larva to dragonfly, the miracle of transformation.

He'd taken his friend, the groom's son, to their garden pond at night to watch the insect's rebirth. They hadn't needed candles, as the April sky was luminous under a three-quarter moon. Two larvae had crawled from the pond; not in company, for dragonfly larvae were solitary creatures, but at a similar place and time. One had grabbed onto the first grass stalk. The other had crawled further, cleaving to brick on the boathouse wall. It had seemed an eternity but was probably minutes as the larvae swelled, splitting apart the backs of their dull yesterday skin. With a creeping, pausing, pushing, they had heaved out gross knobby heads hunched above furled wings. They had stopped, arched back and rested in absolute helplessness. A whooshing owl had snatched the one on the grass stalk. Indifferent to its not-companion's calamity, the one on the brick had righted itself and clasped its old skin with four new legs. Ten feet: four trembling with life, six inertly adhering to brick. It had curved its new body forward and shrugged apart sluggish wings, then rested again. Nothing had happened, and the boys had returned home. The next morning, Latham saw weightless shapes darting from plant to plant: iridescent, filled with the spirit of angels, mating deliriously. Was the survivor of the previous night among them?

Why was he remembering dragonflies now? Saint-Denis Cathedral, the dazzling transcendence of sun through stained glass, reflecting on thin grey stone, was a little like the iridescent weightless flying insects. But that transcendence was aspiration, not reality. Being a double agent meant he'd stay half-ugly, half-beautiful, always arched in extreme vulnerability. So far, he'd cleaved to brick. Was his London counterpart on an exposed grass stalk? *Thank you mould, for cautioning me*, he told the ceiling.

On the way to Boulogne, he stopped at the Louvre Palace laundry and begged Hélène Michaud to help Marie.

"I can't hire her," Hélène insisted. "She's too like me, with her ill manners and peepholes. I suspect you made the problem, so fix it."

But she agreed to send a tutor to teach Marie to read and write in French and Latin, and she'd buy their surplus grain for two seasons, giving Latham time to find a permanent solution. Grateful, Latham kissed her hand and returned to his self-appointed task of preserving Europe's balance of power.

CHAPTER 21
WATERZOOI, WICKS AND FLINTS

Boulogne, August 1584

Latham's two lives crashed into each other the afternoon he received letters from Pieter Boels and David Hicks, both announcing imminent arrivals. Latham read Pieter's letter after he'd prudently burned Hicks's note from London, saying he had urgent instructions from Walsingham. The collision was so sudden that Latham stumbled around dazed, his dread obscuring the arrival dates specified in the letters. Only at night, when the sentient world retreated, did he remember to rummage in the fireplace. When he found an unsinged scrap of David's letter, the problem solved itself: the letters had come within an hour, but Pieter would leave before Hicks disembarked in Calais. *How much life force did I expend on this panic?* he laughed.

I need phlegm to be a double agent.

He was pleasantly phlegmatic in early September, when, from his first-floor window, he watched a rider propel through the gate of his current lodgings and haul on the reins of a stretching bay. Lanky Pieter Boels uncurled from the saddle, dismounting in one motion.

Pieter and Joris embraced with full hugs, Joris spinning like a dervish. As Joris led the horse to the stables, Pieter tossed questions at him, tumbling words into each other with no space for answers. The flinging language was the point, affirming closeness, rather than communicating anything. Latham pulled on his boots and ran downstairs to greet his sub-agent. Pieter was so focused on the joy of their reunion that he didn't notice Joris's pained reserve as the youth stepped back with pursed lips

He hates dissimulating to his godfather, Latham thought, deciding to avoid future awkward meetings. Joris bowed and left for the harbour while Latham led Pieter upstairs.

"I'm so proud of my godsons," Pieter gushed. "Here's Joris, well placed with you who serves our king. And William's doing military logistics with Don Cristobal, serving Admiral Santa Cruz in Lisbon."

"Joris is a good man. Now, what's urgent?"

"I need money to send an agent to Antwerp. Dunkirk and Nieuport are already ours, and we're besieging Antwerp next. After years of reverses, we're winning, but Antwerp is formidable. The walls are five miles around, thick with bastions. There's a rumour they'll be built even stronger. An engineer traitor from our side has a new design that the English support. Any improvement in the walls means more of our men killed. Also, a ship's being built big as a castle and loaded with cannon. I'm a known grain supplier to the Spanish army, so I can't go. Nor can you. Huguenots still call you the worst man in France. Antwerp's falls will crush rebel confidence."

Latham nodded. The rebel leader, William of Orange, had

been assassinated by one of Philip II's agents. The rebels had sought French help, but their champion, the French king's brother, had recently died of fever.

"They have no prince, and we have Farnese. Morale is high," Pieter added. "I have relevant news about trade, too."

"Later. I'll consider money for Antwerp," Latham responded. "Meanwhile, we usually dine at a harbour tavern, The Swooping Gull. There's interesting recent military detritus on the way."

In the main square, migrating chaffinches clustered about a fountain, shrieking over seed. Latham led Pieter through crowds at the vegetable market. As they exited the squat archway of the ancient walls, Latham showed him new stones laid by masons where Henry VIII's cannon had breached the fortifications in 1544, and where English engineers had tunnelled under the wall. Henry VIII had held Boulogne for five years. Hardly a structure was undamaged, evidence of the consequences of modern sieges. Pieter studied everything attentively.

On a switchback path down the grassy hill to the lower town, Latham pointed out the jagged remains of a big hulk the French had sunk during their blockade, trying to drive the English out.

"Did their blockade work?" Pieter asked.

"With one ship? The English laughed," Latham replied.

"Then," Pieter said, grabbing Latham's arm, "our Farnese is wise where the French were stupid. He'll make a bridge of boats across the whole River Scheldt."

This was specific intelligence. Latham raised his eyebrows sceptically. "That's beyond anything ever done."

"He's Farnese, and has the plan."

By now they were near The Swooping Gull Tavern.

"It's famous for waterzooi, a local fish stew," Latham explained. "Your godson feeds the day's catch to the gulls. The legend is that the longer the gulls feed, the better the stew. The tavern has gained so many new customers since he started, they serve us for free."

There was a crowd watching the tavern door. A minute later the door opened. No one emerged, the entrance just gaped. But a swarm of gulls–yellow-legged, black-backed, white-herring patterned, grey-winged—rose into the air, circling nothing in near-military order.

Then Joris came out, a small sack tied to his chest. He walked the few yards to the jetty and thrust his left arm into the air, holding something between his second and third fingers. Bareheaded, his ordinary brown hair waving in the wind, he looked like an ancient wizard exhorting pagan gods.

A courtly ritual ensued: a single gull swooped to retrieve the thing from Joris's fingers, his right hand pulled a replacement from the bag, the left hand lowered elegantly to meet it and elevated for the next gull. He moved serenely, and the gulls were exquisitely courteous. Not a single gull tried its luck on the ground because they knew Joris never dropped anything, and they never mistook human for fish flesh. When the bag was empty, he walked inside. Before the door closed, the gulls broke formation and swarmed a heron in the estuary, to snatch its hard-won dinner.

Inside, Latham and Pieter were soon slurping up perch, mussels, eel and carp, stewed with carrots, beans and spices. Joris chewed stolidly at another table, and played with a narrow faced kitten.

"Your news on trade?" Latham asked.

Pieter had thrust a toothpick into his mouth. "Farnese pressured his Walloon Hansa merchant on the Lubeck Council to secure votes on high tariffs on English goods throughout the Hanseatic League, on pain of Farnese commandeering that Walloon merchant's ships," he mumbled through the obstacle. Then, his teeth clear, he added: "The council voted the tariffs, and is also writing to the Imperial Diet in Vienna, petitioning them to expel English merchants from the Holy Roman Empire. Clothiers are already hoarding cloth. English merchants will have much less money to help the Dutch rebels. This is an economic war."

"Do you have documents?" Latham asked.

Pieter pulled out a roll of papers.

Latham tucked them under his shirt. "I'll look later. Summarise."

Smugly, Boels answered, "Minutes of meetings and the letter to Vienna. First: by unanimous agreement to *act against any Hansa town extending trade privileges to English merchants, on pain of seizure of ships and cargoes of transgressing towns.* Hamburg, with its Lutheran bankers, is particularly put on notice. Second: the letter to the Vienna Diet."

Latham whistled. Many English privy councillors were in business with London merchants. They would be angry.

"You can have funds for Antwerp, Pieter. I need accurate reports and details on your agent."

Back in the main square, the market was closing, trestle tables dismantled, unsold livestock led away. Bells tolled for vespers, and people filed into Notre-Dame Church.

Pieter bowed to Latham and embraced Joris goodbye. He mounted and was soon gone.

Latham put his arm around Joris's hunched shoulder. "I'm sorry, Joris, that was hard for both of us. I'll send you on a courier run next time."

Joris relaxed, and his eyes lit up. "Travel good. *Her...* not in here."

Three days later, a woman accosted a man in the cemetery of Wimille's squat ancient Church of St Pierre. The man was muscular, with green eyes and greying auburn hair, wearing one gold-hoop earring. The woman was tall and shabby, matted brown hair straggling from a faded blue kerchief draping her shoulders and chest.

"Would the gentleman want powder of acorns and pomegranate blossoms for his back? Or, I can see from my lord's protruding freckles that he needs dried sparrow brain to strengthen his wool-droop cock."

David Hicks blushed. Grabbing Latham's cloak, he growled, "Dung tongue with a dried-thistle cunny!"

They parried competing insults, though with the wariness of spy and handler. Hicks bought pomegranate powder, turned his square shoulders and strode under a long row of chestnut trees to the street. Latham plodded in the opposite direction, following Hicks's servant to an abandoned house. The English had sacked the town, which was between Calais and Boulogne, during their invasion in 1544. Walsingham kept this house decrepit enough to be safe for his spies to meet, but unattractive to squatters.

It was Latham's first visit. Window holes gaped, and the walls were cracked. The interior had been burned, the only remaining furniture wood planks so crumbly that the termites had left. Insect skins and tiny bones told of foxes, cats and raptors hunting. Judging from the patter of tiny feet in the attic, prey was abundant. Hicks spread a blanket on the floor, while his servant stood guard outside.

Latham took off the scarf and scratched his hair. "Dye's a torment. David. I'm tired of working for Spain. Let me just work for you."

Hicks sighed. "Impossible. Your value is foreign contacts. Writing that we 'imbue our cause with viciousness' caused an uproar. Sir Francis showed it to Her Majesty. She cursed him for a bigot who'd ruined her reputation. Of course, we know she signs warrants for interrogations, accepting the burden of hard deeds. She calls you an arrogant rogue, and ordered me, your pathetic kin, out of her sight. She threw an inkpot at Sir Francis…"

Latham hooted with laughter. "Empty or full?"

"Half-full."

"What colour? I must see it."

"Red, hitting his ear and ruff." Hicks tried to keep from laughing.

"Then she's just decorating dour Puritan black. You're trusted, so what's amiss?"

"My family's alright because we're Protestant, and Sir Francis needs you. But your sister's paying fines for not attending Protestant services. She was arrested for meeting Campion. Have a care her woes don't multiply."

Latham's laugh vanished. He smashed his fist on the blanket. Through the swirling dust, he snapped, "Don't take me to task over Katherine. We're soul-fasted. Elizabeth uses her as a pawn to get my best efforts. If you haven't lived the conflicts besetting Katherine and me, you're nothing more than a farter of moral judgments. You know nothing at all."

Hicks stood and massaged his back. "We're not actors. Farting moral judgments! What a cliché. You used to be more inventive." He wanted to say: *Your love for Katherine is easy from across the sea. I'm the one who intercedes when she harbours priests*, but Latham was unravelling, and he needed him in good shape. "Listen," he said, softening, "your family loves you, mould brain. I'll put your outburst down to the vigilance you must apply to every minute. After this assignment, you can have a break from us. We've had reverses and need your help."

"What?" Latham knew but wanted the English view. He was calming down.

Hicks poured out his concerns. "Well, rebel leader William of Orange was murdered by Philip II's man, who got into his house masquerading as a supporter and shot him with a concealed pistol. We panic for Elizabeth's safety. The Dutch lost French support when King Henry's brother, François, died. Farnese seems unstoppable. Her Majesty thinks Antwerp can hold–it *is* Europe's largest city–many think it won't. If Antwerp's falls, the pressure on us to send soldiers will be irresistible."

"You don't favour intervention?" Latham asked.

"I hate it, but I'm of no account. Her Majesty hates it; she's refused for seventeen years. Everyone else pants for it. We also hear rumours that the Hanseatic League will keep high tariffs on our exports, a financial blow."

"I can confirm high tariffs were voted," Latham offered. "In addition, the Lubeck Hansa Council is petitioning the Imperial Diet in Vienna to expel English merchants from Holy Roman Empire ports and lands. Apparently, Farnese threatened to take the boats of a key Walloon Hansa council member if he didn't succeed." He handed Hicks the papers Pieter Boels had given him.

Hicks groaned. "Aaah, more bad news." After reading, he said, "There's nothing we can do about tariffs, but we have leverage in Vienna. Spain and England aren't at war, and expelling our merchants hurts everyone. Our Florentine and Genoese banker friends can threaten to call in the loans the Diet members owe. That will make them huff and puff, and do nothing."

Latham grinned. "Your very *pragmatic* friends: Francesco, Grand Duke of Tuscany; his Medici kin; and his advisor, Giovanni Figliazzi."

Hicks nodded, slapping a flea on his wrist. "Something like that. At the right time, we can threaten ships, too."

Latham shifted topics. "My sub-agent says Farnese plans to bridge the whole River Scheldt. He also says an engineer defector from the Spanish side is in Antwerp to work on its defences, subsidised by you. He's sending a man to see. He can't go himself, being a known vendor to the army. I can't, either."

Hicks's face turned cunning. "Why not, mistress herbalist?"

Latham was appalled. "My disguise won't withstand scrutiny; Huguenots bay for my blood after Genlis. Besides, I must help one of my informers. You stopped Guise's machinations, but as a result, an innocent maid who led me to proof of Guise's plot has fallen into poverty."

"Help the maid after this assignment. You owe us service.

You facilitated the return of Spain's army to the Netherlands, which is highly damaging to our security. You're going to Antwerp to check on the engineer we're subsidising. He's supposed to be strengthening the walls but isn't doing it. His name is Federigo Giambelli. He blames the Antwerp Senate for refusing to let him, but he doesn't return our money. He's up to something. What? Stop worrying about skirts and scarves. You won't be mistress herbalist. Here…" He pulled out travelling papers from the privy council.

An English safe conduct document in his name Edward Latham, though no *Sir*. Latham let out a depths-of-the-belly chortle.

"We've set it up," Hicks pressed. "Go to Spanish-controlled Nieuport as Piso Prosperino. A boat of ours will get you to the Dutch rebel fleet at Zeeland. Dress as a farmer. We have an excellent farmer's wife who'll get you into the city with boats running the blockade. In Antwerp, you'll be Edward Latham. We'll have a man follow you. Some of our allies should realise you're on our side."

"Why don't you go?"

Latham didn't know which terrified him most: the physical danger of sailing into Spanish fire; being discovered by vengeful Huguenots; or not understanding the engineer's project. "You know this Giambelli," he urged Hicks. "You have status in Antwerp. I don't know mathematics. I could misinterpret his work."

"No English official should be in Antwerp," Hicks said dismissively. "If the burghers surrendered, I'd be a bargaining chip. You also forget that at Oxford, I traded algebra for tavern learning. I'm worse than you."

They were both silent. Then both spoke at once.

"Antwerp citizens are divided, a third papist," Hicks said, while Latham said, "Not all in Antwerp are Protestant. A third, the rest unbelievers or Catholics.

Hicks clapped his hands. "See, from opposing doctrines we agree. Her Majesty, being generally popular, may not grasp

Antwerp's condition. Size, wealth, proud traditions, and thick bastions count for little if the city's heart is spongy."

"If I go…" Latham's resistance was crumbling; braving Antwerp would be really interesting. "I must avoid my sub-agent's informer."

"Did you get a description and name?"

"Yes. Papers as Justin Timmerman, a mason thirty years old: middling height; blue eyes; brown hair; stocky. He'll have funds in excess of his station, and stay in artisans' quarters."

"He'll get food vomit and lose his purse. Now, before I describe Giambelli, we also need help in Constantinople." He showed Latham a name. "Ahmet Gul, tax farmer of foreigners and non-Muslims. Do you know him?"

Now Latham laughed with frank pleasure. "Little Ahmet? He lives! I'm so happy." He remembered Gul thumping the flank of the stinking camel skin in which Latham and Joris got into the guarded warehouse. "A boy in the household of my great former friend, Ibrahim, of the Bureau of Diplomats, may God rest his soul."

Hicks nodded. "Good. We need an agent beyond our envoy. When King Philip inherited Portugal four years ago, his navy doubled. He also sent his most ferocious inquisitor to Lisbon to, well, run its Inquisition. Portuguese refugees are flooding into Constantinople. We need contacts in Lisbon to learn about Spanish military contracts, so we can best allocate our own limited resources. Gul would know them all."

After a moment, Latham suggested, "My manservant can go. He was friendly with Gul. As a boy, Gul had a big tilting head, and Joris had muddled speaking. They shared an affinity against the world's scorn. Joris knows Dr Afonso Gomes too, who informs for you. Gomes treated Joris's speech defect, and they kept in contact."

Hicks sighed happily at Latham's capitulation. "Spain's truce with Sultan Murad III expires this year. Our envoy will persuade the Sultan to make difficulties about renewing it. That will give Philip something to worry about, apart from us. Policy today requires wide thinking: in this case from the Lubeck Hansa to infidel Turk. Now, don't forget to report to us as if you're Catholic."

"David, when will you accept I *am* Catholic? Your engineer defector, is he Catholic?"

"Of course."

"He works for you. He's not English."

"Mantuan."

"Mantuans are fervent for the Pope. Why is he working for a Protestant regime?"

Hicks spread his hands. "I concede. Here's what you must know. He arrived in London recently with plans for strengthening bastions in Antwerp and London. Her Majesty liked his ideas after our engineers praised them. But she wouldn't alter anything at home, saying it gave false impressions of fear. He also made her uneasy."

"Did she think he was working for Farnese?"

"No. He was never Farnese's man. He's a little man, certainly a papist, because he sought out a priest we know. He first offered his services to King Philip in Madrid but was denied audience. He resented this to the point of changing sides. His low height is countered by soaring vanity. He vows that the next time Philip hears of him, the king will remember his name. Given his quickness to take offence, Her Majesty wanted him in Antwerp, near the Spaniards he wants to avenge himself on."

"Wise," Latham smiled. "Mantuans have long memories."

"She granted him a pension and recommended his design to Antwerp's Senate. But bastions aren't being altered. He says he's making something more powerful, but naught is visible."

"So, a Catholic driven by wounded pride to vengeance; that's a low enough motive to trust. I *long* to meet a man who winkled a pension out of clutch-purse Elizabeth! Learn his art! You know I'll report to Idiaquez, too."

"Of course," Hicks replied. "Send what your sub-agent's mason finds out."

Antwerp, 1584

Joris began his journey to Constantinople in a party of merchants and their servants. With money, good clothes and a sturdy horse, he was so excited by his new opportunities that he forgot the misery of dissimulating to his godfather.

His master was less comfortable. At midnight, face-down in a mucky boat, he hugged an oilskin-wrapped chest containing one change of clothes and his English travelling papers. A squall soaked him as the floodtide swept twenty-two blockader-runners at a cracking pace towards Farnese's unfinished bridge of boats. Latham was terrified, thrilled, aching, sodden, truly alive. Yet all this intensity didn't stop seasickness: from time to time he turned his head to dry retch.

His boat was crewed by two oarsmen and Hicks's excellent farmer's wife. Unlike the other boats, they had no lantern, intending to coast in amidst the bobbing lights of others. The woman sat erect, her mouth spread in a fierce toothless grin. One of her muscular hands was holding a pistol, while the other motioned the oarsmen to keep to the river's centre. Spanish forces controlled the forts of St Martin and St Philip on both banks. Their guns blazed, roiling water in front of, or beside, the boats. One ball hit its prey, and Latham heard screams as wood and grain exploded.

There were shouts in Spanish and Dutch as Spanish soldiers tried to snare ill-steered boats with pikes or nets, and boatmen pushed back with poles and axes. Two boats were captured, their crews hauled out. When their own oarsmen shouted exultantly as they got through, the farmer's wife fired her pistol in raw delight. Latham sat up and looked at the receding bridge as the current thrust them toward land. He shook with excitement, again the young adventurer who'd escaped England by hauling himself hand by hand from plank to plank under Berwick Bridge. Around a curve, jetties came into view. With shouts of relief, the oarsmen tied up and hurled their cargoes onto solid stone.

Everyone staggered to the nearest tavern to wait for the ebb tide or the one after that. Latham sat in a corner drinking alone, wondering how far the bridge would extend when he made the return run. A scruffy man in clerical robes pushed open the door. Latham blocked his ears against the thoroughly heretical funeral service the cleric improvised for the dead sailors. The cleric—Latham wouldn't refer to him as a priest—knew the blockade-runners, and when the ritual was done, talk turned to freeing the captives. Farnese, everyone agreed, was less brutal than his predecessors. He didn't mind captives escaping; it served his current interests for them to run back and fill their officers' ears with his mighty fortifications. Latham spent the night in the common sleeping room, dozing on a straw pallet.

The next morning, he dressed in brown breeches and a brown doublet with black satin slashed sleeves and onyx buttons. Freshly barbered, he bowed to a short gentleman blazing in a magenta doublet with alternating ruby and emerald buttons. The rubies didn't match the magenta, although the emeralds did match his slashed green satin sleeves. Federigo Giambelli's vivid torso was topped by a three-layer ruff, ridiculous for a man of his size. He led Latham into his workshop and spread out his plans for strengthening Antwerp's bastions.

"Certain *great* foreigners recommended them," –his version of discretion about Elizabeth's patronage–"but the Senate rejected them. Cities shouldn't be run by burghers, Sir. They know nothing of war. They adore their stupidity, would erect statues to it instead of prudently defending their city. Only engineers and fighting princes should rule besieged cities."

Latham grinned. Engineers ruling kings; Giambelli was so vain, it should be easy to learn his project. "Farnese's unstoppable," he said provocatively.

"He wouldn't be unstoppable for *me*," Giambelli retorted. "Antwerp is building a huge ship and stuffing it with artillery. They promise that when they sail their monster at the enemy, it will destroy their bridge and other siege works, and blow apart every last Spaniard. But their mathematics is bad. I show them their errors, but do they listen? No. The nonsense is four times normal size. It won't blow things up because it can't reach them. It won't sail, it won't steer, it won't float when loaded. They plan to support it with cork. Cork! They know nothing of buoyancy. They call it *War's End*. It will be, for Farnese! *River's Bottom*, I call it. Down to the bottom, it'll plop, taking Antwerp's best cannon with it; or ground on a sandbar without a single powder puff fouling Spanish nostrils. How they'll laugh! Then the burghers will run to me to save them!" Agitated, he jumped in the air, landing with a thump. Then he chuckled. "And what is this poor engineer to do?" he asked mockingly, hands spread.

He relishes the failure of "War's End," and has a backup plan, Latham thought. He eyed the engineer curiously. When Philip II refused to employ him, Giambelli was so angry he'd changed sides. Now the Antwerp Senate had rejected his ideas, but he didn't seem dismayed. On the contrary, he was maniacally excited.

"Your workshop has the look of a project nearly finished," Latham ventured. "What exactly are you doing?"

Giambelli turned coy. "Honoured emissary, look around and draw your own conclusions. I deny you nothing; all doors and drawers are open to you. I have a meeting and will be back in an hour. We'll talk then." Bowing, he left the room.

The first thing Latham noticed were three clocks, each in a glass case, hanging from the ceiling close to holes in the wall. Bellows behind the gaps made them sway. When Giambelli called his apprentices, the cases stilled. Feet scurried, and everyone left.

Alone, Latham wandered around. On a bench below the clocks were hourglasses, presumably to monitor clocks accuracy. All the clocks had three hands: hours, minutes, seconds, like the ones he'd seen in the Sultan's observatory in Constantinople. The aim there was to calculate the motions of the planets, but Giambelli must have a different purpose. On the next table, five clocks were attached to lamps. He watched, amazed, as a lamp flared every few minutes. Self-lighting lamps were a new luxury only the wealthiest could afford. One clock was detached from its lamp and lay unwound, next to a flint and wicks.

Latham's logic was cryptography, and he was out of his depth. His emotions took over, and he floated back to the transcendent sky during the comet's visitation to Constantinople, transfixing the astronomers; Ibrahim's generous love for him; the importance clocks had for both. Wiping a tear, he brought himself back to besieged Antwerp.

"Talk to me," he begged the clocks.

No inspiration came, so he went to the office. Small tables were piled with papers. One contained a model two-masted ship labelled "72 tn." Moderate size. Beside it was a drawing of a pyramid, with dimensions that showed it would fit on the ship's deck.

The office led to a third room. Its thick iron-plated door, with a lock too intricate for even his picklocks, was open. He saw boxes of marble slabs, mortar, nails, chain-shot, pike blades. When he rubbed his finger in floor dust, he tasted charcoal: explosives.

Concluding that the clue was in the writing, he went back to the office. Pages were filled with equations and chemical symbols in elegant black script, notes in Latin. Latham suspected Giambelli's self-opinion swelled in direct proportion to how much he humiliated his interlocutor. That equation Latham grasped. Giambelli would only explain what Latham discovered for himself. Now he regretted his neglect of algebra at Oxford; he couldn't make any sense of the scribbles.

He went back to the drawing of the pyramid. Here was the only writing that wasn't elegant. Emphatic arrows scrawled sideways were in furious red, with the admonition *Sideways, not up!* three times in Italian. Latham reasoned: he is devoted to his art. His calculations had failed in application, and Giambelli wouldn't tolerate error in himself. That was what the raging scrawl, the change from Latin to Italian, meant. But Latham couldn't link explosives, equations, pyramid, clocks, and lamps.

Under the drawing of the pyramid was another mystery: a ship that had a mast attached to its bottom. Giambelli had inked a "?" next to it.

Latham was blowing out his cheeks in astonishment when Giambelli strode in. "I've been with a great clockmaker who agrees my plan is sound. Was your contemplation profitable?"

Latham hoped he wouldn't utterly shame himself. "You'll blow up the Kowenstyn dyke. A sideways explosion would be more potent than vertical, if it could be managed."

Giambelli cocked his head to the right. "Ah, you saw my scribbles. A good notion, but too late. The generals told the burghers two years ago to blow the dyke, but they wouldn't flood their own lands. The Spaniards control Kowenstyn. It's three miles long, and they patrol constantly. You'd need several breaches. You're very impractical, Walsingham's man."

Latham flushed and tried again. "Then, use fire-ships. But exploding forward rather than sideways would surely favour fire-ships."

Giambelli now cocked his head to the left.

Latham burst out, "You have the advantage of me, master engineer, and you abuse it dreadfully with your hints about clocks. Are you fixing the motions of planets? In

Constantinople, I saw Tariq-El-Din use clocks like this for astronomy. Remember the great foreigner who pays your pension. Her Majesty deserves an answer."

Giambelli blushed. He even bowed. "Sir, I've mocked too hard." His tone had a touch of sympathy. "No, I'm not doing astronomy. I'd never amuse myself disproving Ptolemy amidst the misery of a dying city. Besides, Copernicus has already done it.

"What I'm doing is amenable to logic. If you don't see what I'm making, with the freedom I gave you of my workshop, you're unfit for confidences. If you can't imagine my innovation, why would you believe it? I must be discreet. A loose tongue could ruin its effectiveness. However, I swear the Spaniard will grieve. Tell Sir Francis I've made a secret new compound for gunpowder. It's part of the truth."

Latham left the infuriating engineer and went to join a crowd ogling the monster ship, *War's End*. He hadn't spotted Hicks's promised tail and wondered if Hicks had invented one to let him feel safer than he was.

Everyone was staring at the huge ship. They looked happy, talking confidently about the monster's ability to put an end to all of Farnese's mischief. How it would annihilate both the bridge of boats across the River Scheldt and breach Kowenstyn Dyke, no one explained. *War's End* lived as myth: its brooding height; bulwarks thicker than two adolescents lying end-to-end; four soaring masts, tops reinforced with iron to make them bulletproof; three helms with rudders. Rafts piled with cork were anchored nearby, ready, theoretically, to float it.

War's End wasn't built for living. There were no visible cabins. Great caverns between decks gaped, hungry for cannon, balls and powder. Its pennants fluttered brazenly, proclaiming mind-scrambling vengeance, as if guided by archangels of the netherworld.

The dimensions of the ship reduced men crawling along its cross-trees to caterpillars, while the boats circumnavigating it, carrying clerks making notes, looked like toys in a child's model. The oars looked like tree trunks. Who could ply them? Latham hadn't seen any Samsons; food was getting short.

He imagined the ship in action: caterpillar muscles and minds touching wicks to powder, huge barrels gulping in the burning fuel, hurling off their caterpillar-size restraints, roaring their freedom to make their own maximum malice: choosing what flesh to shred, which spines to shatter, which structures to crumble. How different from the intimate hostility of sword fighting, or the close aiming of a gun at an enemy's unarmoured patch of cloth, or the hack and heave of pike. There you saw your enemy, could reckon your odds. Antwerp's monstrosity was something different: an undiscriminating mass annihilator.

That night he slipped out with the excellent farmer's wife, sweeping down the Scheldt on a pre-dawn ebb tide. The boat bridge had grown in the last two days, but Latham's boat, now empty of provisions, easily evaded Spanish nets. Using his Piso Prosperino papers again, Latham reached Boulogne two days later.

Meanwhile, in the common sleeping room of a workman's inn, a mason reached for a bucket and puked out his guts. He'd been sick for a week. When he recovered, he discovered that his purse had been stolen. The solicitous tavern owner called in a constable, but told the mason he must understand the authorities had more urgent things to do. Out of funds for bribes, Pieter's informer did his best, sketching Antwerp's walls showing no alterations in progress. Like the rest of Antwerp, he ogled *War's End*. He inquired at the Guild houses near Grote Market about a foreign engineer. He even found Giambelli's workshop, but couldn't get in, and learned nothing. He, too, took a boat down the Scheldt, deliberately bumping the Spanish bridge. He used Boels' letter of identification, and after a cordial debriefing, was allowed to leave.

Latham used the mason's report in his letter to Idiaquez, confirming the bastions were not altered, and naming Federigo Giambelli. He described *War's End* as '*the mightiest artillery*

platform ever devised. If it swims, you'll have grief.' He added his
unsought-for advice: *His Majesty should negotiate, rather than
let such monstrous innovation be loosed upon the world.*

When he met Hicks again, he drew their monster ship,
and repeated Giambelli assurance that it would sink from
bad mathematics. "The ship will test his credibility. If it sinks,
you can trust him. If it steers and fires, Her Majesty can stop
his pension."

He described all he'd seen in the workshop: clocks,
equations, self-lighting lamps, model ship, pyramid cone, the
ship with a mast on its bottom. "I'm glad I braved Antwerp,
but didn't grasp his project. He said I couldn't read the clues
he spread around."

Hicks was as puzzled as Latham. "Who'd think the fate
of Antwerp depends on scribbled equation?" They concluded
that explosives with a new compound would be used against
the dyke or any tunnels Farnese built. They couldn't imagine
anything else.

"David, did you invent a follower? I didn't see anyone."

Hicks smile. "That's the commendation I'll put in his
files." He described a drayman who cleaned the street outside
Giambelli's workshop.

Latham gave a start of belated recognition. "He was good.
Tell Her Majesty that Antwerp will fall. These citizens aren't
built for endless sacrifice. They rely on their inventions. It
seems to be Dutch nature."

He described Don Cristobal's *looker*. "It brings distant
objects closer. But the apothecary who built it was hanged
for not paying the tenth penny tax. The monster ship is an
extraordinary artillery platform, but will it steer? What are the
clocks for? Or a ship with an under-water mast and sail? These
things can't stop Farnese. In the end, he wants victory more."
He read out the conclusion of his written report: *Thus you
taste the harvest of your harshness. With foreign Catholic princes
dismayed by your treatment of recusants, the burden of saving the
Dutch falls on you.*

Hicks laughed. "What do you gain by endless nagging?"

"Princes shouldn't be obdurate when the ingenuity of annihilation grows by the day. I write the same advice to Idiaquez."

"Well, God protect you! Rest now. The next fighting season, you'll watch the siege from Spanish lines, as Piso Prosperino."

With that, Hicks retrieved Latham's English travelling papers.

CHAPTER 22
SIDEWAYS, NOT UP!

When Latham ran the Antwerp blockade in October 1584, Farnese's bridge of boats was a quarter done. By December, it was half finished. Construction stopped when carpenters hammering planks joining two moving barges slipped on ice, fell into the River Scheldt, and drowned. The fighting season also ended. Latham, returned to Boulogne from the Spanish camp, looked forward to mulled wine, placid dinners, and a soft bed with heated bricks.

A few days into his rest, a cart driver rattled into the snowy courtyard, shouting for the landlady and the foreigner, Signor Prosperino. Servants unloaded sacks of salted beef, root vegetables and barrels of candied fruit. There was one box for Latham.

In his rooms, Latham inspected it. Two Ottoman forms glued to the sides showed it came from Constantinople. The first paper, a coloured icon called *Damga Resmi*, certified the quality of the goods. A second paper, *Capitulation*, in two languages, approved Master Joris Boels, Fleming, as a trader with favourable customs duties and safety guarantees throughout the Ottoman Empire.

Latham jumped up, full of relief and trepidation. He was thrilled to hear from Joris, but afraid he'd reverted to his mercantile roots, neglecting his duty to recruit informers.

To postpone the reckoning, he did errands: checking his horse; visiting a barber; ordering new shirts and a doublet from a tailor. Finally, in mid-afternoon, he opened the box. Lined with tin under linen, it contained several sacks and a flat oil-skin-wrapped packet. Latham smelled coffee beans, very welcome. A licence for Master Joris Boels to export coffee and plant seeds to Europe was attached to each sack. In Latin and Arabic, it was signed by Ahmet Gul.

The licence wasn't the only paper. A completed order for more coffee awaited a buyer's signature and banker's note for payment, the inked-in price allowing for no haggling. Latham pursed his lips. Was he now his servant's agent? Find a buyer, send forms and payment back. What an enterpriser he'd hired out of misery eight years ago! He wondered if Joris was cheating him, as he did to others the breadth of Europe, or whether this was the best price he could get for Frankish buyers. Coffee in Constantinople was cheap; the government set the price. But Ibrahim had told him Sultan Murad hated monopolies. To mitigate their influence, he allowed traders to export commodities to Europe for whatever buyers would pay.

The flat packet contained drawings. In one, a bowl of figs had the figure eight among the fruit. In a drawing of a lemon tree, the lemons looked so ripe that he wanted to scrape off the rind and savour the bitterness. If the number eight was a letter key and lemon signified invisible ink, then Joris hadn't neglected his duty.

Relieved, he took time to study the other drawings. The grown-up Ahmet Gul was standing by a carriage. His oversized head now sat on a sturdy neck. It still tilted, but no longer looked as if it would topple off if you shoved his shoulders. He was about five feet eight inches, judging by the carriage, which was why Joris included it as a prop. Gul wore the green gown and two-tiered turban, black roll on top of white, signifying a secretary to one of the Grand Vizier's lieutenants. He stared at the world with frank delight. A chief assistant to an assistant chief wielded considerable power, and tax collectors had little need for subtlety.

The last drawing was Joris's self-portrait. The gangly resentful adolescent that Latham had hired was now a confident twenty-three-year-old. A hint of coiled violence still came from the bare hands clutching his preferred weapon, a crowbar. He'd adopted brash European fashion: short breeches and a padded codpiece. His features were as bland as ever, and, characteristically, he had a wounded beast on him. Nestling on his collar was a black lizard with brilliant yellow dots, whose tail had been bitten off. Still, looking at Latham was a confident young burgher.

He found the coded papers in a double layer of burlap. It took him until the next day to make sense of them, because Joris still reversed letters and numbers. As Latham ached through a night of crossings-out, he remembered Walsingham's code-breaker, Thomas Phelippes, saying the hardest decryption was when a writer botched his own tongue. It took Latham until dawn before he had any plausible content: Gul's list of new Portuguese refugees.

As he heated the blank paper, which was Joris's communication, he hummed,

And can the magician a secret divine
From bonfire and lemon brine?

Five nonsense names emerged in lemon-juice ink, and Latham sighed. After a break, he compared them to Gul's list and found five approximate matches. Five new informers. Latham stood and rubbed his eyes. Joris had done well, but if he couldn't code, he'd never be safe. He had to come back.

He copied both lists for Walsingham. To Idiaquez, he sent only Gul's list of Portuguese refugees. He believed that their departure was already known to Spanish authorities, and he couldn't harm them more. He used the information to make his customary exhortation to more moderate behaviour. *This list should grieve you. His Majesty sent the most rigorous inquisitor in the world to Portugal, Cardinal Granville who brought the Inquisition to the Netherlands twenty years ago. New Christians in Portugal quake, no matter how long ago their ancestors converted. They feel the flames before Granville furnishes his new office. You lose their taxes and skills, gaining only the likelihood they'll do mischief against you, resenting their displacement, as most men would.*"

Latham was in a good mood when he returned to the tailor's shop. "Signor Prosperino," the tailor said, "do you know a thin, olive-skinned man, a chin wart poking through his beard? He named you. He's proud because he wears current court fashion, but sateen not satin; cotton that cleans with streaks."

Latham knuckled his temple. The man sounded familiar. Then it came to him. Cheap copies of court fashion. This man had spoken to him in Saint-Denis Cathedral the morning that Campion's death was announced. Assistant to a Spanish official, he'd let slip that he was involved with the Duke of Guise, and presumably his plots. "I met him long ago. He's not a friend."

"He came into the shop and asked if Signor Piso Prosperino was well now. It was a monstrously rude question."

Latham's good mood vanished. Did Spanish officials suspect him of double-dealing already? Larva of the dragonfly, his mind screamed, *half transformed, where's your shadowed brick?*

The tailor was watching him, curious.

Neutrally, Latham answered, "We met once in Saint-Denis Cathedral. I had gut sickness, and he offered me the monks' remedies, which I didn't need. You describe him aptly, Monsieur."

"Tailors have sharp eyes, Signor." He laughed. "God give you joy in avoiding him." Latham clapped him appreciatively on the shoulder and paid for his clothes.

The next morning, an unseasonably warm sun dried the ground. Latham put on his mirrored hat, and, dodging dripping gutters and trees, walked down to the harbour. Near the Swooping Gull tavern, a thin olive skinned figure shrank against the wall. It was the man he'd met in Saint-Denis, older, of course. An amateur. Latham grinned.

After dinner at the tavern, he went back to his rooms, threw his cloak on the bed and collected coffee beans and Joris's papers. On his damp walk back from the harbour, a plan to help the Beaumonts and Joris had come to him. He intended to visit Hélène Michaud. She'd heeded his warnings about the rupture between the French king and her kinsman, the Duke of Guise, and had left the royal laundry and bought an inn five miles away.

When he picked up his cloak, he saw the letter on the bed. A touch of the seal showed that it had been opened and resealed. It was a stinging rebuke from a clerk; not even Idiaquez himself. The secretary had reviewed Latham's file, the clerk wrote. His reports were thin compared to earlier work. If Latham desired continued wellbeing, he must provide materially useful information forthwith.

Latham breathed raggedly. He hadn't been uncovered as Walsingham's agent. On the contrary, it confirmed that he served Spain, badly. But there was no way around its ominous message.

He tucked the letter under his doublet, hired a guard and rode inland, pulling up at the entrance of a grey stone mansion. Scaffolding at the sides and hammering from within suggested major renovations. A petticoat repair girl he remembered from the laundry showed him to Hélène's office.

Hélène stood, delighted to see him. Despite the mess, she looked relaxed.

"Mademoiselle, I'm relieved to see you well and your chief

girls with you," Latham said. Kneeling for his customary exaggerated reverences, he intoned, "But I'm heartbroken I wasn't the gallant…"

"Ha, ha!" she laughed. "Ah, Gidon, I miss our games, but they belong to an earlier time." "Seriously," she added, "I am glad to be safe, but confess I'm bored. I thought courtiers were narrow primpers, passing off scraps from the attic of their brains as learning. But they did glitter. They amused me. My clients here will be narrow and dull. Stupidity is more enjoyable when it shines."

"Poor tragical maid," Latham laughed. "I can't turn dross to gold plate, but I can get you some glitter. I'm here because I have a commodity that will entice the better sort of clientele to your inns. I also want to discuss your kinswoman, Marie Beaumont."

"I can't give her a position here. I sent a tutor. She has her alphabet in French and Latin, and numbers come to her naturally. I can't hire a pouter and eavesdropper. Her best quality is tenderness to her Papa. She's a shrew to her Mama. I can't employ her, ever."

Latham laughed. "I heard you the first time, Baroness. I have a solution. Be patient as I explain. It has three parts. First, smell this."

He pushed coffee beans at her, expounding on their wonders as a tonic. They went to the kitchen, where he made a steaming dish in the Ottoman style. The cook and plate washers drank the sludge first, their faces passing from distaste to gratification. Then Hélène tried it, her grimace curving into delight.

"You see?" Latham urged. "It vanquishes melancholy. Glittering ones will come, to find they're even more marvellous than they thought."

Back in Hélène's office, they enjoyed a discussion of various stimulants: coca leaves, tobacco, coffee, and how they complemented alcohol. Finally, she spoke the words Latham hoped to hear: "How can I buy this in quantity?"

Showing her Joris's licence, he offered her a reliable supply.

"Well," Hélène said, "It's a pretty project, but how does it help my ill-starred kin, the Beaumonts?"

Latham hesitated. Manipulating the future of two young people he was bound to by affection, but not blood, seemed outrageous. But every day marriages were arranged for worse reasons. "I've found a husband for Marie. I ask you to get her parents' approval."

"Marriage?" Hélène sat back, pulling her lips. "This is a surprise, Gidon. You've livened up my day. You know she has no dowry now? She's not a great beauty and has an obstinate nature. Who'd marry her?"

"My manservant Joris Boels, which will have the benefit to me of bringing him back to France. With his licence, he can hire a factor to import coffee. Auguste and Jeanne need a man of substance. Joris will earn enough to support the family."

He hesitated again. How to put this? "No man can ever guess woman's suffering…"

Hélène looked at him attentively.

Latham plunged on. "I have a regard for Marie. I've seen that she burns with desire, as maids past first menses do. But she has a terror of the marriage bed, death from childbirth or childbed fever. Or if she and her husband live, the decay of affection. This seems wise in one so young. She wants a man who'll often be absent. Joris will travel for me, and she can go with him or stay. I promised Marie that if I saw a man with enough substance to satisfy her parents, who would also be absent, I'd make the introduction. Joris fulfils these requirements."

"As I remember," Hélène said, "he barely speaks."

"He has a defect, yes, but it's somewhat improved. He's resourceful, loyal and brave, and has qualities not obvious at first sight." He grinned inwardly, thinking of Joris's competence in a brawl, his apprenticeship in the arts of love in Constantinople's better brothels. "If you agree, I'll propose the match to his uncle-godfather, who'll get his parents' approval."

"And will this odd paragon like the girl?" Hélène asked. "A grown man won't be ordered about by one not his father."

"He looks for his ideal *her*, a blonde Madonna. A whore. Marie doesn't fit his notion, I concede. But he really wants a clever maid of high temperament. Besides, she has a little noble blood. The Boels have none."

Hélène could find no fault in the plan. She signed a banker's note for coffee for all her inns and promised to write to Auguste and Jeanne.

While Latham was putting the papers in his bag, he added, "As mistress of a large female empire, you must know how a man's seed can be blocked. Marie is terrified of giving birth. I rely on you to advise your kinswoman."

Hélène sucked in her breath. "It's illegal, Gidon."

Latham gave her a hard stare.

"Well, as to that I say nothing, nothing, nothing," she grumbled.

Taking the grumble as assent, he kissed her hand and took his leave.

When she was alone, Hélène took out a third unofficial book, one she'd never shown Latham. Of course, she knew dispensers of potions and devices to spoil or block male seed, and midwives willing to scrape out womb tissue that was the beginning of a bastard. There was always some scandal in a royal laundry. In the book was a drawing of a plump young girl, intelligent looking, almost pretty. It was Hélène Michaud, newly pregnant with a married noble's baby. She rubbed her finger over the round belly, a young innocent whose prospects had been wrenched apart. She wept a long time for the long-ago scraping and bleeding that had made her thin again, and impervious to male interest ever since.

Approaching Boulogne, Latham had to edge around black-robed Benedictines on a pilgrimage to the Virgin of the Sea at Notre-Dame. A stocky man with one arm in a sling and an eyepatch was begging blessings and alms. Latham fished a few billons from his waist pouch then gasped. The beggar was Hicks's manservant, seeking Latham. They muttered tersely. The beggar instructed Latham to return to Antwerp to report from Spanish lines. Latham whispered that a Spaniard was following him; a letter to him from Madrid had been opened and badly resealed; that the letter was a rebuke from Idiaquez, that for Latham to keep his head, he needed true intelligence for Spain. Hicks must meet him in Wimille with it in May. They broke apart, Hicks's man bowing with gratitude for alms, Latham loftily waving him up.

Back in his rooms, Latham wrote to Joris. He enclosed Hélène's purchase order, and instructed him to hire a local factor to handle future contracts. He also told Joris to put his recruits in touch with the English envoy and return to Boulogne. "Be pox-free," he ended.

To Idiaquez, he tossed caution aside, writing that he was close to military secrets of urgent interest to Spain. His quill jabbed the page as if its honed edge would induce Walsingham to disgorge a shining item. At the harbour the next day, he paid a courier to take his letter to the Spanish Embassy in Paris, repeating the address loudly. He chuckled when he glimpsed wart-chin through his mirrored hat approaching the courier. Then he started for Antwerp.

"So Pieter, Joris can enjoy the felicities of marriage," Latham concluded, after outlining the benefits of the match. He and Pieter Boels were in a Spanish officers' tavern, a hut near Farnese's boat bridge. Pieter had made his April grain delivery, and he and Latham were relaxing over wine.

There was now a settled feel to the siege: Farnese controlled both river forts, St Martin on the Flanders bank and St Philip's on the Brabant bank. The boat bridge was finished, and on the other side of Antwerp, his men controlled Kowenstyn Dyke. Antwerp was sealed. Latham and Boels were the only customers, and Latham had to wave away the serving boy who hovered, offering refills.

Pieter was on the point of approving the marriage when the door banged open. He said nothing, instead listening to three infantry officers who burst in, mid-argument.

"They'll attack tonight."

"We've seen no scouts."

"We caught their divers cutting boat cables, brave bastards."

"That's rumour. There are no prisoners."

"Still, it's coming."

"Yes, they're coming. We're done for if both fleets attack at once."

They stopped when they saw civilians. The last soldier had spoken with a roughness Latham knew well, the growl of a street thug grown to authority. He jumped up, arms open. "Juan Alvarado! Assistant sergeant-major. Congratulations. I'm amazed to see you here. Last time we met was on Monte Viso. Whose colours do you wear?" Alvarado had an insignia featuring a black eagle in flight, a red castle in its claws.

Alvarado's face creased in a near-toothless grin. "Ninth Company, Signor Prosperino, though I miss Don Cristobal." He tailed off, realising that he sounded ungrateful for his promotion. He introduced Latham and Boels, winking at Latham to acknowledge his mistake at Mons years earlier when he nearly hanged Latham as a saboteur. Latham inclined his head, thinking: *wrong then, right today.*

The soldiers joined Latham and Boels, calling for wine and the advertised goose pie.

"Sir, you sounded melancholy, as if the oracle spoke ill," Pieter Boels said to Alvarado. "Surely nothing can break our bridge. Farnese says it will be his sepulchre or path to Antwerp. It's his path. Alexander Farnese's as invincible as his ancient namesake."

Alvarado scratched his head, puzzled. He didn't recall Alexander the Great besieging Antwerp. The oldest man, a colonel, explained. "Our fear, Master Boels, is that the Zeeland navy, a large and wicked force, is waiting to sail through any breach made by the Antwerp fleet, trapped on the other side of our bridge. The Antwerp fleet is smaller, but also wicked. A joint attack would destroy a blockade it took a year to make. A gap wide enough for two galleons could mince us up. We're just fifteen hundred defenders because most of our forces man the dyke."

"But with the distance between Dutch fleets, how could they coordinate?" Pieter asked.

"That's the question," Alvarado grunted.

There was silence.

"Beacons," the youngest officer offered. "And this is rat pie, not goose." He spat a mouthful onto the floor.

"You'll be happier and fuller if you call it goose," Alvarado snorted. "Beacons can't be made out in a firefight, fool. There must be pre-arrangement, with some method for verifying."

The rat pie-eater's vivid clothes suggested he'd arrived recently. Latham smiled, remembering Alvarado's disdain for well-to-do raw recruits, like William Boels.

"Pre-arrangement, beacons, devil's arts doesn't matter. Alexander has cancelled all leave," the colonel declared. "We're to bring pikes, nets, hooked poles, chains and buckets to the bridge. See guns loaded, everyone on alert. Come, time to get it done."

Latham and Boels bowed as the officers left, wishing them safety in God's care.

Boels wanted to step onto the bridge, so they went outside. Despite the weapons poking out of every archway, and on every surface, it was hard to imagine in the fragile early spring, that the metal was real. Or hear cannon belching and screams of the wounded intruding on fields glowing with tentative green, interspersed with impudent yellow daisies and delicate white or lilac hollyhocks.

"New life," Pieter said with an expansive gesture. "I approve Joris's marriage,".

Latham thanked him as they passed the fort and approached the first barge. A sentry stopped them, despite passes that allowed them freedom of the camp.

"I'll take you, Signor." Alvarado's rough growl again. He'd seen them approach, and wanted to show them the fortifications. Proudly he ushered them onto the first wooden plank of the road across the barges. At this stage, the war's momentum was balanced between Farnese's military prowess and the geography of a revolt sheltered by tricky waters, along with periodic help from Spain's rivals.

The bridge was astonishing. Barges, each sixty feet long, spanned the river's twenty-four hundred feet. Each barge was joined to the next by cables and iron chains, the thick wooden planks over them making a road. The distance between barges was about twenty feet, allowing for flexibility at ebb and flood tides. Alvarado explained the design, for practical details came easily to him. Latham whistled. He'd experienced tidal violence on his last visit and had wondered how Farnese could accommodate it. "Brilliant," he said.

Alvarado swelled with this praise as if he'd designed the bridge himself. In this pride of ownership, he was like everyone here. Any man who'd participated in the body-numbing work believed that the bridge's completion depended on him. And the men's women, who cooked, loved, sewed, and applied herbal doses, also took pride in the bridge. As Alvarado threaded between soldiers readying weapons, he told them that the piles anchoring the barges were seventy-five feet deep. Leaning over a barge, he showed them a gun platform attached to a pile; its guns could hole a fishing boat at sixty yards. Two wooden bastions on the bridge bristled with artillery. These batteries complemented the fort cannons and the guns of two galleons anchored by the forts. There was nowhere beyond gun range. Alvarado pointed out a second boat bridge some distance away. A bridge to protect the main bridge, eleven groups of three boats cabled together.

Latham wondered how Giambelli could breach these defences. Relieving the siege was now his job, since Antwerp's monster ship, *War's End*, was being re-built to correct its faulty design. Did the Mantuan still think his invention would make the Spanish king remember his name?

Dusk greyed the horizon, bringing lookouts with torches, and Alvarado escorted Pieter and Latham back to the hut. Again, they were the only customers.

It wasn't long before trumpets signalled lights on the water. Drums throbbed, boots pounded stone. "I'm going," Pieter announced, strapping on his sword. He grabbed a pike leaning against the wall. "Will you?"

"No. I fought at Saint-Ghislain. I'll help move the wounded if there are any. You mustn't go, Pieter. You know nothing about repelling fire-ships."

"These soldiers are used to it. It's my chance for action," Pieter insisted, racing outside. Latham's last view of him that night was of a lanky frame twisting into a trotting helmeted horde. He understood Pieter's excitement–the spirit of Mars had once suffused him too–but his feeling tonight was bleak dread.

More trumpets blared. There was a sudden stop in the rush, the crowd compressing as a path was cleared by shoving guards. To cheers, Farnese and his aides took positions near the first barge. Farnese wasn't shy of the front lines, and his men adored him for it.

Latham wandered to the stables. Seeing an abandoned horse and cart, he mounted and rode along a track by the river bank. At the water's edge, soldiers were holding poles and pikes. They looked tense and experienced. Some sat on moored rafts which had hooks along their sides. *Did one of them try to net me last year, when I hurtled through the bridge's gap on the flood tide?* Latham mused. *Curious thing, being a double agent. I would have killed them then. Tonight, I'd carry them to the surgeon. So, are they enemy or friend?*

The water glowed with tiny lights. At first, they approached in a controlled progression. Then one after another meandered, thrust by an uneven current, but inexorably gliding towards them. What caused the motion? A sailor would know, Latham realised. He narrowed his eyes, wishing he had Cristo's *looker.* Dimly, he made out tiny figures scrambling down ship sides or diving off decks to reach small boats alongside, and pulling away. As they left, sails, rigging and decks burst into flames. A breeze wafted acrid tar and the sound of crackling fire at him.

"Fire-ships!" shouted the men on the rafts, echoed by lookouts down river. Distant trumpets and drums summoned every available soldier. It was slow, eerie, serene. Latham had no idea how many ships were coming. With the multitude of lights, he couldn't tell fire on a ship from its glowering watery reflection. He assumed the veterans could.

"Right, men. Three close and small," shouted a soldier on one of the rafts. His group of eight men picked up their hooked poles and stood. A minute later they jeered. Two boats entangled with a log and were drifting toward the middle of the river, while the third was caught by spears jutting from the raft sides and burned out harmlessly. There were many fire-ships—the shout "Right, men, three close"—rang out again and again. But there were also many logs and rubbish. Over the next two hours, more ships came, in groups of various numbers. Some bumped the river banks, fizzling out before they reached the bridges. Others bumped Spanish defences. Troops on the rafts and bridge shoved them away or hooked them close and doused the fires. It seemed futile, but as time went on and on and on, it exhausted the defenders. Latham thought at least fifty burning vessels had floated by, but of course, he still couldn't tell substance from reflection.

There was a pause, the river returning to a normal inky look. Alvarado rode up to join Latham. He was grinning. "Our generals say we've beaten them back. What a waste of tar, wood, hemp and turpentine. Ha, ha, ha! We're dancing and singing on the bridge." Dismounting, he shouted out-of-tune:

Antwerp may be joyful,
But great should be its grief,
For Spain has doused its fire-ships,
Or tangled them in weeds.

Don't you remember us singing a version of that ballad when we beat Genlis, Signor? There's no sign of the Zeeland fleet. Your friend was knocked over by the smells. Ha, ha! Hello, what's this?"

They stared at two new ships approaching, one behind the other. They were burning lightly, wisps and flickers, and looked unmanned. Latham shifted uneasily; he saw no ant-sized men scrambling off. These ships had two masts, a weird construction on the decks, and were much larger than the others. He recognised the pyramid he'd seen in Giambelli's drawings, with the scrawl *Sideways, not up.* A sudden burst of rain blotted out his view. Then, as quickly as it came, it passed. The first ship loomed opposite them, mid-channel. With a 'pfft' stink of wet powder and smouldering tar it grounded on a sandbar.

"What's its name?" Alvarado asked. The boldly painted name was in Dutch, which he still couldn't read.

Fortune, Latham replied.

Men untied a raft, preparing to pole to the grounded ship.

"It'll make mine," Alvarado chuckled. "They'll get iron if they douse the rigging fire. I want a share for my men. We can sell it."

"Juan, don't go." Latham grabbed his arm.

"Why?"

Latham couldn't explain because he didn't know. The ship resembled the model he'd seen in Giambelli's workshop, but he wasn't sure. Even if it was, it might be as much of a flop as it looked. "What if there's a bomb?" he asked Alvarado.

"If there is, rain drowned the wick. You can help me take the iron back in the cart." He scrambled down the bank and leapt onto the raft.

Assuming the raft men knew what they were about, he watched admiringly as they scrambled up the ship's side. While they were milling around the quiet deck, the second big ship drifted past. "That one's called *Hope*," one of them shouted, laughing.

Latham watched *Hope* drift past the grounded *Fortune*, avoiding logs and sandbars. It slid through a gap between three-boat formations in the bridge protecting the main bridge. A freshening wind thrust it toward the main bridge's second barge.

"The wick's out, comrades," was the last human sound Latham heard before *Fortune* blew up in a roar muffled by slapping waves. Fire and a lateral eruption of metal and stone annihilated the boarders in seconds. Burning body parts and chunks of debris hurtled into the air, and then tumbled down, swept away by an angry river. How did the bomb go off if the wick was out and the ship unmanned?

Then he understood what he should have seen months ago. Clocks had sparked flints to fire the powder at a set time. Giambelli had invented a timed, self-detonating bomb. Latham had seen clocks being tested for accuracy; clocks attached to lamps that self-lit; flints beside them. *Sideways, not up.* Lateral annihilation. He hadn't had the imagination to put it together.

Shouting warnings, he cantered to the main bridge, the cart bucketing. No one turned his way. All were watching *Hope* glide ever closer, while a few near Farnese's party, after a sudden agitation, led the governor and his aides ashore. Trumpets summoned reinforcements.

Seconds scrolled by but felt like hours. Latham dismounted and ran, puffing, along the road beside the diagonal fort wall, around a curved bastion to the door. He was waving and shouting, but everyone on ramparts or aiming their guns through windows stared at the bridge. When he reached the sentries, he babbled the danger.

"Brainsick," the sentries concluded, hauling him through the doorway and shoving him behind the stone wall. He fell, winded. A sentry kicked him and told him not to move, or he'd be skewered.

Hope struck close to where Farnese was moments earlier. And nothing happened. Latham heard a sentry cheer that soldiers were on the deck, yells from the soldiers that the smoke was wispy and there was no wick, and there was a huge strange stone cone on it. Hearing the ping of axes on stone and suspenseful quiet, he got up and crouched by the fort door. The sentries had gone to the bridge.

Then a tall wild glare obliterated the stars. Unimaginable horror was unleashed. With a calamitous roar, as if the world's every cannon fired at once, the earth heaved and shook and the air filled with missiles. Latham, dragonfly larva clinging to shadowed brick, saw chunks of rampart stone hit the ground around him, throwing up choking dust, stone shards and earth. Chain-shot, stone slabs, marble pieces, plough-coulters, spearheads, pike blades, cannonballs, anything that could crush, shatter or dismember, flew, finding targets in screaming flesh, tents, walls, and wooden stables. Latham looked up. Severed limbs swirled like a flock of migrating birds. A whimpering page boy crawled close to him. He held the boy close, but he twisted away in panic and ran for the stable beyond the fort. A hurtling armour-plated leg decapitated him, sending his head with its bright blue pin-fastened cap over the wall.

Latham fainted. When he came to it was quieter, the air still. He patted himself: chest, thighs, shoulders, ankles, head; to his amazement, he was whole. Unsteadily, he stood, grabbed a lantern and walked through the doorless entrance. On the way to the bank, he passed bodies. Somewhere a dog moaned, and he kicked away a cat clawing his torn hose. A strange sky greeted him, sparse stars winking through streaky clouds that moved in an indifferent procession from west to east. It was moonless, with Mars an orange blur. The banked clouds that had unleashed rain earlier had moved north, blackening that part of the sky, while around him smoke twisted up in tendrils as if to meet the gauze above. Glowing red blobs on the river marked fire-ships burning out.

Latham seemed to be alone, the sole survivor of Giambelli's apocalypse. The ship, the blockhouse, the men, many barges, and large sections of the plank road were gone, a huge breach in the bridge smouldering. Picking his way around embers, wood bits, torn pennants and debris, he found a stable part of a barge and peered down. There were countless bodies, some floating face up, some snared in nets or jammed against the pile, some being swept downriver. Most horrible was the detached arm wrapped around a piece of plank, identifiable only by scraps of insignia of half an eagle clutching half a red castle: Ninth Company colours.

Not everyone was dead. Two wounded men cried out. Latham put his hand in the water then snatched it back. It was scalding hot. He took off his shirt and lowered it, pulling the nearest man onto their tiny patch of stability. The man shrank back, crying pitiably as Latham shone the lantern at him. His face and arms were pink and puckered by the hot river, but he could walk and lift. Together, they helped the second man. Miraculously, he had grabbed the pile strut, hung monkey-like with his legs and hands, avoiding getting boiled as the water rushed by. He staggered, his mouth opening and shutting noiselessly. With no other visible damage, befuddlement seemed to be his malady.

Despite hearing more cries for help, they had to rush to higher ground. A new terror had begun. This *thing* Giambelli had made wrested from nature control of the tides. The Scheldt ebbed, not according to moon time, as Latham knew it from when he ran the blockade, but in minutes instead of hours. The water sucked out violently and roared back just as violently, pouring over the barges and flooding the bank. Astonishment at water slapping his knees brought the shocked soldier back to consciousness. "Them ships got us here," he muttered.

That's when Latham finally grasped the satanic brilliance of Giambelli's plan. The engineer never expected fire-ships to breach the bridge. Released slowly, their job was to crowd the bridge with troops, and exhaust them with long snaring, dousing and pushing, readying them for the bomb ships. King Philip would certainly remember the Mantuan's name.

More survivors arrived. One soldier, shrugging off water-logged breeches and boots, babbled that the saints had saved him. Tossed into the air near St Philip's Fort, he had flown across the river, had been deposited by St Christopher in weeds near St. Martin's Fort, and had paddled ashore. He twirled his arms, laughing maniacally and singing, "I'm a bird." He had nothing more than a bruise on his forehead. Another man joined them, pulling hay out of his hair; he, too, had flown and landed in a haystack. Apart from scratches, he was healthy. Camp women also joined them, emerging from huts beyond the fort, faces smeared with stone dust and ash.

Everyone who could stand collected the wounded. *Hellburners*, they called the bomb ships. No one had ever imagined such a weapon. They believed Farnese was dead. A barber-surgeon who teamed up with Latham had been near the governor's party. In a quivering voice, he told his story as he and Latham loaded a moaning man onto a cloak-covered door and slogged through calf-deep water to a makeshift sick room on the first floor of the fort.

He said the same thing over and over, repetition pinning him to reality. "When *Hope* glided to the bridge, a young officer rushed up to Farnese, weeping that he had a dread vision of carnage; he insisted the general leave the bridge. He clutched Farnese's sleeve, violating all protocols, and wouldn't let go. "Farnese is, oh, my Lady of Mercy, was, as superstitious as the next man. He and his aides backed ashore. But they all fell when the ship blew up and couldn't be roused. They're dead."

Back at the bridge, more survivors were joining the rescue efforts. Every few minutes they paused, staring downriver, dreading the Zeeland fleet they expected to sail through the breach, guns blazing unanswered, mincing them up. They stared upriver, expecting to see the Antwerp fleet, the joint attack that logically should follow the explosion.

On Latham's third trip, he heard a wholly unexpected sound: cheers. And an astonishing sight. Farnese had woken up. He was rallying soldiers, his voice raspy with dust. "It's not what was done to the bridge that matters, comrades, but what the enemy sees has been done. The enemy, comrades, hasn't appeared. We have terrible losses. My chief officers are dead; hundreds of your friends are dead. But I'm here, and you're here. Almighty God spared us for His Divine purpose. Where is the Zeeland fleet? Where is the Antwerp fleet? Not here. The enemy doesn't know his success. Success not carried forward is failure. Plug the gaps. Make a line, no matter how thin. We'll know its frailty, but the enemy won't. Spare no effort. There's time to grieve later."

The next two days and nights disappeared in unrelenting salvaging, patching and hammering. By the time rebel scouts came close enough to realise that their bomb had made a great enough breach to break the blockade, the bridge looked repaired. Why they delayed was a mystery, but the Zeeland fleet stayed away. Antwerp was again sealed up.

His help no longer needed at the bridge, Latham began to look for Pieter Boels, his two servants and grain carts. When he got to the field where vendors pitched tents, Pieter's tent, servants and carts were gone. The field was gouged by tombstones and metal missiles from the bomb, and shredded canvas and broken poles were strewn everywhere. There was a busy din of boys and women putting up flimsy shelters from the debris. A gawking chattering crowd stood around one great hole. A marble slab from the bomb had penetrated the earth beyond the height of a man. Latham hired a camp boy to dig with him around Pieter's vanished tent. A day's work yielded one book of sodden tables of commodity sales and another of symbols that were Pieter's code keys, which he burned.

On the fifth day, he found Pieter in a farmhouse three miles from camp. A cannonball had shattered its barn, but the house was undamaged, its inhabitants safe. The farmer's wife, a sturdy shapeless woman of middle years, led Latham to a makeshift attic bedroom, where he found Pieter in a sad condition. He was under a wool blanket, shivering, despite the warm day.

He smiled weakly at Latham. "A tombstone hit me," he whispered. "Never saw it. They say I was unconscious for two days. A joke, no? To be laid low by a death marker. I have a piece. Use it on my gravestone."

Latham demurred. "Pieter, be optimistic. You'll be up in a few weeks."

"No. It pleased God to take my arm." Latham pulled back the blanket; Pieter's left arm had been amputated below the elbow. It was freshly bandaged.

"That's no hindrance," Latham assured him, but Pieter had fallen asleep before he finished the sentence. He stayed, sponging his sub-agent's face with a vinegared towel. For hours he sponged every fifteen minutes, listening to the sleeping man's unintelligible mumbles, in the interim searching his clothes and the furniture for compromising papers. There were none.

When he descended the uneven stairs to the kitchen, the farmer's wife, a person of obvious grace, explained that her husband, away tending relatives at the moment, had found the unconscious Pieter in a field, beaten off thieving urchins and brought him back. They'd sent for the surgeon, who took the arm off when gangrene appeared. "The poor man bore it with utmost bravery," she said. Latham thanked her profusely. The purse he gave her brought stunned gratitude to her seamed face.

A week later, Pieter deteriorated. His hosts moved him to their bedroom and put pallets on the kitchen floor for themselves. Pieter breath was light and rapid, and he gave off a fetid smell. "I'm so relieved to see you, Edward," he got out, then dozed for an hour. As weak as he was, he was lucid. When he woke, he continued his thought as if there'd been no interruption. "The surgeon's long face tells me all. Please take my will from my saddlebag and give it to my lawyer in Cambrai. Also, my written approval of Joris's marriage."

Latham stayed all day, helping the farmer's wife lift Pieter from soiled sheets, wash him, change his bandage, and hold him over the close stool. That evening, Pieter woke. "I'm a widower, Edward, and my sons went to Geneva to be Calvinists. They repudiated me. You didn't know that, did you? I'm leaving everything to Joris and William. Now, tell me everything about the bomb and the bridge."

"Is that what you want?"

"A story will keep me alive." His eyes were intent.

Latham nodded. "First, dear friend, your carts and servants are gone. I believe they fled."

Pieter's eyes crinkled in amusement, "Thieves. I can't blame them." Then his face went opaque with pain. "Tell me my bedtime story."

"It's grim, Pieter. A thousand killed. There's never been a weapon like this, the first timed self-detonating bomb. Giambelli invented it, and we are still seeing its effects. Days after the attack, horses went sick. When the water trough was emptied, they found a decomposing toe at the bottom. The siege continues, but the misery is intolerable. The rebels now understand the opportunity they lost. Almost every night fire-ships come; there are trumpets and drums every few hours. The word *Hellburners* is on every tongue. Two new breaches were made by small bomb ships, but the men repaired them. I don't know if the rebels are low on powder and missiles, but the explosions weren't as strong. One ship was amazing. A lookout described it to me. It had no sails rigged and no crew. Another rebel innovation. It steered straight for its entire journey, unlike normal gliding vessels. When it hit the bridge it broke apart. If it had had more powder it would have been very destructive. The next day, our divers explored it. It had a mast and sail attached to its bottom so that the current drove it. No sailors needed and not at the mercy of the wind. What else can they think up? Patrols are constant; no one sleeps more than two hours a night. There are no reinforcements because we expect an attack on Kowenstyn Dyke from that monster ship, *War's End*. It must deploy soon. Who knows if it will float or steer? There's terror of disease and desertions, but Farnese shares the men's hardships. That keeps everyone together."

Pieter had regained colour during Latham's description. "Farnese will take Antwerp," he whispered. Latham left, feeling hopeful.

Next day, Pieter said, "I don't regret my wounds. I've stared into hell. I'm better for it." After a pause, he added, "Did you know that the farmer's wife is an atheist?"

"No!" Latham cried in astonishment. "I know some rebels are unbelievers, not just Calvinists."

"Edward, I've been wrong on many things: applauding heresy burnings and being so partisan. I'm grateful I saw hell. This war is madness. Giambelli is Catholic, like us; he used the Dutch to avenge a personal insult, while this angel atheist cares for me like kin. She brought a priest to shrive me. Work for peace; that's my revelation. I survived to see your face and tell you. Do you see?"

"Don't repent your fervour. What did any of us know when we swore our youthful oaths?" Latham yearned to confide in the dying man but refrained. "I'll try for peace."

Latham couldn't tell if he was satisfied. Pieter died peacefully that night. Latham wrote to William in Lisbon and Joris in Constantinople, then had the body embalmed. Before taking it to the Boels family tomb in Cambrai, he sought out the priest who had shriven Pieter. He made a long, fraught confession of his own, begging forgiveness for the tangled loyalties that made up his life.

CHAPTER 23
DEBRIEFINGS
AND A
MARRIAGE

Wimille safe house, late May 1584

That shocked him, Latham thought, watching Hicks trying to get his mind around what Latham had just said.

Hicks had disembarked and ridden straight to Wimille. Now he was leaning against the wall, one leg bent, flicking Calais sand from the soles of his boots. "Say that again, Edward. You're telling me that one of Giambelli's ship bombs broke the Spanish blockade and Antwerp's defenders didn't notice? God save us from allies!" He started working on his other boot.

Latham said it again. "I was there. *Hope* breached the boat bridge, and Antwerp scouts didn't come for two days or nights.

DEBRIEFINGS AND A MARRIAGE

Galleons from the Antwerp or Zeeland fleet could easily have sailed through, killing most of us. Over a thousand of Farnese's men were dead, just a few survivors. Reinforcements weren't possible because Kowenstyn dyke had to be manned. The Spaniards were stunned, just stunned, that God was granting them time to make enough superficial repairs so that the bridge looked continuous when rebels did finally look."

Latham gave Hicks a detailed account of the devastating *Hellburners*.

Hicks worried the fact, frowning. "So Antwerp's rulers had the *notion* that Giambelli's invention wouldn't work and clung to their monster ship, which was being rebuilt to correct their own engineers' mistakes. Off to battle go fifty fire-ships and the ship bombs. There's conflagration, explosions, massive destruction. But because of their *notion*, no authority checked the bridge." He looked at Latham in shock.

Latham shifted subjects. "Being eyeball to the bomb ships was to visit hell. I survived, but Idiaquez is threatening me unless I get him substantial intelligence.

Hicks sat on the blanket, looking evasive. "My man got your message though."

Latham watched, nervously pulling the tassels of his gipsy scarf. "Do you have intelligence for me?"

Hicks met his eye. "I do." He sighed.

Whatever I get comes at a steep price, Latham realised.

"You'll take it personally to Madrid," Hicks said.

"Madrid? Right into the hands of Idiaquez, who suspects me of false dealings?" He paled.

Hicks nodded. "A risk, I agree. It gets worse. Her Majesty says you must fund the journey yourself. She won't pay for your report on Giambelli's workshop, because you didn't see what was in front of your eyes; nor for the *Hellburners* account, which she called an apple of gold, but out of season, worth less than an unripe one in season. She insists she'll only pay for timely accuracy, otherwise, her coffers would be emptied by any rogues with guesses. Walsingham defended you. He said the nature of innovation is that it can't be compassed by lesser men. But that just played to her argument. Sniffing, she retorted that *lesser* men don't merit rewards."

Latham chewed his lip, then started laughing. "Is that all the bad news?"

"Yes," Hicks replied. "I do have excellent intelligence for you."

"Well," Latham considered, "my Spanish salary funding the trip has ironic appeal."

His relief palpable, Hicks rummaged in his saddlebag, talking as he searched. "Listen, we know more about Antwerp than you do now. Let me fill you in. Giambelli was right about *War's End*. When it deployed–sailed is the wrong word–it hit a sandbar. Never fired a shot. The Spaniards took the guns and burned the hull. They call it *Bugaboo*, laughing their heads off. Antwerp calls it *The Lost Penny*. Lost 100,000 pounds, in truth. They're begging us for more help, with an aggrieved air of having been done ill by, which sends Her Majesty into paroxysms of fury."

He was tossing shirts, books, papers, hose, soap, a scent bottle, to the floor. "Found it. For your spymaster, Idiaquez, in Madrid. May God thwart his practices. We're impressed by how the Spaniard quakes at the thought of *Hellburners*, which you described vividly in the days after the attack. It suggested a strategy."

A woodpecker tapped the wall outside, summoning a mate; further off came the ascending shrills of woodland ducks. Hicks shook his head as he broke the seal. "Ah, to be an unthinking bird. No summer joy for us this year. Giambelli fled Antwerp, which shows the state of things. Farnese has proven he's cleverer than our allies. We pray that our Elizabeth is cleverer than Farnese."

"Where did Giambelli go?"

Hicks gave a faint smile. "He's with us."

"He's not making bomb ships?" Latham got up and paced the room. "You mustn't."

"No. We don't have powder reserves, for one thing. Those pyramid cones take seven thousand pounds. Also, he's too touchy. He's designing improvements to our fortifications. We keep him busy and much praised.

"But that brings me to strategy. There's a note in your package from Sir Francis Drake to Giambelli, thanking him for his help with specifications, marked *approved* by Sir John Hawkins, head of the admiralty. It's fake. The idea is to hint that he is building *Hellburners*. They think Elizabeth is Satan incarnate. Pretending we have them is almost as good as having them. That's our strategy: moulding perception. We'll have other agents dribbling confirmation to them."

Am I merely part of something? Latham thought, affronted.

Reading Latham's mind, Hicks chuckled. "You're not Atlas, holding up the world. Put self-opinion aside and let me finish."

Latham blushed. "The rest of the packet?"

"Naval documents, with Her Majesty's consent. All true. She hopes that seeing our strong condition will deter Philip." He handed it over.

Latham flicked the pages: a ship plan, costs, construction contracts, crew complement. He whistled. It was a generous haul.

"Hawkins was a pirate, as you know," Hicks explained. "He's building new royal warships, refitting some existing ones for speed and manoeuvrability. Spanish naval doctrine, with its tall ships stuffed with artillery and soldiers, is simple: close, grapple, board, annihilate. The design of our ships is now shouting: 'No. You can't get close enough.' This ship plan should make Spanish captains nervous. Our crews will also be a third smaller, sailors working the guns as well as the ship, instead of embarking separate army artillery units. Hawkins says this makes the rate of gunfire much faster. It's also cheaper."

Latham stared at the plan which certainly suggested a vessel sleeker than Spanish warships he'd seen. He raised his eyebrows.

Hicks read his thoughts again. "Yes, Walsingham is unhappy with the high quality of this offering, but Elizabeth rules. Still, he sees one possible advantage. Watch for any sign this intelligence is *confirmatory*, not new. Confirmatory means they have a spy in London. You wrote last year that little-known details in the account of past invasions of England done by a Spanish officer suggested that there was a pro-Spanish spy in London. He'd be in the comptroller's office or admiralty, hence these particular documents. You delivering them personally to Idiaquez will help us to find him. We've created a character for your source: mythical Master Robert Stanford, a disgruntled pious man of the old faith, toiling in obscurity in the admiralty. It's all here. This packet is gold, Edward; Idiaquez will love you. I hope you're grateful to Her Majesty. Despite her rants, she wants you to have good offices with Spain, for our country's sake.

"There's one more thing, Edward: Mary's son, King James, has ended three years of vacillating; he refuses any co-rule of Scotland with his unhappy mother. He prefers us bearing the cost and risk of maintaining her. Keep an ear alert for reactions to this in Spain."

Latham rolled up the packet and put it away. Dread braided his gut for Mary. '*I would rather lose all than stay in the same case,*' she'd written to him when sending him to Barbara Blomberg to help secure her marriage to Don John. What next? "You're throwing me into the lions' den with a thin rope!" he said.

"Complex mission, I know." Hicks blushed. "You get back in high favour with Idiaquez using our naval plans, denting Spanish enthusiasm to invade us in the process; while watching out for Spanish or Marian mischief. Good luck. When will you go?"

"Next month," Latham replied. "After my manservant's marriage."

"Marry barely-speaking Joris? No! No! No!" Marie shouted, stamping her foot. She was in the attic, confined for a second day, in order, as her mother said, to think reasonably about things beneficial to all. Drumming her heels didn't break the reinforced lock. Her protests gradually weakened, and she wept softly then slept.

At midnight, the servant girl, Yvette, unlocked the door, whispered for the ladder and brought in a tray of food. Hélène Michaud had promised Yvette two ducats if she could "bring Marie around." Yvette was fond of Marie. Three years older and more worldly, Yvette thought Marie's rejection of Joris came more from fear than revulsion. So after Marie had wolfed down rabbit stew, the girls compared their experiences kissing Jean, the caretaker from the Beaumonts' former inn at Saint-Denis. Soon they were giggling and hugging.

"The Fleming mightn't be as awful as you think," Yvette urged. "I've seen him appraise women: young, old like my mama, plump, thin, as if he sees through their clothes, but in a friendly way. He's kind to animals. That's rare. Jean's all slop, huff and push, dear." At her authoritative tone, Marie hooted, remembering how she'd watched them rubbing and panting on the inn stairs through her peephole.

"I know Jean's handsome," Yvette persisted, "but he's not husband material. Besides, if the Fleming barely speaks, you need barely listen. That's a happy position for a wife."

"So I could order him about?" Marie hadn't considered this and started to laugh.

"Of course. But you won't have to. Your mama says he'll travel for Monsieur Prosperino. He won't even be here, though he'll send money. He trades coffee, and just inherited something elsewhere he'll have to supervise. Please say yes and come downstairs. We need you desperately in the fields."

After three nights of conversations like this, Marie dried her eyes and walked into the parlour with lofty, if grimy, dignity. She had a long talk with her mother, while her father stayed slumped in his chair. Jeanne assured Marie that, while Joris might appear simple, he was clever in special ways; she knew of no young man who traded with the Turks who'd not been born to it, and Signor Prosperino said he was a fighter who could protect her. Moreover, he'd often be elsewhere. When Marie leaned her head against Jeanne's shoulder and nodded yes, her father's hands jerked up as if to clap. But the distance between them seemed vast, and they dropped. Still, his body had momentarily animated. Marie took it as approval, almost an order.

"If it helps Papa, I'll do it," Marie cried. She looked again at the self-portrait Joris had sent Latham, shuddering at the injured lizard nestling at his collar. "I suppose he's not so very ugly. I don't know how I can put up with his beasts." She thought wistfully of Jean, who knew what animals were for. "But if he's so busy saving them, he'll leave me alone."

'*Elsewhere,*' to Yvette and Marie's mother, Jeanne, was the not-near- Épinay house in Cambrai that Pieter Boels had bequeathed his nephews and godsons, Joris and William Boels. In its near-empty quiet, Joris, prospective groom, faced his fears. Since dawn, he'd been making little wooden altars. Three stood on the dining table, varnished pine with decorative moulding at base and top. Joris pinched his nose at the smell, took a turn around the room, then started making two more.

As he sawed, graded and varnished, the lawyer's voice reading Pieter's will and last letter rolled around his mind.

With the grace of God, Amen. Except for this house in Cambrai, fruits of my marriage, all I possess was gained by my own efforts. The two sons of my seed and deceased wife Magda's womb became Geneva Calvinists and repudiated me for not following them. Not knowing their whereabouts, my equal heirs are my godsons and nephews William Boels, son of my brother Albert; and Joris Boels, son of my brother Jacob. They may divide the estate as they wish."

In a separate letter to Joris, Pieter blessed the union with Marie Beaumont. *Joris, my beloved fellow, consider the benefit of having France as a place of refuge. You can have no concept of this war in the Netherlands if you hadn't seen the new satanic machines of death. The further from our birth soil, the happier you can be. Then there is her class, which is superior to ours, the maid being connected distantly to the House of Guise. Further, Sir Edward described her as a young woman of unsullied purity and other virtues. I am shriven and die at peace, grateful to the Almighty for having granted me a time on earth free of disease and poverty, and the chance to serve sovereign and state as best I understood the right course. I grieve Magda's death and the estrangement from the sons of my blood, but these losses opened my heart to you and William. Dance on my grave, dear boy. May your life be what you most wish.*

A list of assets had been attached: one warehouse for lease; five commercial partnerships; an eighth share in a trading ship; two houses with tenants; horses; jewellery, silver and gold coins; accounts receivables. It was complex but standard; the lawyer would untangle it.

William had written from Lisbon to say he was needed for vital work there. He instructed the lawyer to sell everything except the Cambrai house, to which he'd someday bring a noble Spanish bride, but that would have to wait until the wicked Dutch rebels reconciled with their anointed King. Meanwhile, rents should be sent to his lodgings. William sternly advised Joris to take his portion in annuities, so he wouldn't have to satisfy any employer, the impossibility of which had embarrassed the Boels family in the past.

That William's odd cousin might marry well and want the Cambrai house never occurred to him.

To Joris, this condescension was very old. He'd long grown beyond erupting in punches. He'd get his revenge someday not by violence, but by coney-catching William with some trick. Private vengeance was alright; the important thing was for it to happen. His determination was coolly soothing, like fig sherbet on a hot Constantinople day.

His business today wasn't William, but his own future. After finishing the altars, he drew fine past loves. The first was of the dirty-blonde Lutheran girl he'd proposed to after she had been raped by the local inquisitor. She'd refused him, but he'd sent her money until he lost track of her whereabouts. The second picture was the issue of that vile inquisitorial crime, a skinny boy with black mop-top hair. The third was his favourite whore in Constantinople, a sensualist with caramel-coloured skin and slanted green eyes, who taught him the arts of sexual pleasuring and drama. His fourth drawing was his ideal *her*, a virginal maid with long blond hair and blue eyes gazing over budding breasts. The fifth was Marie as he remembered her: pert and stocky, with unruly auburn hair. He was to marry her. He didn't want to, but his godfather had urged the union from his deathbed. His parents had died during a spring plague before getting Pieter's proposal, so Pieter's urging had the sacred character of a last wish. Latham, his master, said that if he looked properly at Marie, he'd be deeply engaged. He'd gain French citizenship and ennoble the blood of Boels heirs. There was nothing more to say.

He placed a drawing on each altar and bowed to the first four. Then he intoned appreciations and renunciations individual to each, in jerky phrases. When he was done, he tore the four drawings with slow, reverent rips, broke the four altars, and laid the pieces by the fireplace. That left Marie.

He knelt and prayed to God to fill him with notions proper for husbands.

There was a knock on the door; it was the head-servant. William had instructed Joris to dismiss all the servants, shifting the cost of maintaining the house to the hypothetical tenants whose rents he expected to enjoy. Joris had relished countermanding that order, winning gratitude from the head-servant, cook, gardener and scullery maid. Anxious to please his new employer, the head-servant, a grizzled man in his fifties, pretended to understand what he'd heard. "A fine worshipful maid," he said, pointing to the intact drawing of Marie. He held out a letter, adding, "From France, sir."

Joris read painstakingly. It was the Beaumonts' agreement to the marriage. He drew a finger across his throat and grinned ruefully. "Send…box," he ordered. Anticipating acceptance, he'd bought fabrics: damasks, velvets, linens, sateens, and leather of different thickness for boots and shoes. He'd chosen colours that would highlight Marie's grey eyes and auburn hair: alabaster whites; dark yellows; pale blues; magentas; near-black purples. When the servant left, Joris threw wood and torn paper into the fire. To his amazement, some spirit invoked by his incantations entered him, erasing memories. Past breasts blurred, perfumes got lost in wood ash; trilling voices got entangled in his inner debate over what it meant to be a husband.

Three weeks later, the bride and groom stood in the parlour of the Beaumonts' farmhouse. Long-faced puppets, they were rigidly separate, responding only to the invisible strings their elders pulled to join their lives. Latham was shimmering in dark greens, his flaxen hair tinted with grey, beard growing in skimpily after his gipsy disguise in Wimille. Marie's father, Auguste, leaned on the stable boy's arm. His daughter's marriage had brought him a wondrous recovery, as Latham had predicted to Marie. Jeanne, her long-suffering mother, glowed with relief at seeing her daughter placed and her husband sensate. Hélène Michaud, freed from fostering a girl uncomfortably like herself, was liberal with gifts. Yvette as bridesmaid enjoyed one of the sateens Joris had sent. The local priest, who knew nothing of their lives, complacently intoned God's sanctifying rivet. After the ceremony and meal, Hélène gave Latham the names of two witches in Paris who had helped her girls at the laundry avoid pregnancy. He handed it quietly to Joris when the couple left the farm.

At the wedding, Joris had brushed Marie's lips with his moist warm ones, to be met with a dry pursing of her own. Now they faced a week together in Paris, in Latham's old suite above the Petit Pont, for which the Englishman had paid. After the excitement of raucous streets, a prolonged unpacking and washing of face, hands, privates and feet, taking longer than the setting of the sun and rising of the moon, he tried again. The tip of his tongue probed her mouth, but he withdrew when she tensed in apparent repulsion. His ideal *her* had always been a virgin, but now he'd married one, he realised he had no idea what to do. Using his superior strength didn't seem proper.

He'd always sensed something feral in Marie during past encounters when he was Latham's courier, and she was the inn's produce buyer and hen strangler. Even reckless. Now, as he stepped away, he thought about animals: dogs liked sloppy; cats and lizards didn't. Not that he'd tongue-kissed a dog, as the green-eyed whore in Constantinople did. But the analogy suggested letting his wife, feline or reptilian, come to him. Enlightened by his insight, he drew an implausibly flattering sketch of her. After giving it to her, he bowed, got into bed, turned his back and slept.

Marie lay awake in a welter of confusion. She'd been disturbed and aroused by his kisses; he smelled nicer than any male she knew. Jean gave off hay and leather; her beloved Papa was yeast, which she'd always assumed was the proper man smell; Signor Prosperino moved in an aura of cedar oil. Joris smelled of sandalwood, jasmine, and loam from his boots. It was intoxicating. But her insides coiled: the thought of full humping revolted her. And its purpose, being wrenched open by childbirth and dying of childbed fever, terrified her. Huddled at the edge of the bed, she hummed plainchant–was it too late to flee to a convent?–then a favourite lullaby, *There was once a little boat*. Soothed by imagined rocking on river currents, she dozed.

For the next few days, Marie chose what they'd see. Finding, as Yvette had promised, that a barely speaking husband could be ordered about, she pulled Joris to Wednesday and Saturday livestock markets, amazed by the number of hares, rabbits, pigs, boar, goats and poultry that sold in hours. She told him that she'd bought molasses and fish for the Louvre Palace kitchen with its steward, and pulled him to the river docks. There they watched firewood, fodder and charcoal sold from boats, then followed their resale in streets and shops. She was fascinated by the business of feeding three hundred thousand urban Parisians. She questioned fishermen, butchers and grain carters on costs, mark-ups, and the general fleecing of Parisians, particularly foreigners. She told Joris which prices were fair, which extortion; bargaining for the bread, sausage, cheese and wine they ate for lunch on the grassy hillock overlooking Notre-Dame Cathedral. She was indifferent to the buildings, which she'd seen during her work for Hélène Michaud.

Joris believed in social degree: servant to master; knight to baron; wife to husband. But he was content to follow his wife's interests and beat off cut-purses, in the spirit of letting her come to him. One morning, he swivelled to twist the scrawny neck belonging to a boy cutting her belt. She'd had no sensation of being robbed. His aggression, cruel enough to send the thief away sobbing, but not enough to bring a constable, impressed her. Whatever this husband lacked–she was puzzled by his restraint, even frustrated–he wasn't weak.

At a street corner, he surprised her again. A card player was inviting bets. Standing among the apprentices, street boys, tourists and students, they watched his winnings grow. When three disconsolate players left, plucked of their valuables,

Marie saw her husband's face sag into a dreamy stupor as he threw a testoon and some billons on the ground, seemingly not knowing the difference. The card player bit the testoon and grinned as Joris sat beside him. There was a flurry of cards. In the end, Joris had four aces, and the street player did not. The spectators cheered. They all knew the card player cheated but had never been able to beat him. Joris scooped up coins worth four testoons, led his wife at a fast pace around a corner and into a tavern. In the dim light, she invited his kisses: luxuriant, probing, awakening yearning in her every pore. "How did you do it?" she eventually asked. He peeled apart lightly glued sleeve cuffs and showed her the street player's aces. She laughed, and they enjoyed their meal. He knew she wanted him, but in their rooms, she tensed, and he refrained.

He spoke little. He yearned to describe markets in Constantinople, which he knew she'd like; to explain about lizards re-growing broken tails, and so many other things, but his speech had deteriorated. The technique Dr Gomes had taught him, of seeing dancing pictures on a ceiling, deserted him; he couldn't assemble in anything like reasonable time.

In the end, that saved them. Infirmities brought them closer. Marie was paralysed between desire and terror—a convent wasn't what she wanted—and her confusion made her sympathetic to Joris's inarticulateness. Before the family's poverty, before her father had collapsed into depression, she would have scorned her husband's defects. Now she offered him the tender patience she gave her father. Slowly he scrunched his face less as he grabbed phrases. When he finally got out his first string, they clapped, him in triumph and her with curiosity. "Saw poster... fake execution. Tomorrow... take you...to an effigy hanging," he shouted.

Executions were frequent, but there'd been none recently. So a crowd hungry for edification was gathering at the plaza outside the Hôtel de Ville. It was drizzling and cool, so Marie and Joris drew cloaks around them as they disembarked from a commuter wherry and climbed the stairs of a tavern where Joris had bought balcony seats. They looked down on two scaffolds guarded by helmeted soldiers. More soldiers protected a dais from which an official would read the sentences. Threading through the crowd were food vendors and the ubiquitous cut-purses.

A bell tolled single-spaced tones. Drums beat, coming closer. Mounted constables cleared the way as forcefully as if the plaster replicas of the convicts had armed supporters in the crowd ready to spring the condemned men loose. Two carts carried effigies; hands roped behind their backs, feet chained, propped in place by wooden blocks, so they wouldn't slide as the carts jerked over cobbles. The effigies were dressed as prisoners, including jail grime. As the carts trundled below the tavern balcony, Marie shrieked and clutched Joris's arm. He leaned over to her. "Avocat Lamont and his clerk!" she mouthed, not wanting anyone to hear. "They were in the plot that ruined us. Lamont vanished."

"Trial anyway," Joris mouthed back.

Marie nodded. The Duke of Guise, who'd bought the Beaumonts' inn and plotted against the French king, must have hidden them to stop them from testifying. She glanced at Joris. He didn't seem to know anything; Signor Prosperino must have kept what she told him about the box in the storage room to himself.

The ceremony began. Two magistrates mounted the dais and listed the crimes of the convicted men. They proclaimed it an execution in absentia, to be implemented if the criminals showed their faces anywhere in France. With a flourish, two soldiers unrolled paper images of Lamont and his clerk and nailed them to the gallows, to loud cheers. A priest, who'd been walking with the carts, approached the gallows and intoned last rites, asking the papers if they had any last words. They didn't. He shouted "Long live King Henry!" and stepped away, crossing himself. There were *Ahs* from a crowd entertained by the formal ritual. But *Ahs* tailed off in frustration, for there was no blood. The sense of having been delivered from terror and chaos by hard justice was thwarted by the prisoners' absence. The execution ended with soldiers chopping up the effigies, leaving the pieces for souvenir seekers. To end the terrifying and ridiculous ritual, the procession wended its dignified way out of the plaza, drums beating and bells still tolling.

Marie sat with Joris quietly while the crowd dispersed. "I knew them," Marie finally offered. "Lamont was awful. He got Papa to buy the farm. But his clerk? He just copied..." She searched for her meaning. "To end in a show like a wizard's curse. Listen, I just made them dead."

"Punishment a show...yes," Joris replied. He pulled a stitched booklet of his drawings from his doublet and showed her an Ottoman impalement gallows, vertical poles and cross beams, one midway down with two protruding metal hooks With hand gestures and rushed phrases he described how the prisoner, hands bound, was hoisted high, then dropped. Falling where? It was chance: instant death, days of torture, a miss and repeat. The unpredictability horrified, entertained and instructed Ottoman subjects.

Signor Prosperino had refused to describe Ottoman punishments to Marie. Now she knew. They hailed a boat, for it was Wednesday, and Marie wanted to see Place Maubert market again. Hand in hand, they wandered around poultry pens and goat cages. A laughing group was advising a farmer whose sow was giving birth. A young boy and girl held the rear legs of a half-emerged piglet; the farmer was pulling back on his sow's shoulders. The sow squealed, and in an explosion of fluid and tissue three piglets plopped out. Marie had experienced symbolic death and real birth within hours. She knew her duty in the cycle. Everyone was slapping a back or cheering, except Marie. Her shoulders heaved, her face mottled, and she convulsed in desperate sobs. Joris finally understood her terror.

Back in their rooms, he showed her a sheath. It was soft; the outside oiled, its open top threaded with a ribbon tie. "Venus glove. Stop...baby. No more...scared," he said. He drew her again, this time with one side of her face scrunched in fear, the other slack with desire. She remembered Latham saying years ago: "One day your February revulsions, by maturity's alchemy, will become July's hot urgencies, soothed only by the marriage bed." It sounded horrible then. But here were February and July together, in this accurate picture of her. She had a husband who saw who she was, and she opened to him. He was careful: the sharp pain of ruptured virginity was muted by the oiled pig intestine, a trickle of her blood, and it was done. Her whole body tingled with newly awakened intensity.

When he took her back to the farm and left to join Latham in Madrid, Marie was relieved to see his back; it had all been so concentrated and strange. Kneeling by the bed that night, she added to regular prayers for her family, the king and the harvest, gratitude to God for marrying her to a man who'd go away often. But later she woke and patted the quiet, cold void beside her. Her fingers slid under her nightgown to pull her nipples, then crept down to the springy hair guarding her cunny. As she rubbed, her awakened insides ached for sustenance, a new mouth frantically pulling on the barely-understood emptied teat. When she spasmed in release, she lay back, relieved yet depleted. For the first time, she understood the paradox of human aloneness and union. At breakfast, her first words were: "I like this husband. He must come back."

CHAPTER 24
INTO THE
LIONS' DEN

Madrid, September 1585

"How that man gets around! He's as nomadic as you and me," Latham exclaimed, studying the drawings that Joris had brought him of the thin, olive-skinned Spaniard he'd detected following Latham to Calle Cuchilleros, Madrid: the same intense eyes and the same cheap copies of court fashion. Latham and Joris had rooms on the residential first floor of a plate shop in Cutlers Street, and Joris had been watching Latham's back for three days. Other drawings showed the man near the Royal Alcázar talking to couriers, and embracing a tonsured clerk at the south gate, whose face was turned away, but not entering the courtyard with him.

"Good work," Latham said. "While you were in Constantinople, he hung around Boulogne and might have opened my letters. I met him in Saint-Denis Cathedral once in 1582. He has dubious friends. Try to find out who he serves, where he lives."

Joris left, and Latham chewed his lip, worrying. In Saint-Denis, he'd spoken a few words to this man in Spanish. If he was intimate with Idiaquez or his clerks, that could be dangerous. All these years, Latham had communicated with his Spanish masters in Latin. He was relying on hiding his fluency in Spanish to manage his interrogation and get the information Hicks wanted.

Well, throw the dice! He had no choice. Next day, he rode to the hilltop Alcázar to meet Idiaquez. On his previous visit, he'd met his employer, Secretary Antonio Perez, at home, and was lauded for bringing intelligence that the young French king was mortally ill. This time, his intestines braided with fear; he was gaming to avoid exposure for double-dealing.

The royal family was in Aragón, but, unlike most monarchs, Philip did not take key administrators with him. Business was managed from Madrid. A constant stream of mud-spattered couriers flung themselves in or out of the gates. Latham knew that Philip wanted to decide everything: military, fiscal, clerical, personnel, landscaping, architectural details, even resolving squabbles between monks over cell allocations.

At the gate, royal halberdiers searched carts and people for weapons. They waved workmen and cart-drivers to the east gate, where renovations were underway at the East Wing Queen's galleries.

Latham dismounted and joined a line of visitors and petitioners inching toward the south gate. To take his mind off his nervousness, he gazed at the palace. It had been built around an old Moorish observation post and fort, even retaining *Alcázar*, Arabic for fortress, in its name. Latham was surprised how incomplete the transition from infidel militarism to Renaissance grand living was. A semi-circle of terraced stone slabs, topped by a soaring slate spire, formed one tower. But the two other towers retained their original squat oblongs, with ancient archers' slits, and crosses incongruously plopped on top. He visualised infidel sentries shivering in winter storms or licking dry summer lips as they searched for Christian soldiers poling across the River Manzanares, or hauling siege engines up the hill at night.

His historical excursion ended when a guarded shouted at him; he was at the gate. His name was marked off a list, and a stable boy took his horse. It was a sign of favour to use the Royal Stables instead of outside posts, but Latham knew that by the day's end he could still face the rack master. He shivered as he followed a page through the courtyard. Again, he saw old and new melded: graceful Moorish archways letting in a brilliant light that draped European columns, and spectacular statues and paintings.

The guardroom was at the head of a dazzling spiral staircase of alternating black and white marble steps. There, Latham was searched again, and waved on to follow a new page, who led him to Idiaquez' office.

Despite having reported to the powerful secretary for years, Latham had no idea what he looked like. But he had a mental image: tall and lean, with an aquiline nose and black hair whose severe barbering reflected the coiled menace in the rebuke his clerk sent Latham in Boulogne.

He was startled to bow to a very different man. Flesh-and-blood Idiaquez conveyed complacency. He radiated comfort with himself and his role in running the empire on which, the saying went, the sun never set. His figure was full, not lean; his clothes were plush but plain and loose. He didn't advertise his greatness with jewels or trumpet his virility with cod-piece padding. His frowning bushy eyebrows, grizzled hair and beard were grey and neat. Certainty was his effect; this man wasn't subject to doubts. His memos to Philip would be clear, affirming what his sovereign already thought, and wanted to hear. That was Latham's sense of Idiaquez, as he rose from his bow and deliberately mangled his Spanish obsequies. Idiaqez indicated a low stool.

Flanked by two tonsured clerks in clerical robes, Idiaquez sat behind his desk, tapping a thick file. A prop to throw him off balance, Latham assumed: his file, full of his excoriations of Spanish cruelty. Idiaquez must be angry at his presumptuousness. Heart pounding, he began delivering his report in Latin, resorting to French for technical terms. Ship plans, cost structures, crew complements, all furnished by the mythical informer Hicks had invented: poor, pious Master Robert Stanford of the admiralty. Rattle, rattle, he went. The diplomat who'd recruited him to work for Spain in 1569, Francis de Alava, had advised him that Latin was the only language for avoiding misunderstandings, since King Philip read only Latin and Spanish. Latham was hoping fervently that his file hadn't been updated to reflect competence in Spanish.

"Wait here," Idiaquez said neutrally. He picked up the documents and left the room, leaving his clerks. Amazed he'd said nothing yet about Latham's presumptuous criticisms, he looked down, studying his shirt cuffs. He played with them; the lace offered many threads to pull or smooth.

He was uncomfortable on the stool, but wasn't going to let that provoke him into speech. The clerks weren't as disciplined. They were quiet for a few moments. But the younger clerk couldn't tolerate silence and leaned over to his superior. Dark circles around his eyes signified the peculiar animation sparked by exhaustion. When he started to murmur Latham looked up with infinite discretion.

"We'll see what the military advisor says," the clerk said in Spanish, as Latham read his lips. "These documents confirm what our fat *Trojan Horse* wrote. They exactly correlate."

Latham smoothed a thread. One question answered. Did Idiaquez have a spy in the English controller's office or admiralty? Yes, code name *Trojan Horse*, and fat. *God forgive me*, Latham thought, *but my London counterpart larva clings to exposed grass.*

After a half hour, Idiaquez returned. "Helpful," he said flatly. Latham inclined his head humbly, blood thrumming with relief. Idiaquez continued, "My adviser, veteran artillery captain of the army of Flanders…"

Wait, why consult a land soldier about ships? Latham wondered.

"…and I agree that these reforms weaken, not strengthen, the enemy. Sailors can't work ship guns. Specialised artillery units are needed to clean and reload the guns; know when powder separates and prevent accidental explosions. Men of rank should account for expending royal ordnance, not low-born rigging scrapers. What English ships gain in manoeuvrability they'll lose to bad crewing, as sailors scramble from mast to cannon. These papers show that an enterprise against England, should we mount one, will take fewer resources, not more. We're very satisfied with Master Robert Stanford, and you."

His words fell on a Latham staring at his boots, absorbing the blow of having failed in the primary goal of his mission. Elizabeth hoped to deter a Spanish invasion by showing the efficiency of her ship-building program. It had been interpreted as weakness. Would she blame him rather than herself? In his mind's ear she was already yelling: "'Swounds, that cur Latham brought the whole might of Spain and Portugal down on us!" He nearly missed Idiaquez' next words. Then he caught them. Straightening up, he realised he'd been holding his breath.

"…but this packet puts our suspicions entirely to rest."

Latham had never fully admitted to himself how certain he was he'd be in prison tonight. Exhaling, he thought, *Safe for now.*

Idiaquez went on. "A few questions. This letter from Francis Drake to Giambelli mentions specifications. What does that mean?"

"I know nothing beyond what Master Stanford sent," Latham said neutrally.

The senior clerk interjected, "He's building *Hellburners*. There's no depravity beyond England's Jezebel."

"I won't conjecture," Latham added. "A spy who guesses has no integrity."

There was a pause.

"But what do you think? What's Master Stanford's opinion?" the junior clerk persisted.

"What's in the documents is all I can attest to."

Idiaquez said, almost kindly, "We don't often meet in person a man of rank who survived the ship-bomb *Hope*. We've got many written accounts, but tell us the smell, the feel of it."

Latham thought: *They've planted Hellburners in their own minds, which to them is evidence. At least I succeeded in that.* He offered granular details of the dead, wounded and burned; the rubble and far-flung destruction; the debilitating aftermath, until he left the camp.

A new clerk came in and handed Latham an invitation to a ball that night, and two purses of coins.

"Can you get the smaller purse or equivalent funds to Master Stanford?" Idiaqez asked. Latham inclined his head.

"Good. A courier will bring your next assignment. You may go."

Latham wondered if he should ask Idiaquez to call off the Spaniard who'd followed him in Boulogne, and here, now that doubts about Latham's loyalty were resolved. No, better to have a tail he knew. He was stunned Idiaquez hadn't mentioned the many harangues in his reports. Working to keep his expression reverential, Latham bowed and withdrew.

I gulled Spain's Secretary of State, he thought, feeling almost numb as he walked to the guardroom. Elizabeth would demand to know why Idiaquez saw her naval reforms as evidence of weakness, rather than efficiency. Perhaps the reach of Spain's empire—territories over three continents; multiple languages and races; constant wars—made being simplistic the only way to get through the day. Spain had a vast network of spies. But getting information, and using it best, were two different things. Style filtered down a hierarchy. If keeping things smooth guided how information travelled from clerk to secretary to king, then Idiaquez never read Latham's criticisms. He grinned, remembering how his hands shook when he gave his impudent missives to couriers. Some clerk's clerk had extracted the facts and filed or destroyed his originals. What a waste of fear.

There was a rustle as Idiaquez' senior clerk grabbed his elbow. "'*You imbue your cause with viciousness,*'" he hissed in Spanish, quoting Latham's most presumptuous criticism, and pulling him behind a column.

Latham tensed, forcing himself to look perplexed. "En Français, s'il vous plaît."

The clerk stared hard but obliged. "How dare you criticise us without the name of counsellor? Did you think my master would see them? I've filed your rot, in case opinion turns against you again. Gentlemen show gratitude."

Latham handed him two escudos with a smile, retorting, "Good day, Father. How happy with your generosity the poor will be on dole day."

He yearned to bolt from Madrid now, but knew he'd arouse suspicion if he didn't go to the ball. When he got back to his rooms, he found Joris. "Can you use this?" he asked, tossing him the purse meant for the mythical Master Robert Stanford. He laughed at his servant's puzzled delight. "It's a ghost's fee."

Joris counted the coins, whistled, and put them in a leather pouch he wore under his shirt. "Spend it very slowly, when we've left Madrid," Latham said, "and please guard my purse."

Dressed in black velvet breeches and doublet with magenta satin slashed sleeves, he arrived at Ambassadors' Hall after the dancing had begun. The checkered marble floor seemed to gyrate under the flickering of hundreds of candles, while dance movements created oscillating light and shade that obscured bodies as fabrics swirled. He had no idea who was there, except for Idiaquez and a phalanx of black-robed clerks. The secretary sat on a tall-backed chair, watching. *Maybe*, Latham thought, grinning, *that's why this stately pavane is followed by another pavane, instead of the lusty galliard that usually follows it.* The plaintive tenor invented embellishments to his tune, while viols and tabor beat out the slow duple rhythm.

Eventually, Idiaquez stood. After a cornett blared for silence, he pleaded paperwork. He commended the gathering on its decorum, then swept out with his clerks. The night got livelier: the tenor sat down and wiped his brow; cornettos, viols and tabor blared out a galliard, and intricate steps and jumps began. Laughter swelled. Latham longed to join them—his feet tapped the rhythms—but he held back, sensing someone wanted to talk to him.

The nearby light dimmed as candles burned down. The musical instruments changed again, tabors now supported by citterns and a penetrating double-reed shawm. A galliard segued into the risqué volta. Men held their partners by busk and hip, women clasped their partners' shoulder then launched themselves trustingly into the air, female thigh coming down to rest on the male thigh that rose elegantly to meet it. It was sensual; a few couples donned eye masks and sidled out of the hall. Latham laughed out loud. Off to private dalliances; religious Spain made as many bastards as other places. As servants replaced candles and the hall brightened, Latham felt a tap on his arm and heard the last sound he expected: a soft Scots burr.

"Edward Latham! I thought I recognised you. When you laughed, I knew. I can scarcely believe it! You're here for poor Queen Mary, too."

Latham turned to embrace a man he hadn't seen for eighteen years. When he was Mary's courier in 1567, Latham had ridden to Stirling Castle several times to check on the royal son, James, who was under the care of the Catholic Earl of Mar. The man who'd tapped his arm was Mar's courier, and Latham had shared his quarters during these visits. They'd enjoyed several conversations over rough wine. The light was tricky, but Latham thought his red, yellow and purple sash signified Vatican service.

He felt the tingling that presaged a major discovery. But if Mary was plotting again, did he want to know? He struggled with this for a moment, but, as usual, curiosity won. Music and stamping feet muffled their words from the nearby guard. "Our revered Queen Mary…" he began and then tailed off, waiting for the former courier to complete his sentence. When he didn't, Latham threw his dice. "Our beloved Mary Stuart, at last, has the right plan to free herself and gain her rightful crown." He was careful not to say which crown, Scottish or English, was rightfully hers. He added, "She informed me someone from Rome would be here. I'm relieved it's you. How did you get your distinguished position?"

The courier swelled. "I went to Rome with kind letters from Queen Mary and my master."

Latham nodded. "Mary is solicitous of her servants. When I went to Paris, she placed me under the protection of her cousin, Henry, Duke of Guise."

Mar's former courier leaned close to Latham. "I'm a papal courier now. His Holiness approves King Philip's marriage to Mary when all is done. That's what I'm here to say."

Another marriage for Mary? Latham recalled trying to secure Mary's marriage to Philip's half-brother, Don John. Suddenly, he missed Don John's mother, Lady Barbara. *Marry Philip now?* What did *when all is done* mean? "When all is done," he murmured. "What assurance does she have? This is no small venture."

"The Vatican will support Philip's invasion after the London gentlemen do what's necessary. We have no correspondence with Queen Mary, she's too carefully watched. You'll have to get the message through. Who are the London gallants?"

'Do what's necessary' could mean only one thing: assassinating Elizabeth. Latham had thrown a dice, called three and won three: regicide; foreign invasion; Stuart/Hapsburg union. How he wished he'd lost! He shivered for Mary. She

was planning a terrible crime. He couldn't help her; the most he could do was pray that she'd back off. "You know I mustn't name the London gallants," he answered. He forced a smile through his turmoil.

"You're right," the courier conceded. "Medals will be struck for them soon enough."

They embraced and said goodbye, as the courier had an early start the next morning. Latham hurled himself into galliards with the frenzy of one who wished tomorrow would never come and was long gone. He rode back to his rooms with Joris, distraught and silent; and his fitful dozes, in what remained of the night, were a jumble of warm memories and visions of hell.

When Latham finally got up, Joris was out. He was relieved, wanting to get his letter to Hicks over and done with. Using code was dangerous; he had to embed his news in a plausible-sounding letter between merchants. After several minutes, he wrote in French as Signor Piso Prosperino, acting in Madrid for Monsieur Antoine Minard, merchant of Wimille. Minard was an informer for Hicks.

Esteemed Monsieur Minard, You will be pleased to hear I delivered your consignment. I was much embraced, as your goods were as fine as their factor's earlier advisory promised. While here, I commissioned a sculpture of a fat little Trojan Horse for your beloved Lisa, remembering how dutiful she is at her Greek studies...

Latham hoped Hicks would connect the factor's advisory with a hypothetical spy in London sending intelligence to Spain; the fat Trojan Horse as a clue to his identity, and Lisa with Elizabeth, who read Greek. He got up, paced the room then drank some wine. After whittling a fresh quill, he continued.

These customers are great persons, and while I waited for my sculpture to be finished, they entertained me with a play composed by their Fool, in which Cassandra's revelations were made pretty lullabies that wouldn't affright a child. 'Twas funny and sad, for when did truth become less so for being mocked? But they are devoted to this Fool, thinking him wise, as great persons are wont to do…

He leaned back in his chair, tapping his lip, willing Hicks to understand that Elizabeth had become Cassandra, and that the naval documents meant to discourage Spanish aggression had the opposite effect. Now came the most painful part. He bent to it.

When I was leaving, your customer's protégé showed me a tapestry they wanted me to buy. A unicorn—unicorn being on Mary, Queen of Scots' coat of arms, and she was renowned for needlework—grown somewhat plump from being caged, is released by several gentlemen. The beast was done after the old Fleming design, but the hunters wore three-layer ruffs done in silver thread. In the background, a choppy sea, done with blues and greens with white tips, two ships and mounted knights. It is a grand design, and they have great ambitions for their weavers. My host urged me to take it for you on credit, my offices with them being in good order. I demurred until I consult you. May I suggest you give their enterprise serious consideration in the future? And further, if this letter reaches you by 20ᵗʰ October, the courier merits consideration.

With gratitude for your continued commissions,

Respectfully, Piso Prosperino, in Madrid, this eighth day of September 1585

It was the best he could do. Sighing, he crossed himself and sealed it. Before caution could set in, he went out to hire a courier. At the palace, he had noticed that a private service took letters and small packets from lesser officials and merchants to contacts in the Spanish Netherlands and ports on the way. They advertised travel times three times as long as the royal relay, which was still good. He promised a bonus if delivered in less than six weeks.

Joris greeted him when he got back to Cutler Street with drawings of Latham's follower entering the palace by the east gate, going to the stables.

"Mid-level lackey, as I thought," Latham said. "No threat today, but could be in the future. We're leaving tomorrow."

He intended to sail to Boulogne from the northern ports of Santander or Ambrosero. As he hadn't received orders from Idiaquez, he sent his itinerary to the palace. The next few days passed in leisurely travel, in company with merchants, pilgrims, tourists and soldiers on leave. For once, he had no need for frantic haste, and he delayed a few days at a monastery, using most of his salary to secure prayers for Mary's soul.

Wherever they stopped, Joris bought gifts for Marie, and he began a book of drawings for her. In ancient Segovia, while he was at the aqueduct, Latham went to mass. It was a glorious service, but he didn't line up for communion. On the church steps, seeing priests talking easily to parishioners, he realised he hadn't gone to confession in—how long? He didn't have a ready date. After Giambelli's *Hellburners*, yes, when he'd saved many wounded. In Cambrai, after the long, dangerous ride with Pieter Boels' embalmed body. He'd been timing confessions for when he had virtuous actions under his belt, which was a perversion of humility before God.

He shook his head. He'd left England because he was afraid of dying without being shriven by an ordained priest. Now he had hourly opportunities to cleanse his soul. But if he did confess, he'd be in the Inquisition's hands within a day. This was Fortune's greatest jest on him.

At Ambrosero, the mountain town overlooking the

harbour where Lady Barbara Blomberg had settled, he left Joris to get travelling schedules by sea and land and went to visit her, unannounced. He rode up a twisting cobbled road to the town, then took a gravelled track that ended at a handsome estate with iron gates. He'd brought a lute. *Why not?* He thought.

Red roof tiles and brown stones glowed radiantly under the late afternoon autumn sun. In the courtyard a fountain bubbled, enticing in the dry air. Red and lilac flowers, yellow ferns and grasses in garden beds and balcony baskets looked as if the flora of the nearby forest had walked here and claimed the best resting places.

But the place seemed near-empty. Where were the gardeners and stable hands needed to manage this place? And quiet. Where was sound, the trilling voice and guttural curses?

An elderly servant came to the gate, responding to a barking dog. Latham explained how he had met Lady Barbara in Brussels, and showed his lute.

Shaking a grizzled head, the servant let him in. "Lady Barbara and her maid aren't here. It's no use waiting. You can have some wine, Signor, then you should leave."

He led Latham to the hall, clacking on bare wooden floors cleared of rushes. The hall was A-frame, with brick walls and a wood-beamed ceiling. *What exquisite resonance*, the musician in Latham thought, *made for intimate concerts*. He put his lute on a chair. Everywhere were signs of female predominance: a tapestry of a female saint; panels of paintings of women cooking, weaving and brewing; unfinished needlework on a bench; a statue of Madonna and child; portraits of Lady Barbara in court glory. But the musical instruments were crowded into one corner: a spinet; small organ; lutes; a recorder set; two tabors. All were dusty. A pile of music on the floor was covered with a grimy cloth. What paper Latham could see had been chewed.

Shocked, he asked, "Did Lady Barbara's voice sicken permanently?"

"No, Signor," the servant replied. "Never more ethereal and brilliant. Nightingales despaired. She came to see music as worldly vanity and has given up such things. She's in retreat at Convent San Sebastian de Haro, arranging an endowment so that prayers will be said for her soul after God takes her."

"Is she ill?" Latham asked, alarmed.

"She's in sanguine health, praise God. But you and your lute would be unwelcome." Latham kissed the hem of her gown on the portrait and left a respectful note. Returning to the harbour, he thought: *you can't go back.* He reflected on the journeys of souls. Lady Barbara, so sensual, gifted and tempestuous, and not apt for the nunnery, had muted her angelic voice and was planning for eternal life, in a convent. Mary, Queen of Scots, was journeying, tragically, to a dark place. This was goodbye to both.

At his inn, were orders from Idiaquez. Hitting his forehead with his palm, Latham laughed, "Joris, I'm on the wrong coast of Spain. I have to ride east tomorrow, to Barcelona, for a ship to Naples. Go and see Marie. I want you to be in Lisbon next spring. Your cousin, William, is logistics clerk for Don Cristobal, serving the Spanish admiral, Santa Cruz. He's involved in war planning. You're to get all William knows."

Idiaquez asked Latham to find out what loans Genoese bankers were making to Spain's enemies. Giovanni Figliazzi, Idiaquez wrote, the Duke of Tuscany's principal adviser, was Florence's new ambassador to Spain. Figliazzi's aide, Benedetto Landolfi, whom Latham had met in Florence six years ago, would work with him in Naples.

Yes, Latham remembered Landolfi and his master, Figliazzi, the pragmatic men of Florence, far friendlier to England than Philip understood. Walsingham would also benefit from knowing what loans the bankers were making to England's enemy, Spain.

Leisure was over. On balance, he was relieved.

CHAPTER 25
TULIPS AND A
BATTLE PLAN

Lisbon, Spring 1586

Dawn seeped through a small round window in Marie's and Joris's bedroom, allowing Marie to find the towel on the headboard, push it up her vagina and retrieve the vinegar-infused wool ball that averted pregnancy.

Joris was asleep. She was careful not to wake him as she felt her way to the close stool and cleaned herself. Her innards stung, but that didn't lessen the pleasure she got from their lovemaking. It was a blessing that her husband had the money and willingness to buy the amulets, wool balls, and sheaths of oiled animal intestines that kept her barren; otherwise, they would have had to commit buggery. She'd heard peasants did it when they had too many children. It sounded horrible. Marie looked at Joris fondly, knowing he'd have an *I stole the marchpane* expression when he got up.

He was still a mystery to her: a gambler who coney-caught

any opponent who underestimated him; he was thuggishly quick to anger, but tender to animals and her; a stumbling speaker and backwards reader, yet meticulous sketcher of people and scenes; lusty, as Mama said all men were, yet disciplined in using devices to block or spoil his seed. She put on cloak and slippers to sit outside; early mornings were still frosty.

After passing the kitchen, where their odd-job boy slept, and a room that had once been a commercial store, where Joris stored coffee beans and exotic plant bulbs, she unlocked the back door and walked under a stone arch to the enclosed courtyard, waiting for sunrise.

The neighbour's rooster shrieked, and myriad smaller birds twittered. Stretching her arms in delight, Marie watched her favourite plants delineate: red myrtle leaves, yellow acacia, and turquoise lavender bushes whose fragrant purple blooms tried valiantly to mitigate the city's stench.

She knew their cook and day servant, Isabella, would soon be here, carrying baskets of steaming bread and a pail of milk, puffing from the steep street stairs. Their rented house was in the *Alfara* district, under the glowering shadow of St. George's Cathedral. Isabella was what Joris called new Christian, and she had an anxious seamed face. Descended from Jewish merchants and scholars, her grandparents had been burned by the Inquisition, their wealth taken. But she retained ancestral learning. Knowing several languages, she could interpret, and was honest. Somehow, she'd been hired before Joris and Marie arrived.

As she gazed at the flowers, Marie's thoughts raced back to her decision to leave her parents to travel with Joris. It wasn't her plan when they married.

When Joris had returned to Épinay after Madrid, their reunion had been a clutching, laughing, panting affair, and when it was time for him to leave for Portugal, she begged to come. Surprised, he lifted her chin to search her eyes, then walked her into a snow-crusted field.

"Foreign lands…different, not safe," he got out in his laboured way.

"I want to be with you. Ask Signor Prosperino how I told him about wicked people hiding things in Saint-Denis."

Joris stopped and scratched his head. Latham had said nothing about her helping him. "Would…like it," he said, wiping a tear from his eye. He guided her around the field, one hand on her shoulder, as if she was a prize filly he was showing to a royal horse master.

He looked to a cloud-banked sky, grabbing phrases as Dr Gomes had taught him. "Conditions. I can stop… get with child. But…degree. Dust to stone to plant to tree…"

"What are you talking about? I want to go with you to Lisbon."

"Degree. Knight to baron, priest to bishop, servant to master, wife to husband. You do…as I say. I serve Signor Prosperino in Lisbon, you too."

"What will I do?" she asked eagerly.

Joris shook his head, muttering, "Later."

In bed that night, Marie tossed for hours. Her parents were frail. Sometimes she thought death had already found a home in their blue-veined skin. She imagined that the grim reaper was peering out of their rheumy eyes, saying, "We're partners now." But they insisted she go, expressing happiness she'd be at her lawful husband's side.

It wasn't until they'd settled in their Lisbon house, after a journey full of new experiences, that Joris explained his assignment.

"S…see cousin William. Learn all his work," Joris said.

"The cousin who's rude to you," Marie replied. She hadn't met William Boels. "He's here?"

Joris nodded. He launched into practised sentences. "William clerk to… Don Cristobal Covarrulejo d'Avila… aide to… Alvaro de Bazan, Marquis of Santa Cruz… Spanish admiral."

"Pretty names," Marie mused, rolling her tongue

around their long strangeness. She remembered William's condescending letter to Joris after their mutual godfather, Pieter Boels, had died. *You must buy annuities, cousin, so you won't have to satisfy any employer, the impossibility of which has embarrassed our family in the past. Annuities, once taken, demand no judgment.*

She hadn't forgotten William Boels. "Will I make a dinner for him?"

Joris shook his head in a negative.

Marie gathered that Joris was to extract something military for Signor Prosperino from his cousin, without William knowing he'd been practised on. Joris longed to avenge himself on William for a lifetime of contempt; perhaps this would satisfy him.

"Get all of what from William?" she asked.

"Spain…war plans."

"Why? Signor Prosperino serves Spain. That king knows his own plans. Why would anyone pay him or you for this?" She always calculated the value of things.

Joris tensed. His wife was clever, but not ready for the complexities of the trader she knew as Signor Prosperino.

After a silence, she asked, "What am I to do?"

"Shop." He unfolded a list: salt, iron, grain, flour, meat, seasoned wood, hemp, charcoal.

"We don't need all these," she said, frowning.

"Want *prices*: last season's; now; next. Go up much, means war. Like five inns…in street when one …before. Linen… soap, oats price up."

She wasn't satisfied but agreed. "Very well, I'll take Isabella and the cart. She says the sweetest water is near St Vincent's monastery, up the hill. With the cart, I can buy several barrels and fill them. Our well pumps muck."

Hearing the maid work the front door key, she went inside, reflecting on how the judgments her priests and parents had sealed in her had been shaken up since leaving Épinay. Meeting all kinds of strangers, initially, her Catholic absolutism had kept her unfriendly to any she deemed different. But sustained hostility was hard work. If she and a Lutheran blacksmith were the only ship passengers clinging to deck ropes during a storm, was she to fling off the protective hand on her shoulder? She tried packing her condemnations away. To her surprise, she liked it. She'd accepted a new Christian as a servant, privy to their intimate lives, while Joris believed she still followed Jewish rituals. Marie wouldn't have kept her secret in Épinay; she did here.

She liked the old Moorish house; its foibles and decorations told exotic stories. Cracks in the stone spoke of earthquakes at different times and different violence. Ceramic wall tiles were eloquent, too. Geometric patterns, blue and white in the passageway, brown and yellow in the kitchen, were Moorish, Isabella said. She'd pointed out newer Christian ones–fish; crosses; a crèche–where settling had broken original tiles. Haphazard replacement connected Marie to the past, as if she was gaining those years of living. She imagined ancient householders whispering their loves, terrors, struggles with the oven and the well. These ghostly new friends offset her loneliness. *Buy war materials and sweet water. That's what I'll do today*, she thought, going to rouse the kitchen boy.

Naples, the same hour.

In a tavern bedroom, Edward Latham was trapped in a nightmare. *A naked man hung from ceiling hooks, his wrists manacled. He was large, fat even, the skin, muscle and tendons of his poor shredding hands mangled by his weight on the manacles, as he swayed to the thud of cudgels on his back, legs and chest. The cell was bare stone, large enough for three jailers to have elbow room to swing a whip. The floor was slick with piss and blood. The man knew he was bruised all over, encased in pain, but the purest, shrieking agony was his arms, chest and shoulders, an unspeakable internal tearing. This fat man had Latham's face, the cudgellers yelling English curses.*

He woke yelling, frantic with the certainty of pain. Moaning, he rolled over onto soaked sheets. A chambermaid banged on his door. Hearing no answer, she unlocked it, rushed in, looked once and started screaming. She grabbed Latham's knife, staring around wildly. There was no intruder. She lit a candle and shone it on the bed linen, and the nuisance guest. "Blood," she cried. "Where are you cut?"

Latham sat up. Wonderingly, he touched his nose. It was wet, and so were his beard, chin and moustache. Still half in his nightmare, he saw his bruises leech colour, felt torn joints knit and the swelling of his wrists subside. He was whole and pain-free; he'd merely had a nosebleed.

He did what he could to calm the maid, and after standing and walking to show he was healthy, he dismissed her. Alone again, a thought entered his mind, meandered around it. Enough time had passed for his letter from Madrid to reach London. In that report, he'd confirmed the existence of a pro-Spanish spy in London, code-named *Trojan Horse*. Had he dreamed his counterpart's torture in real time? He shuddered. Was there another possibility? It made more sense for Walsingham to feed the Trojan misinformation than eviscerate him. Had Latham symbolically taken his counterpart's punishment? He couldn't know for months, if ever. Irritated, he cleaned himself up and went to find an apothecary. The gorgeous Neapolitan sun, hitting harbour whitecaps, Mount Vesuvius presiding over all with a shockingly innocent look, brought him back to physical reality. There was still information on bankers' loans he needed to pursue.

Lisbon, the same day, 11:00 a.m.

Don Cristobal and logistics clerk, William Boels, were working in an office in Estaus Palace. Abutting Rossio Square, the palace had been built early in the century to house royal visitors and diplomats, and its style was clean Renaissance lines. A more diverse population lived there now: military aides like Don Cristobal had suites, and soldiers, clerkly purveyors, and brocaded officers bustled in and out of offices or clustered in corridors. Black-robed clerics were ubiquitous, ominous squads whose smile muscles seemed ossified, for the Spanish Inquisition had its Portuguese headquarters here, overlooking Rossio Square's execution place.

Don Cristobal was preparing a contingency plan for King Philip to invade England. While he perused William's inventory of Spanish and English military forces, several pages with columns and charts, William leaned back in his chair and studied his manicured fingernails. Looking forward to praise of his meticulous work, he'd dressed well, in a blue summer-velvet doublet with pearl buttons over a white cambric shirt with blackwork cuffs and a flat lace collar. By contrast, Don Cristobal was wearing black breeches and an open-necked beige shirt. Paperwork didn't inspire him to dress formally.

Although William knew his work was excellent, he couldn't shake off a premonition that all wasn't right. In the arched walkway, he'd slipped on warm dog dung, falling on his knees. Why hadn't it been cleaned up? He'd come into the office scowling, tossed his cloak on a chair, then wiped boots and hose with a gloved hand. Cursing himself for ruining a good glove, he'd thrown them into the fire. When Don Cristobal came in, wrinkling his nose, he saw his clerk burning expensive gloves, and raised his eyebrows.

That's what happens when you come to work exhausted, William thought, bowing to Cristo. Rising from a raw recruit, a bisono, at Mons, to senior logistics clerk in the *empire on which the sun never set* took work. Becoming indispensable meant backaches, eye strain and fatigue. "Phew, that's better," he muttered, breathing through his nosegay.

Don Cristobal snorted, "Can't have a war without animals and their dung, Boels." He didn't like William, although he couldn't name his fault. In a fighting soldier, he'd admire the man's ambition. But he relied on his mathematical ability and had reluctantly approved his betrothal to one of his daughters after lawyers verified William's inheritance.

When Don Cristobal finished reading, he said, "Good. Figures from our observers and spies on English resources agree. If we land, we face about twelve thousand trained troops. More will be mustered, but they'll be raw, like you at Mons, Boels, shooting to miss. Ha, ha, ha! They'll flee when it begins. I'd add seven thousand battle-hardened veterans now fighting with Dutch rebels. The English queen will recall them if she knows we're coming. Assume she won't be caught by surprise."

"Secretary of State, Don Juan de Idiaquez," William expounded, "writes that our London spy, *Trojan Horse*, numbers 125 to 170 English ships, sixteen royal galleons supplemented by impressed armed merchantmen and patrol boats. He writes that the crews on warships will be a third reduced to save money, weakened by having to sail and fire guns. Edward Latham's report confirmed crew complements."

Don Cristobal paged through, looking for the submissions of *Trojan Horse* and Latham. He was infuriated when he found summaries, instead of the raw data he craved. *Why didn't I know that Edward was in Madrid?* he thought. *I'm sure he wrote; the messenger must have had an accident. My oath-brother that I haven't seen since climbing Monte Viso? What a neglectful cur he'll think me.*

Deeply regretful, he turned to Idiaquez's judgment of English capabilities and jeered. "Boels, English sailors are pirates. Of course, they can sail as well as shoot. We'll assume good crewing, short supply lines, and some of these appalling *Hellburners* that Madrid thinks Giambelli's building for Drake. Can we land? That's always the crucial issue with Albion."

William's job was to calculate costs and locate provisions. Feeling warm, he took off his doublet and collar. He reached for quill and ink, asking, "Sir, what ratio of our ships to theirs?"

"The issue with England is always 'can we land?'" Cristo restated. "4/1 in ships. 550, starting with the best Portuguese galleons. Order favourable winds, too. Ha, ha, ha!"

He got up, pulled a soft-bound pamphlet from a bookshelf and pointed to one paragraph. "My analysis of years ago." The pages had greasy fingerprints, obviously much shown. He pointed to passages near the end.

'The French king's navy reached the Solent in July 1545. His 200 ships faced Henry VIII's 80…One galleon of each side was wrecked, but only by accidents of their own side. A 2.5/1 advantage still did not allow the French to land.'

"Also," he said, "add money for foreign cannonballs. Our best gunmakers in the Netherlands fled to Protestant lands. Bunch of heretics. We'll have to buy ammunition from Italian states, which means customs duties. Now, infantry…"

He pointed to his pamphlet again: 'Tactics cannot depend on an internal Catholic uprising, despite what dream-touched exiles promise. The English queen's rule generally pleases her subjects, certainly more than a foreign invader.'

"What ratio for infantry?" Boels asked, sighing.

"3/1. 60,000 men. What, Boels? You're green at the gills."

William's mind was racing to calculate costs. He was feeling hot. He didn't know if putting his name to the price of this plan made him sick, or if his humours were awry. Perhaps a latent malady had caused him to slip in the dog dung; he was usually nimble at dodging street filth. "Madrid will hate the cost, sir," he said soberly. "Surely mighty Spain can knock over the English with much less?"

"This is a contingency plan."

Boels relaxed. "Then it's a starting point for negotiation."

"No. It's required to win. No one can make me say what's needed isn't necessary. Ha, ha, ha! Now, I have leave for a month. It will be your privilege to present the plan to Admiral Santa Cruz. He'll agree; he knows the situation. If his aides tremble and scale it down, give them my paper."

William undid his shirt ties and fanned himself with a hand. Don Cristobal saw sores below his neck. They were pale, but to him their foul nature was unmistakable. Appalled, he shouted, "Boels, you're whore-poxed!"

William blanched and ran his hand over the sores. He'd thought they were insect bites.

"Your betrothal is cancelled," Don Cristobal fumed.

William struggled to grasp that his only bedmate, respectable married Doña Maria, had infected him. He hadn't patronised brothels; he was the victim of perfidy. He opened his mouth to say so, then shut it. Putting the horns on a famous ship captain wouldn't advance his cause.

"Pack your bags and get out by midday." Don Cristobal took a breath. "Work from your villa and take mercury. But you won't be marrying my daughter when you're cured."

He strode out, slamming the door. Losing Boels' inheritance, which would have solved many financial problems, upset him. But he was also dismayed by having to put into honest writing what it would take to break the English navy. He had no illusions about easy wins.

In the empty library, William sat, devastated and angry; he knew that Don Cristobal had bedded camp girls at Mons. Having union with Spanish nobility unfairly ripped from William hurt him. Ever since Alvarado had told him, after the ambush at Saint-Ghislain, to be on the winning side, which was Spain, he'd served them devotedly. Nothing thrilled him more than the inscription on the new Spanish/Portuguese customs house in Lisbon: NON SUFFICIT ORBIS, The World is Not Enough. Infinity. A little of this greatness rubbed off on him. Don Cristobal had rebuffed him, but he'd still write and deliver this plan, and there were other noblewomen to court. Resolved, he got dressed and prepared to leave.

Joris had been in Rossio Square for over an hour, watching for William. He was standing outside a complex on the east side, All Saints Royal Hospital. No executions were scheduled, so the ground was bare of gallows, faggots and wood blocks. Military officials and clerics bustled in and out of the palace; poor patients were being helped into the hospital; tourists, artisans and workmen bought food, drink and fabrics from vendors. A few customers were haggling over dubious gold-streaked nuggets with fishermen whose boots reeked of salt and sea muck. Constables watched for pickpockets and abusive beggars.

Sometime past eleven, Joris saw a cloaked stocky figure ride into the square, followed by loaded carts. It was Don Cristobal, apparently in a glowering temper as he shouted at his carters to "move along, and don't tip on the way to the dock." Latham had told Joris to avoid meeting Cristo this time, so he pulled his cap down and waited.

William soon rode out on a chestnut mare. He had a leather satchel strapped to the saddle and was accompanied by one cart whose driver wore livery, so it was an official journey. William's clothes looked expensive, but to Joris's surprise he was slumping, the picture of pained defeat. When a beggar grabbed his mare's reins, William pulled a stone from his pocket and hurled it at the beggar's face. He missed, and his bad aim told Joris his cousin's wits were disordered. This wasn't the time for a reunion.

Instead, Joris untied his nag from the hospital horse posts and followed, keeping well behind. They left Lisbon through the Gate of the Duke of Bragança, close to the river. William took a road, at first cobbled then gravel, veering uphill. Lush fields opened on both sides, and the elegant spire and square complex of Our Lady of Hope came into view. Joris looked up the hill: a forest of spreading pines led to the summit, which had been cleared for two windmills. Travellers peeled off, some to the church, some to farms or villas. Joris turned back, not wanting William to spot him. He was sure he could bribe William's address from the carter.

He said nothing about his day to Marie, but listened eagerly to her tales of vendors she'd found, and the barrels she'd bought from the cooper, now full of sweet water. "Prices for seasoned barrel wood and iron are double two years ago, the cooper said. I wept and ranted, but only beat him down a bit. When I said I didn't need the barrels after all, that I'd come back next year when he'd be on his knees begging for my trade, he just hooted, saying it would double again, his order book already being full." She yawned. "I was all over today. I'll get grain and hemp prices next week." She was soon asleep

Joris stared at the ceiling. He'd seen mobilisation in Constantinople when Sultan Murad III went to war against Persia. Price surges suggested it was happening here, too.

Joris continued watching Estaus Palace, but William didn't appear. However, liveried couriers with stuffed satchels came out and left the city by Duke of Bragança Gate. Hours later, they returned carrying stuffed satchels. William was working from his lodgings. This continued absence suggested that he was sick or out of favour, maybe susceptible to money. With Joris's Ottoman trading licence, he had value in coffee beans and exotic plants. Whatever setback William had encountered wouldn't lessen his contempt for his cousin; he was more likely to talk unguardedly to one he considered dust-brained.

Joris retreated to the old storeroom and played the memory games Dr Gomes taught him until he was sharp. Then he hired one of the professional scribes working in Old Pillory Plaza, who called themselves notaries. Close to the docks, but north of the former royal palace at the harbour, the Plaza was a hub for merchants, citizens and visitors who needed a recorder of their thoughts: love in prose or verse, chaste or illicit; petitions of grievance phrased with a delicate balance of deference and outrage; glowing obituaries by hopeful will beneficiaries; testimonials for employment; personal prayers. Imperial Lisbon was bursting with vitality, but most citizens couldn't write. These scribes, with their stock phrases, flamboyantly penned, kept social interactions flowing. Joris selected one of two advertising services in Dutch, in addition to the standard Portuguese, Italian, Spanish and Latin.

8 April 1586
Most worthy and esteemed cousin,
Whereas I have come to this city…

William began to read Joris's letter and laughed, despite the pain around his lips. Grimacing, he read on. The secretarial style, akin to a royal proclamation, had set him off, so at odds with his idiot cousin. He'd recognised the penmanship at once: Flemings wanting favours from him always turned to this fellow.

…to prepare lodgings for my master, Signor Prosperino, with whom you are also happily acquainted. I find I have fallen into a troubling circumstance…

Fallen. Of course, Joris had fallen, William thought.

...wherein mistakes I have made, you, in your kindness, could remedy with benefits accruing more to you than me...

Imagining the starts and stops Joris must have inflicted on the scribe, William laughed again. He wondered if the scribe, who charged by the page, one rate for text and another for figures, had added a surcharge for time. He should have!

I confess I did not buy annuities, as you recommended, with our uncle's bequest (God have mercy on his generous soul), but through a high-placed slave official in Constantinople, I invested in an exotic plant that our countrymen and other European notables seek. My licence is in order, but the proper cultivation of this subtle plant eludes me. An erudite like you, esteemed cousin, could make something of it, and relieve me of an unsuitable labour...

Did Joris have tulips? William remembered him trying to cure tailless lizards and birds with broken wings. Most died; he was no physician. The scribe must have been astonished when he unscrambled Joris's meaning. This notion of that man's face lighting up with greed worried William. Thievery was rampant; if word got out, Joris could be robbed of the plants before William got them. He should meet his cousin at once.

Further, I will visit you on 9th April about the Cambrai house. It has tenants but no profits, because of the salaries for uncle's servants. I could not fire them as you instructed, they looked at me so melancholy.

With respect,

Master Joris Boels, City of Lisbon Jrosi B

Joris had signed with his usual letter scrambling, while Pedro Nunes certified the date and accuracy of his rendition of the customer's intent.

Late morning on 9th April, Joris rode up a gravelled driveway to a three-storey stone house, followed by a carter with trays of seeds and pots with bulbs. Overlooking the Tagus River, William's lodgings were far enough from the city to have sweet air heavy with the scents of spring. Noisy blackbirds swirled around fruit trees, and a dog burst from the stable and bolted after a bobbing white rabbit tail. Beyond the driveway, the ground cover was dry and scrubby, a fire hazard confirmed by buckets and ladders near the well. Still, it was peaceful.

He followed the servant to William's ground floor suite. His first view of his proud cousin was a bent shape by the fire. It was warm, but William sat hunched under a thick blanket, hands and neck bandaged. He drooled as he gingerly touched a loose tooth. The air stank of metallic sweat. Having never seen William struggling for dignity, Joris was overcome with pity.

They exchanged almost empathetic glances, kinship with Pieter Boels visible in both. Joris had his uncle's kinetic energy and dishevelled grooming, while William had his sharp blue eyes and learning. Pieter's love for them both jolted them to momentary fellowship.

But it didn't last. Asserting intellectual primacy, William pointed to shelves crammed with books, pamphlets and ribbon-tied scrolls. "I've read them all, three languages: military manuals, prices and currency equivalencies, mathematics, astronomy," he said loftily,

"You ...learn...ned." Joris scrunched his face.

William affected modesty. "There's always more to study." *How sad to need a scribe to communicate*, he thought. "But today you find me low," he continued. "Last week I was sealed in a long container and smoked with mercury vapour; a foretaste of the coffin. How I prayed. But the doctors say I'm near cured. I'm finished with overly friendly women."

Joris was looking at William's desk: there was a closed oak box on it with iron bands and two intricate locks. Writing materials filled the rest, except for an open jewel box containing a gold ring in which a small ruby was set.

Joris pointed to the ring. "L...look good...on... you."

William smashed his fist on the side table. "Fool!" he snapped. "Opening and shutting your mouth like a beached fish. That's a betrothal ring returned to me after I got sick.

That damned Don Cristobal cancelled my engagement to his daughter. It's her loss; they have no money. I'm fed up with how the fighting gentry treats foreigners from commercial backgrounds. 'Hey churl,' they say, 'lend me money. It's your privilege. I might pay you back if the sun slants right.' Bah, curse them all. Any man can get the pox."

Although William usually gave his countrymen short shrift, today he was in such a rage that he couldn't stop. "I'm five times the gentleman he is."

Joris assumed *he* was Don Cristobal.

"I let him think I bedded whores," William said, "but it was the wife of a galleon captain. She had other friends I didn't know about. Married women generous with their favours– what serpents. With the king a purist, they couldn't survive the scandal, so I kept quiet. I'm the noble here, not Don this or Doña whore. I work for the greatest king in Christendom, yet struggle on half-pay." Colour returned to his cheeks. "We can help each other, Joris."

Joris took a turn around the room, his attention seemingly riveted by wood nails securing the floor planks. Then, as if it had taken him all this time to think what to do next, he handed William instructions on caring for the plants, along with the prices Ahmet Gul in Constantinople had set for European buyers. William rang a bell for the servant to bring in the plants. After finding them in better condition than he'd feared, he asked, "What do you want for them? I don't have cash. The doctors are thieves. What percentage of the profit?"

Joris pointed at the ring.

"No," William retorted. "That's for a Spanish noble widow I'll court when I'm cured."

"Why... Sp...Spaniard? Spain...weak," Joris got out. He filled a goblet with wine and brought it to his cousin.

William burst out, "How can you say such stupid things? We retook Antwerp and Brussels last year! Our empire is so vast, the sun shines on part of it every hour."

Intuitively, Joris had stumbled on how to get William talking. "Or…m…moon," he grinned.

After a moment, William asked slowly and emphatically, "Joris, did Edward Latham say Spain is weak?"

Joris rolled his head ambiguously. Yes or no? William couldn't tell. After a pause, Joris held up his hand. "N…not b…beat…rebels… so weak."

William was so astonished to be arguing facts with Joris that he forgot about who'd given him the absurd notion of Spain's weakness. "I'll prove Spain's strength," he shouted. Opening a coffer by the fireplace, he took out a heavy brass ring with several keys. Selecting two, he unlocked the oak box on his desk. Joris would forget everything, William knew, but might retain a sense of greatness. He read out Santa Cruz' battle plan: 550 Portuguese and Spanish ships, their type and locations, artillery units, to blow apart 170 English ships; provisions and ammunition; infantry of 60,000 to beat 20,000 trained English troops.

Joris stared at the ceiling with a seraphic smile. Using Dr Gomes's memory techniques, he visualised or felt everything: Philip's great ships at their various ports; smelled the sweat of infantry hordes; ran his hands over gleaming guns; bent under sacks of cannonballs he alone loaded under a baking Mediterranean sun.

When William finished, Joris wriggled his back to relieve the ache from hauling sacks. "S…such big ships, b…boom bang, many soldiers be…below…much vomit. Ha, ha, ha!"

"Yes, cousin, much vomit," William agreed, almost politely. He was tired, and willed Joris to leave. "Spain isn't weak at all. It's the greatest empire ever, see? NON SUFFICIT ORBIS. The world is not enough. I wrote that battle plan. Never forget it."

Joris sensed William wanted him to go. He sat, and sat. "N…no c…cost…plants. Glad r…rid of them. Not… dismiss …Uncle Pieter…servants."

"Agreed," William said instantly.

At last Joris stood. William waved him out indifferently, eying the tulips.

When Joris got home, he banged the table triumphantly, raving that he had had his revenge on William. Marie ran for pen and paper, and they worked all night, burning candle after candle, as Joris called up his dancing pictures and Marie wrote numbers and names. Some things seemed muddled, but it amounted to a 4:1 ratio in ships and 3:1 ratio in soldiers, supplementary ammunition to be bought in Naples. She encoded it in French.

Joris drew William's box and tricky locks for Latham, expecting that he'd come and check everything himself. Marie added price increases for war commodities. They addressed their package to Signor Prosperino, care of his banker in Naples.

CHAPTER 26
BEER BARRELS
AND ASSASSINS

Greenwich Palace, London,
March 1586, one month earlier.

T he common swift in season could migrate from the Mediterranean to England in seven to ten days. Human couriers, winging their way in all seasons, were less predictable. Latham's report to Walsingham from Madrid, the previous September, arrived in nine weeks. Using images on an imaginary tapestry, it exposed a plot by Mary, Queen of Scots to be freed by a group in England, in coordination with a Spanish/Papal invasion to restore Catholicism. In addition, Latham confirmed the existence of a pro-Spanish spy in London, code-named *Trojan Horse*. This report was David Hicks' central concern.

In April, back in Lisbon, Marie and Joris were waiting for an acknowledgement of getting Spain's battle plan from Latham in Naples. Latham had been learning about loans that Genoese bankers planned to make to the warring Dutch and Spanish parties. Both of Latham's employers wanted this information, Idiaquez because Philip needed new money to mount any large expedition, and Walsingham because he thought he could persuade bankers not to lend to the Spanish king. For his part, Latham waited eagerly for a package from Joris and Marie.

It was normal, in the murky world of espionage, that time seemed to jerk back and forth, while actions marched inexorably toward their consequences

Thirteen hundred miles from Naples, David Hicks was pulling his earlobe as he argued with code-breaker, Thomas Phelippes. Hollow-eyed from the stress of staying ahead of Elizabeth's enemies, they weren't discussing Latham's report that he'd sent from Madrid. They were arguing about papers in wooden tubes swimming in fluid inside more wood: more precisely, whether wooden tubes containing letters inserted into beer barrels were waterproof enough to keep the writing intact.

England's spymaster, Sir Francis Walsingham, had a new way to spy on Mary, Queen of Scots, now imprisoned in Chartley Castle. A handsome ex-seminarian, dissipated and morally foggy, had changed allegiance when his English captors showed him the rack. Gilbert Gifford had persuaded Mary that letters could be smuggled in and out of Chartley without interception, using tubes inside beer barrels. The local brewer was compliant, paid by both Mary and Walsingham. Whether Gifford told himself that if Mary *did* no harm she'd *come* to no harm, wasn't known. At any rate, Phelippes decoded letters coming out, sent them to their destination, decoded the replies, and sent them to Mary in a new barrel. After an innocuous beginning, the content had turned conspiratorial. Thus Mary's letters from Chartley and Latham's dispatch from Madrid about a developing plot to free her, with foreign support, were the same story.

It was crucial that no letter from or to Chartley get spoiled. The question worrying Hicks was whether the sealing on the tubes was strong enough to last through a normal consumption cycle, in case a mark from the brewer signifying that a barrel had letters was overlooked. In Walsingham's office–he was away–they were testing a tube's durability through slow consumption of a full barrel.

"Do we have to drink it all?" Phelippes asked, grimacing. It was the second day.

Hicks chortled. "Queen's beer. Enjoy it."

After one more mug and a belch, Phelippes summoned pages. To their puzzled delight, he ordered them to drink the barrel dry, then take the day off. When they left in wobbling good humour, he took off his doublet and rolled up his shirt sleeve. Opening the bunghole, he inserted tongs and pulled out a tube. The test letter inside was smudged. "Alright, we need better waterproofing," he grunted, drying his hand and rolling down his sleeve.

He picked up Latham's letter and Hicks' summary, glancing from one to the other "I know our Daniel had to be careful in the lion's den and use plain text, but I hate metaphors. You did well, attaching logic to tapestries and so forth, but that kind of writing shifts the burden of interpretation to us. What if we're wrong? His principal image: the caged unicorn is obviously Mary; men of rank free her, pictured as hunters with modern ruffs; galleons on a choppy sea suggest invasion. A Papal courier says the pope approves Philip marrying Mary when the attack succeeds. God's death, the notion of wedding Mary makes even me pity Philip."

Phelippes put the papers back. "Our first worry: who are the men of rank? Can they get to Elizabeth before we get to them? Do they have access to court gardens or the presence chamber?" He hit his forehead with his palm. "It's no light task, protecting Elizabeth. Who *are* they?"

"The gang isn't finalised, is my guess," Hicks pulled his earlobe again. "Latham's clever, don't you think? He's my kin by marriage."

"You claim him when he does well. Not when you have to get his sister, Katherine, out of trouble for harbouring priests." Phelippes spoke gently as he looked up at the taller Hicks. "Her Majesty won't raise his fees. She's a clutch-purse."

Hicks shrugged and looked at his timepiece. Noon. He ordered dinner for two from the kitchen. The rest of Walsingham's staff were at Windsor Castle, where the court would soon assemble for Easter. Walsingham was at a private audience with Elizabeth, and not expected back.

"What will he tell Her Majesty?" Hicks asked.

"Nothing about letters in beer barrels." Phelippes laughed, then paused for a rumble outside. Carts carrying tapestries and furniture were being wheeled along bare floors. Greenwich Palace was being stripped for seasonal cleaning.

"Walsingham won't be caught a second time," Phelippes continued when it was quiet. "Last time we had a window on Mary's letter, you were abroad. You don't know how *she* messed us up."

He paused as a crash sounded from outside. "When Sir Francis told dear dread Elizabeth that we had a spy in the French Embassy intercepting Mary's letters, she told the French ambassador that she knew all that was afoot. She was desperate to stop Mary from going too far, lest she had to act against her. We got nothing good after that. He'll describe what we know about this plot, not our methods. Otherwise, she'll pre-empt us again."

Two exhausted kitchen servants delivered a modest stew with bread, the kitchen already short-staffed. Hicks stuck his finger in the glutinous gravy. "Archival venison." He dismissed the servants with a rueful smile and tip.

"They must agree on tactics," Phelippes said when the door shut.

He never mislays a thought during interruptions, Hicks noted admiringly.

"Walsingham wants to let the plot ripen; identify every

conspirator and supporter," Phelippes expounded. "But letting the plot ripen requires Her Majesty to be *bait*. Is she willing to put herself in danger, seemingly nonchalant, relying on the quick reflexes of guards who don't know there's a plot to murder her? We can't tell them, in case one of them is part of it. Should Elizabeth take the risk, since the realm depends on her safety? We're determined to catch Mary plotting assassination in writing. Her Majesty won't want Mary caught, because there'll be a universal bray to put her to trial and execution. Legally trying a monarch appalls her. And Mary is her cousin."

"I see her objection," Hicks said. "It upends social order. Mary was forced at knifepoint to abdicate. If you believe an anointed sovereign is still sovereign by birth, there's no jury of her peers."

"It would be a precedent, and ends only one way." Phelippes smiled. "Mary should have felt the axe years ago."

"But, Tom," Hicks persisted, "if common law can take Mary's head, it can take any monarch's head. Where would authority issue from?"

He was talking to air because Phelippes had left the office. *How can he be so meticulous about the minutiae of plots, and so casual about upending all society?* Hicks wondered.

When they met again, before leaving for the day, Hicks began, "I thought about Her Majesty telling the French ambassador she knew what was in Mary's letters. She's forewarned plotters before. She forewarned the Duke of Norfolk twice; executed him only after his second treason. I say she performs her function as a divinely anointed earthly ruler, offering free will, agency, as God offered Adam and Eve. That's not an indiscretion."

Phelippes wasn't willing to imbue female tattle with theological subtlety. "Agency forsooth," he snorted. "Yes, she's forewarned high-ranked traitors with retainers, to mitigate dangerous opposition from factions to the traitor's punishment. I haven't seen any forewarning of the poorer sort of rogue. But you proved my point. We can't tell her about letters in beer barrels, or she'll forewarn Mary, the greatest traitor of all."

Hicks shifted tack. "Still, trying to deter war is always a virtue."

"I'm not sure I agree," Phelippes mused, pulling his cloak off the wall hooks. "I'm of the faction for a cleansing reckoning. Anyway, I'll be busy with Mary's cyphers for the duration. We'll get her this time!" He scraped a finger across his throat.

"No reckoning is clean, Tom!" Hicks shouted to the open door.

Naples, May 1586

In his private inn room, Latham opened Joris's box from Lisbon, untied the bitter- smelling sack and chewed some coffee beans. From a false bottom, he retrieved Marie's pages. An apocalyptic scale of warships, infantry and weapons emerged from his letter-by-letter decryption. He gasped and sat back on his heels, not quite able to visualise this armada of 550 ships and 60,000 infantry. He stood, kneaded his aching back. Joris and Marie had done brilliantly. Still, some dispositions were garbled, and it wasn't his own work. He began his letter to Hicks:

I can't confirm these military details until I see the document myself. That I risk a rending burning death is of no account, given this matter's importance. I pray the realm will not be dismembered. He put the unfinished letter away, as he was expecting a visitor who might add useful information.

Nervous, he tidied up, dabbing himself with perfume of moss, mushroom, twigs and violets, then filled bowls with washing water. *He's comely*, he thought admiringly of the sailor who'd soon arrive. Charles was wiry, with freckles, a broken nose, curly red hair and a brindled beard. Latham was flattered that Charles was eager to come to his rooms, and was also hoping that an afternoon of sport would yield intelligence.

He'd met Charles by chance. The week before, he'd gone to Molo Piccolo, the city's compact new mercantile and tourist docks, to hire couriers to take his report to Idiaquez on loans bankers might make to the rebel Dutch and their allies; and his report to Hicks on loans bankers might make to Spain.

He was about to return to his lodgings when he saw a merchant convoy bound for Molo Piccolo. But one ship turned toward the ancient docks of Molo Grande, abutting the administrative centre Castle Nuovo. A pilot boat sped out to guide the ship in, while soldiers lined up to supervise unloading.

The breakaway ship was a Mediterranean carrack, which was normal. But Latham's attention was caught by the square white sail on the mainmast. Its double black eagles of the Lubeck Hansa was unusual. In the months he'd been here, Latham had learned that Hansa merchants typically didn't run their own ships in the Mediterranean; they chartered local boats instead. A long white pennant with the red cross of St George signified that this carrack was on official business for Spain. A Hansa ship working for Spain now meant hurting England; Latham had to learn more. English merchants hadn't been expelled from the Holy Roman Empire, as Farnese wanted; despite the petition two years ago from the Lubeck Council. But Hicks would certainly want Latham to investigate the carrack.

He walked to the end of the dock, crossed a wide, busy boulevard and entered a piazza. A few yards in, a street vendor was selling flowers and herbs. Latham bought violets, put them in his breeches pocket, and walked to the dock entrance of Molo Grande. Some of the carrack's crew were already going on leave. He followed them into the bawdy areas of town, watching as they peeled off into gaming houses and brothels, hoping to find one seeking male rather than female company. The signal was violets pinned on a cap, jerkin or cloak. Latham was about to give up when one sailor looked about nervously, consulted a scrap of paper in his hand, pinned dried violets onto his jerkin, and bolted into a tavern called the Huntsman's Bow. Latham grinned, relieved and nervous; the sailor looked pleasant.

For a while, he walked the streets and dock then came back to the Huntsman's Bow, a violet pinned to his feathered cap. The sailor was drinking alone, on a bench near the serving hatch. Between sips, he looked around with anxious disapproval.

Latham put him at ease with his obliging manners. For the time being, he avoided pointed questions. He gathered that the sailor had ten days leave, while new cargo was being loaded, and he was in Naples for the first time. Charles Groen was a Fleming, and had sailed on Dutch or Hansa-owned ships since boyhood. He was incurious, good-natured and voluble; the perfect source, if he knew anything.

Over their first dinner, Charles had helped Latham understand what kinds of vessels were suitable for different waterways. Latham had sailed often but had no technical grasp of nautical issues.

The next day, Charles had walked Latham along the docks. "That wobbling Spanish castle will run aground in our harbours," he said, pointing up. "Galleons, even galleasses, are no good." He indicated a boat with a shallow draft. "Now, that's what I'd take to escape Nieuport coastguards. I wasn't always on the whitest shade of law; done some smuggling in my time." Charles laughed; he thought that hinting at petty crime gave him colour. Latham grinned in response.

At their next dinner, Latham tried a direct question. "So if Farnese threatens to commandeer the smaller boats of Fleming

Hansa merchants, to make them do what he wants, they bow, sweat, quake, and say 'yes'?"

"Right," Charles confirmed. "Under his pressure, we ship official cargoes from Naples to Cádiz, Brussels to Lisbon."

They'd arrived at what Latham needed. He tried for specifics. "What cargo, exactly?"

Charles scratched his beard dubiously. "Not sure I should say, exactly."

Latham took a reckless breath, suggesting that they meet in his private rooms the next day. He was mildly alarmed when Charles whooped. "I was getting worried you're just a looker! A sensible fellow does nothing onboard, see."

Latham's current lodgings were in the old city, an area of curving tree-lined streets whose buildings blotted out the sun. Many structures were handsome: two or three storeys, with arched entrances and intricate lintels. Scents of citrus fruits and figs wafting from back gardens spoke to settled life. But the chipped walls and grime showed that the district's glory days were over. It was a far cry from magnificent Palazzo Como, where Latham had stayed while getting his initial information about banker loans. There he'd been the guest of Benedetto Landolfi, aide to Florence's ambassador to Spain, Giovanni Figliazzi, whom Latham had met in Florence. But moving from elegance to tawdry always amused Latham.

Casa del Buono Vino e Sogni (House of Good Wine and Dreams) served food, had a common sleeping room, a yard for performances, and private suites. It practised the subtler arts of thievery: overcharges; counterfeit coins; a haven for illicit trysts with the potential for later blackmail. Two prostitutes in gaudy overskirts and fantastically dyed, twisted hair lounged regularly at a corner table in the tavern. But it was safe from violent crime.

When Latham answered Charles's knock, they dispensed with preliminaries. The first rut was fast, fierce, and in near silence; the second was slow, tender and teasing. Latham was astonished by his own performance, then very smug. The food he'd brought in got cold. Wine was another matter; they emptied three flagons.

A couple of hours later, Charles was chuckling over something he'd just mumbled. Latham rolled over to face him, stroking his thigh. Unbelievably, he was hardening again. "Charles, did you say that, in addition to the hemp and iron you've been shipping to Spain, that the Spaniards are buying Neapolitan cannonballs that don't fit their own ship guns?"

"That's right," Charles laughed. "It's funny. Spain's guns are Dutch, see, from when Spain ruled all the Netherlands. But Fleming gun makers, best in the world, ran away because most were Protestant. Italian guns, which the Spaniards aren't buying, require a different calibre. You wouldn't know calibre; it's the diameter of the ball. They have to match the barrel, see. Be a snug fit, like you up my arse."

"Shh." Latham put his hand over Charles' mouth, pointing to a hole in a dark knot of the wood panelling that he'd stuffed. "Someone here likes blackmail."

Charles blanched. He was voluble but careful.

Latham whispered, "But if they're too large, the cannonballs I mean, isn't it just a matter of chipping?"

"Could be too small," Charles rasped. "Me and my mates just heard the corporal warn the purveyor. No secrets on a ship, see. The purveyor didn't give the corporal the time of day. Low rank, see. Didn't ask the big or small of it. Purveyors just want bribes. Our owners don't care. The contract says 'Move cargo.' We do, to wherever. They don't tell us deckhands until we're at sea." He brushed Latham's thigh.

Latham pushed him away. This is what he was meant to learn. With his intellect satiated, his lust abated. He handed Charles a florin, "Time for you to go, dear fellow." He lay back and stared at the ceiling, barely noticing Charles's startled pulling on of trousers, shoes, a hasty misaligning of shirt ties.

How bad could ammunition mismatched to its gun be? Latham visualised wrong Italian cannonballs exploding Dutch gun barrels, the guns bursting their breeches, careening about the deck, mashing crew, devastating fires. Could it change a battle's outcome? Marie's letter had mentioned custom duties for buying foreign ammunition. It all made sense.

He'd add this to his report to Walsingham, who'd tell Drake. He also had to tell Idiaquez. But if his assumption about how information was handled in Madrid was right, the clerk's clerk would dismiss a common Fleming's account of a dispute among his betters, not even conducted in his own tongue.

By now, Charles had aligned his shirt ties. He broke Latham's reverie. "You're a strange one, Signor. Hot member, cold heart. Will I see you again?"

Latham got up and punched him playfully on shoulder. "I like you, Charles. Not here; I'm leaving. But maybe in Lisbon or Boulogne. Ask for me."

Mollified, Charles left.

Feeling wonderfully energised—even hoping more chance meetings were in their future—Latham watched Charles lope toward the piazza. Then he finished his reports. Letters sealed the following morning, he arranged passage on a ship to Barcelona, intending to join a courier relay to Lisbon, to check on Marie and Joris's report.

Six weeks later, he was congratulating himself on having made the journey. William Boels was in Madrid, courting a new Spanish bride, so Latham had time to go to his house, open the tricky locks, and study the battle plan. Joris had done amazingly well at memorising, but he had muddled some things. There were also notes in the margin—by Idiaquez' clerk's clerk?—that looked fresher than the original script: *His Majesty says this is a 'well-thought-of plan, that will be considered when*

right occasion arises.' What right occasion, Latham wondered with a shiver, could trigger this mammoth enterprise? Then at the bottom, the cryptic word: *less.* A window into Spanish thinking, it was incredibly valuable. He decided to deliver it personally in a few months, which meant re-entering England with as little authorisation as he'd left.

After giving Joris and Marie leave to see her parents at the farm near Épinay, France, Latham watched the Lisbon shipyards and harbour. Everything he saw and heard gave the impression of systematic refitting, but not mobilisation. Whatever occasion Philip thought right for triggering Santa Cruz's invasion plan hadn't yet occurred. A letter from Don Cristobal explained Spain's lack of direction. He'd sent it to Latham's banker in Naples, who forwarded it to Lisbon. Dated 2nd April, Latham got it in late September.

> *Esteemed Midas Mithridates,*
> *Your oath-brother mourns such long separation and*
> *absence of letters, praying daily no palsy or fever has taken*
> *you.*

Latham stopped, remorseful that open-hearted Cristo was now an unknowing adversary. He went for a walk. St George's Cathedral glowered over the steep staircase street. He longed to seek the confessional, but his duplicity wasn't something he could open to a Lisbon priest without lying, compounding his sin. It wasn't the first time he'd felt spiritual deprivation in a place so abundant in opportunities for it. He settled for private prayer in a side chapel.

After busying himself with errands, he girded himself to Cristo's letter.

I had home leave after finishing a contingency plan…

Latham chewed his lip; the fruits of that work were inches away, in his desk drawer.

My daughter Isabella was betrothed to William Boels. We planned a wedding during my leave, but mutual reconsideration ended it. I hardly know the whelps, my children, so little am I home because of our accursed wars. But thanks to Teresa they grow splendidly in health and spirit, which I beg God's favour to continue. How I yearn for my oath-brother to admire them, and to run his fingers through the tricky crumbly soil that makes us who we are. Still, feeling a stranger on my own ancestral estate, I applied to rejoin the Army of Flanders. The captain delivering my commission had no clarity: policy is divided over finishing the Dutch rebels off first; attacking their foreign supporters first; taking more Americas land for silver. All depend on the Turks renewing our yearly truce. I recall you were in the infidel capital. Do you know their mind, at all? I long to serve Farnese and embrace you again, in equal measure.

Yours fondly,
Cristo.

Latham put Cristo's information together with his observations in Lisbon and sent them to Hicks. *The Ottomans have a proverb*, he wrote: *'the mouse, though it could not squeeze through the hole, had a pumpkin tied to its tail.' To you, who are so vicious to Catholics, and to Philip, vile persecutor of Protestants, thinking refuge lies in the dark hole beyond, I say 'behold two brainsick mice.'*

He paused, looking at the side table where he'd put Ibrahim's clock with the silver falcon on top, its hands at 2.00, the hour of his death. "Did you just speak through me, love?" he murmured. A floor tremor set the clock shaking. The hands moved then stopped, a small earthquake.

"Think with subtlety," Ibrahim had advised him. *Very well*, Latham thought. He replied to Cristo with a plea for patience with the rolling stone that was his friend, always on the move from Boulogne to Naples to Madrid and back, ahead or behind his pension and letters from kin and friends. As to a Turk/ Spanish truce, with apologies, he'd heard nothing.

But the policy significance of the Turkish truce sparked his curiosity. He wrote to Ahmet Gul in Constantinople, asking him to reply to his last rooms in Boulogne. He burned a finger as his hand shook heating the wax; giving a Boulogne address committed him to leaving the centre of activity here, where Hicks wanted him; and going there. That meant he really *was* going to slip into England. Against orders.

Hampshire, one month earlier, August 1586.

David Hicks was enjoying the second day of his first holiday in years. He lay back on the picnic blanket, gazing up at a five-shade rainbow while his children played. They were at the bucolic estate of his wife Isabel's cousin, Mark Ashley, in Hampshire. In truth, they were all damp, as were the roast chicken and pies they hadn't finished before the squall, but no one cared. In the estate's woods, he saw a falcon soar into the sky, hover and dive; his oldest son was hawking for the first time with Mark and his falconer. Down the hill, two of his daughters were whooping on ponies with Mark's three girls; his two younger sons were at the archery butt with Mark's son; under umbrellas, Isabel and Mark's second wife, Mary, talked as they played cards Servants were everywhere, watching the children, clearing away the food, drying things off, replenishing drinks.

Ours is a felicitous marriage, Hicks thought. He looked at Isabel fondly: the passionate attraction he'd felt at the beginning had muted. Her obsessive focus on minutiae of lace, thread, hat feathers, gems woven into hair and clothes, which made her always a work of art to contemplate, had worn thin after a while. Just as the romance of his work in the spy service wore thin on her, since he couldn't talk about it. He couldn't mock village portents of doom to allay her fears or warn her about how fragile the country's stability was when the public mood was complacent. But she hadn't denied him her bed, and they were blessed in health. None of their offspring had been lost to miscarriage, disease or accident; a miracle in itself.

Hicks closed his eyes and dozed, waking abruptly to the bearded face he least wanted to see. "Robert, you're a nightmare," he grunted to the messenger who handed him two letters. He got up, and they walked inside. Hicks sighed at Latham's enumeration of the 550 ships and 60,000 men that was Spain's first written invasion plan. The second letter was worse. In haste, Phelippes had resorted to drawings, which he normally scorned as imprecise, compared to cypher. However, there was no ambiguity in these scrawls. Seven stick figures with fish-like gasping mouths were netted; a caged unicorn stood, eyes rolled up, a knotted noose around its neck. The text read: *Return immediately. Facts, persons proven. Research needed for unprecedented legal trial.* The full stop was a crown atop a disembodied smile. The seven gentlemen plotting to assassinate Elizabeth had been captured, Mary implicated in writing. She'd be tried, conviction and execution assured. The awful precedent.

Hicks went outside again, spread his arms and howled at the rainbow, now just a smear across the sky. He held Spain's war plan in his left fist, Phelippes's triumphal missive in the right, which could provoke what was in his left. A few minutes later he was in the saddle, holiday over.

CHAPTER 27
THE ENGLISH QUEEN AGONISES, PONDERS AND POUNCES

Greenwich Palace, London, early February 1587

So it has come to this, nineteen years after it began, with my wretched cousin, Mary, Queen of Scots, fleeing her land to protective custody in mine. I, Elizabeth, Queen of England and Ireland, am pressed by my subjects to execute her, after her conviction and sentencing to death for plotting to kill me and to cause foreign armies to invade my realm. In a flood tide of rubbish from gabby mouths and pens, my subjects say I must cut off her head. Forthwith! Councillors, Parliament, learned judges and pettifogging lawyers, prate the same words. I am not ready for such a repugnant act.

Weeks have passed since the proclamation of the verdict and death sentence, along with my speeches to Parliament about this tragical affair. Copies are seen abroad, and I am importuned by all Europe. If there is a noble or cleric without loud opinion, I am sadly unaware of him.

My loving subjects say my wits have wandered because I haven't signed the warrant of execution. They call me womanly weak. It's true that I sit on cushions sucking my finger for hours (my finger, not my thumb, I protest to God, who understands all). I care not for food or sleep. I meet foreign envoys when I must, lend a solemn ear to their pleas to spare my cousin's life.

The King of Scotland, Mary's son, sent a dutiful letter lauding my mercy and proclaiming his natural love for the woman who bore him. His envoy whispered, "A dead bitch doesn't bite." Was that also his authorised message? I retorted "What, and put a worse in her place?" The mother's death removes the last block to the son's claim to succeed me. Other ambassadors say I should put Mary into their prince's care, who guarantees to keep me safe. Nonsense. I ask why I would take my security and that of my realm out of my own hands and place it into the hands of another, whom God takes at His pleasure. Yet others say there's no law by which to try and execute an anointed monarch. To them, I say, "I know best the laws of my land." My councillors cheer at this, thinking the axe at Mary's neck. To them, I say, "I cannot perform such a repugnant act." I rebut all proposals, so they whisper I am mad.

My ladies have earned many shillings telling diplomats that I pace the nights, muttering "Strike or be struck at." It's true. I don't resent their profits. I tell them to charge extra to say my bowels are out of order and I'm in fierce temper. But my night pacing isn't because of lost wits. On the contrary, I've never seen as clearly. I debate myself because there's no one else with sense to whom I can open my mind. I repeat "Strike or be struck at" because Almighty God has not illumined my understanding of which is better: Mary dead and no further threat; or alive, confined for my spies to monitor. What benefit comes from removing her, when watching her catches the delirious supporters who must kill me on her behalf?

My subjects love deductive reasoning. Firstly, Mary, deposed queen and vile murderess, plotted against you. Secondly, she is the threat at the centre of all plots to topple England's government. Therefore, thirdly, eliminate Mary and the threat is gone. This reasoning is nonsense. The threat is never eliminated, it just shifts.

I would laugh if these were university debates. There were innocent days before Mary fled misery in Scotland to bring misery here, before Dutch subjects and their Spanish king came to blows, when compromise seemed possible. Gusman de Silva was Spanish ambassador then. We could deal. He was my guest in 1566 for the debates at Oxford. My champion, Edmund Campion, soon to be a Protestant deacon, argued: a) The moon's magnetism influences the motions of the tides; b) the mood goddess is the highest body in the sublunary sphere; c) therefore, she rules all below. No one dismantled his artifice. But that reasoning has naught to do with life. Who could have imagined then that Campion would turn into a prating Jesuit, stirring disputation in my realm, disembowelled as a traitor? And that the Catholic courtier, Edward Latham, who left me that day to serve Mary and other Catholic princes, would now spy for me? No, these debates are all a futile attempt to bridle an untamable world. Still, when a small state faces mighty foes, as we do, cunning words can be good defensive weapons. I am well-practised in wielding them.

Consequences are the issue. If I am seen to sign, seal and expressly release the warrant to execute Mary, her son, James VI, King of Scotland, her ferocious French cousins, the Guises, and her kinsman by marriage, the French king, could join Spain and attack us. I rule half an island; if these nations combine, we're done. They could march under colour of vengeance; religion; or the cause of monarchy itself. If I, an anointed queen, execute by law another monarch, I have struck them all. There's no king, queen, tsar, margrave, elector or count of any religion who won't clutch his neck when the messenger gallops in with the tragical news. England will be the world's pariah.

Spain looks to war with us at some time–I've seen the plan–they could mobilise 550 ships against our 170. I showed it to Francis Drake. He proposed preemptively attacking ships in Cádiz. I refused. But if Mary dies by the axe, I'll have to send him for the realm's immediate protection, which in itself is provocative. My subjects, of course, have infinite confidence in Drake. He's a brilliant raider–all Spaniards quake at El Draco–but he's *never* fought a massed fleet action. When I remind Walsingham of this, he twists his mouth down even more than usual, as if I'm being disloyal to my own servant.

I don't believe the kings of Scotland and France want war; they have their own problems and have benefited from peace with us during my reign. But they'll be so sore pressed by their Catholic nobles that they may fear for their own crowns if they stay neutral. To protect my northern border and eastern coast, I *must* help them preserve their manly honour by creating ambiguity. My councillors won't see this. "Strike or be struck at" is no simple choice. I'd be mad if I weren't sitting on cushions sucking my finger.

I told everyone involved in Mary's trial that we princes were set on stages in the sight and view of all the world, and that our proceedings had to be just and honourable.

They were.

Thirty-six of the greatest persons in England heard evidence in Fotheringhay, where she was held, instead of a common law jury of twelve local men of no distinction, which would have been absurd for her case. I forbade the commission to issue judgment, instructing them to return to London and try the case again in the Court of the Star Chamber. The verdict of 'guilty' was thirty-five to one, both Catholic judges convicting her. Both Houses of Parliament examined the evidence separately and came to a unanimous verdict of 'guilty' and a sentence of death. They met together. Same result. Thus the present stand: my subjects say I must execute her, forthwith; and I demur.

If Mary and I were two milkmaids, a pail on each arm, I told them, if my life only were at stake and not the religion and security of the realm, I would not harm her. I like milkmaids as a metaphor. I often called one up to excuse myself from marrying suitors or refusing favours. I don't know any milkmaids, unless there's one among the poor women whose bare feet I wash each year. If my principal nobles know milkmaids, it's in the biblical sense of sin.

But this, indeed, is to let my wits wander. Milkmaids aside, what holds true is that this crime, my royal kinswoman seeking my death and the ruin of the realm with its religion, is a rare case to put to law. I had desired to avoid the "public ripping up" of the matter by offering her life if she'd confess, repent and disclose all her conspirators. I asked her no more than I already knew. I knew everything. She refused twice. How I wept. She pushes me to kill her, *to bring to an end the weary tribulations of her life*, she wrote. In her mirror, she sees a Catholic martyr, which is a twisted patterning of her errors that led to her present condition.

There *is* another way to protect both realm and monarchy. Two years ago, the nation's great nobles made an Oath of Association binding them to kill any potential successor to my throne who sought my life. They were in a panic for the realm when Philip's agent assassinated the Dutch leader, William of Orange, and Walsingham thwarted two plots against me. I didn't know about the oath until they showed me the signatures and seals, and asked me to help them make it law. It was meant, not as a trap, but to forewarn any claimants to my throne of the consequence of seeking my death. Mary saw the law.

The *Act for the Queen's Safety* has two parts: the first established the procedures under which Mary has just been tried. The second part makes it lawful for a citizen to kill a convicted person *after* publication of the death sentence. It doesn't state that I must be dead to come into effect, though its writers probably envisaged it so. The realm would be safer if Mary's death could happen quietly; foreigners *beg* me to do it this way.

In my speech, now published here and abroad, I reminded my petitioners of their oath: *I am not unmindful ....that you would swear to pursue to the death...every person who should seek my life and the place which I hold...a perfect argument of your true hearts.*

But having made this law, my subjects run from it in a faint. Speaker Puckering gave a stinging repudiation: "Either we must take her life from her without your direction, which will be to *our* extreme danger by the offence of *your* law, or else we must suffer her to live against our express oath, which will be to the uttermost peril of our own souls."

Peril to their souls? I had nothing to do with their express swearing, except to moderate it as it became law. What silliness. And what whirling prepositions! *Their* law is now *my* law, which they are in terror to offend. Well, I admire their ingenuity; they take advantage of their ancient privilege of parliamentary free speech. I tell you, Spanish Philip, if you defeat me, you'll find your new subjects marvellously unruly. Puckering had the nerve to say to my face that if they killed Mary, I'd make them scapegoats for state security. Would I? I'm not estranged from my manifest sins. To secure the northern and eastern borders, I might. But they scapegoat the entire realm for principles they've suddenly discovered because of this accident, and God's pleasure, that I still breathe. What's virtue, what's sin, in such a case?

I had to think quickly to counter Puckering: *by your leaves, you have laid a hard and heavy burden upon me...for now, all is to be done at the direction of the queen—a course not common in like cases.* I told them that we had to look to persons abroad as well as at home, but that I would do what was best for the realm..

Which is delay.

I didn't expect instant agreement from one of them to honour his oath and kill Mary. Rather, I used my womanly weakness, on which they opine so expertly, to arouse their chivalry, hoping for a discreet message later. I told them I would play the blab, and disclosed a new plot in which evil-willers had written an oath to kill me within a month or hang themselves. I dwelt on my death. *If the stroke were coming,* I said, *perchance flesh and blood would seek to shun it.* Moving on to Mary's vile plot, I added that *I should not have found the blow before I had felt it, and though my peril should have been great, my pain should have been small and short.* I borrowed from Sophocles, telling them that as a subject, then a sovereign, I had found treason in trust and seen great benefits little regarded. My trial of this world made me think that an evil is better the less while it endures, and them happiest that are soonest hence. Though I would be loath to die so bloody a death I doubted not but God would have given me grace. It was for my subjects' sake, not mine, that I desired to live, to save them from a worse.

There wasn't a dry eye in the hall. All knelt, professing their love. Still, despite tears aplenty, none offered to relieve my burden. So I asked for a further debate. I said that in common law, conviction and sentence in a capital crime usually bring a swift death. In this rare case, I asked them to separate guilt, which none could dispute after seeing her incitement in cyphered writing, from the sentence. I wished them to try to devise a way for Mary to live and for me and the realm to be safe.

They argued for five days, for which I honour them. They consulted laws and customs on refugees, prisoners of war, and hospitality, delving into precedents from ancient Greece to Saxon custom to present law. Walsingham's fellow, David

Hicks, with the one earring and chipped teeth, did much research, I'm told. No precedent they found applied to Mary. I prayed for just one dissent. What I could have done with one doubter! There was none. A second unanimous petition: I must cut off the head of my royal cousin, forthwith.

To justify my signing the warrant, they defined Mary. Who is she? She's my royal cousin, anointed Queen of Scotland. Not to them. She's no longer anointed because she abdicated. I demur: abdication coerced at knifepoint, as hers was, doesn't have the force of law. She's an anointed queen, illegally deposed.

My Lord Burghley always contended that being forced to abdicate for turpitude is legal. What is this undefined crime? One sin Tuesday and another Friday? She was accused of plotting the regicide of her husband, my cousin, Lord Darnley. To which I replied that her role wasn't legally proven.

"She's merely a cousin to you in a remote degree," they say. Hardly. King Henry VII was my grandfather and her great-grandfather. I laugh when the same wits advocate the succession claim of her Protestant son, James, as closest in blood. How can the son be close and the mother remote? Word by word, my garrulous subjects, even the vile murderess, squeeze me to the wall.

But canny vixens can find a gap.

I had to respond to their second petition. This time I put away milkmaids and images of my death. Instead, I turned to fate. *There falleth out this accident*, I conceded, *that only my injurer's bane must be my life's surety*. I praised their reasoned judgments, but all the answer I gave them was thus: *if I should say I would not do it, I should peradventure say that which I do not think, and otherwise than it might be. If I should say I would do it, it were not fit in this place and at this time, although I did mean it. I pray, therefore, let this answer answerless content you for this present time.*

I left all unresolved. I am charged under God first to protect His true religion, then to apply justice without preference and to preserve the safety of the realm. Can I keep Scotland and France neutral, while upholding justice and the express will of my subjects? I revere our laws. As princess, during the reigns of my brother then my sister, I was accused of treason. Twice I stood in danger of my life. But my answer always was, "Put me to trial." They did not, because there was no evidence, and I became queen in the proper order, after my brother and sister died naturally. There *is* evidence against Mary. As odious as the matter is, the death sentence is just. Her co-conspirators are dead.

Why was I thinking of Sophocles' *Oedipus Rex*, which I studied in Greek as a girl? It's the claw of fate. There's a saying that if you save a person's life, the beneficiary owns you forever. That's true of wretched Mary and me. I saved her life in 1567 when rebel lords deposed her. I threatened war if they harmed one hair on her head. I was the only prince to support her. Her French Catholic kin lifted not a finger. When I proposed a joint English/French trade embargo until the rebels reinstated her, the French king, Mary's brother-in-law, refused. Ironically, the Scots rebel lords feared for their southern border as I fear for my northern border today. Why did I have the passion for helping? She was kin of the same sex; deposed illegally; she bore a son who could inherit both our thrones, freeing me from the same. Would I have waged war if they had killed her? I don't know. In the end they didn't hurt her. So when she escaped, she ran to me, ushering in unquiet here; for wherever Mary sits, mayhem follows.

Despite her many plots, I kept her confined but safe. My subjects made law enabling them to kill her. Now they say only I must direct it. Mary won't cooperate with my preference that she lives. She owns my reputation as the virgin queen who kills a prince, her kinswoman. She owns conditions in my realm since war will likely follow her execution.

A few days ago, Walsingham went home sick, but not before regaling me with a new plot to free Mary. At his side was my ambassador returned from Paris, nodding like a puppet with a welded scowl. I question its advancement, but it's really too much. I sent a message to Mary's guardian to honour his signature on the oath. He refused, citing a horrified conscience. So be it.

Sir William Davison, a radical, is filling in for Walsingham as my principal secretary. I sent for him and signed the warrant. I told him, well, many things, not all consistent. I told him that he could get it sealed; that he should tell Walsingham, who'd die of grief, by which I meant, sarcastically, happiness; that I wished to hear no more about it; that he should not let it out of his possession or show it to anyone until after the Lord Chancellor had sealed it.

The next day, I said if it wasn't sealed, to delay; he said it was and I complained about his unseemly haste. I added that I had had a dream about him; that I had done him a mischief. He didn't probe; he could have. Did disdain for my sex withhold him?

If he obeys my instruction to keep the warrant in his possession, Mary lives awhile, perhaps to die of the wait. How wonderful that would be. But if he runs to my councillors and implements the warrant, I've got my scapegoat. I don't know what will happen. Never in spoken or written word have I *ever* consented to this deed. Even saying *my injurer's bane must be my life's surety* is ambiguous, because bane means harm, not death. I haven't expressly released this warrant. So if the accident falleth out that Mary's head is struck off, I can wail long and loud enough, to keep Scotland and France neutral. I'll have to send Drake to attack Cádiz, then try hard for peace with Spain. Surely my good brother Philip, deep in his heart, cannot prefer war.

What will Secretary Davison do? I forewarned him. I gave him agency. A seasoned courtier would see what I'm about. Yet I judge him stiff-necked, holding in his hands the document of death he and his faction have panted for, for fifteen years. Yes, destiny is in Davison's hands. Perhaps, now, I can sleep.

Boulogne, 10 March 1587

Latham woke to the shattering jangle of bells. From the old Church of St. Nicholas, Notre-Dame, monasteries and smaller churches, the raucous summons to wakefulness was continuous. He dressed hurriedly and ran to the market square. The ear-splitting tolling announced a royal death. Proclamations of the execution of Mary, Queen of Scots were pasted on walls. Town criers rubbing sleep from their eyes were giving places and times of Te Deums to her martyrdom. Pamphlets excoriating Elizabeth were everywhere, and balladeers reminded the crowd that the martyred Mary, executed in an unprecedented application of common law, had been Queen of France, wife of King Francis II until he died, then Queen of Scotland. Latham wandered around, numb. The queen he served had finally killed the queen he had once served. His grieving for Mary was long done: for months he'd hoped and prayed that she would draw back from trying to assassinate Elizabeth. But no; she'd ventured all, and paid the price. He barely registered the assault on his ears, as he pondered the consequences of this shocking event. Eventually, he returned to his rooms, where he found a letter from his sister, Katherine.

20th February 1586

Beloved little brother,

I know not if this reaches you, ignorant of which country you're in. I use the address I have in hopes that your good landlady will send it on. What terrifying days! Mary, Queen of Scots, was executed on 9ᵗʰ February (our calendar) at Fotheringhay Castle, her petticoat the red of martyrdom. A ghastly rumour is that espying all this solid red so disordered the axeman's wits that he had to chop thrice to end it all. The witnesses were two hundred local gentry and some courtiers. It ended months of suspense. I have enclosed publications from the queen's speeches to Parliament on the matter, which are printed abroad too, so you can see how the weeks unscrolled in mystery and tension. Bonfires, church bells, dancing and drinking of celebration by the stupid and barbarous filled the streets on news of Mary's death. There was a signed warrant, but Elizabeth denies she expressly released it. Secretary Sir William Davison, who got the warrant implemented, is in the Tower, to be tried for disobedience to his sovereign in the Court of the Star Chamber, the court that convicted Mary. Privy councillors who signed a memo sending Davison to Fotheringhay are banished from court. We hear of rioting in Paris, the French alliance tattered. God protect us; I pray there's no war. If you get this, dear Edward, please write to say you are safe,

With love forever, Katherine.

Latham read the publications twice and found no phrase in which Elizabeth agreed to execute Mary. There was ambiguity, a lick of fog shrouding what had happened. In the queen's summation: *let this answer answerless content you for the present time* he even sensed contempt.

He decided to stay in Boulogne for a while. How the kings of France and Scotland reacted to Mary's death was critical to whether four or two nations (Spain and the Papal States) would eventually attack. He expected Benedetto Landolfi, aide to Giovanni Figliazzi, Florence's ambassador to Spain and an informer to Walsingham, to let him know Spanish thinking, and was waiting for Ahmet Gul's reply to the letter he'd sent last October, asking about the Ottoman/Spanish truce.

Latham got Benedetto Landolfi's letter in April.

…Paris street friars and pulpit clerics preach vengeance on England. Mary's cousin, Henry, Duke of Guise, demands war; the French king demurs, giving deference to written assurances by

Elizabeth that it was a horrible accident; she never intended it to happen. Which faction prevails will ultimately be contested in blood, but for now, French royal policy is neutrality, and we hear of no immediate Guise mobilisation. Scots King James, Mary's son, sings neutrality too; he got Elizabeth's letters bemoaning the horrible accident. Thundering silence from Philip, who prays day and night. Military officials here buzz about whether the Turks will renew the truce with Spain. Thus far, uncertain.

Yours in haste, but with devotion to the common interest,
Benedetto Landolfi

A few days later, the letter from Gul in Constantinople arrived. Dated 8ᵗʰ January, it was sent before Mary's execution, but with knowledge of her arrest.

…Do you remember that moonless night in 1579? You and Joris stumbled along inside the stinky two-humped camel skin we borrowed from Father Jerome's church. I played the grey-haired clerk with a wrinkled face who got you into the guarded warehouse. There you found evidence of our trade preferences and policy. Brass, silver and gold Catholic artefacts that Elizabeth of England secretly sent our Sultan were used for his Persian war. She has done us other kindnesses. Her enemies will gather if the execution of that Catholic queen proceeds. We would return a kindness. In that case, our glorious Sultan will not renew the truce with Spain. Philip will have to keep one hand cupping the hole in the back of his breeches, not free to marshal all his forces against her. More explicit understandings could be written if the axe falls on that queen's neck.

Latham tapped his lip. He must be the first European to know this. Being first was everything, and he was now ready to risk going home.

That night was clear, with a crescent moon. He climbed to the roof and leaned against the chimney. Cupping his birth sign Scorpio in his left hand, Elizabeth's birth sign Virgo in his right, he told himself he was holding them in place. Separating Scorpio and Virgo was Libra, its scales winking balanced successes and failures. He stood for hours, moving his hands as the constellations shifted infinitesimally slowly. When the moon dropped below the church spire, he went inside. In a buoyant mood, he packed his bag.

CHAPTER 28
REUNIONS

Sussex to Surrey, England, June 1587

Edward Latham returned to England as he'd left twenty-one years earlier, without travelling papers and at night. But with a difference: he carried Santa Cruz's battle plan, with margin notes indicating King Philip's thinking, and Gul's advice that the Ottoman/Spanish truce wouldn't be renewed. A French smuggler deposited him on a mud-bank of the River Rother, the deep bells of St. Mary's, Rye's ancient church, beckoning with exquisite resonance. The river was unusually shallow this summer, so Latham had to get out of the boat before reaching a jetty. Easing himself over the rail, he clambered down the side and waded, his boots sucking in mud.

He'd prepared a disguise as a peddler, and daybreak found him carrying a sack of fabric scraps, cutlery and pot scourers, wearing a brown tunic and a hat with flaps covering his flaxen hair, and a short sword at his belt. After three days of hiking on muddy roads, interspersed with kind lifts on carts full of oats, caged chickens and hare carcasses, he reached familiar woods. He followed a deer track through, emerging onto a gravel road. His heart started to thump as raucously as the summer birds when he glimpsed Katherine's border hedges. Here he was unannounced. Katherine might be away; he had little money; he needed Hicks to square a permit, but Hicks could be abroad.

Would this reunion be a farce, like the one he'd attempted with Lady Barbara? In letters, he and Katherine had projected soul-fasted intimacy. But who were they to each other, really?

Through the iron bars of the front gate, the timber framing of the house's two fifteenth-century wings was unchanged. Two of the five red brick chimneys smoked, and healthy ivy snaked up walls. Someone was in residence; that was promising. The vegetable gardens, apple orchard, stables, dairy and brewhouse looked the same, and the maze they'd played in as children was still there, a grey striped cat at the entrance licking its paws. It was bucolic, but his skin rasped with apprehension.

A hound and mastiff charged before he lifted the gate latch. He stopped, offering his hands through the bars. They sniffed, barked without much conviction and backed off. Latham opened the gate and took a tentative step. The dogs growled continuously but let him walk to the front entrance. He wondered if he had a family scent, or if the dogs were trained to announce, but never maul. Katherine was known to have harboured Catholic priests, including Campion, and was often raided. Whether the visitor was a priest or the queen's priest catchers, it made sense for her to own circumspect dogs.

Memories triggered by his slow walk: Katherine was just nine, and he was three, when their mother died, yet his sister had taken on a maternal role whose bossy solemnity masked her generosity. She'd never relinquished instructional roles; of course she'd train polite dogs.

A second-storey shutter flung open, and the window opened—old mullioned glass had been replaced with glazed glass—and a shrill female voice directed him to the servants' entrance. A stable boy ran to tend a horse, frowned at the scruffy pedestrian and disappeared with a disgusted shrug. When Latham got to the maze, he saw that the plain hedges were now sculpted into twisting spires, pyramid-like towers or rounded tops. Topiary was costly. Along with new windows, the estate displayed prosperity. Whatever the differences between crown and Katherine, the house radiated settled confidence.

A rheumy-eyed servant opened the back door and looked at Latham's neck for a priest's collar. Finding none, he was about to order him gone, but Latham pulled out a paper seeking pot scourers and knives. The forged writing resembled Katherine's, which Latham knew intimately. Despite the oddity of Lady Katherine writing to a common peddler, the servant led him to the kitchen and sent a maid upstairs with a message. He hadn't said Lady Katherine was away, and he hadn't probed. Pulse racing, Latham hungrily eyed a half beef on a long wooden table waiting to be sectioned and spiced.

The maid returned and led Latham to the family wing, showing him into a parlour. Along the corridor, leather shoes and boots stood outside doors, and belts and bags hung from wooden wall pegs, more than this household would require. Strange. Then he forgot to think, as a familiar refrain caused his heart and soul to nearly burst his rib cage.

"Send him this purge and tell Williams to let blood a quart. Black bile is slowing his carving," the voice trilled. Purge: Katherine's cure for every ill. With crisp but uneven footsteps, she strode into the parlour. In the millisecond before explanations were required, Latham saw that her long blonde tresses, once as flaxen as his, were white, with an exquisite silvery shimmer hinting at pewter. She'd thickened, her skin seamed, and she carried a cane. But evidence of mortality only made her blue eyes more brilliant. She looked healthy and comely.

Carrying the forged letter seeking pot scourers, she stared with puzzled hostility at a peddler she hadn't sought. After years of managing a life of discreet religious dissent, she never made assumptions about visitors. She stood and stared. Latham swept his hat off to expose his hair.

She locked onto his hazel eyes and gasped. "Edward? It can't be. Edward? Oh, God be praised, my wayward wandering brother."

Latham opened his arms to embrace her, but before he could close them around her chest, she was on the floor kissing his shoes. Weeping, kissing, laughing hysterically. He pulled her up, his face mottled with embarrassment. He was as shocked by her devotion as she was astonished by his presence. A few minutes later he was upstairs, a fragrant bath being prepared for him. When he was clean and dry, they dined privately and went deeply into the frankest talk they'd ever had.

He said little about spying, except that, in his own way, he served Elizabeth.

"How do you live, Edward? Papa, God rest his soul, went to his grave never understanding why you rejected the match he negotiated: a virtuous lady, a fertile family with title and lands adjoining ours. I had a notion, but never said…" She looked at him, eyebrows raised. "Come, it's time for honesty. We might never see each other again. I know you're here unauthorised."

He pursed his lips, then pulled out of his sack Ibrahim's little clock with the silver falcon on top. He poured out his love for his great Ottoman friend, tragically executed. He described the comet that had oppressed the sky for a month, the emasculated clacking of wood on wood or iron that was the only sound Christian churches could make.

Katherine got up and walked to the window. Then turned. "Edward, it's as I thought. You scampered so hastily to Scotland at Lord Darnley's invitation. All knew Darnley's… um…flexible nature."

Latham blushed. He'd never realised he was such an open book.

She paused. "Men who prefer their own kind aren't a

mystery to me. My second husband, Roland, returned to those ways after we had our son. We live separately. At first, I was angry and insulted. But it's God's will. It has pleasant aspects: no voice supplants mine."

What followed was a rambling account of all her progeny: their marriages, positions and progeny, kin Latham was unlikely to meet. He tried to memorise the connections as she talked, but eventually gave up. Finally, she crossed herself and gave a great sigh. "None of my children serve in the Queen's church. We obey the law, and skirt corners a little." With a smile, she returned to his life. "Edward, dear, I hoped your closeness to Lady Barbara Blomberg had inspired you to more wholesome practices, despite her being so much older?"

Latham shook his head. "Lady Barbara is magnificent, but not my destiny." He described their intimacy as part of a heady mix of divine music and dabbling in high policy. "From the way I tuned my lute she knew my capabilities, and adapted her virtuosity down, so I could succeed at her concerts. That's a kind of love. I visited her in Ambrosero, Spain, recently, imagining I could renew the relationship, but the house was silent: rat-chewed music and dusty instruments. She was on a convent retreat, living for prayer."

They both laughed.

"I met a sailor I like in Naples," Latham added, tentatively.

"I love you absolutely, Edward," Katherine said. "Your sins are between you and God. All I can say is that you seek His forgiveness every day."

Latham chewed his lower lip. What he'd taken as unconditional affection contained a great deal of censure. But what did he expect? Religion, and abandonment by her second husband, naturally made her wish her brother was like other men.

Her confession was more immediately dangerous: while she attended weekly Protestant services, as the law required, after each service she visited a priest in the village for mass, confession and absolution. He was a tanner, but had graduated from Rheims seminary and was ordained. Few knew his secret because he didn't proselytise or foment rebellion.

"A tanner priest. So that explains all the leather?" Latham asked.

"Yes." Katherine smiled mischievously. "I buy each visit. You'll understand why it's relatively safe if you stay a few days. When Pope Gregory XIII issued his directive that English Catholics could obey their heretical sovereign without risk of damnation, I made that my guide. I yearned for you to come back, and thought you would. But perhaps you were wise. Pope Sixtus V now agitates against England more than other Protestant states. Why? Is Sixtus infallible? Was Gregory infallible? I honour you for throwing all up for your faith. I couldn't. This land, the children's status, our name. I'm too attached to them."

"I'm relieved you're healthy and in funds," Latham said, grabbing her hand. "I was terrified after I gave Campion your name; his charisma moved me beyond thought. He promised a covert mission, and I believed he could ease your fears, but all I did was get you arrested. I read his *Brag* and *Ten Reasons* in Saint-Denis cathedral, after his execution."

"He did conduct mass for us. It was transcendent to touch God through him. I'd never be without that experience. I'm grateful. But did he *have* to make such a blatant public fuss? He bragged that he could prove the rightness of primary allegiance to pope over crown while a papal/Spanish army took Smerwick in Ireland, and our forces were trying to recapture it. He gave up names. Of course, there's no blame; they racked him cruelly. Many of us were arrested, in terror for weeks."

"When I heard," Latham said, "I went to Walsingham to bargain your release for my knowledge of a plot against Elizabeth."

"Edward, how brave. I never knew. When, exactly?"

Latham knuckled his forehead, trying to pull a date from his skin.

When he found it, she exclaimed, "Oh, dear brother, I was released long before then. No charges, just lice and black-browed warnings."

"Walsingham never told me."

"Ah, we're all projectors selling the Philosopher's Stone," Katherine mused. "Walsingham, me, you, certainly the queen, Campion, the pope. It's fitting you came as a peddler with a forged letter. Pray for forgiveness."

After a companionable silence, Latham said, "I heard a ballad about Campion's execution: *A dew mist of his blood baptises souls new sprung.* Was your soul new sprung?"

"Yes, exactly!" Katherine agreed, happy for a more idealistic discourse. "There are different ways to faith. I chose a survival path, but new sprung. Since Luther, some great old families have split and gone to extremes: one branch obsequious servants of heretical governments, another branch assassins and traitors."

"I pray God lets us live beyond this reign," Latham said. "With Mary dead, her son James is next in line. Some say he's for true faith, despite heretic tutors. My vision is the peaceful succession of a Catholic Stuart king, and open worship for Catholics. That sustains me."

I'll earl you in England, Mary had exhaled when she had knighted him in Scotland. Perhaps James would fulfil that promise.

Latham's theoretical future didn't interest Katherine; she had a practical question. "When you sought Walsingham to trade my safety for your information, how did you get to him? One doesn't just walk in on England's spymaster, especially one serving Philip."

Latham frowned. Eros he'd confess, not spying. "I got kidnapped."

Katherine noted the hardworking word *got*, hinting at double tricks, the hunted becoming hunter. She reassessed the hazel eyes she'd always thought windows to a wounded heart needing protection, now seeing their hard, lived-in look.

Edward wasn't her wayward little brother, whose unbalanced humours could be cured by purges. He'd done secret work in foreign countries for years, and was a cunning manipulator and survivor. He didn't need her worry. Feeling sorry for him had always been a proof of her virtue; realisation of his toughness opened a void.

Servants cleared dinner plates. Katherine put a finger to her lips and showed him a panel behind a bookshelf. "I'm going in person to cousin Isabel, to send for Hicks. She's over fifteen miles away, and who knows where he is? I'll be away for a few days. If constables come, hide here."

They embraced. Ten minutes later, Katherine, a maid and the stable boy armed with a sword rode out of the gate.

She returned with Hicks the following week, both sweating from the July gallop. Sitting, Hicks mopped his face with his sleeve. "I've got a letter from Phelippes, good for thirty days. I'm glad you're alive, but marvel you came. Her Majesty ordered you to stay abroad."

Latham handed him Santa Cruz's plan. "This is the Spanish invasion plan, David, with King Philip's comments. I sent you my servant's summary, and braved Lisbon to verify it."

Hicks started to read, then looked up, face creased in disappointment. "It's out-of-season stale. Philip's note: *the right occasion to consider it?* Mary's execution. *Less?* We're getting hints of a different plan."

"Then read this," Latham said, thrusting Ahmet Gul's letter at him. "Sultan Murad won't renew his truce with Philip. No one in Europe knows."

Hicks read again. "Now that, dear kinsman, is gold." He paused to drink iced ale. "Let me lay out the situation. Drake's raiding Spanish shipping in Cádiz, but we don't know the results yet. Meanwhile, the Scots and French kings will remain neutral; they pretend to blame Davison for Mary's execution."

Latham grinned. "James pants to inherit England."

Hicks nodded. "The long and short of it, yes. Mary will be buried with full royal honours in Peterborough Abbey on 30th July. That mollifies James's sense of precedence, without specifying the succession. French King Henry is terrified of being toppled by the Guises, so he keeps the alliance with us. He could never beget..." Hicks looked slyly at Latham.

"Don't link me with that impotent self-flagellator," Latham retorted, pushing his chair back and getting up. "If I were king, I could beget."

"Yes, we don't need to duel over it. I'd never demean the *universality* of your lust."

The solid family man and nomadic spy stared at each other. "The point," Hicks persisted, "is that King Henry is the last of the long Valois dynasty. His blood heir is the Huguenot prince, Henry of Navarre. For King Philip and the Guises, this is catastrophic. If King Henry won't make a Catholic his successor, Guise will depose him before he dies of natural causes. So King Henry III, kin by marriage to decapitated Mary, stays neutral. Elizabeth saw all this before Mary's death. Her obfuscations and manipulations were to get us where we are today: everything terrible, but could be worse."

Latham sat. Hicks clapped him on the shoulder. "Wait for instructions, you brazen fool."

"One question," Latham said as Hicks buttoned his doublet. "What happened to *Trojan Horse*, the spy I exposed while I was in Madrid?" He held his breath, recalling his nightmare of torture and nosebleed in Naples.

"Describing him as fat helped. We showed him the manacles, then let him persuade us we'd made a dumb mistake. He feels safe, and we feed him falsities. He was never a plotter."

"When?"

Hicks wanted to go, but Latham grabbed his sleeve.

"A few days before Easter. Why?"

That was enough for Latham. His nosebleed had coincided with showing torture implements to *Trojan Horse*. Latham *had* symbolically taken his counterpart's punishment. "Never mind. Thank you." He released Hicks, feeling amazed, and oddly absolved.

As Katherine walked Hicks to the stables, he murmured, "Stop worrying, Kate. He's strange, both patriot and Catholic. He can't stay, though."

For the next two weeks, Latham lived Katherine's rhythm, braving the tanner/priest for mass and confession. The congregation was just seven adults. His eyes stung and throat rasped from chemicals, but he left spiritually renewed and bought one more leather belt to add the house's oversupply.

"His stink discourages all but the truly faithful," Katherine said as they walked home. "He baptises babes at night, after their Protestant dip."

This was the alternate life, Latham thought. "Katherine, you'll laugh at this, but I, who live in Catholic lands surrounded by priests, am constrained in full confessions. It wasn't that way for years, but since I serve England in my own way, it is now."

She laughed. "Nothing's pure for Lathams. What's the name of the sailor you like? I'll add him to my prayers for you."

Hicks sent a messenger, requiring Latham to meet him at the grotto at Theobalds, Lord Treasurer Sir William Cecil's country palace, fifteen miles north of London, on 19th August. It was time for Latham and Katherine to say goodbye. There was no shock of separation–they'd lived apart too long–but a profound emotional wrench. The passion of kinship had initially overwhelmed the reunion: their biological parents were the same, unusual in an era of early deaths; they'd had the same wet nurse; shared memories of the spreading oak tree with green lichen they glimpsed from the nursery. As separated kin, they'd each cherished the other as a muse. For Katherine, her wayward, beloved little brother needing support had been her lodestar; for Latham, Katherine's unconditional love had anchored him through peripatetic geographical travels and romantic attachments. Reunions brought them to love each other more realistically.

Still feeling the glow of their hard-won honesty, Latham dismounted three days later at Theobalds gates, waiting while crowds of poor people received daily alms and food. After his name was marked off on a visitors' list, he rode through the gates, handed his horse to a stable boy, and looked for the garden where Hicks expected to meet him.

In a small wood-panelled room that served as the privy chamber when Elizabeth visited Theobalds, she picked up a paper from a battered box and held it up. Her face was wan with the pain of an infected tooth. "What do you advise me to do with them, my lords?" she asked her councillors. A sardonic smile curved her lips. The delicious irony of having these particular papers distracted her from the dread of imminent tooth-drawing.

Everyone laughed. Looking at each face, Sir William Cecil realised that this was the first laugh that councillors and queen had shared since Mary's execution. Elizabeth's rage had started to abate after the Scots and French kings had signalled neutrality. Banished councillors like Cecil had tip-toed back into her peripheral vision and survived her rants. Of course, no one could resist laughing at the ridiculousness of her having these scrolls. They were papal indulgences; new ones, not historical documents from a library.

English pirates had been hunting in the Caribbean, but had got nothing but scurvy and two crates of documents. A falling mast had killed the captain during a storm that nearly destroyed the ship, which was drifting alarmingly close to Cádiz. Survivors had been thrilled to get Drake's protection, giving up papers for food, dry hammocks and grog.

The logbook had told Drake that the pirates had plundered

a Neapolitan merchant ship commissioned by Pope Sixtus V to sell indulgences in Hispaniola. Grasping the delicacy of the find, Drake had sent them back immediately, convinced that the Pope was raising cash to help fund Spain's attack on England.

There were two hundred indulgences, meant for Hispaniola's elite, signed and sealed, with spaces for recipient, sin and payment. The secretarial cover letter decried the vicious sins rotting islands blessed with riches, with correspondingly large payments required to absolve them. Proceeds were expected by return ship.

"What am I to do with them?" Elizabeth repeated.

At the back of the room, David Hicks prepared to take notes.

"Give them discreetly to our loyal subjects of the old faith," Lord Chancellor Hatton proposed.

"Who are they?" Elizabeth asked innocently, a finger on her lip. She listened poker-faced as arguments over this or that person heated up. Hicks scribbled names, crossed them out and added them back. He knocked the inkpot onto Cecil's new Turkey rug. Humiliated, he knelt, begging forgiveness.

Elizabeth laughed. "No harm, Master Hicks. It was inevitable." She looked spitefully at Cecil.

She's still enraged that I helped Davison implement Mary's execution, Cecil thought. He'd bought the rug for her visit; its exquisite golds, greens and silver would be hard to clean.

"We have two hundred indulgences, while I continue to believe the Almighty blesses me with hundreds of thousands of dutiful Catholic subjects," Elizabeth said.

Charles Howard of Effingham, soon to be Lord High Admiral, urged displaying them in London, to expose papal corruption, and stiffen the spines of God-fearing Protestants.

"That also tends to division, my Lord," Elizabeth rebutted. *Why can't they see that nothing can be done in England with the indulgences?* she wondered. *After all these decades, don't they understand that governing is polyphony, not monody?*

Her long-time favourite, Robert Dudley, Earl of Leicester, was quick to sense her drift. He suggested publishing them in Rome. "Jesuits hate the corruption of indulgences, and these, with their blank spaces, will be highly offensive. It will divide our enemies."

Elizabeth sighed. "It will purple that pope's face for an hour. I'll devise a remedy." Discussion turned to port defences and other practical matters.

She knows what to do with the indulgences, Hicks thought as he left the meeting. *She was playing.* But what can she do with them?

He looked for Latham. He'd proposed a place that couldn't be missed: the grotto in the garden open to general visitors, its entire stone surfaces glistening with overlaid metal and winking with embedded crystals. But Latham wasn't there. After an hour, Hicks gave up.

Latham had arrived at Theobalds on time but had no concept of winking metal. He went to the garden reserved for Cecil and honoured guests. Small garden plots, rich with flowers in full fragrant bloom were being weeded. Latham meandered along neat stone pathways, rested at the fountain, and meandered back again.

A door from the towered court opened suddenly, and Elizabeth strode out, accompanied by a tall, grey-haired slender man whom Latham recognised as Charles Howard, admiral of the navy. All four gardeners bowed and made for the servants' gate. Their swift backwards zig-zag scuttle was skilled. Deep in conversation over a paper the queen was waving, neither she nor Howard noted their existence.

Heart pounding, Latham stayed, bowing deeply.

Elizabeth was wearing a simple black velvet dress embroidered with silver thread and pearls. The fabric was gorgeous, but she had no farthingale and little make-up. *She moves like a predatory gazelle. Still.* Latham was amazed at her litheness.

"We thought to be private," she said to him politely, not

trying to name him or risk a mistaken guess about his rank. Clearly, she didn't remember him. "Please withdraw." She and Howard walked on, talking intimately and with animation, following the same paths Latham had taken to the fountain.

He bowed again, took a couple of backward steps, tried to catch her eye, but she looked right through him.

He heard her say, "He must be the new signet clerk."

"Ma'am, I don't know him, but that man's not the new clerk," Howard rumbled.

Elizabeth swivelled to stare at Latham while keeping pace with Howard and still talking, her piercing gaze drinking in Latham's character. Three times she did this: swivel and stare, while walking and still listening or talking. Latham saw in the swirling pearl-infused black skirt a firmament, a night sky running through seasons with each turn: Ursa Major and Draco atop Lupus at one moment; Andromeda pointing down at Orion at the next.

Here was his destiny: to serve order against chaos, through this divinely-anointed predatory gazelle, who didn't know who he was and told him to go away. She has lasted, he murmured, straightening up from his bow. To my old eyes she's beautiful: lined, intelligent narrow face; relaxed regality; bad teeth; innate fierceness. *This is the day Ibrahim predicted; the day I'd like my country better.*

They were out of sight, and he hurried away before they returned.

He looked for Hicks at the bowling alley, tennis courts, the Great Hall, where a mechanism propelled constellations across the ceiling, and at the lake and hothouse, finally finding the grotto where he'd been meant to go. Hicks wasn't there.

Hicks eventually found him taking supper with the stable hands, listening to the boys' accounts of how they got their position. Chattering excitedly, Hicks led Latham to his room, where there was a cot long enough for a man of Latham's height. "I sent my man to sleep in the gardener's cottage so we can talk," Hicks started. "First, you're to go to Madrid.

Our friend Figliazzi is Florence's ambassador there, in Philip's confidence."

Latham nodded, listening.

"You'll penetrate Spanish plans," Hicks continued. "Drake's on the way back. We won't have confirmation until he submits his logbooks, but a merchant docking last week said he had destroyed several dozen galleons at Cádiz, and burned near one hundred ships with supplies for Spain. He's taken a Portuguese treasure crammed with enough bullion, jewels and spices to fund the expedition. Philip's ships are searching their coastal waters for him; they have no idea he's nearly home. Spanish ships will have to refit, so no Armada can attack for months."

He started packing. "I'm leaving now, messenger duty. You stay the night."

"What's afoot?" Latham asked.

Hicks started laughing. "I'm to find a Portuguese physician in London and hand him a peculiar gift and opportunity." He described the captured papal indulgences, with spaces for sin, sinner and payment, and reprised the arguments over what to do with them. "What would you do with them, Edward?"

Latham thought. "Nothing here. Exhibit them in Rome."

"That was Leicester's suggestion. Her Majesty's dreamed up something more wickedly subtle. She's giving them to a Portuguese converso physician who's occasionally brought us intelligence. He attends our services weekly, but is a Friday Jew. He wants money, having lost everything to the Inquisition. She believes that this Jew will enjoy writing names, sins and payments in a pope's spaces. He'll sell the indulgences in Hispaniola, as Pope Sixtus intended, but split the proceeds with her. They're lending him a ship and crew. If Sixtus honours the indulgences, he'll please Hispaniolan nobles, but have empty coffers. If he repudiates them and insists they pay again for forgiveness, he'll alienate them, and they'll like us more. Either way, Elizabeth gets paid, and the doctor takes the risk. Walsingham says it's the prettiest political spite he ever saw. We have to make the most of anything that floats our way."

He tramped out, chuckling. Latham snuffed out the candles. *They were discussing the indulgences when I saw them in Cecil's garden*, he decided. *How vast the world is. To gain advantage at little Plymouth, a queen must dabble in Hispaniola and Constantinople.* Trying to visualise the infinite map, he fell asleep. Swirling black pearl-infused skirts and a narrow face telling him to go away, moved across the night sky of his dreams.

CHAPTER 29
A LETTER AND
A MURDER

Madrid, February 1588

L atham opened the window of his suite in Calle Cuchilleros, the same one he'd rented on his last visit. He threw the shutters apart and leaned out to inhale early morning street life. Snow-tipped roofs were kissed by salmon-orange clouds, with the promise of an imminent blatant sun. He cherished the green leafed balcony plants with their orange and red berries, emitting a faint freshness. The first street vendors were setting up carts, begging chambermaids tossing waste from windows to be careful. Bells rang for Prime mass, drowning out barking dogs chasing produce carts. He looked for his favourite vendor, an olive seller with a green and gold parrot that shrieked *Baked fishvomit, baked pigshit, Maryfullofgrace* at the bakery across the road. The olive seller heaved into view, hauling sacks, a table and a birdcage.

It was a normal day, except it wasn't. He'd been here for

months, failing to "penetrate Spain's plans." For the first time, those willing to talk knew nothing, while top officials remained unbreachable. Madrid was mourning the death by fever of the expedition's leader, Admiral Santa Cruz. But even appointing his successor hadn't shaken out specifics. Latham was expecting Benedetto Landolfi soon, aide to Giovanni Figliazzi, Florence's ambassador to Spain, also an informer to Walsingham. He fervently hoped that Benedetto had something worth reporting.

Marie had written from the Beaumont farm that both her parents had died while she and Joris were travelling, and she was grief-stricken. She was also now with child. Latham assumed the loss of the woman and man who'd birthed her, the desire to continue their line, had prevailed over her horror of pregnancy. He replied, expressing sympathy and joy, with prayers for God's blessings. He gave Joris leave and asked them to return as a family to his service when they were ready.

Although war preparations were being carried out in Lisbon, the information Latham needed was in Madrid. He didn't need a sub-agent in Lisbon. He knew that the repairing of ships and re-provisioning after Drake's attacks were fast and furious, but no destination was announced. Orders from Madrid had gone out to Lisbon and other ports that judges were to sentence criminals and heretics to the oars, rather than hanging or burning. An expedition was certain, but it could be to the Americas, the Netherlands, Ireland or England.

Latham knew England was the target, but couldn't prove it. Hicks sent frantic letters saying he must have the crucial papers by now. Thus the price of success: high expectations. What terrified Walsingham was that Elizabeth was insisting on proof of Spanish intent before mobilising herself. But since English and Spanish diplomats in Bourbourg were discussing peace, overt war moves weren't visible.

A cheerful greeting floated up. Landolfi's lips curved in his usual laugh as he pointed to the cursing parrot. A minute later, boots pounded upstairs, and he burst in. "I don't know why

I'm in a good mood," he said, reaching for the watered wine. "For the first time ever, King Philip doesn't confide in my master. Is he suspicious of us, or making peace talks look real?"

Latham sighed. "The talks are a sham. My orders are 'penetrate Spain's plans', and I'm failing."

"Well, I have an *anecdote* for you," Landolfi said. "Idiaquez heard from one of his peace negotiators that Elizabeth's astrologer cast a chart showing that peace is possible. She was thrilled. Idiaquez told the king in my master's presence. His Majesty retorted, "My astrologer has a stronger stomach.""

"Sarcasm isn't proof," Latham objected.

"I also have the latest published naval promotions," Landolfi added. They pored over them, noting the officers' careers. All had fought in the Mediterranean, none in the Americas.

"The destination isn't the New World, then," Latham said. He said nothing to Landolfi about one name on the list: Don Cristobal, liaison in Calais, no date set. That, more than anything, suggested that Cristo, now back in Spain's Army of Flanders, might be integrating a joint attack by forces from Spain and Parma's army in the Netherlands. But not proof.

Landolfi commiserated, finished his wine and left, eager to get back to the royal palace before everyone was up and about. Latham cobbled together bits and pieces for Hicks. To mollify Walsingham's anxiety about prolonged diplomacy, he wrote: *If Prince A gulls Prince B by not charging warlike, and if Prince B gulls Prince A by not charging warlike, both sides' eyes swivelling everywhere, then surprise invasion can't be compassed. Although long talks logically favour the mightier and richer in men and munitions, static hordes assembled for offence are prone to disease. If talks wander to the hot season, decimation by plague favours defence.*

On the third Sunday in April, under a cerulean sky, he stepped into a side alley and mopped his forehead. It wasn't hot, but the previous week had been bitterly cold, the contrast unsettling his humours. He was on his way to his rooms after

Sext mass when he sensed eyes on him. His mirrored hat revealed several possibilities. He leaned against a wall to see if his humours were playing him, or if he was being followed.

These were days of frenzied excitement. The sermon he'd just heard was a prayer to Almighty God to help his devoted servant, King Philip, by raising his friends and smiting his enemies. The friend to be raised was Henry, Duke of Guise, in a power struggle with the King of France, Henry III. A milquetoast Catholic and English ally, the French king was King Philip's enemy. If Guise could grab part of France–Paris wasn't out of the question–it would be the best thing since Antwerp's surrender, the bishop preached. Guise would help Philip attack England, if that was the mighty fleet's destination. Tales flooding the city affirmed the fleet was ready to put to sea, but still the purpose hadn't been declared.

Behold Latham's first follower: a stocky fellow in the brown monk's habit, hood covering his cheeks, fingering his rosary with a rough suntanned hand. A youth aping an old man's gait. The monk turned into Cutler Street, heading, Latham suspected, to his rooms.

He stayed put. Behold the second follower: a thin man with olive skin and black eyes, armed with a sword, following the monk. Or was Latham his target? He stopped yards from Latham, ran his tongue around his lips, then turned into Cutler Street. Latham knew him well: from Saint-Denis Cathedral in 1582, when the Spaniard let slip he'd secretly visited Henry, Duke of Guise; from following Latham in Boulogne in 1584; from Madrid in 1585, where Joris sketched him near Latham's rooms, and hanging around the Alcázar.

Latham waited, intestines braiding with terror. Landolfi had speculated that Philip was getting suspicious of him and his master, Figliazzi. Latham thought that he, personally, had put all doubts about him to rest after giving Idiaquez English naval plans–but perhaps not.

Eventually, he lifted a foot, then the other, and braved his rooms. He saw neither man. After eating dinner in the common dining room, he returned to his suite. An hour later, there was a knock on his door. Sword drawn, he opened it. The monk rushed in and threw up his hood. "Sir, do you remember me?" he asked in English.

Latham's mouth dropped open. He sat down hard on his bed. "The stable boy and courier from Theobalds! Ben Martindale. God have mercy, you risk everything. You're a terrible monk. You walk like a courier pretending to be a scholar. Look, you're being followed."

He took Ben to the window and pointed. Three shops down, the thin Spaniard was rejecting olives while the parrot squawked. "I don't know if he's after you or me. He's followed me before. Where do you stay?"

"I got work and board at a stable near the south wall, a pallet in the supply outhouse. It's near a new slaughterhouse. The ostler was desperate because two of his lads got kicked by horses upset by the blood smell. Said I was on a pilgrimage but would help as a penance. He saw how I calm horses. That gentleman won't go there."

"Don't be complacent," Latham cautioned. "Weren't you hand-fasted to a lass with child? What's this about?"

"It's such a secret mission that Master Hicks, with Sir William Cecil's agreement, decided it should be handled differently."

"It has been," Latham sighed. "You're incompetent."

"I got here with my package."

Latham poured him a cup of wine. "Dear boy, getting back's the hard part."

He took the box Brother Ben offered. The carved ebony exterior had indentations where embedded jewels had been cut out, while inside, the cream satin lining cradled a vial of ancient blue-green pitted glass that displayed a finger bone. A false bottom gave up two letters, one with a red wax royal image.

Latham put them on his bed and sat, arms folded. "Explain."

"The box is a relic Thomas Cromwell took from a dissolved monastery in old King Henry VIII's day. For my cover, not to sell."

"That's a relief. Whose finger is it?"

Ben grinned. "Well, sir, it depends if I'm asked in France or here. But the letters are the thing. The queen's message is wrote direct by Sir Francis Walsingham, Secretary of State, to his counterpart, Don Juan de Idiaquez. It is to be delivered unopened to Idiaquez by Giovanni Figliazzi, Florence's ambassador here, and given to Figliazzi by you, because of your good offices with this Figliazzi and the Spanish king. The other letter is to you from Master Hicks, so you'll understand any answer you get. You bring the answer to me, and I rush back, eat and sleep in the saddle. Then I marry Rosemary, all proper and with goodly funds."

Latham asked, "Do you know the matter?"

"No. I'm just the courier."

Latham put a blanket on the floor for Ben and went out for meat pies. While Ben dozed, he decoded. Hicks wrote that Farnese, Duke of Parma, told English peace commissioners that Philip would never make peace, but that Parma could briefly halt his attacks on English soldiers in the Netherlands. Having failed to win a general truce, the English commissioners pleaded for permission to come home, but Elizabeth ordered them to stay and talk without pre-conditions. She hadn't fully mobilised, because she still lacked proof that the Spanish fleet was bound for England. Everyone was tearing their hair, bewailing her irresponsibility.

However, she *had* listened. She'd hit on the way to verify Philip's intent. Going around her commissioners, she was sending a direct message to Philip through Walsingham, using Latham's connection to Figliazzi and Idiaquez, that she was sincere in wanting to negotiate all points at conflict without pre-conditions. The implication that "all points at conflict" included tolerance for English Catholics floated there, but wasn't specified. A man of true faith wouldn't disdain peace.

If Philip agreed, and the Armada was bound for England, he'd stop it, and save money and men; any other response meant war.

Hicks summarised the arguments Figliazzi was to present: there were ongoing efforts in Rome for reconciliation between England and the papacy, led by a Jesuit who had good relations with both parties and loved peace. An Anglo-Spanish alliance was traditional; Elizabeth appreciated Philip's early support of her when she first became queen, and thanked him again, but her offence at his later plots against her was justifiable. Finally, her negotiators in the Netherlands would talk without pre-conditions.

Was it a cynical gambit, or a very desperate last throw? Latham woke Ben, got directions to his stables and sent him away. Then he rode to the Alcázar to find Landolfi. Philip, Idiaquez and Figliazzi were at the El Escorial Palace and Monastery, twenty-eight miles from Madrid. But Landolfi was expected back last night.

Latham barely registered the beauties of the Alcázar; in fevered impatience, he suffered searching by royal halberdiers. He ran up the spiral staircase to the first-floor diplomatic apartments. Landolfi's manservant answered his staccato raps, looking mulish. "The master said not to wake him for anything but thunderbolts."

"I am thunderbolts," Latham boomed.

In a few minutes, Landolfi staggered out, unshaven, in a rumpled nightshirt, cap and slippers. "Thor? I got in a few hours ago, mad night ride. What's urgent?"

They went into Figliazzi's study, and Latham pulled out the sealed letter.

"You want me to gallop right back to El Escorial?" Landolfi asked, incredulous. "Can you swear it's even genuine?"

"I can't, but the venture's so mad that I believe it is. It's a sacred duty to deliver a ruler's message that can stop thousands dying."

"Duty?" Landolfi queried. "It's a risk to me and my master, who aren't parties to the quarrel."

"Take it to Figliazzi. He'll give it to Idiaquez. The fleet will sail at any moment, so you have to hurry," Latham insisted.

Landolfi grumbled. "Thousands are going to die, Edward. As Musselmen say, 'their names are inscribed by Allah.' Philip won't waste the millions he's already spent. I'll be in trouble if it's forged, more if it isn't."

However, minutes later he was in the saddle.

"The knight's ridden off on his quest," Latham wrote to Hicks's agent on the Spanish/French border, paying for a fast courier.

Landolfi was gone for ten days. Excited and nervous, he met Latham outside the South Gate at dusk and walked him to the park. Softly, he said, "The answer is 'Too late.'"

Latham made to leave, but Landolfi grabbed him. "It took days after decoding for handwriting experts to pronounce it genuine. When they did, Idiaquez was perturbed that Figliazzi had a letter from Walsingham, which bespeaks long, deep intimacy. We made up enough to slide out of trouble, but you should leave. I don't think Idiaquez even showed the letter to Philip. He muttered that months ago something might have been done, but Figliazzi believes they were always set on war. Spain's ally, Henry, Duke of Guise, is chasing the French king out of Paris, which Philip takes as proof of God's favour, since Guise could bring France in on Spain's side. Idiaquez says it's reckoning time. The fleet sails this week."

"Well, I've got what I need," Latham said. "I must tell the courier."

"Be careful. That area's rough."

Latham rode toward the south wall. He tied his horse to a tavern post a few blocks from the stables then walked. It was getting dark, candles blinking from windows here and there. He was armed with a sword and knife and had adopted Joris's way of sheathing a crowbar between his shoulders. A dark lantern hung from his belt.

He sniffed blood, wondering if the slickness on the cobblestones was slaughterhouse gore or street filth. When he came to the stables, the turning, huffs and neighs of nervous horses filled the air. No wonder they hated it here. He had the impression there were five or six, but didn't hear any soothing stable boy murmurs.

Where was Ben? The outhouse was several yards from the stables, separated by a well and trough. There was no adjoining house, so the ostler and his family lived elsewhere. Latham was hopeful that Ben had picked a good spot to hide out.

He lit the lantern and approached the outhouse, a large rectangle that might have been a second stable during lucrative times, before municipal officials built the slaughterhouse. It was darkly quiet. He had no sense of anyone inside snoring, scratching, pleasuring himself or reading. He touched the door, it gave, and he eased in.

It took a few moments of holding the lantern up, noting tackle, barrels of oats, blankets, hay bales, before he understood the extreme violence of Ben's death. His foot hit clothed flesh. He looked down and gasped at the boy sprawled on his back; his throat slashed so deep that his head was attached by gristle alone. Beside him lay the relic box, smashed and empty. Latham bent and touched pallid skin. It was still warm.

At the other end of the building, a ragged breath sounded. Latham's nerves shrieked. He wasn't alone. He longed to run for the open door, but the murderer was too close. He was certain it was the thin Spaniard. Leaving the lantern by the body, he eased up and back, drawing sword and crowbar. His moves were answered by the click of flint. A gun; good. Latham would have the advantage when it fired, because the killer couldn't easily re-load.

With a whoosh, a net fell where he'd stood a second ago. A sneeze, not far away. So there were two, and they meant to capture him. He hid behind a post and kicked a stone in the direction of the sneeze. The gun roared, and the ball thudded into the post, sparking hay on the ground. The sneezer panicked and ran for the door. Latham put out his foot. As the sneezer stumbled–he seemed callow–Latham plunged his sword deep into his back. He threw the dying body onto the hay to smother the fire. Latham yearned for the door, to pull his sword out of the corpse, but both were too far away.

He drew back behind a post. The Spaniard came forward slowly, sword swinging. Latham's knees shook. The olive seller's parrot came to him. "Bakedfishvomit, baked pigshit, Maryfullofgrace," he squawked. The Spaniard had been in Cutler Street when the parrot was there. For a second, the Spaniard looked around, puzzled. Latham threw the crowbar at the roof.

The crowbar dislodged droppings and dust. In the confusion, Latham rushed his attacker. His knife hit metal-studded leather. He twisted from the Spaniard's sword slash, turned and hacked his wrist. The man advanced, ignoring blood coming from his sleeve. Latham backed away, tripped, and sat down on one of the corpses. He saw the glint of the Spaniard's blade as it rose. He grabbed the Spaniard's calves and pulled him down. The blade clattered out of the attacker's wounded hand, and they rolled together, punching and kicking. Latham found himself on top. He pounded his knuckles into the Spaniard's soft throat. Blows later, he had no idea how many, the body went still.

The outhouse door opened wider. A lantern probed, its holder took a step in. *I'm done.* Latham thought. *Can't fight again.* He grabbed the Spaniard's sword, staggered up, and looked into Benedetto Landolfi's astonished eyes.

"God be praised, did you kill three?"

Latham laughed hysterically. "Only two," he corrected, when he could speak. "Look at what those bastards did to Ben." He wept.

Landolfi shone his lantern on Ben's corpse. His cheeks were seared by burns, and his fingers smashed. He'd been tortured, presumably by the other two dead men.

"Do you know the Spaniard?" Latham asked.

"I do. He's the brother of the senior clerk to Idiaquez. I heard him insisting to his brother, the clerk, that you spoke

Spanish to him in Saint-Denis years ago. That clerk hates all three of us; he's been running his own little network. It's God's blessing you weren't captured. Get out of Madrid with your message of hostilities now. I'll dispose of the Spaniards' bodies, borrow horses and the cart. The horses will be glad to leave."

Indeed, they were bumping their stall walls. Landolfi tried a joke: "Edward, if you must kill senior servants' kin, deserted stables near a stinky slaughterhouse are a helpful location. Thank you."

Latham didn't respond.

"Leave Ben," Landolfi continued. "The ostler will call the constable tomorrow, and the investigation will be about who killed him and smashed his holy relic."

London, Whitehall Palace, late June 1588.

"Well, Master Hicks," Elizabeth said, "Confirmation from Latham that it's war, though we are mobilised; you all persuaded me. 'Too late' isn't the plan, which I expected. But I'm told that those two words were hard-won, and Latham will go to Calais. Tell Walsingham to pay him a regular salary. Where *is* this accursed Armada?"

"It left Lisbon in April, Your Majesty. Right now? We have no idea where it is."

CHAPTER 30
ARMADA, PALAMON AND ARCITE REDUX

Calais, 4 August 1588

L atham took his eyes off the harbour and bent to pick a strand of seaweed off his boot. A moist, stinky twist displaced from its natural setting, made him think about the tangle facing him today. He was going to meet Don Cristobal for the first time since becoming a double agent. Letters couriered over distance and time had allowed for calibration; dissembling when they were eye to eye, flesh clasping flesh, was much more challenging. Latham revered the sworn blood brother who'd once saved his life. But England and Spain were at war now, and he and Cristo were on opposing sides. Committing some subversive act against Cristo seemed inevitable, although he had no idea what it would be.

Girding for betrayal, he straightened up again and looked out to sea, The scale of the conflict amplified his anxiety. Somewhere out there, beyond lapping waves and patchy fog, the largest naval battle Europe had ever known was raging. Rumour held that the fleets were roughly equal. Would God's favour, policy, tactics, or luck prevail in a frontal battering? No one had any idea who was winning so far. Latham's pulse raced with the fierce urgency of crews working sails, oars and guns. Yet he could do nothing. His was the shackled passivity of the spy, who teased out information, manipulated enemy perceptions and delegated action to others. Their names would be chronicled; his might not.

Mist fuzzed the gulls into undifferentiated blobs swooping in troughs of grey waves. Between gull shrieks was what sounded like a distant crump of cannon. It continued for a while, then stopped. He strained to listen, leaning forward on the jetty until he nearly fell off. A wind gust clean-scrubbed the view, revealing a sea empty of great vessels, and a hint of Dover's cliffs. Had he imagined the gunfire? Then mist fogged everything again.

It was time to go. His life was a quill inking a circle, he reflected, the parchment resistant at times, causing spatter, the lines not closed. If the end was cannon fire in the English Channel, the beginning was Elizabeth's visit to Oxford and the play, *Palamon and Arcite*. Two knights bound by sworn oaths and fighting for a common cause, fall out lethally over the chaste Princess Emilia. How ironic that Elizabeth's guest for the performance was the Spanish ambassador. As Latham walked to the town centre, fragments came back to him.

Busy in his memories, he didn't notice salt marsh giving way to encroaching bushes until a feathery, white-blossomed Tamarix branch snagged his hose. It took delicate manoeuvres to disentangle twigs without tearing the cloth. The play's resolution had been the death of one of the knights, the survivor marrying the princess. But however he subverted Cristo, Latham determined it must be with policy, not violence.

His raw appetite returned when he reached Rue de Quatre Coins. Perhaps it was the smell of spitted meat–he'd missed breakfast–or the bustle of civilians going about ordinary life despite the monumental event taking place over the horizon, that gave a sense of status quo.

Because almost no one knew that he served Walsingham, he'd disguised himself for protection from Huguenot spies. *One of Fortune's ridiculous jokes*, Latham thought, entering the tavern where he was to meet Cristo. He was wearing scuffed boots, had a dirty sling on one arm and a worn insignia on his other sleeve suggesting he was a veteran soldier.

He recognised Don Cristobal at once: stocky build, coal-black eyes, close-cropped bristly hair and the sticking-out ears always alert for danger. But he was no longer clean-shaven, a black beard streaked with white hid the chin dimple that softened his fierceness. It took a moment for the Spaniard to recognise his blood brother, but then he roared with laughter and folded Latham into an embrace of python-like intensity.

"Pitiable wound, good disguise," Don Cristobal chuckled. "You never know who the French favour on any day."

He'd reserved a private room for their midday meal. Over it, they reminisced: tender inquiries about acquaintances; laughter at the translucent bugs in the Monte Viso tunnel; disdain for the foibles of certain others, magnified by the passing of time. Latham veered between relaxing into the warmth of shared adventures, and feeling that his buttocks were perched on a razor.

He was relieved when Don Cristobal moved a candlestick to a packet of reports. Tapping the pile, he sneered. "Have there ever been wilder rumours? A fisherman tells a tale to a clerk, who writes it on parchment, ties it with ribbon, forcing officers like me to waste time on it. I have to decide which rumours make sense and send them to Parma, who's waiting in Bruges. My report is one of several, but I cling to the vanity that my opinion matters. Being far from action is strange. I'd like your opinion."

"I'm no expert on battle," Latham said doubtfully.

"You know more than the blabbers who've sent this rubbish," Cristo snorted, organising the pile. Latham was startled to see his face in repose settled in bitter frustration. When Cristo put on reading glasses that masked the eyes that could veer instantly to affection or humour, the lines around his mouth amplified his negativity.

"What ails you?" Latham asked.

"I loathe this battle plan, Edward. It wasn't what I wrote, or what Admiral Santa Cruz proposed before he died, God have mercy on his soul. But as an admiralty officer, my reputation is attached to this travesty. Santa Cruz would twist in torment at the chanciness of the enterprise. I proposed 550 ships and 60,000 men in a unified force, with provision to defend against the diabolical Antwerp *Hellburners* that Idiaquez warned us the enemy could have. But the king whittled it down by three quarters..."

Latham's knees stiffened under the table. He'd delivered that plan to Hicks. Still talking, Cristo hadn't noticed Latham's tensing.

"Instead, our king dreamed up a perfume fantasy that on the perfect day and hour, tide and weather smiling, God disposing all in our favour, Parma would lead thousands of infantry on hundreds of barges to join the fleet from Spain, making up the complement in Santa Cruz's plan."

Latham wondered if the English knew about the change in Spain's plan. He yearned to commandeer a boat to Dover, or by sorcery induce a vision in the English admiral's brain. His reporting had suggested fewer than 500 vessels, but he hadn't been able to be precise. "150 are not as many as 550, but all say the fleets are roughly equal," he offered.

"Parity doesn't an invasion make. God's blood, Edward, my paper said that clear as clear. King Philip's plan ignores the Dutch pirates waiting to pound Parma's barges the moment they move. Drake. All Madrid ever screams about is Francis Drake. But there floats Justin of Nassau, Dutch rebel admiral, a little menace with lots of flyboats, blockading our waterways while fever ravages the troops. King Philip painted the Dutch navy out of his pretty picture. Pah, I told them so. And for that, they're blocking my next promotion. Well, here's to rumours." He took a drink.

Cristo couldn't help laughing as he read aloud the reports, with their flamboyant contradictions: the English navy destroyed, Elizabeth captured and being taken on a donkey to Rome (this from a Hansa cog that saw few English ships off Portland Bill); most Spanish warships destroyed (this from a fisherman who saw a mighty explosion and fire destroying the *San Salvador*, all hands believed killed); the Armada intact nearing Calais; Spanish troops landed on the Isle of Wight and the Armada there; and both fleets out of ammunition and drifting silent.

"What do you make of all this?" Latham asked. He wondered if the annihilation of the *San Salvador* was true; perhaps Neapolitan cannon balls mismatched to Spain's Dutch guns–the problem Charles had told him about–had caused the fire.

"First, what do you think?" Don Cristobal countered, drumming his fingers on the table.

"I heard distant gunfire this morning. Neither side has won."

"Of course it's a nonsense. The English are fighting in their home waters, close to resupply," Don Cristobal agreed. "Now, silent drift makes sense. We used Lisbon ammunition first and could have run out. Switching to new ammunition takes time, while the English have less to begin with. I inventoried all that in Lisbon. I believe an explosion destroyed *San Salvador*. A fisherman doesn't mistake fire at sea."

"Could that be caused by ill-fitting ammunition?" Latham asked.

"Yes. Or an English cannonball could have hit their

powder room. Or one of our sailors could have dropped a lit match in the wrong place. If all hands are dead, we'll never know. But it's just one ship. Now, establishing a beach-head on the Isle of Wight is good strategy."

"Didn't you say the order is to join with Parma?" Latham asked.

"I did," Don Cristobal said, "But a forward commander seizes the chance to win, orders be damned. The Isle of Wight offers that. I would have landed."

"*Orders be damned* isn't loved by today's precise generals," Latham said mildly. "That's why you're a glorified clerk."

"True." Don Cristobal gave a faint smile. "I violated the Treaty of Arras with unauthorised guerrilla raids. And they succeeded. Ha, ha, ha! *I'd* seize the chance to win and land on the island, but I have no confirmation that the Spanish Admiral thought correctly. The fleet may come here, as instructed. I must urge Parma to wait until he knows. He loves his men; you saw that at Antwerp. Throwing them into Justin's guns while they hunch unprotected on barges, sheep to the slaughterhouse, is no small matter."

"You've chosen your rumours, then."

"Yes, and expect our Armada to be short of ammunition, pleading for more. Let's go to the harbour with my *looker*."

When they got there, only the sun's angle had changed. Gulls cried, and there may or may not have been a rumble of gunfire. Wind gusts made it hard to keep the *looker* steady, but when they did bring distance to eyeball, no giant ships loomed in the lens. So far, Latham hadn't had to do anything against his oath-brother.

Three days later, some things were clear.

Both the English and Spanish fleets had anchored near Calais, beyond gunshot range of each other, at parity and stalemated. Obviously, the English fleet wasn't destroyed, and Elizabeth wasn't on a donkey plodding to Rome. The Armada, clustered close to the Calais cliffs, looked vast and mostly intact. It hadn't established a beachhead on the Isle of Wight. Calais politics were resolved: neutrality. The Governor of Calais refused to welcome the Spaniards officially or to sell them weapons, but allowed the purchase of fresh food and drink.

Don Cristobal invited Latham to join him for dinner aboard a fighting galleass captained by a childhood friend of his from the Gredos mountains, Don Felipe Pasqual d'Avila. Latham's first sense of Spanish morale came before he met Cristo for the ride out to Pasqual's *Juana*, which was anchored in the inner thigh of the Armada's half-moon formation.

Latham had been wandering Rue de Quatre Coins, looking for a suitable gift for Pasqual, when five men carrying baskets of oranges ran into a tailor's shop. They were dressed in blue breeches tied at the knee over white hose, and loose blue jerkins with a grey armband. They didn't come out, and after a few minutes, Latham peered in. They weren't there. The plump, pasty-faced bearded tailor affected ignorance of the three languages Latham tried. Curious, Latham walked down a filthy lane to the back of the shop. Three men in brown novice robes, without baskets, were leaving; looking about amateurishly, splitting up to go separate ways. *Deserters*, Latham thought, no doubt with the king's escudos under the oranges. If he read their clothes right, they were musketeers from one of the galleons.

He said nothing when he met Cristo at the jetty. But as they were being rowed between galleons, armed merchantmen and supply vessels, Cristo said, "All this naval power doesn't mean happy crews. I'm sure I saw a couple of sailors desert at a seaman's cemetery. They ran into the church asking for sanctuary. I just pray they weren't from Felipe's ship." He frowned morosely when Latham described what he'd seen at the tailor's shop.

They stared up at rigging, hulls and gun ports, awed by the power, discipline, and relatively minor damage inflicted by days of fighting. True, on several ships, crews were suspended in nets, frantically stuffing cannonball holes in hulls, or crawling along cross trees repairing rigging–lighter galleasses seemed to have suffered the most damage–but mainmasts looked intact. This fleet could swim. There was a lot of fighting ahead.

Don Cristobal grunted. "English ships must be even sounder than ours because they fire from further off. Edward, if Santa Cruz were alive, we'd be dining on flagship *San Martin*. Still, Pasqual's a solid man, admirable rather than admiral, ha, ha, ha! He's also an *orders be damned* fellow, if it advances the cause. Growing up in the Gredos mountains does that. The air helps a man sees clearly. His promotion is stalled, too."

They looked back at the town. Tiny human figures crowded the cliff tops and ramparts, enjoying the monumental display of Spanish might, the dark wooden hulls and, by contrast, brass guns dazzling in the late day sun. Those spectators could also see what he and Cristo couldn't: the sprawl of the English fleet.

"Speaking of *unwholesome*," Don Cristobal began, wrinkling his nose, "did you know that William Boels sails as purveyor and courier? Last week, the admiral sent him with Rodrigo Tello on a pinnace to Parma's camp. They should be back today. If Boels ingratiates himself with Tello, he'll be promoted again, maybe above me. What a thought!"

His expression, animated when appraising the galleons, darkened. He didn't have to explain his rift with Boels. Latham knew Cristo had cancelled William's betrothal to his daughter when he discovered that the Fleming had the pox. After his cure, William had won the hand of a Gredos noble widow with liens on Cristo's lands. Nothing could have humiliated Cristo more. Latham had to give Boels credit: he had a gift for vengeance. *It runs in the family*, Latham mused. William had no idea that Joris had gulled him into getting Santa Cruz's battle plan for the English. He reached over and touched Cristo's arm. "Bah," he retorted. "Forget Boels. I'm relieved you're not on any ship. You'll live while he may not."

When they reached the *Juana*, Latham arranged for the same boatman to pick them up before midnight. They looked up at the galleass, a broad three-master bristling with guns, as well as twenty-six oar pairs. To Latham, it looked ferocious, lethal and nimble. But Cristo said as they climbed the rope ladder, "Its bark is worse than its bite. None of the guns can throw a nine-pounder; the planks can't take the recoil."

As an officer helped them over the rail, the purveyor raucously bargained with two boatwomen, each in her own skiff. Hams, cheese, bread and fruit came up from one boat; caged hens, lambs, and eggs from another. At the deck's bow-end, the galleass's shackled oarsmen were being aired and exercised. Supervised by guards preemptively snapping whips, they shuffled in a circle, their faces blank with fear and shock. The air reeked of sweat and waste.

How did anyone survive the oars? Latham wondered. He took another look to estimate their fitness. They looked stringy but sound; Pasqual evidently took adequate care of his human tools.

An officer escorted Cristo and Latham to the sterncastle cabin, where Pasqual waited. Set up for dining, the captain's cabin was large and pleasant, with curved glass windows offering a view of a multitude of taller ships rocking at anchor.

They interrupted a conversation crackling with nervous excitement. After Don Cristobal greeted his friend and introductions of officers to guests were done, Pasqual explained the agitation. The Governor of Calais had sent his nephew that morning to advise Admiral Medina Sidonia that it wasn't safe to anchor long so close to the cliffs. Tidal currents from the North Sea or Atlantic could sweep in and meet with sudden violence, making sailing very tricky. But between the Armada and open water was the English fleet. A lanky, grey-haired man with calm grey eyes, Pasqual spoke in an indifferent monotone, pitched to alleviate anxiety.

It didn't work, because one of the officers said to Latham and Don Cristobal, "Our admiral is a respected *land* general." His implication was shockingly close to insolence. "Beg pardon if I speak out of order, sir," he added hurriedly, with a deep bow.

Pasqual deflected firmly. "Our renowned admiral understands our location perfectly, gentlemen. It's Monsieur Gourdan, the town governor, who needs to make known he issued us a public warning. There's renewed civil war in France. The French king calls for neutrality between us and England, while our ally, the Duke of Guise, calls for supporting us. Guise has chased King Henry out of Paris, to Chartres. But there's a royal army with the king. The end of this rebellion isn't written yet. Gourdan is covering his arse, if my honoured guests will forgive my crudeness."

In the ensuing laughter, Pasqual motioned them to sit. "My experienced crew would like to propose remedies," he murmured to Latham and Don Cristobal, seated on either side of him. "But a galleass officer doesn't advise a flagship."

"Oh for the days of *orders be damned*, Pasqual," Cristo whispered. They exchanged rueful grins.

Pasqual then turned to his officers, his tone brooking no contradiction. "There's one item of business before we enjoy fresh food. Our admiral has advised that the English might attack tonight. An English pinnace came close this afternoon. We chased it away with a few shots, but it was clearly on reconnaissance."

His upraised hand silenced the communal groan. "Our position is not ideal, but the admiral has taken defensive measures."

"Permission to speak, sir?" The question came from the man sitting on Latham's left. Bent and elderly, his piercing green eyes defied ageing. He'd been introduced as the chief navigator. At

Pasqual's nod, he asked, "What kind, sir? It couldn't be a major action at night. Plundering a sickly hulk? Fire-ships?"

"Whatever they do, our orders are to stay put," Felipe responded. "No breaking formation. Patrol boats are positioned to tow away or beach any fire-ships."

The priest said grace, and everyone bent to eat roast goose, preserved ham and salad. There was less fear in the snatches of conversation Latham heard than he would have expected. It dawned on him that lesser officers wouldn't know Giambelli was in London, purportedly working on *Hellburners* with Drake. Idiaquez must have confided only in the admiral and senior captains.

Don Cristobal stripped the complacency away. "What about that Mantuan's diabolical machines? Signor Prosperino here was at Antwerp, and lived through it. Never saw the like, he says."

All eyes turned to Latham.

Had he arrived at his subversive act against Spain and his blood brother? He had no idea what the English planned, if they even had a plan. They didn't have *Hellburners*; Hicks had assured him of that.

"Essentially, the diabolical machine ships have to be big enough to bear the mass of stone slabs and metal they throw. The fire-ships I saw at Antwerp were much smaller."

Pasqual pressed him to be more precise, reaching over to a side table for writing materials. Latham took time to drain his goblet. Describing that night still traumatised him. He tried to recreate the scene at Parma's boat bridge as landscape, as if he was a painter dispassionately choosing how much of a white crest to put on the waves, how steep to draw the river banks, how dim or bright the night sky.

"Self-detonating bomb ships are unmanned for much longer than fire-ships, where crews light the tar then jump off the side into waiting boats."

Latham went on to describe the eerie serenity of the night, how the water glowed with tiny lights from burning barges, fishing boats and small cogs, the water reflecting the fires so that he couldn't tell rigging flames from their below-surface echo. "The Dutch sent more than forty fire-ships. Some snagged on rubbish; others were hooked or netted by Parma's men. *Hope* and *Fortune*, the bomb ships, were big, maybe 100 tons. But they also had rigging fires. Please spare me talking about the destruction by the actual bomb," he concluded.

"Forty?" the green-eyed navigator gasped. "With us and the English fleets being equal, there's no sparing such quantities." The other officers nodded agreement.

Pasqual sanded his notes dry, and ordered a messenger to deliver it to the admiral.

"We trust God Almighty to favour His own cause," he said, signalling an end to the discussion. Don Cristobal looked attentively at him; he could have sworn he'd heard sarcasm. While the priest added a Latin prayer, the green-eyed navigator muttered to Latham in German. "God Almighty indeed. Oh, to be a privateer!" Latham winked at him.

For the benefit of the guests, talk turned to describing the journey so far: the solemn, prayerful launch in Lisbon; the wrecking storm that forced them to stop and refit in A Coruña; blow-by-blow battles against the English, with some disagreement over the sequence and results. The end was the beginning: mountains of shot expended but little gained; parity then and parity now. From time to time, an officer came in to report on the wind, anxious faces swivelling to him.

While the cheese was being passed around, William Boels arrived. He'd been going from ship to ship, reporting conditions at Parma's camps. Don Cristobal looked away, willing the Fleming to disappear. Boels looked healthy, prosperous and as pompous as ever, but tense.

"Two weeks," Boels said tonelessly, with an air of being thoroughly sick of his news. "Sirs, two weeks before the Duke of Parma can embark."

His words fell into an appalled silence. As far as it was possible for olive-skinned, weather-beaten, drink-flushed complexions to go white, they did.

"At least two weeks," Boels added, rubbing it in.

The silence was prolonged. It was the captain's prerogative to speak first, but Pasqual was mute, thinking furiously. Boels couldn't stand the verbal vacuum he met every time he delivered his news. "Sabotage," he offered, his voice rising in agitation. "Dutch sabotage at shipyards; crumbly planks mixed with sound ones, all to be undone and redone."

Pasqual waved Boels to sit, which he did, helping himself to bread and cheese. In the tense quiet his stolid chewing was audible. Having an explanation didn't help. Everyone turned inward, chewing a lip or fingernail, massaging a thigh through breeches. It was only a partial explanation, Latham thought, pushing a goose bone around his plate. Boels must have heard in Dunkirk and Nieuport about the threat Justin of Nassau's boats posed to Farnese's barges. It was odd that he hadn't mentioned it; as if Spain's servants had painted the Dutch navy out of the picture of the invasion plan, just as their sovereign had. Cristo looked stricken, his eyebrows pulling together in a glowering frown, as he contemplated the rape of his original proposal.

Deciding hospitality required a happier atmosphere, Pasqual challenged everyone at the table to describe the most useful innovations they'd seen, a prize to be awarded at the end. Why not? There was nothing else to do but wait. He promised a pig to his officers, or a barrel of wine to Latham and Cristo if they won. Conversation turned lively and went on a long time. Latham noticed that Don Cristobal kept quiet about the *looker* in his bag, talking about the Monte Viso tunnel instead. If Cristo showed off the *looker*, Pasqual might commandeer it for Admiral Medina Sidonia.

From time to time, the green-eyed navigator interrupted with "What will we do for two weeks?" But Pasqual ignored him and kept pulling the conversation back to innovations.

He declared an officer, who'd said that the Armada's half-moon formation was the best innovation in modern times, the winner. It was the appropriate decision, to boost morale.

Shortly before midnight, Latham and Don Cristobal said goodbye to Pasqual and climbed down the rope ladder to their hired boat. They entered an amazing seascape. A freshening west wind stripped cloud puffs and veil-like strands from the heaven's constellations. At sea level, the man-made environment was all enchantment and menace. Their little boat was rocking; the castle-like monstrosities towering all about them were rocking, prows and sterns marked by orange lanterns fuzzed by wisps of cooking smoke. The language the monster shapes spoke was a primal song of wood groaning and creaking; interspersed with swishing water thrust out by pumps; discrete sharp-edged voices; bells ringing the turn of sandglasses.

"Pasqual runs an efficient ship," Don Cristobal said, rummaging in his bag for the *looker*. "But I grieve at the low trust the officers have in their admiral, not to mention the deserters we saw in town. When a battle hangs in the balance, trust in a commander makes victory or defeat."

He assembled the *looker* and wiped spray off the lenses. Astonished by the device, the boatman forgot to row, causing the boat to bucket. Don Cristobal cursed him as the lenses got wet again. After another wipe, he steadied himself on the bench and trained it at distant pinpricks of light. "English ships," he said, passing the *looker* to Latham.

The tide was coming in, and the boatman rowed more easily than on the way out. He turned chatty, without being asked. "Westerly breeze and incoming tide, a gift, sirs. They carry us at two to three knots per hour before I make a single stroke. But change is coming. My joints scream before the wind turns north or east, and they're moaning now," he warned. "If it's a blow, these galleons will strain their anchors or be sent scurrying to Denmark. Take my advice, use that strange tube on land tomorrow."

Latham was about to ask him a question when Don Cristobal stood without warning, bucketing the boat again. A wave crested over them, and they got drenched. The boatman yelled at him as he worked to regain control. Don Cristobal grabbed the mast to steady himself and focused on trumpets coming from perimeter Spanish ships. Many large lit blobs were heading towards them. Two suddenly swivelled sideways, to cheers from Spanish lookouts. *Our patrol boats snagged them*, Don Cristobal thought. But the other blobs were approaching. Fast.

Cries started coming from nearby ships, their terror palpable:

"Too big for fire-ships!"

"Eight *Hellburners*!"

"Buggers are two hundred tons!"

"Antwerp bomb ships!"

"Diabolical machines!"

Still standing, Don Cristobal peered through the *looker*. Six large ships advanced in a line, about forty feet between them. They were through the perimeter, and would be on top of them in about seven minutes. A ferocious fire started at the prow of the first ship and raced to its stern. In a few seconds all the sails and rigging were ablaze. Just before spray fogged the lens again, he saw men leaping into the water.

He shoved the *looker* at Latham and sat. "Wipe. Quick. What are they? I saw men torch a heap in the prow, run astern and slide into a rowing boat pulling away."

Latham wiped and saw something similar. There were no stone pyramids on the decks, and they were manned; they were fire-ships, not *Hellburners*. Heart pounding, he gave the device back. "The lens fogged. Sorry. They're three times bigger than Giambelli's bomb ships."

Don Cristobal blinked. There had been no new spray; the lens couldn't have got smudged so soon. He waved his arm at the deck of the nearest galleon, shouting "Fire-ships! Only fire-ships." No one took any notice. He shouted again: "Fire-ships, not *Hellburners!*" And again. "Fire-ships."

The approaching ships were burning steadily. One suddenly flared with a cataclysmic crack, its cannons exploding in thunderous double-shotted rolling broadsides.

Don Cristobal kept gesticulating. Finally, a galleon officer looked down, cupping his ear. Don Cristobal screamed: "Six fire-ships! No *Hellburners!* Fakes! Don't let six fakes break what 130 English warships couldn't!" The officer waved at them to escape. Don Cristobal screamed up at him again, and the officer shouted back, "*Hellburners!* Get away!"

Frustrated, Don Cristobal turned to the boatman and yelled, "Turn around. Take us to the flagship."

The boatman shook his head and rowed frantically toward the inner harbour. "No! Are you mad?"

On a nearby hulk, pipes shrilled orders to cut cables, the first ship to disobey the admiral's command to hold position. The sails missed stays, flapping as the current propelled the hulk into its neighbour. Frantic men tried to pole them apart. As if that hulk had signalled general orders to flee, an armed merchantman pulled up anchor. It blundered over a baker's skiff, smashing it to pieces. One woman was cut in two, and a drowning man screamed for help.

Back near the *Juana*, Latham and Don Cristobal heard a shrieking grinding of wood and metal on wood, shouts of

"*San Lorenzo!*"

"*Girona!*"

"Lend a hand. Pole! Axe!"

A pause, cheers, then more shrieking and grinding.

"*San Lorenzo!*"

"*Rata!*"

"Pole! Axe!"

San Lorenzo, flagship of the Neapolitan galleasses, had evidently collided with the *Girona*, freed itself, then ploughed into the *Rata*.

All the while, the burning English ships glided closer. Don Cristobal watched in horror, and Latham concealed his glee, as the once-disciplined rows of great ships disintegrated, waterborne castles cutting cables, abandoning anchors, tottering to sea. Wobbling stern lanterns mapped the scramble to get away. Every captain thought only of himself; the impregnable half-moon formation had been thoroughly shattered.

Resting the *looker* in his lap, Don Cristobal pulled out his knife. He leaned over, pointing it at the boatman. "Turn back! Flagship or die!"

Latham stood, an arm crooked around the mast. Violently he kicked Don Cristobal's knee, knocking the *looker* into the air. It flew up, corkscrewing in the wind. Higher, higher. A gust snatched it and tumbled it into the water, yards from the boat. Gasping in pain, Don Cristobal reached into a trough, a crest, a trough. The *looker* was gone.

Don Cristobal sat back and stared at his oath-brother.

Puzzlement, horror, rage, grief showed on his face. And suspicion.

"Don't kill the boatman, Cristo," Latham said as he sat.

To the boatman's relief, the fierce Spaniard's shoulders sagged. "Go back," the boatman cajoled. "Without anchors, these monsters are dangerous. They'll fly all awry when the wind turns. A king's treasure in iron just went to the sea bottom. I never saw the like."

With a twisted smile, Latham said, "It's too late to go to the admiral, Cristo. You can't prove these aren't *Hellburners* without your *looker*. I'm heartily sorry you accidentally lost it."

"*I* lost it?" Don Cristobal ran his finger along the knife blade, feeling its bite.

Latham persisted: "You will live and fight another day. Many of those sailors will die."

He met a look of hatred.

Palamon and Arcite, falling out over a virgin Queen, Latham thought. "You doubt me?" he asked, offering his chest to Cristo's knife.

Shaking his head, Don Cristobal wearily sheathed his knife.

It's not death tonight, Latham realised. *We are modern, not ancient, knights.*

Don Cristobal suspected that his oath-brother had betrayed him, and Spain, but he couldn't be sure. Losing his *looker* had been so fast, opportunistic, and accidental. He had his own, more urgent dilemma: struggling with the unfamiliar condition of self-doubt. If he hadn't kept the *looker* secret, if he'd done his patriotic duty and given it to the admiral, this night, this enterprise, faulty as it was, might have been saved. Greed and pride had likely condemned his sons to fight the same war.

When they stepped onto a stone jetty, Don Cristobal elbowed his way through the crowds of torch-wielding, chattering spectators brought out by the mayhem at sea. He strode away without a word or backward glance.

Latham watched his receding back with resignation: a piece of his heart lost, one more separation for a larger cause. He followed a crowd eddying up a cliff trail for a better view. By the time he got there half an hour later, shouts and pipes from Armada ships were few, as the anchorage in Calais Roads emptied. Soon, a few lowering flares were the only remaining lights. A fisherman next to Latham explained that the dying fires came from beached English fire-ships. Burning out harmlessly, they'd done no physical damage. Latham marvelled that a notion—*Hellburners*—that he and others had wafted into Spanish ears, had upended thousands of tons of wood and metal, and sent a fortune in iron plunging into the sea. He marvelled at how one small act could shape a mighty event. If Cristo had given Pasqual his *looker*; if a deck officer had heeded Cristo instead of dismissing him; if Spain's captains had had the courage and discipline to anchor long enough to see that the flaming ships weren't *Hellburners*, but fakes.

At dawn, the English would be able to attack the randomly clustering anchorless ships, drifting at the mercy of winds blowing them north, if the boatman's aching joints were right. All hope of linking up with Parma's army was gone.

Surely there was sardonic Divine malice in the sheer mismatch between the Armada's physical might and the collective illusion that ripped it apart. This was a good night's work.

Unable to contain his excitement, he broke into a Volta dance. Locals around him muttered that he was possessed, and edged away to give him space. "The spy's foot *CAN* direct the royal head. I poached Philip's!" Latham sang, mimicking tossing his partner in the air and setting her down. Then he sobered up. There were great adventures to come; he hadn't moved his birth country to tolerate Catholic liturgy. Yet.

Acknowledgements

It is impossible to adequately thank all the people who've helped me bring this project to the point of publication. Insurance agent colleague, Connie Cohrt, introduced me to John Ware, my literary agent who insisted I write. Critique group authors— Christina Britton Conroy, Josephine Diamond (tragically deceased), Jeri Hilderley, Janet Mayes, Julieta Rodrigues, Caroline Thomas, Linda Trice—helped to shepherd me from hope to story. Members of the Historical Novel Society New York Chapter are an unfailingly generous resource. Leslie Wells, an editor, was a critically constructive eye. My neighbour, Dan Young, instructed me in using historic guns, while my Blue Pencil Café mentor at the HNS Portland conference in 2017, Adrienne Dillard, referred me to MadeGlobal Publishing, which took the chance of sending this debut tale into the world. I am indebted to the New York Public Library; Butler Library, Columbia University; and the Beinecke Rare Book and Manuscript Library at Yale.

Many published works were invaluable resources. Sir Roger Williams *The Actions of the Low Countries (1590),* edited by D.W. Davies, Folgers Shakespeare Library, Cornell University Press, 1964, was a primary source for Vitelli's ambush of Genlis in Chapter 5. An English mercenary serving in a nearby Dutch unit, Williams wrote that the Spanish believed Genlis had 7,000 foot, including four hundred cavalry. Modern scholars cite a force of 5,000. However, since Latham was fighting in the Spanish line, I used Williams's perception. For the Constantinople chapters, Orhan Pamluk's *My Name Is Red,* Knopf, 2001, offered an atmospheric fictional depiction of the city, supplementing contemporary travel diaries by European visitors and secondary sources. The drayman's song in Chapter 17 I translated from French, from Frederique Krupa's *Paris: Urban Sanitation before the 20th Century: A History of Invisible Infrastructure,* 2005. The Turkish proverb Latham quotes in his letter from Madrid to David Hicks in Chapter 26 comes from Neeja Muallimoglu's online collection, *The Turkish Delights. A Treasury of Proverbs and Folk Sayings, National Education Press, 1998.* Finally, in *Argument for an Execution,* North American Conference on British Studies, 1992, Allison Heisch analyses Elizabeth's language concerning the trial of Mary, Queen of Scots. I built on her foundation in my first-person portrayal of Elizabeth's tactics. Marcus, Mueller and Rose *Elizabeth I Collected Writings,* University of Chicago Press, 2002, was also helpful. I, not they, am responsible for any errors in the book.

The publisher would like to thank the invaluable team of pre-readers who helped to make this book even better than we'd hoped it would be. We would like to put out a special thanks to Karen Anspach for spotting the last few errors. Without readers, an author and publisher are nothing. Thank you all.

About Loretta Goldberg

Australian-American Loretta Goldberg earned a BA in English Literature, Musicology and History at the University of Melbourne, Australia. She taught English Literature at the Department of English for a year, before coming to the USA on a Fulbright scholarship to study piano with Claudio Arrau. Her discography consists of nine commercial recordings, now in over seven hundred libraries. She premiered an unknown work by Franz Liszt on an EMI HMV (Australian Division) album, and her edition of the score for *G. Schirmer* is in its third edition. Concurrently, she built a financial services practice, which she sold to focus on writing. Her published non-fiction pieces consist of articles on financial planning, arts reviews and political satire. She earned an MA (music performance) from Hunter College, New York; and a Chartered Life Underwriter degree from the American College, Pennsylvania. Member of the Historical Novel Society, New York Chapter, she started and runs their published writer public reading series at the landmark Jefferson Market Library. Commuting between New York City and Clinton, Connecticut, she enjoys a community rich in extended family, colleagues and friends. She lives with her spouse and two charming cats.

You can discover more about Loretta from her website:
https://lorettagoldberg.com/

Author's Note

Several years ago, I was reading in bed at night. My book was tough fare: *Memoirs of the Reign of Queen Elizabeth from 1581 to her Death*, an eighteenth-century edition by Thomas Birch of the papers of Sir Francis and Anthony Bacon, Elizabethan brothers. Sir Francis Bacon is remembered as a philosopher and lawyer, but both men ran spies for Elizabeth I for twenty years. One of these spies was in trouble.

"Oh no!" I cried, struggling with the f/s ambiguities of eighteenth-century printing. "Anthony Standen *if*, no, *is*, blown!" Our two cats scrambled to the floor, and an irritated "Who....*cares?*" rumbled from my dozing spouse.

It was a good question. I had no idea why the career-ending exposure of this obscure adventurer hooked me. Anthony Standen, a young Catholic courtier, left Protestant Elizabeth I's court in the 1560s for reasons of religion and spied for Catholic Spain against European Protestants. Yet, in the 1580s, he became an effective double agent for Elizabeth abroad, while remaining on Spain's payroll. His reasons are unclear.

I am a secular Jew, so why was I intrigued? I believe that we create artefacts—paintings, sculptures, stories, music—to try and make sense of the world we find ourselves in. Eventually, I realised that Standen epitomised, in a pure form, inner conflicts that permeate our modern lives, along with the compartmentalisation we call on to manage them. An insurance agent–my profession at the time–serves an insurer employer and the claimant; a physician gives a nod to hospital budgets, and to a patient who might gain a few months with a stratospherically costly drug; a tobacco company executive putting his children through college knows that his industry is concealing the addictive poison of cigarettes. For most of us, these conflicts are muted. For Standen, they were a matter of eternal damnation. What split could be more profound than a Catholic who believed in transubstantiation and a physical hell, yet risked his life to protect his heretical birth country?

I wanted to wander in his world. Historical fiction is alluring because the known outcomes provide a frame for imagining the experience. What was it *like*? Another incident teased me. During the reign of Henry VIII, English soldiers were besieging a Scottish town. A church spire was in artillery range. Officers called a halt and pored over their bible. Was bombarding the spire allowed? They came to the conclusion that it was and fired the cannon. I wondered if Hamas soldiers consult their Korans before storing weapons in Gaza's UN refugee centres. I decided to incorporate a search for theoretical justifications in my characters.

Other aspects of the century also drew me. The invention of the printing press late in the fifteenth century spawned uncontrollable outpourings of false and true information; opinion; dissent; and often wicked satire. Institutions reeled, their leaders often responding with appalling cruelty. There was a siren call for religious martyrdom. It was a time of anxiety, upending of traditional alliances, a heady excitement at new learning, and the sense of an infinite geographical world. European military technology was such that no side could annihilate the other. Victories and defeats were temporary, thus violence was intermittent but never-ending. However, the era also brought the notion of companionate marriage, secular social welfare programs, and more widespread elementary education.

Onto this messy stage steps Sir Edward Latham, my fictionalised anti-hero, inserting himself into the religious wars and trying to moderate English and Spanish policy. The Reversible Mask is a quest novel. Callow Latham goes out into the world, is battered and bruised, but emerges stronger, bringing benefits back to his tribe. He interacts with forces and people but does not *integrate* with any.

Sir Edward Latham is not Sir Anthony Standen. He does some things Standen did, and many he did not. His loves, hubris and foibles are my inventions, clearer and dearer to me than his elusive model. Still, like Standen, Latham encounters the principal persons of his day. To dramatize these extraordinary historical figures, I have sometimes mingled their documented words with my own. For vividness, I have taken occasional license with chronology. In one chapter, Elizabeth I ponders over what to do with *blank* Papal Indulgences meant by the Vatican for sale in Hispaniola but captured by her pirates. This occurred in the 1590s, not when Latham hears about it in 1587. But for me, Elizabeth's solution typified her slinky statesmanship so deliciously that I included it. Otherwise, I have tried to be faithful to chronology and location.

Finally, treasured reader, who honours me more than I can express by reaching this page, who did I make up? My fictional characters are courtier David Hicks; mistress of the Louvre palace laundry, Helene Michaud, and her cousins, the Beaumonts; Fleming courier Albert Braak; Spanish officer Don Cristobal Covarrulejo d'Avila; Fleming servants William, Pieter and Joris Boels; and Ibrahim with his Constantinople household.

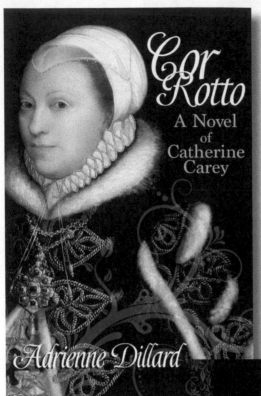

Other Books
from
MadeGlobal
Publishing

Available
NOW!

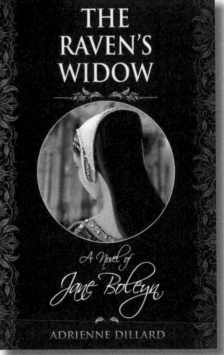

TONI MOUNT

A
Sebastian Foxley
Medieval
Murder Mystery

THE

OLOUR
OF
POISON

TONI MOUNT

Sebastian Foxley
Medieval
Short Story

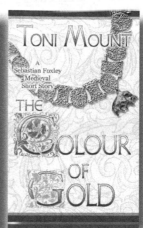

THE
COLOUR
OF
GOLD

TONI MOUNT

The Third
Sebastian Foxley
Medieval
Murder Mystery

THE
COLOUR
OF
COLD BLOOD

TONI MOUNT

The Fourth
Sebastian Foxley
Medieval
Murder Mystery

THE
COLOUR
OF
BETRAYAL

TONI MOUNT

The Fifth
Sebastian Foxley
Medieval
Murder Mystery

THE
COLOU
OF
MURDE

TONI MOUNT

The Sixth
Sebastian Foxley
Medieval
Murder Mystery

THE
COLOUR
OF
DEATH

Book 1 in the Katherine of Aragon story

Falling Pomegranate Seeds

The Duty of Daughters

Wendy J. Dunn

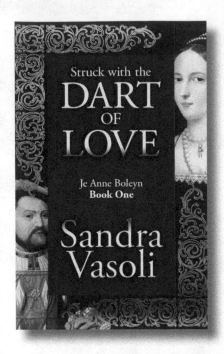

Struck with the

DART OF LOVE

Je Anne Boleyn
Book One

Sandra Vasoli

Sean Poage

THE RETREAT TO AVALON

The Arthurian Age
Book 1

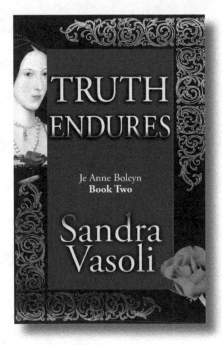

TRUTH ENDURES

Je Anne Boleyn
Book Two

Sandra Vasoli

Historical Fiction

The Sebastian Foxley Murder Mysteries - **Toni Mount**
The Death Collector - **Toni Mount**
Falling Pomegranate Seeds - **Wendy J. Dunn**
Struck With the Dart of Love - **Sandra Vasoli**
Truth Endures - **Sandra Vasoli**
Cor Rotto - **Adrienne Dillard**
The Raven's Widow - **Adrienne Dillard**
The Claimant - **Simon Anderson**

Non Fiction History

Pustules, Pestilence and Pain - **Seamus O'Caellaigh**
Anne Boleyn's Letter from the Tower - **Sandra Vasoli**
The Turbulent Crown - **Roland Hui**
Jasper Tudor - **Debra Bayani**
Tudor Places of Great Britain - **Claire Ridgway**
Illustrated Kings and Queens of England - **Claire Ridgway**
A History of the English Monarchy - **Gareth Russell**
The Fall of Anne Boleyn - **Claire Ridgway**
George Boleyn: Tudor Poet, Courtier & Diplomat - **Ridgway & Cherry**
The Anne Boleyn Collection - **Claire Ridgway**
The Anne Boleyn Collection II - **Claire Ridgway**
Two Gentleman Poets at the Court of Henry VIII - **Edmond Bapst**

PLEASE LEAVE A REVIEW

If you enjoyed this book, *please* leave a review at the book seller where you purchased it. There is no better way to thank the author and it really does make a huge difference!
Thank you in advance.